Cupertino
21251 Steve
Cupertine
408.7

MW00451913

THE INCUMBENT CORONER

BOOK TWO OF THE FENWAY STEVENSON MYSTERIES

PAUL AUSTIN ARDOIN

Cupertino Scenic Center
21251 Stevens Creek Blvd
Cupertino, CA 95014
405.777.3156

THE INCUMBENT CORONER
Copyright © 2018 by Paul Austin Ardoin
Published by Pax Ardsen Books

All rights reserved. Printed in the United States of America. No part of this book may be used or reproduced in any manner whatsoever without written permission except in the case of brief quotations embodied in critical articles or reviews.

This book is a work of fiction. Names, characters, businesses, organizations, places, events and incidents either are the product of the author's imagination or are used fictitiously. Any resemblance to actual persons, living or dead, events, or locales is entirely coincidental.

ISBN: 978-1-949082-03-6

First Edition: September 2018

For information please visit:
www.paulaustinardoin.com

Cover design by Ziad Ezzat
ziad.ezzat.com

Author photo by Monica Toohey-Krause of Studio KYK
www.studiokyk.com

10 9 8 7 6 5 4 3 2 1

TABLE OF CONTENTS

PART I

—◆—

THE WEEK BEFORE

CHAPTER ONE

FENWAY STEVENSON SAT ON THE COUCH IN HER APARTMENT. She didn't know what she was going to do for dinner, but she didn't care. The morning had been spent on an overdose victim in the foothills, the afternoon on the mountain of paperwork that threatened to take over her desk, and she was tired. This was the first night in a week she had left the office by eight o'clock. She picked up the remote and plopped her feet on the coffee table.

The doorbell rang.

Fenway blinked a couple of times before getting up. She opened the door.

Dez stood there, still in her black Dominguez County Sheriff's Department uniform, holding a six-pack of beer.

"Hey," Dez said. "I know I didn't call first, but I was in the neighborhood."

"We just saw each other at work an hour ago, Dez. This can't wait till tomorrow?"

"I guess it could have," Dez said, stepping inside. "But I wanted to let you know in person. The paperwork came back in right after you left. HR approved your vacation for next week."

"Oh." Fenway hadn't counted on that—she had requested the time off at the last minute, and she hadn't yet been coroner for the requisite ninety days to be guaranteed vacation time.

"I know," Dez said, reading her face. "You must live right. It's like you've got a rich daddy or something." She chuckled as Fenway shut the door behind her. "I'm going to put these in your fridge. You want one?"

"What is that? Querido Falls Brewing?"

"Yep. Their Hefeweizen. Hope that's okay."

Fenway nodded. She hadn't had their Hefeweizen, but she liked their pale ale. "But I thought you were all meeting at Winfrey's for happy hour."

Dez shrugged as she disappeared into the kitchen. "Bunch of sticks in the mud. After you said you weren't coming, Mark cancelled because Randy needed help running lines for his audition. Migs and Piper got tickets to some concert down in Santa Barbara."

"I'm glad they're finally together."

"Hah. Sure. If you don't mind disgusting public displays of affection."

Fenway heard the sound of two beers being opened and the caps swirling to a stop on the counter.

"And Rachel said she had too much work to do."

"P.R. work seems to agree with her."

Dez came back into the living room holding two of the beers. "You know she's just keeping busy to keep her mind off her father's trial." She handed a beer to Fenway.

Fenway wanted to pour it in one of her nice beer mugs back in the kitchen—but her exhaustion won out and she stayed put. "Plus, it's hard being a widow at twenty-four."

"Can you name a better age?"

"Ninety-five."

Dez tilted her head, nodded, and raised her bottle. "Cheers."

Fenway and Dez both had a swig of their beers.

"Thanks for the beer, Dez."

"Don't mention it. I didn't feel like going home and this six-pack cost about as much as a decent vodka tonic at Winfrey's." She had a second swig and set the beer on the coffee table. "You mind hanging out with an old lady like me on a Tuesday night?"

"Oh, please, Dez. Don't be giving me that 'old lady' crap. I think *I* have more gray hair than you do." It was true; Dez's short black curls didn't have a trace of gray. "And I'm exhausted. This week already feels like I've worked a hundred hours."

"Oh, it's so nice for you young'uns to make me feel spry." Dez shook her head. "Fifty's right around the corner."

Fenway waved her hand. "Stop whining, Dez. You've got a few more years. And besides, fifty is the new thirty."

"Spoken like someone who hasn't seen the wrong side of thirty yet." Dez smiled. "Okay, speaking of old ladies, my bladder seems to shrink with each passing year. Be right back. Don't do anything I wouldn't do." She went into the bathroom off the hallway, closed the door, and turned on the modesty fan.

Fenway shook her head and put a coaster under Dez's beer. Her phone rang in her purse on the kitchen table. She walked in and dug it out; the incoming caller read *Nathaniel Ferris*. She sighed and answered it.

"Hi, Dad."

"Fenway! Glad I caught you."

"This isn't a great time." She walked back into the living room and took another drink of her beer.

"It'll just take a minute. Listen—you haven't changed your mind about running for coroner in November, have you? You know you're doing a hell of a job since you've taken over."

"No, Dad. I'm a nurse, not a politician, and you know my boards are next month."

Ferris sighed. "Dr. Klein is going to run."

"I figured. He's announcing on Monday, right?"

"That's what I hear. News travels fast."

"And I also heard you have some pharmaceutical executive you're going to support."

Dez came back into the living room, sat on the sofa, and picked up her beer.

"That's right," Ferris said. "Everett Michaels. But only if you're not running, Fenway. You're my daughter. I'm not going to promote another candidate over you."

Fenway hit mute. "Sorry," she whispered to Dez.

Dez nodded.

Fenway unmuted. "When I accepted the appointment," she reminded Ferris, "it was strictly babysitting the position until November. You promised me that."

"Okay," he said, "I just wanted to make sure before I ask you to introduce him when he announces his candidacy."

"Introduce Everett Michaels?"

"Right. I'd like to you introduce him—and give him your endorsement."

"But I don't know anything about him."

He chuckled. "You know enough, Fenway. You know he's the VP of development at Carpetti Pharma, you know he's got a great medical research background, and you know he's a lot better for the county than Barry Klein. What else do you need to know?"

"For one thing, I've never even met the guy."

"We can fix that. It would really help Everett's campaign if you would endorse him," her father said. "Or, if you don't want to go that far yet, you don't have to be partisan for this—just say it's your pleasure to introduce him."

Fenway's mind raced to figure out how to decline politely. "That puts me in an awkward position, Dad. I've still got to work with the *whole* board of supervisors until I'm replaced—and that includes Klein. And besides, won't it look better for the press coming from Nathaniel Ferris? You know how much half this town loves you." *The half you own*, she thought.

"And you know better than anyone how the other half of this town hates me." She thought she detected a note of pleading in his voice. "But many, many people like you, Fenway. The people who like me like you because you're my daughter. And the people who *don't* like me like you because you arrested my right-hand man for murder."

"I think you've got that backwards," Fenway said, fighting to keep the anger out of her voice. "The half that don't like you don't like me either. And the half that *do* like you think I'm some sort of traitor for catching Stotsky."

"Look, if there's one thing I know, it's how to read a crowd. Your endorsement would be a huge boost."

"I think my endorsement would probably hurt more than it would help."

"Not according to our latest poll."

"Poll?" The idea that her father already spent his own money to conduct polling on this, she realized, shouldn't have been a surprise to her. And yet it never ceased to amaze her how Nathaniel Ferris had no clue how to behave like a normal father.

"You've got an eighty-one percent positive rating," he said.

"You ran a poll? You do realize this isn't a national election, right?"

"There are dozens of companies who do this for smaller campaigns, Fenway. It's not a big deal. And if you introduced Everett on Monday, we'd have a sure thing in November."

"Oh, Monday's no good," she said, trying to sound as disappointed as she could. "I have to drive up to Seattle this weekend, and I won't be back."

"Drive to Seattle? Why in the world would you do that?"

"I'm getting some of Mom's paintings out of storage. My favorite painting of hers, in fact."

"Which one is that?"

"The one of the ocean and the cypress tree growing out of the rock, the one right by the butterfly waystation."

Ferris sighed audibly. "Isn't that only a mile from your house? Don't you jog there every morning? Can't you see the real thing any time you want?"

Fenway gritted her teeth. "Coming from the man who fell in love with her because of a painting? That's pretty rich, Dad."

"I suppose," Ferris said. He didn't speak for a few seconds, then cleared his throat. "Can't you just fly?"

"Nope. The paintings are too big to take on the plane."

Her father paused. Fenway could hear him turning everything over in his head.

"You sure you won't be back by Monday morning?"

"No, I won't be back till at least Tuesday or Wednesday. Maybe even later."

"Well, why don't you take *my* plane? You'd be back in plenty of time."

"I'm not taking your plane to Seattle, Dad."

"Why not?"

"Because it costs you something like twenty-five grand whenever you take off and land."

"Having you speak at Everett's announcement is worth twenty-five thousand dollars to me, Fenway."

She wanted to scream at him. She still had ninety-five thousand dollars in college loans to pay back, which he had never even acknowledged. He barely acknowledged that he hadn't given Fenway or her mother a cent in alimony or child support. But he threw around a fifty-thousand-dollar weekend trip to Seattle like he could pay for it with the change he found under the sofa cushions.

"Oh, there's the doorbell, Dad," Fenway lied. "I've gotta go. Talk to you later." And she hung up before he could protest further.

She looked at Dez, who took another drink of the Hefeweizen.

"Nathaniel Ferris, I take it," Dez said.

"You should be a detective."

Dez cackled. "You may just be the only person in this county who won't give him what he wants."

"I may just be the only person in the county he doesn't own," Fenway said.

"So, you're going to drive up and get your mom's painting?"

"Yep. I leave Friday morning. I should get there on Saturday."

"I'll be interested to see the painting. You sure talked about it enough. I hope it lives up to the hype."

"Well, if it doesn't, take a happy pill and pretend it's the most beautiful thing you've ever seen. That's one time I won't need your disturbingly accurate candor."

Dez smirked. "So where are you staying up there? Some fancy hotel?"

"I'm staying with a friend."

"A friend?" Dez looked sideways at Fenway. "That's suspiciously vague."

Fenway blushed.

"Oh, girl, you're hooking up."

"I wouldn't call it a *hookup*," Fenway said. "He's an ex-boyfriend."

"An ex-boyfriend?" Dez narrowed her eyes. "Is this Akeel?"

Fenway's mouth fell open. "How do you know about Akeel?"

Dez laughed. "Rachel tells me more than she should, I guess." She lowered her voice. "Is he still hot?"

"I don't know if I think he's that hot."

"Rachel said you talked about his abs and shoulders and eyes for ten minutes. I stopped paying attention, but I got enough to know you think he's hot."

Fenway paused. "Okay, fine. I'm going to try to hook up with him." She lowered her voice, although no one else was in the apartment. "Look, you know and I know that sleeping with McVie a couple months ago was a bad idea, but I, uh, I haven't really been able to get him out of my head. But I have to work with him, and I don't want to screw that up just because I've got a big schoolgirl crush on him."

"Plus, he's trying to make it work with his wife," Dez said pointedly.

"Right," Fenway agreed quickly. "So I thought maybe it would help me get over him to spend a night with Akeel."

"Or three or four nights," Dez said.

Fenway couldn't help the grin that spread over her face.

"He's that good, huh?"

"Oh, Lord, Dez, we were only together for about six weeks two years ago, but damn, we couldn't get enough of each other. Seattle had a heat wave that summer, and we barely left his apartment. I lived with my mom and she called me a couple times to see if I was okay." She rubbed the sides of her mouth to get herself to stop grinning, but to no avail. "Hoo boy, I was *more* than okay."

Dez rolled her eyes and made a face. "You *know* I didn't need that level of detail."

"Oh, please, Dez," Fenway said. "I didn't go into any detail at all."

"And yet, somehow, I still need to wash out my ears with soap."

Fenway laughed. Dez, the one person in Estancia who didn't expect anything from Fenway, never tried to put a claim on her. She was just there for advice and support—like how her mom had been in Seattle, before the cancer.

"But just six weeks?" Dez asked. "Did he ship out or something?"

Fenway stopped laughing. "No. It just, uh, didn't go anywhere. We had this heat between us, but once we actually hung out together, we didn't really click."

"What needs to click?"

"For one thing," Fenway said, "he didn't have any books in his apartment."

"None? Not even *The Da Vinci Code* or Tom Clancy or something?"

"Nope. He didn't like reading."

"Huh. I guess that *would* be a problem." Dez glanced at Fenway's overstuffed bookshelves.

"And when I met his friends," Fenway started, and then shuddered.

"Oh," Dez said.

"Yeah. I mean, I know Akeel and I had a physical relationship, but when I met his friends, they looked at me like—I don't know. Some sort of trophy. One of them said Akeel only liked me because I acted like a white girl."

"A white girl, huh." Dez's mouth became a thin line.

"I know. Some crack about the color of my skin, too."

"The color of your skin?"

"I wasn't black enough for them, apparently."

Dez paused. "Did Akeel know your father's white?"

"What does that matter?"

Dez shrugged. "It doesn't really, I guess."

"I mean, I liked the fact that Akeel was so attracted to me, but he didn't say anything to his friends. Never defended me, just let me take it. They only said a few things, but it bugged me. We started spending a couple nights apart and then we just sort of stopped seeing each other."

"But you called him up?"

"Um," Fenway said, "he lives really close to the storage unit."

"Did you call any of your other friends?"

Fenway averted her eyes.

"You better hope he's still hot," Dez said. "And you better hope he's not rooming with one of those assholes who said you weren't black enough. Or you better start thinking of excuses why you need to sleep on the couch."

"This is a bad idea, isn't it?" Fenway said, biting her lip.

"You're driving a thousand miles in your new Accord for a booty call," Dez said. "I don't know, I'm terrible with relationship advice. But he's not married, and he's hot. At least that's something."

PART II

---•---

SATURDAY

CHAPTER TWO

———◆———

SEATTLE. SATURDAY AFTERNOON. FENWAY FLIPPED DOWN THE
visor and looked at herself in the mirror. In the hotel room in
Grants Pass that morning, she had spent a long time getting ready.
Her hair looked fantastic in spite of the six hours in the car, still
cascading in ringlets on either side of her face, almost touching
her shoulders. Her eyeliner and mascara accentuated her large,
dark eyes, but she hadn't overdone it. Her lipstick needed just
a little touching up, but other than that, her makeup was great;
not overdone, just a clean, put-together look. All the stars were
lining up.

She looked one last time at what she was wearing. She had on
a scarlet polo dress, with five buttons below the navy blue collar. It was contoured to her body, which she knew Akeel would
like, but wasn't too forward in its sexiness. It was a little shorter
than she might usually wear, but the cut of the dress was casual
enough to wear sneakers with it—she wasn't in the mood to wear
heels, hot ex-boyfriend or not.

She hated herself a little bit for caring this much about how
she looked for Akeel. She wouldn't care this much how she looked

for McVie. McVie who read novels. McVie who liked concerts. McVie who looked in her eyes when they were talking. Not all their talk was about their work, his as sheriff, hers as coroner. But McVie had made it clear he wanted to work things out with his wife. So here she was.

She looked at the small apartment building—Akeel had one of the three upstairs apartments in the converted Victorian—and saw him at the window, watching her car, watching her.

And, she saw clearly, not wearing a shirt.

Apparently he wasn't interested in pretense.

She shook her head, popped the trunk, and opened the car door.

She took her suitcase from the trunk, keenly aware that he was watching her. When she'd walked up the seven steps to the landing, Akeel was already there, behind the door.

"Hey, babe," he said. "You changed your hair. I like it."

"Hey, Akeel," Fenway said. "Didn't your mom ever tell you you'll catch cold if you don't put on a shirt?" Cold? Hell, the danger was fever: his abs hadn't lost their definition in the two years since she had seen him. She thought of what Dez had said and breathed a sigh of relief.

"What my mamma told me was that I better have someone to keep me nice and warm." He pulled her to him. Even in her sneakers she had two inches on his five-eight frame. "I can't catch cold when you're so hot."

Fenway rolled her eyes. "Oh, please, Akeel," she said, stepping out of his embrace.

"That's a great dress, too," he said. "Looks all innocent, like you're about to go on a picnic or something. It's like ninja-sexy."

"Ninja-sexy?"

"Yeah, it looks all sweet and nice at first, not like a sexy dress, and then it sneaks up on you and suddenly, pow! You don't know what hit you."

She could feel the color rise to her cheeks. "Okay, Cyrano, take this suitcase upstairs before we make everyone puke."

"Ain't no one out here but us," he said.

"I hope there's no one in *there* but us either."

Akeel smiled. Fenway smiled back and followed him upstairs.

Her hands were on his muscular back as soon as the door to his apartment closed behind them. Her left hand snaked around to his stomach, then started to loosen his belt. She kissed his shoulder.

"You're not wasting any time tonight," he said. He put the suitcase on the floor. She put her purse on the end table, still kissing his back.

"Only got one night in town," she breathed into his ear. "Wanted to make it count."

"One night?"

"We'll see how it goes."

They made it to the sofa, although his jeans did not.

It was easy to get comfortable with him again, Fenway thought. Their bodies went well together. She liked how they fit. She liked the way his skin smelled, liked how his hands were so strong and confident on her back, on her shoulders, on the sides of her face as he kissed her deeply.

Her phone rang in her purse.

When she realized where the ringing was coming from, their clothes were mostly off, and he was kissing her, up and down her body. The phone stopped ringing after about twenty seconds. Then it rang again. She ignored it again, and it again went to voicemail. They were in a rhythm, and she didn't want to lose it.

The phone rang again.

And, excruciatingly, Akeel stopped. "You got a boyfriend in Cali wondering where you are?"

"No," she said. "I hardly know anyone there except co-workers. And they know better than to call me on vacation."

"You gonna get that?"

"No, I'm not going to get that," Fenway said. "I want you to keep doing what you were doing."

"Your phone is breaking my concentration. And believe me, you want me to have my full powers of concentration for this."

Fenway sighed. "Fine. I'll tell them to go away."

She pulled herself up on the sofa and grabbed the phone out of her purse. "It's Dez," she said.

"Who?"

"She's my co-worker." Fenway answered the call. "Hey, Dez. This better be important. You don't have any idea what I'm—"

"Mayor Jenkins is dead, Fenway."

Fenway stopped. "Wait, what? The mayor? Dead?"

"Yes."

"What happened?"

"Stabbed," Dez said. "They found her at Cactus Lake Motel about fifteen minutes ago."

"Cactus Lake Motel? Was she trying to stop a drug deal? Was she trying to *make* a drug deal?"

"I can't say," Dez said. "Where are you? Have you made it to Seattle yet?"

"Yeah, I'm here. With Akeel."

"Good. We booked you on the next flight back. Five-thirty. Coastal Airways flight out of Sea-Tac."

"Out of Sea-Tac? But I've got my car here."

"Just leave it in long-term, Fenway. The county will pick up the tab. You can go back and get your car in a few days."

"No one else can do this?"

"Are you or are you not the coroner of this county, Fenway? You don't think the mayor getting murdered is important enough to cut your vacation short?"

Fenway stood up and padded half-dressed into the kitchen, away from the disappointed Akeel. She lowered her voice. "Is there any way I can leave tomorrow instead?"

Dez's voice was sharp. "Did you hear me say who died? Alice Jenkins. First black judge in this county. First black mayor in this county. First black anything-that-matters in this county. Not the first black *woman*, the first black *person*, period."

"I guess I didn't know that. I'm sorry. I'll be on that flight."

"I'll see you when you land."

Dez clicked off.

Putting the phone in her purse, Fenway avoided Akeel's eyes. She had to be out of the apartment in thirty minutes. And she had caught a chill.

CHAPTER THREE

THE SECURITY LINE AT SEA-TAC WAS LONG, AND SHE REALIZED AS she sat on the airplane that she didn't even have a book to read. She just stewed about Akeel complaining about how the talk of murder had ruined the mood, wasting their remaining half hour together. And then she thought about the mayor, murdered in a motel room, and her mood grew worse.

At eight o'clock, Fenway walked out of the baggage claim area at the Estancia airport. She saw Dez waiting for her in her red Chevrolet Impala and got in.

Dez's silence spoke volumes about her dark mood as well. Fenway braced herself for a snarky comment about her too-short dress or the casual white sneakers, but it never came. Fenway had never seen her so quiet—Dez just nodded in greeting, then drove out of the airport straight to the freeway and exited onto the state highway, up into the hills toward Cactus Lake.

As dusk approached, the fog settled in, as it did around Estancia nearly every evening in the summer. They drove on the winding uphill road in silence for twenty minutes until they burst through the layer of fog.

Fenway blinked, barely believing the stark contrast between the fog and the sudden clearness, even in the twilight. She looked behind her; the grey mist obscured the town, the beach, and the ocean as far as she could see.

She turned around and out of the corner of her eye saw the sign for the turnoff for Cactus Lake. Fenway would have missed the turnoff had she been driving. Dez turned her wheel to the right and braked for the stop sign at the foot of the exit.

The pine and ironwood trees became scrubby along the side of the road, a thousand feet above sea level. Dez made a left turn onto the frontage road and pulled the Impala into the cramped parking lot of the Cactus Lake Motel. The motel sign had lost two of its letters, but their dust-ridged outlines were still visible. They pulled in next to a Dominguez County Sheriff cruiser; it had to be McVie's. He would certainly lead the investigation for a death as high-profile as this. The crime scene unit van was already on the scene. Fenway wondered if Dr. Yasuda had made the trip from San Miguelito, or if she had sent one of the techs.

Dez killed the engine and they both got out of the car and walked toward the motel office. Through the open door, she could see Sheriff McVie, tall and muscular and chiseled, looking professional in his black uniform. Fenway felt her mouth go dry. Even from this distance, she saw the gold band still around his left ring finger.

A middle-aged white man with a large pot belly stood heavily behind the counter. He looked sad and a little bit nervous.

McVie looked up when Fenway and Dez stepped through the threshold of the office.

"And this is the coroner with one of our sergeants now," McVie said.

Dez stepped up to the counter and pulled out a business card. "I'm Sergeant Desirée Roubideaux," she said to the man, who grew more pale by the second. "Did you make the 911 call?"

"Look," the man said, "I don't want any trouble. This place already has a bad reputation. We took your advice a couple of months ago and we're trying to keep the junkies away."

"We're not gonna worry about that just now," Dez said. "Rome wasn't built in a day, am I right?"

The man squinted. "What?"

"I mean, I don't think the junkies will all just leave overnight. It's a process."

He shrugged. "I guess so."

"All right," Dez said. She turned to McVie. "I understand our people are already in the room?"

He nodded. "Celeste secured the scene as soon as she arrived. CSI got here about an hour ago. I was just finishing up with Mr. Colburn here."

"Cliburn," the man said.

"I'm sorry. Cliburn."

The man grabbed a key off the set of hooks behind him and handed it to the sheriff. "It's room 26. Up that first flight of stairs to your right."

Fenway stepped aside and let the sheriff take the lead. Grim-faced, McVie strode to the stairs and started to climb, Fenway and Dez following close behind.

"What's the story on this?" she said to McVie as they stepped out of the office and started up the stairs.

"The 911 call came in at just after three. He said the house-keeping staff found her on the bed when they went in to get the room ready for the next guest."

"Can we talk to the housekeeping staff?"

"They didn't stick around," McVie said. "Afraid of the cops."

Fenway nodded.

She looked down the outdoor hall. Officer Celeste Salvador stood guard about halfway down between the staircase and the room.

The sheriff stopped in front of Officer Salvador, next to a tan door with brass numbers reading 26, yellow police tape across the door frame. "Thanks, Celeste," he said to her.

Celeste cleared her throat. "Not a problem, sheriff. Hi, Dez. Hi, Fenway."

"Who caught CSI on this one?" asked Fenway. "Did Dr. Yasuda come down herself?"

"No. The new guy caught it."

"Kav?"

"Right. He's still in there."

Too bad Dr. Yasuda hadn't made the trip, Fenway thought to herself. But Kavish Jayakody, although the newest crime scene tech, had gained Fenway's trust by pointing out evidence in a couple of cases they had worked together.

McVie unlocked the door and pushed it slowly. It creaked as it swung. "This is kind of hard to see. You might want to prepare yourself." He stepped backward and nodded to Dez.

"Okay," Dez said as she lifted the tape and stepped inside, followed by Fenway, then the sheriff. McVie closed the door behind him.

On the bed lay an African-American woman of about seventy-five, dressed in a light blue business suit. She wore matching flats, but no jewelry. Her silver hair, though disheveled, looked like it had been recently done and styled. Her right arm rested at a right angle next to her body. Her left arm dangled partway off the bed, and her legs hung off, as though she had been standing, tried to sit on the bed, and collapsed. A large, wet-looking bloodstain had soaked the comforter, and several large splatters stained the carpet in the three feet or so between the front door and the bed. Fenway took a few soft steps toward the body and leaned over the bed. The woman was definitely Alice Jenkins, with the same kind brown eyes Fenway remembered from the board of supervisors' meeting, when they discussed Fenway's appointment as County Coroner. Alice had been an ally—or at least someone who treated her like her own person, and not as the daughter of the most powerful man in the county. Now those kind brown eyes stared, unseeing, at the ceiling.

She tore her gaze away from Mayor Jenkins' face and down to her torso. The white blouse under her suit jacket was completely blood-soaked from just below her collar down to her waist.

An Indian man came out of the bathroom, about five-eight, with large, dark eyes, a square jaw, and slightly graying temples. He wore a black San Miguelito Medical Examiner jacket and blue nitrile gloves.

"You made it," he said.

"Hi, Kav," McVie said. "Thanks for staying."

Kav nodded. "Certainly, Sheriff." He exhaled. "As you can see, those are stab wounds on the body. I've identified four distinct wounds, two in her abdomen and two in her chest. She would have bled out quickly."

Fenway continued to look at Mayor Jenkins. "Liver temp?" Fenway asked mechanically.

"Already ambient when I got here. Rigor puts time of death around one o'clock this morning, give or take an hour or two. Salvador arrived first on the scene this afternoon."

Dez wrote quickly in her notebook. "You say you got a good look at the wounds?"

Kav nodded. "Yes. I took pictures already. Do you want to look for yourself?"

"Hang on for a second, Kav," Dez said, averting her eyes and putting her hand over her mouth. Kav waited several seconds before McVie broke the silence.

"What else did you find?"

"Not much in here," Kav said. "About three hundred finger-prints. A ton of DNA—hair, skin cells everywhere. Guests didn't choose this motel for room cleanliness. I haven't moved the body, as you can see."

"What the hell was she doing here?" Dez murmured. She shook her head, as if trying to clear her mind from a bad dream.

"I've been over this room thoroughly," Kav said. "I haven't uncovered a reason why Mayor Jenkins came here."

Fenway thought for a moment. "Is the room in her name?"

"No," McVie answered. "This room should have been vacant last night. The housekeeping staff did a sweep of the room this afternoon, since it had been rented for this evening."

"Who reserved it for tonight?"

"Someone named William Matisse. There's a note in the motel files that he prepaid for the room in cash, but doesn't say when, or who at the motel made the transaction."

"Well, that's not suspicious at all," said Dez wryly.

"Will Matisse," McVie mused. "I know that name." He put his hand up to his chin thoughtfully.

Dez kept writing. "It sure rings a bell," she said. "But I can't place it."

"Called Yasuda yet?" Fenway asked Kav.

"I let her know," he said. "I thought I'd wait till you got here to schedule the autopsy. I figured you'd want to attend it with the M.E."

Fenway nodded. "Thanks, Kav."

Dez pointed her pen at McVie. "Sheriff, we should talk to Celeste if you haven't yet."

McVie pressed his lips together and stepped over to the door and pulled it open.

"Officer Salvador?"

"Yes, sir."

"Can you come in here a moment?"

"Yes, sir." She stepped in through the police tape and closed the door solidly behind her. She nodded to Dez and Fenway. Kav gave her a half-smile and went back in the bathroom.

"You were the first officer at the crime scene?" asked McVie.

"Yes, sir. I received the call from dispatch at 3:23 p.m. I arrived at the motel at 3:40."

"We didn't have a closer patrol car to the motel?"

"Not in the afternoon, Sheriff. Things don't usually start heating up here until the sun goes down."

"All right. What did you do once you got here?"

"I spoke with Mr. Cliburn at the front desk."

"That's the man who's there now, right?"

Celeste nodded. "I asked him if he made the 911 call. He answered affirmatively, then walked me to the room and opened the locked door with his key."

McVie nodded.

"I asked him who found the body, and he said one of the housekeeping staff."

"Did you get a name?"

"No, sir. Mr. Cliburn didn't remember who reported it, and when I got here, most of the housekeeping staff had already left."

Dez crossed her arms and shook her head.

"I asked Mr. Cliburn if anyone had been in the room except the housekeeping staff," Officer Salvador continued. "He said he didn't know. Many members of the staff have the key to these rooms."

"I see," said McVie.

Officer Salvador hesitated. "Sheriff, if I may offer an observation, security is pretty lax here. Keys go missing frequently, and I don't believe the doors are re-keyed on a regular basis."

"Thanks, Celeste," McVie said. "What did you notice when you entered the room?"

She took out her notebook and flipped two pages. "First, I swept the room to make sure no one else was here. When I entered, the shades were drawn and the overhead light was off. I drew my weapon, and I turned on the overhead light with my elbow. The bathroom door was open. I also checked under the bed."

McVie nodded.

"Then I performed a visual check on the body. I recognized Mayor Jenkins right away. The victim was clearly deceased due to her open eyes and the, uh." She cleared her throat and blinked hard.

McVie's voice was quiet. "Do you need a minute, Celeste?"

She pinched the bridge of her nose and closed her eyes. She cleared her throat again, then opened her eyes. "I'm fine, Sheriff. As I was saying—due to the amount of blood on the bedspread."

"Did you check for a pulse?"

She hesitated. "Not at first, sir. I thought it was clear she was dead. I couldn't wrap my head around it. Probably a minute or so later, when I remembered protocol."

"That's all right, Celeste. What else?"

Salvador looked down at her notebook. "The room was quite warm, but it didn't seem unusually so for July. The bathroom fan was on, but that was the only sound I heard."

She flipped back a page. "I continued my sweep. I didn't find any weapons or other hazards. I also didn't find anything belonging to the victim in the main room, though. No purse, for example. No jewelry. No suitcase. No clothes hung up on the rod on the side there." She motioned to a lonely-looking wooden curtain rod just outside the bathroom door.

"Anything on the bathroom counter?"

"Nothing but a wrapped soap and a plastic cup."

"The motel provide those?"

"I assume so, but I haven't confirmed it yet."

"Okay."

"I left the room, leaving the overhead light on. The door locked behind me. Then I used my radio at three forty-seven to contact dispatch."

"Wow, you didn't waste any time," Fenway said to Dez. "I got the call before four."

Dez nodded, thin-lipped. The mayor's death had sapped her usual snarky, sarcastic mood.

"Did you call Rachel too?" McVie said.

"No," said Celeste, "but I assumed that dispatch would take care of it. Either her or someone else in public relations."

"And Rachel didn't show up?" McVie asked, surprised.

"If there *is* a reporter here," said Dez, "they're probably renting a room with a hooker or a crack pipe. They're not here to get a story. Probably a good thing Rachel *didn't* show up. Keeps it out of the media another few hours."

"No reporter waiting for his big break camped on the police scanner?" asked Fenway.

"Sometimes we get lucky," McVie said.

Celeste continued. "I stood outside the door of the motel room. Mr. Jayakody arrived at, uh, let me see." She flipped another page in her notebook. "Approximately four forty-five. I didn't get the exact time of arrival."

"You were there the whole time?"

"That's right, Sheriff."

"No one went in or out?"

"Not through this door or window. And I don't see another point of entry to the room."

"Okay, thanks, Celeste," McVie said.

Kav stuck his head out of the bathroom. "I'm almost done here. The ambulance is on its way, and we'll get Mayor Jenkins transported to San Miguelito."

Fenway nodded. "I'll call Dr. Yasuda."

She stepped out of the motel room, with its harsh fluorescent light, into the dampening twilight. At almost nine o'clock, the sun had dipped behind the horizon. She drew a deep breath. The motel had accurately earned its horrible reputation. The sheriff's department constantly responded to incidents at the motel—drug busts, overdoses, prostitution. Cactus Lake itself was gorgeous—and a misnomer, as a cactus couldn't be seen for miles, but rather pines, ironwoods, and sturdy bushes. A turnoff, five minutes down the winding road from the motel, led to a beautiful state park frequently photographed for travel magazines.

A woman in a light blue uniform down the corridor watched them with a fearful look in her eye.

Fenway thought a member of the housekeeping staff had been brave enough to stay. She smiled and waved as non-threateningly as she could. The woman jumped, startled, and disappeared around the corner.

Fenway followed. She turned the corner and the woman had unlocked a room next to a housekeeping cart.

"Hello?" Fenway called.

The woman wouldn't make eye contact.

Fenway tried again. "*¿Cómo está, señora?*" Bits of high school Spanish trickled back into her head. She had read Borges in the original Spanish her senior year, but she had forgotten so much that she doubted she could get a conversation going with this woman, much less ask her what she saw.

"*No quiero ningún problema,*" the woman said. Fenway had to translate in her head—the woman didn't want trouble.

"*No hay problema aquí,*" Fenway said. There's no trouble here.

The woman looked up and finally met her eyes.

Fenway struggled with the next sentence. "*¿Está usted trabajar aquí el sábado por la noche?*" She knew she had butchered the verb tense, but hoped the woman would answer whether or not she had worked Saturday night.

"*¿Anoche?*"

Fenway grimaced. "*Sí, anoche.*"

"*Sí, cuando la alcaldesa fue asesinada.*"

Alcadesa, alcaldesa—Fenway dug through the files in her brain for the translation. What was it?

"*Señora Jenkins,*" the woman said.

It clicked into place—*alcadesa* meant a female mayor. The housekeeper had been working the previous night, the night of the murder.

"*¿Has visto algo?*" Fenway asked, hoping the housekeeper had seen something else.

The woman stepped out of the room and took a long look down either side, and answered in broken English.

"I see something," she said. "A man. He look strong. All black clothes."

"He wore all black?"

"*Sí.*"

"Like a suit?"

The woman looked at her strangely.

Fenway fought to remember the word, then got it. "*¿Un traje? ¿Un traje de negocios?*"

She shook her head. "Not, how do you say, fancy. Clothes for the running."

"A running outfit?"

"*Sí.*"

"Long sleeves and long pants?" Fenway mimed this.

She nodded.

"Where did you see the man in the running outfit?"

"At the room."

"With Señora Jenkins?"

"No. Um, how do you say. Outside. Outside the room."

"Did you see any blood? *¿Hay sangre?*"

"On the running clothes? No, I don't know. He had all black clothes."

"Can you describe the man?"

The woman shook her head. "He was no white," she said. "But I no see his face."

Fenway asked two or three additional questions, thinking more and more that she'd be embarrassed if her old Spanish teacher Señora Francisco showed up. But the woman had no more information. Fenway thought about asking her name, but decided against it; she didn't want to scare her off. Fenway thanked her and let her get back to cleaning.

She hadn't known Alice Jenkins very long, but the few interactions they had had were good. Not only had Mayor Jenkins deflected several attacks from Dr. Barry Klein when they had first met, but she also gave Fenway a special commendation for solving the previous coroner's murder. In Dominguez County, Jenkins was popular with the university liberals because of her stance on inclusivity, and accepted by the rural conservatives because she championed farm assistance and additional resources to fight wildfires.

A few weeks ago, Celeste had joined Fenway for lunch at Dos Milagros, Rachel's favorite *taquería* on Third Street. They had run into Mayor Jenkins leaving as they were arriving. "Afternoon, Celeste!" the mayor had said, beaming at her as she got in her car. "Good to see you too, Fenway."

Over their tacos, Fenway asked how long Celeste had known the mayor.

"Since the first day I got to town," Celeste had said. "She got me through my initial interview. The sheriff before McVie didn't really like, uh, people of color. He kept calling me Mexican."

Fenway had nodded through her own mouthful of *pollo asado*. She knew the feeling.

"The mayor is one of the good ones," Celeste had said. "And she talks to people about her ideas in a way that the people who originally disagree end up thinking it's *their* idea."

"My mom was like that too," Fenway said. "I bet the two of them would have totally gotten along."

And now both of those strong, outspoken African-American women were gone. Fenway came back to the present, shook her head, and walked toward Dez's Impala.

She took her phone out of her purse and called the medical examiner's office. Dr. Yasuda picked up. She, too, seemed uncharacteristically distraught by the news of Mayor Jenkins' death. They agreed to meet for the autopsy the next morning.

This hadn't been a good day, and it didn't seem like it would get any better. Fenway looked up and saw the ambulance from San Miguelito turn off the mountain highway. The body of Mayor Jenkins would soon disappear from the motel room.

CHAPTER FOUR

WHEN FENWAY AND DEZ GOT BACK INTO THE IMPALA, THE LIGHT
had completely gone from the sky, giving the motel a dreamy,
dreary look. All the way down the mountain highway, Dez stayed
quiet; she didn't crack any jokes, she didn't tell Fenway anything
that she had done wrong at the crime scene.

Finally, as they turned onto the freeway, she spoke. "I just
can't believe it, Fenway. I can't believe she's gone. The mayor! Just
gone. And I can't *imagine* why she went to that motel."

"She wouldn't stay there, I don't think," Fenway said. "No
purse, no suitcase, no cosmetics bag."

"Could have been taken," Dez said through gritted teeth.
"Whoever did it could have taken them."

They drove for a minute in silence.

"Hey, Dez, would you mind stopping at Rachel's apartment on
our way?"

"Rachel's apartment?"

"Yeah," Fenway said. "I finally gave in a couple of weeks ago and
bought a few houseplants. Rachel said she'd water them for me when I
went to Seattle. Now that I'm back, I can get my extra key from her."

"You can't get the key later?"

"Well," said Fenway, "I kind of want to see how she's doing."

"Ah, okay. Not a problem." Dez turned off at the Broadway exit and went the opposite direction from Fenway's apartment. "I wouldn't mind seeing her too. Her dad goes in front of the grand jury in a week or two. Can't be easy for her."

"Has she been holding up okay since I left?"

"She called me late Thursday. Having a rough night."

"I guess I'm not that surprised."

"Yeah. Mostly I think she's doing better, but she's still not sleeping. You know, bad dreams, can't get back to sleep, that kind of stuff."

"She told me she was getting better." Fenway paused. "Has she said what bothers her the most? Her father killing Dylan? Shooting her father to save me?"

Dez clicked her tongue. "Now, Fenway, you're not getting all guilty over that again, are you?"

"I know I shouldn't," Fenway said. "I mean, in my *head* I know I shouldn't feel guilty. It's just my emotions don't always follow logic."

Dez nodded. "Yeah, I get that."

"She's still going to counseling, right?"

"Yeah, and I can see the difference. But I'd be lying if I said she didn't still have a long ways to go. Yesterday was pretty good even though she hadn't slept too well. She seemed upbeat, kinda enthusiastic. And you know what I think it is?"

"Besides the counseling?"

"Yeah. It's that promotion. She jumped into that new job with both feet. And I'm glad for her. I'm glad she has something to take her mind off everything. She was so depressed."

They pulled into the parking lot of Rachel's apartment complex.

"Looks like the girl's in," Dez said. She pointed to the BMW parked in space 19, right in front of Rachel's townhouse.

"Saturday night and she's spending it at home," Fenway said.

"Oh, Fenway, she's still grieving. Leave her be."

Dez parked the car. They said nothing as they approached the door. Fenway rang the bell, stepped back, and waited. Fifteen or twenty seconds passed.

Dez stepped forward and knocked soundly. "Rachel, it's Dez and Fenway, girl! Come on down here! Let's go get some burgers!" She knocked again. "Or whiskey!"

Still nothing.

"Maybe she's in the bathroom," Fenway suggested.

Dez squinted. "Or maybe she's out with her friends."

Fenway looked sideways at Dez. "Maybe. But you know her friends are all weird around her. Especially that one girl Jordan. She's supposed to be her best friend, but hasn't even seen Rachel since all of this happened."

"Ring the bell again," Dez said, a note of urgency in her voice.

Fenway did. Thirty seconds passed. Fenway and Dez looked at each other.

"I don't like this," Fenway said. "It doesn't feel like she's just in the bathroom. It's too quiet."

Dez began to pound on the door. "Rachel!" she called.

There was no response.

Dez opened her purse and dug around in it.

"What are you doing?"

"Got a key," she said.

"How come you have a key?"

"Because Rachel was a *complete* mess a couple months ago. I came over here every day, bringing her dinner, making sure she got her ass out of bed, you know, that kind of stuff."

"I didn't know that." Fenway felt a little pang of jealousy.

"Unlike some people I know, I don't broadcast everything I feel all the time."

Ah, Fenway thought, *there's the Dez I know and love.*

"There you are, you little shit," Dez muttered, pulling a small keychain out of her purse. She unlocked the door and swung it open. "Rachel?" she called. "Rachel, it's Dez. Are you okay?" She stepped in, Fenway following closely behind her.

"Rachel?" Fenway called out. The dread nipping softly behind her brain suddenly screamed for attention. Fenway bounded up the stairs, her long legs taking three steps at a time.

At the top of the stairs, she threw open the bedroom door.

Rachel's petite frame lay on top of the covers, not moving. Fenway didn't see any blood.

"Dez! Up here!"

Fenway dropped her purse on the floor and grabbed Rachel's wrist and felt for a pulse. She felt it—weak, but she felt it. She pulled up Rachel's left eyelid, revealing a dilated pupil. Rachel, taking shallow breaths, didn't respond.

"Call 911!" Fenway yelled. "We need an ambulance!"

Dez appeared in the door, a look of horror on her face. "No ambulance. Get her in my car."

Fenway, running on adrenaline, bent over and picked up the five-foot-nothing Rachel and put her over her shoulder in a fireman's carry.

"Get your car open," she gasped. She hoped she could carry Rachel all the way to Dez's car. She was glad she had decided to wear the white sneakers that morning instead of heels.

Dez sprinted down ahead of her. Fenway took the steps cautiously at first with Rachel over her shoulder, then a little faster as she leaned against the wall for balance and gained confidence in her footing. She hit the ground floor and ran out the door. Dez pulled up on the sidewalk. Fenway got the rear door open and laid Rachel in the backseat, trying not to do it too harshly.

"Turn her head," Dez barked. "If she throws up, she's gonna choke otherwise." Fenway turned Rachel's head to the side and closed the door.

"Lock it up and meet me at St. Vincent's," Dez shouted to Fenway, tossing her Rachel's keys. Fenway caught them in midair, and Dez threw the car into reverse as she put a globe light on her dashboard, spun around, and drove off.

Fenway hadn't even been home yet.

She turned around and went back into the townhouse, walking upstairs. She went into Rachel's bedroom and bent down to get her purse from the floor.

She saw a pill bottle lying next to the nightstand. She picked up her purse, then walked over to the pill bottle and picked that up too. She turned it around in her hand. *Buprenodone Hydrochloride Tablets, USP, 150mg.* There was no label on the bottle, no patient or doctor information. Fenway shook the bottle. Empty.

She pulled her phone out of her purse and called Dez.

"Kinda busy now, Fenway," Dez said, picking up.

"Found an empty bottle of buprenodone by her bed," Fenway said.

"What are those, sleeping pills?"

"Not exactly, although it's an off-label use—"

"Dammit, did she overdose on sleeping pills or not?"

"Just tell the ER it's buprenodone," Fenway said. "They'll know what to do."

"Buprenodone, got it." Dez clicked off.

Fenway, dazed, sat down on the bed.

She knew the last couple of months had been hard on Rachel. Fenway couldn't help but think of herself as one of Rachel's closest friends, especially since Jordan and some of her other friends had all but abandoned her.

But the self-doubt crept in—and started to overwhelm her. How did she not see this? How did all the signs of this elude her? And why did Rachel open up to Dez and not her?

Fenway couldn't believe Rachel would choose to kill herself, though. She had just gotten promoted to work in the public information office, as close to a dream job as Estancia offered. Rachel had sketched out her five-year plan to Fenway over dinner at Zorro's on Thursday night before Fenway left for Seattle. Fenway didn't like the plan—Rachel intended to move to D.C. around year three—but it showed that Rachel thought about long-term goals.

And instead of sadness or depression about her father, Rachel felt only anger. She had only visited him once, after his arraignment, after they had denied bail because he was a flight risk, and she had screamed at him, she had sworn at him, and the officers working at the jail had escorted her out.

Nothing Rachel had done in the last two months were the actions of a woman about to kill herself. Not that there was any way to be sure.

Fenway decided to find Rachel's health care card. At the very least, the insurance companies could be notified sooner rather than later, hopefully saving Rachel a mountain of paperwork.

If she survived.

Fenway closed her eyes briefly, then stood up and walked downstairs to look for Rachel's purse. She found it on the coffee table, a receipt from Dos Milagros sticking partway out of the top.

Fenway supposed that if Rachel wanted a last meal, it would be from her favorite *taquería*—but, still, something about that seemed off. She went to the kitchen trash and opened the lid. The telltale foil and plastic salsa containers were on top.

Fenway sighed and turned around. And saw the note on the kitchen table.

To whoever finds this:

If you know me at all, you know my life has completely fallen apart the last two months. I wake up every day and I don't want to spend it without Dylan by my side.

When I close my eyes at night, all I can think about is shooting my father. The sound of the gun in my hand haunts me.

I can't sleep. I can't stay awake.

I don't want to face another day without Dylan.

We'll be together soon enough.

Tell Ana that I love her and hope she finds the strength to go on without me and Dad.

Fenway picked up her phone again and dialed a number.
"Kavish Jayakody."

"Kav, it's Fenway. I hate to tell you this, but there's another crime scene. It's Rachel Richards. Someone tried to kill her."

———————◆———————

Fenway called dispatch as well, and Officer Donald Huke arrived within ten minutes.

"Ma'am?" he said to Fenway. "I'm going to have to ask you to wait outside until the crime scene technician gets here."

"Officer Huke," Fenway said, "I know we've had discussions about you calling me *ma'am*."

"Yes, ma'am—Miss Stevenson."

She shook her head and left the apartment. Huke followed her and stood guard at the door.

Kav had told Fenway it would take him over an hour to get to Rachel's apartment, as he had to help the paramedics get the mayor's body into the ambulance for transport, then needed to bag up the sheets and comforter, as well as properly store all the other evidence. Fenway didn't relish spending quality time with Officer Huke. But Fenway felt out of sorts. Twelve hours ago, she had been expecting quite a different way to spend her evening.

She thought of her Accord in the Sea-Tac long-term lot, costing Dominguez County taxpayers twenty-seven dollars a day. She thought of her suitcase in the trunk of Dez's Impala, with her cosmetics bag and that sexy white tank top. And she thought of Akeel's gorgeous stomach, and the way his body trembled when she climbed on top of him.

The phone rang. It was Dez. She walked about thirty feet away to have at least a little privacy.

"Thought you'd want to know that they've got Rachel stabilized," Dez said. "She's gonna pull through. Oh—sorry. Gotta get back in there."

"Thanks, Dez," Fenway said, exhaling fully. The tension started to come off her shoulders as Dez hung up.

She walked back to the door.

"Rachel's going to make it," she said, and surprised herself by having to fight back tears.

"That's great news," Officer Huke said, the relief visible on his face. It was the first time Fenway had seen him display an emotion.

She took a deep breath. "Don," she said, "is this how you pictured spending your Saturday night?"

Officer Huke winced.

"You don't like 'Don'? I'm sorry. What do you prefer?"

"My parents named me Donald, and that's what I go by," Officer Huke said. "Though, I think at a crime scene, it's best for peace officers to be as professional as possible."

"You'd like me to call you Officer Huke."

"If that's not too much trouble, Miss Stevenson."

Fenway sighed.

A breeze had started, cool air coming from the ocean.

"Were you on duty tonight?"

"Yes." Officer Huke didn't move his head when he answered Fenway. "If you don't mind my asking, Miss Stevenson, what were you doing here?"

"I got called in from vacation, and Rachel was looking after my place. You know about the murder up at the Cactus Lake Motel."

And for the second time in two minutes, Fenway saw Officer Huke express feeling. "I heard. What a horrible thing. Did you know the mayor takes all the officers and detectives out to lunch on their first day on the job?"

Fenway smiled. "No, I didn't know that."

"I really can't understand who would do that to her." Huke shook his head.

"Did you know her very well?"

"Not really. But I attended most of the Board of Supervisors meetings. She had a real knack for diplomacy. Talked Dr. Klein off the ledge more than a few times."

"You went to the supervisors' meetings? Were you assigned security or something?"

Officer Huke looked at Fenway and furrowed his brow. "No. I'm involved in the community. Why wouldn't I go?"

Fenway looked in Officer Huke's eyes, searching for the joke.

He cleared his throat. "Do you know what she was doing at that motel, Miss Stevenson?"

Fenway shook her head. "The room should have been vacant. Someone named Matisse rented the room tonight. The housekeeping staff found her."

"Did you say Matisse?"

"Yep," Fenway said. "Like the painter. Only not Henri. I can't remember the first name. Something ordinary. Michael or Robert or something like that."

"William?"

Fenway's head snapped back around. "Yes. William. How did you know that?"

"William Matisse died fifteen years ago," Officer Huke said. "When he turned, I don't remember, nineteen or twenty, he got caught in a drug bust with a few other people—including Alice Jenkins' son. It was a big scandal, although she wasn't the mayor at the time."

"What happened to William Matisse?"

"Another inmate killed him in prison, only about a month into his sentence, I think. A prison fight, or stabbed in the shower, I can't remember. Didn't have the connections that Jenkins' son did, though. What was that guy's name? The son was older, like twenty-five." Huke tapped his temple. "It's right there. Some unusual name. Not super crazy, but one you don't hear very often."

Fenway looked it up on her smartphone. "Fletcher?"

"Yes, that's it. Fletcher."

"So who would have used the name William Matisse to rent that room?"

"I don't know."

"It must have been someone who knew William Matisse, don't you think?"

"I guess. Someone who was on a bender and used to do drugs with him, maybe. As sort of a dedication."

"Someone like Fletcher Jenkins, maybe?"

"Maybe. I know they sent Fletcher to rehab instead of jail. I heard he got straightened out, though."

"How do you know all this? Weren't you a fetus when this all happened?"

"I was ten. We did a big class project on current events."

They were silent for a moment.

"Does Fletcher still live in town?" Fenway asked.

"Yeah, I think I heard he stuck around after getting out of rehab."

Fenway and Huke stood in silence for a few minutes.

"When do you suppose the CSI tech will get here?" said Huke.

"I don't know. He had to make sure the evidence was all bagged up properly." Fenway looked at the time on her phone. "Ugh. It's already ten. This is going to be one of those long nights, and I've gotta be at the autopsy early tomorrow." She sighed.

"Miss Stevenson?"

"Yes, Officer Huke?"

"Is Rachel going to be okay?"

"Sure. Dez called and said she'd pull through."

"No—I mean, *after* this. Organ damage, or even, you know, suicidal thoughts?"

Fenway looked at the ground. "I don't know. She overdosed on some pills. I don't know if she took enough to do permanent damage."

"But you don't think she tried to commit suicide."

"Absolutely not," Fenway said firmly. "First of all, the note's not in her handwriting. She doesn't make her g's like that. Plus the note got her sister's name wrong—it's *Anne*, with two n's, not *Ana* with one. Someone staged this."

"What kind of pills were they? Sleeping pills?"

"Buprenodone," Fenway said. "Anti-anxiety medication, mostly. Sometimes it's prescribed as a sleeping pill."

She thought for a moment.

"Sometimes it's prescribed to combat addiction, too," she said softly to herself. Fenway remembered it as an older medication, but one that had been popular with rehab doctors ten or fifteen years earlier.

Just about when Fletcher Jenkins served a stint in rehab.

Another awkward silence came between Fenway and Huke, and Fenway could barely tolerate it until Kav pulled up in the CSI van. A young woman was in the passenger seat.

"Thanks for coming, Kav," Fenway said as he got out of the van.

"Hey, did you hear they stabilized Rachel?" Kav said.

Fenway nodded. "Yeah, Dez called me."

"Have you met our crime scene tech, Melissa?" Kav motioned to his passenger. Melissa got out. She wore a sparkly sleeveless top, a short black skirt, and stiletto heels; her dark hair cascaded in curls down to her shoulders. She smiled sheepishly at Fenway. Fenway couldn't place her at first. Then it hit her.

"She's a crime scene tech, huh? I thought she was your prom date, Kav."

Melissa blushed. "Okay, I guess I deserved that."

Kav looked puzzled.

Fenway explained, "Just before you started, Kav, I went out to a site in the middle of the woods in a black dress and high heels."

"What were you doing in the middle of the woods in a black dress and heels?"

"I had to go to a memorial service that afternoon. And Melissa had a little fun at my expense." Fenway smirked. "Little did I know she just played the long game until she could outdo me with the fancy outfit."

"Very funny, ha ha," said Melissa, putting her hands on her hips.

"Melissa has brought the finest designer blue nitrile gloves with her to the red carpet this evening," said Kav, playing along. "These are the same gloves worn by the glamorous starlet Roxanne McFarland on *Memphis Medical*."

"You can stop now," Melissa said, trying to appear annoyed, though a smile played at her lips. She handed the box of blue nitrile gloves to Fenway and took a pair for herself. "Some people go out dancing on Saturday nights."

"I'm sure we all had plans more fun than analyzing a crime scene," Fenway said. "I'm sure you've all had to cancel plans for work before." She glanced over at Melissa. "And if you have to wear uncomfortable heels, collecting evidence in an apartment sure beats walking through a dry riverbed in the middle of the forest. I think the judges would still score me higher on degree of difficulty alone."

Officer Huke stepped aside from the front of the door.

"Hey, Donny," Melissa said. "Missed you at the club tonight."

"Duty calls," said Huke.

"Maybe we can catch a drink later."

"We'll be here pretty late."

"Maybe the drink can be at my place," she said in a low voice as she passed him. He smiled and his ears got a little red.

Once they were inside, Fenway cocked an eyebrow at Melissa.

"What?" Melissa said, shrugging. "Donny's a lot of fun."

"If you say so. I thought he always colored inside the lines."

"Mmm," Melissa murmured, turning her head to get one last look at Officer Huke. "He can color inside *my* lines any time."

Fenway rolled her eyes.

Melissa went straight for the letter on the kitchen table. "Did anyone touch this?"

"I don't think so," Fenway said. "I picked up the pill bottle off the floor upstairs to check if there were any pills left. I didn't think at the time that it could have been foul play."

"But you didn't touch the note."

"No, I didn't touch the note. But I've been over here six or seven times since May. My fingerprints will probably be on a bunch of stuff in the kitchen and family room."

Melissa set her mouth in a tight line and went to work.

Kav and Fenway went upstairs to search the bedroom. They did a grid search of the floor and the bedspread, and searched the dresser, the closet, and the nightstands.

"Here's her .22," Fenway said, remembering Rachel using it to save her life.

"We'll get Melissa up here for fingerprints, but I'm not seeing anything," Kav said, disappointed. "I'll still bag up a few things just in case, but I'm not seeing any other pills. Not even a water glass."

"How did she take all the pills if she didn't have a water glass?"

"You said yourself that someone staged this, Fenway. They must have dissolved those pills in her drink or in her food, and moved her in here."

Fenway was lost in thought for a moment. "You know," she said. "Officer Huke just told me that Mayor Jenkins' son went to rehab after a drug bust fifteen years ago. If he fell off the wagon, that might explain why she went to that motel. Maybe she tried to find him there."

"I guess that might make sense."

"The name on that room reservation—William Matisse?"

"Yeah?"

"Same guy who got arrested with Fletcher Jenkins fifteen years ago. At least that's what Huke says."

"Hmm," Kav said, narrowing his eyes.

"And the pills in that bottle? They can be used for sleeping pills, but some doctors recommend them for drug and alcohol addiction. They used to prescribe them a lot, especially around the time Fletcher went to rehab. And since we're talking about a staged suicide—well, maybe we should talk to the mayor's son."

Kav paused. "You think this is connected to the mayor's murder?"

Fenway thought for a moment. "I don't know, Kav. It's a pretty tenuous connection. But it's still worth asking Fletcher. I can see what the sheriff thinks."

Kav went downstairs. Fenway pulled her phone out. McVie answered on the third ring.

"McVie."

"Hi, Sheriff. It's Fenway."

"Hi, Fenway. Can this wait? I'm trying to get out of here to salvage some sort of date night with Amy."

"I'm sorry, Sheriff, but did you hear what happened to Rachel?"

"What?" McVie said sharply. "What happened to her?"

"I came to pick up my key and she was unconscious and non-responsive," Fenway said. "Dez took her to the hospital. I found an empty bottle of sleeping pills on the floor."

"Oh my God," McVie said. "Which hospital?"

"St. Vincent's."

"I'm on my way."

"Wait!" Fenway said before he could hang up. "I think we may want to talk to Mayor Jenkins' son Fletcher."

"Fletcher?"

Fenway explained everything breathlessly: the name on the motel reservation; the buprenodone pills that could be used to treat addiction; the stint in rehab as a possible reason for the mayor being in that hotel. She finished, almost panting with adrenaline.

"We need to talk with Fletcher right away, don't you think?"

"What's the medication called again?"

"Buprenodone."

"And it's a sleeping pill?"

"It's actually an anti-anxiety—"

"Never mind, Fenway." He clicked his tongue. "I don't know if I agree with you on the medication connection, but we should at least talk to Fletcher about his mother's murder. Let me see where his last known address is. If he's still in town, we'll talk to him together." He paused. "How common is buprenodone?"

"It used to be really common to treat addiction. Today, not so much. But a lot of doctors don't want to change a medication that's working for their patients. Especially when it comes to addiction."

"What about for anxiety or sleeping?"

"It's not that common."

"Okay," McVie said. "You can ask him the medication stuff, but be careful how much you say. I don't want to burn anything on his mother's murder by going fishing with the Rachel thing."

"I understand."

"Where are you now?"

"Me? I'm at Rachel's apartment with the CSI team. Kav is here. So is Melissa."

"Melissa who?"

"Melissa, uh, from the San Miguelito M.E.'s office. I don't think I caught her last name."

"Okay. I'll give you a call back in a few minutes."

Fenway went downstairs.

Melissa examined a plastic half-full Gatorade bottle. "I think this bottle contained the buprenodone."

"Gatorade?"

"Yeah. The sugar and salts would have masked the flavor."

"So you're saying it's attempted murder."

"I sure think it's looking that way."

Fenway paused. "I'm sorry, Melissa," she said, "but I don't think I caught your last name."

"De la Garza," Melissa said.

Fenway nodded.

"Okay. When we get this back to the lab, I'll see if we can push a rush on this analysis."

"Thank you."

Suddenly, the room closed in on Fenway. She closed her eyes and took a deep breath. She opened her eyes and the walls were back to normal. But she had to fight back tears.

"You okay, Fenway?"

She nodded. "I, um, I'm going to walk home. You don't need me for anything else here?"

Melissa shook her head.

Fenway picked up her purse and took a couple of steps toward the door. Her breath caught, her eyes started to water. She pulled the door open. It seemed much heavier. She made it outside and began to take some deep breaths, but a sob caught in her throat.

She took the concrete path toward the sidewalk so she could go home and clear her head.

The tears were streaming down her face now; part of her wished it was day instead of night, so she could wear sunglasses to at least partially obscure her tears from passing strangers, but part of her needed this out in the open so she could cleanse herself of everything. The death of Alice Jenkins—the one member of the board of county supervisors who treated her like a real person. Finding Rachel's near-lifeless body—a victim of attempted murder. She didn't want to include her aborted romantic interlude with Akeel in her list of things that had gone wrong; she felt cheap and selfish for even thinking about it after the mayor's murder. Alice Jenkins' body likely lay on a metal table in the M.E.'s office by now; Rachel, who had shot her own father to save Fenway's life, lay unconscious in the hospital.

She gritted her teeth, clenched and unclenched her fists. The rushing air from the passing cars cooled the hot night air. She welcomed it and hated it at the same time.

A jogger turned the corner and came toward her, lithe and fast in neon green shorts and a white short-sleeve athletic shirt. She had a cap pulled over her face, looking down at the ground. She raised her head and saw Fenway, face streaked with tears, and immediately looked back down and kept going past her, down Broadway.

Fenway concentrated on walking, getting her arms going back and forth, putting one foot in front of the other, and soon she calmed down. She approached the freeway overpass, and the roar of the cars below drowned out the last catches of her sobs.

She pulled out her phone and called Dez. It rang once and went to voicemail.

After the overpass, she caught a green light across Channel Islands Boulevard and walked through a well-lit park to get to Estancia Canyon Road. The traffic noise from the freeway died down, and only a couple of bicyclists on the other side of the four-lane road saved the street from being deserted. The fog that often crept over Estancia during summer twilight had held off until now. In the artificial light of the streetlamps, over the empty field, she saw the mist start to thicken.

It was dark inside the Coffee Bean—the shop had closed a couple of hours before—but the lighted sign above the store had a pale, haloed glow around it. Fenway walked quickly toward the coffee shop, switching the purse to her other shoulder.

A call came in on her phone. She glanced down at the screen; it was McVie. She cleared her throat twice before she clicked *Answer*.

"Hey, McVie."

"Hi, Fenway." McVie paused. "Are you okay? You sound, I don't know…"

"Like I've been crying." She pushed a sob back down her throat and covered it with a cough. "Yeah."

"Yeah." McVie hesitated. "You know they said Rachel's going to make it, right?"

"Yeah."

"I just got off the phone with Dez. They're keeping an eye on Rachel for signs of liver failure. She's still unconscious. But she's stable."

"Thanks for telling me."

There was silence for a moment.

"Did you find out where Fletcher Jenkins lives now?" Fenway asked.

"Oh, right. Yes, that's why I called. He's still in Dominguez County. He's got a place in Vista Del Rincón."

"That little town wedged between that big granite rock face and Ocean Highway?"

"Yeah. He got married about ten years ago. Actually seems to have turned his life around. He's an auditor now at a big accounting firm. His wife teaches at Las Desporadas Middle School. Two little girls, eighteen months and five years old."

"So that would really suck if he fell off the wagon. There are grandkids involved. Alice Jenkins would have definitely tried to get Fletcher out of that motel if he had been back to his old ways there."

"That would be one possible explanation to explain her presence."

"It's unlikely she rented a hooker."

"Unlikely, but not impossible."

"Come on, McVie."

"You haven't worked in law enforcement for as long as I have, Fenway. You see some stuff over the years."

She was quiet.

McVie filled the gap in the conversation. "I'm just getting off the freeway onto Broadway now. I'll be picking you up in just a few minutes. Then we can head down to Vista Del Rincón."

"Oh—I started walking home. I, uh, I couldn't be at Rachel's anymore."

McVie hesitated for a moment. "Yeah," he finally said, slowly, his voice soft and empathetic.

"You can get me now, though. The walk did me good. I've calmed down."

"You can skip it tonight, Fenway. I don't want to put you through any—"

"I want to come with you to question him, Sheriff," she interrupted. "I want to ask him about the buprenodone. I want to see the look on his face."

"Fenway," McVie said softly, "I know you're upset. You don't have to come."

"No, no," Fenway said, "don't mistake that for an emotional reaction. I want you to tell him we found his fingerprints on that suicide note. If he's the one who did it, it'll put him off guard.

Even if he wore gloves, he'll say to himself, *Did I keep the gloves on the whole time?* And we'll see it in his face. We might not get a confession—but we'll know where to start looking."

Fenway could almost hear the gears turning in McVie's head.

"Okay," he said carefully. "You're right. And you know about the buprenodone. You at home?"

"About five minutes away. Do you want to pick me up in front of the Coffee Bean?"

"Sure. See you soon."

Fenway clicked *End Call* and took another deep breath.

CHAPTER FIVE

FENWAY SUDDENLY REALIZED HOW UNPROFESSIONAL SHE MUST look; she was wearing her tennis shoes and the scarlet polo dress she had put on in the hotel in Oregon that morning, the same outfit she wore when she arrived at Akeel's house that afternoon. She pulled her compact out of her purse and tried to clean up her tear-stained face. Despite not having a sink, and only having a few minutes, she hid the signs of her tears.

McVie pulled up, and she opened the door. "Thanks for getting me."

"No problem at all," he said. She saw him look in her eyes—not stare up and down her body the way Akeel had—and wondered if he had a hard time getting her out of his mind too.

It took them about twenty minutes in the cruiser to get to Vista Del Rincón, south of Estancia. Fenway looked to her right—even in the muted foggy darkness, she could see the Pacific Ocean less than fifty feet away from the edge of the highway. As Fenway leaned forward to look out the windshield to her left, she saw the granite wall extend up at a near ninety-degree angle from the ground, jutting into the misty night sky.

Vista Del Rincón comprised little more than a collection of forty modest houses, a general store, and a gas station. As the cruiser slid into the turn lane, McVie had to wait for a while for an opening in oncoming traffic.

"I can't imagine living here," said Fenway.

"You really should come here in the daytime," McVie said. "Get an ice cream cone at the general store and sit on the patio there. The ocean in front of you, the granite wall behind you. The freeway seems inconsequential."

"Until you have to go into town."

McVie shrugged. "It's not for everyone, I guess. I wanted a house here when Amy and I first got married. She wouldn't have anything to do with it."

"Everything going okay?"

"With Amy?"

"Yeah, I know you're working on things."

McVie breathed out. "I guess it's to be expected that when we work on things, it has to be work. It's just really hard work. Maybe I'm not used to, uh, processing that kind of anger."

Fenway tried not to react at all.

"Okay," McVie said, turning onto a narrow street with dirt paths for sidewalks. "Look for house number 64. I think it's on the right."

They wound their way around the next gentle curve.

"That's it. The green house on the right," said Fenway.

It was a small mint-colored house with 64 on the mailbox—the old, traditional kind, with a red metal flag that actually looked like a flag.

"Okay." McVie eased up on the gas pedal and coasted to a stop next to the dirt path, just past the driveway. In front of the one-car garage sat an old Jeep Grand Wagoneer and a tiny Toyota hatchback. The front porchlight shone weakly, its yellowed bulb straining against the encroaching darkness.

"Should we both get out?"

"I think so," McVie said. "They look like they're home."

As she went to open her door, Fenway noticed her hands were shaking slightly; maybe not so bad that McVie would notice. But she knew McVie could tell she was keyed up.

She pulled herself out of the passenger seat, with McVie already halfway up the driveway. She wanted to give herself a minute to shake out the cobwebs, take a few deep breaths. She didn't want to look unprepared, or let Fletcher Jenkins rattle her. Then she had a thought.

"Sheriff!" she hissed.

He turned around and looked at her.

She hurried over close enough so he could hear. "Is this a next-of-kin notification?"

"Of course it is. What did you think?"

"I thought we were going to interrogate him."

"No. I mean, we'll ask him a few questions. You were planning to let me take the lead, right?"

She blinked. She had been so on edge she hadn't thought about it. "Of course."

"I'm going to try to steer the conversation around to the sleeping pills. Once I do, you'll be ready with follow-up questions. This is how we did it for that meth overdose in Paso Querido two weeks ago, right?"

"But that wasn't a murder."

"We didn't know that then." McVie paused. "I'm sorry, Fenway. I don't know why I just assumed this would all be second nature to you. First Mayor Jenkins, now Rachel—I'd be lying if I said this didn't bother me. I'm thinking about how to talk to this guy, but I guess I'm too stuck in my own head."

"Do we need to regroup? Maybe we should go back to the car."

Just then, the front door opened.

"Hi there," said a tall black man who stood in the doorway. "You from the sheriff's office? Can I help you?"

McVie moved out of the shadows into the light.

"Oh, hey, Craig!" the man said. "It's been a long time."

"Fletch," McVie said.

The man moved to the porch and the door closed behind him. He had short black hair and a short, neatly kept beard which showed just a touch of gray at the chin. He wore a rumpled light blue oxford dress shirt, untucked and very wrinkled at the waist and below. He had on a pair of dark tan khakis and his feet were bare.

"Jeez, I haven't seen you since the five-year," Fletch said.

"You missed the last couple," McVie said.

"I'm sure that being the sheriff, you heard what happened," Fletch said. "Stuck in rehab for the ten-year, and I didn't really feel like showing my face at the twenty."

McVie nodded.

Fenway cleared her throat and looked at McVie.

"Fletch, I'd like you to meet the county coroner, Fenway Stevenson."

Fenway took ten awkward steps over to the porch. Fletch stepped forward to the edge of the porch, minding his bare feet, and shook her hand.

When they made contact, she felt how clammy her palm was. Fletch smiled anyway, but Fenway's return smile must not have been very convincing.

"Everything okay, Craig? Why the visit with the coroner?"

McVie walked forward slowly toward the porch. "Yeah, this isn't a social call, Fletch. Is there somewhere we can talk?"

"We can go into the living room. The girls are asleep."

"Your wife home?"

"Yes, but I think she's getting ready for bed. It's past ten, isn't it?"

McVie nodded. Fletch walked back to the door and pushed it open, then stood aside. Fenway went in first, followed by McVie, then Fletch, who closed the door behind him.

A small patch of tile served as an entry, and a built-in bookshelf separated the hallway from the living room. A white toy box sat in the corner. A blue fabric couch and loveseat dominated the small room, surrounded by a few scattered toys.

"Sorry," Fletch said, bending down and picking up the toys in front of the sofa. "We tell the girls to put their toys away before bed, but, you know how it is."

"Yeah," said McVie.

"You have kids?"

"Just one. Megan's sixteen now."

"Man, time flies," Fletch said, shaking his head and turning toward the toy box. "Tomorrow I'm dropping them off at preschool, and I'm going to blink and they'll both be driving."

McVie cleared his throat. "Listen, Fletch, I'm really sorry to be the one to tell you this."

Fletch turned around and straightened up quickly. "Tell me what?"

"Your mother was found tonight. She's dead, Fletch."

Fletch blinked and a toy dropped out of his hand and fell to the floor with a loud thud.

"Dead?"

"I'm sorry, Fletch, I really am. We're all devastated."

"I just—" Fletch started. "I just left her a message an hour ago. We were all going to go out to dinner next week." Fenway could see his easy demeanor collapse around him; his shoulders and eyes sunk down and in, his head drooped as if he had gotten punched in the stomach.

A woman appeared at the end of the hallway. "Fletch?" she said. She was white, about five-foot-six, in a green tank top and grey sweatpants, her brown hair in a ponytail. "I heard a noise."

She saw the sheriff, in his uniform, and Fenway, standing awkwardly behind the sofa.

"Mom's dead," Fletch said softly. He reached out with his left arm to the sofa, and finding the arm, awkwardly smashed himself into the cushion.

Fletch's wife rushed around the bookshelf and pushed her way past Fenway to her husband. She wrapped him up in her arms and rocked him gently and almost imperceptibly. He stayed silent, eyes wide open, staring at nothing.

"I'm really sorry for your loss," Fenway said.

They could hear the clock ticking on the mantel, an old tabletop-style clock with mahogany sloped sides that looked like it had been passed down.

"Listen," McVie said. "I'm going to have to ask you a few questions. You're not going to like them, and you might not like me very much after I ask them, but I've got to ask them anyway, or I wouldn't be doing my job."

Fletch pulled himself up with one hand, although he still had one hand on his wife's arm. "What are you talking about?"

"We found your mother at the Cactus Lake Motel."

Fletch's eyes darkened.

"I don't know what your mother was doing there, Fletch. Did she happen to say anything to you about it?"

Fletch ran his head over his face from his forehead to his chin. He muttered under his breath—Fenway thought she caught a string of swearing—and slowly stood up.

"No," he finally said. "No, I don't know why she went there. And if you're asking me this, it means you think she was murdered."

McVie nodded.

"And I'll save you the trouble of asking me for an alibi," Fletch said. "What's the time period I need to account for?"

"Looks like late last night and early this morning," McVie said. "Between eleven and three."

"Asleep in bed, here, until five-thirty," he said. "Isla woke up then. I got her and we made breakfast. I remember starting the coffeemaker at six o'clock on the dot."

"Anyone vouch for you?"

"Tracey can."

"He's telling the truth," Tracey said. "I didn't look at the clock when he got up, but Isla usually gets out of bed between five and six. Olivia sleeps until eight or nine on Saturday. I slept until about seven."

McVie nodded. "How about earlier this afternoon?"

"Today? I drove the girls to get new shoes up in town," Fletch said. "We went to Drake's. Uh—I think I have the receipt. We got there around two-thirty or three."

"I threw the receipt away," said Tracey. "But I'll dig it out." She left to go through another doorway.

"I'm sorry about all these questions," McVie said, "but I just have one more. Do you have any buprenodone in the house?"

Fletch set his jaw. "Yes," he said. "Dr. Sutherland prescribes it for me. Dr. Miriam Sutherland, office over in P.Q. I've taken them ever since I got out of rehab. Pretty much the reason I'm a functioning adult."

"You've taken it for fifteen years?"

Fletch shrugged. "It's a lower dose now, but yeah."

McVie shuffled his feet. "I'm sorry, Fletch, but I'm going to need to see the last bottle you got from the pharmacy."

Fletch sighed. Fenway could see the exasperation on his face, although he tried not to show it. "I just had it refilled a few days ago. I'll get it. It's in the bathroom."

Fletch walked in a daze around the bookshelf and down the hall, just as Tracey walked back in from the kitchen. "Okay, it's got some grease on it, but you can read it."

McVie took the greasy receipt from Tracey. "You have an evidence bag, Fenway?"

"I came right from the airport, Craig. I mean, Sheriff." Fenway winced at her slip-up. "I might have one or two in my purse, but I didn't take my kit on vacation with me." She started to rummage through her purse.

"Thought you might have grabbed a few from Kav."

Fenway shook her head. Then she found two evidence bags hiding in a side pocket. "Okay, here's one, Sheriff." She handed one to McVie.

"I don't know what you're looking at Fletch for," said Tracey, as McVie slipped the receipt into the evidence bag. "But whatever it is, he didn't do it at 2:47 this afternoon. And I bet the security cameras and the workers at Drake's will vouch for him too."

"I appreciate it, Tracey," McVie said. "Sorry you had to dig through the trash."

"Honey?" Fletch called. Tracey walked quickly past the bookshelf and down the hall.

McVie and Fenway found themselves alone in the living room again.

"What do you think?" Fenway whispered.

"I don't know yet," McVie said. "It doesn't seem like he knew she was dead."

"No. That seemed genuine."

"But drug addicts usually lie pretty convincingly."

"True."

Fenway stopped and listened for a moment. She thought she could hear urgent whispers coming from down the hall. "What do you think they're discussing?"

"I don't know. Their voices sound worried."

Fenway nodded and strained to hear, but she couldn't make anything out.

They waited in the living room for another five minutes. The hallway whispers were becoming more urgent. Fenway caught

Fletch saying, in a frustrated tone, "Don't you think I—" before catching himself and lowering his voice again.

The sheriff took a few steps toward the hallway and leaned over the bookcase.

"Is everything okay?" He said it loud enough for Fletch and Tracey to hear, but not so loud that the girls would wake up. At least, that's what Fenway hoped—she listened carefully, but neither little feet nor little voices could be heard.

Tracey came out of the hallway, holding a small box. "Fletch is still looking for the bottle. We found the box it came in."

She handed the box to Fenway. The CVS Pharmacy logo was clearly printed on the top left corner of the label, and to the right, the address in South Estancia. Fletch's name, the name of Dr. Miriam Sutherland, and the instructions were all neatly printed below. That would explain why there was no label on the bottle itself.

Tracey hesitated. "The bottle isn't, um, it's not where we usually keep Fletch's meds."

"That's the only place you keep those pills?" McVie asked.

"Fletch says he put it in its usual place. He's almost out of the last bottle. I don't know. I didn't pick the prescription up, and I wasn't with him, either. Maybe he put it somewhere else."

"Okay." McVie nodded.

Tracey bit her lower lip and crossed her arms. She stared at the floor. Behind her, sounds of frantic rummaging could be heard—probably Fletch going through the bathroom drawers and medicine cabinet, Fenway thought.

Fenway watched McVie, but he didn't say anything else.

"Do you know a woman named Rachel Richards?" Fenway blurted out.

Tracey looked up. "I'm sorry?"

"A woman named Rachel Richards," McVie said easily. "I think she went to school with one of your daughter's preschool teachers. She works in our office. Fenway's good friends with her. She thought maybe you knew her."

"Oh," Tracey said. "No. No, I don't think so."

"She sometimes volunteers at the preschool," Fenway offered, trying to extend McVie's lie. McVie shot her a look and Fenway clamped her mouth shut.

"I'm going to see if Fletch needs any help," Tracey said.

"Listen," McVie said, "we can get those pills later. I hate to do this, but we'll need Fletch to come with us tonight to identify the body. I promise, I'll have him back here as soon as I can."

"Tonight? It's already really late."

"I know," McVie said gently, "but every second counts here. Don't you want us to figure out who killed your mother-in-law?"

"Right," Tracey said. "Of course. I don't—" and a tear ran down her cheek. "I don't really know what to do. I liked Alice so much. She was so good with the girls. They're going to—" her voice caught; she swallowed and went on. "They're going to be devastated."

"We can give you some resources to help you make arrangements. I can't imagine what Fletch is going through right now. And you too."

Tracey nodded, and walked back into the hallway. The frantic scrabbling noises stopped, and Fletch appeared, dead-eyed, in the hallway.

"You might want to put some shoes on, Mr. Jenkins," Fenway said gently.

Fletch looked down at his feet and nodded. "Right. I just need..." And he trailed off. He turned and walked back, returning a minute later with a pair of grey sneakers in his hand.

Fletch, confused at first why they were going all the way to San Miguelito, settled in for the long ride. Fenway talked at length about the funding for the coroner's office, the agreement that Dominguez County had made with San Miguelito. She talked about Dr. Yasuda, her professional demeanor, and even mentioned the occasional morbid joke that she would tell. Fenway laughed nervously but heard nothing from Fletch in the back seat; she turned around and he was asleep.

"I don't think Fletch had—" Fenway said softly, but McVie immediately raised a finger to his lips and shot Fenway a warning glance.

Fletch didn't stir again until they turned into the driveway at the M.E.'s office. He looked around; he didn't recognize his surroundings. He cleared his throat. "Are we here?"

"We're here, Fletch," McVie said. "We'll try to get you in and out as fast as possible. Get you some information, some resources you can use."

"Have you called Ellen yet?"

"Who?" Fenway asked.

"I think one of the sergeants is calling your sister," McVie said. "I haven't spoken to her yet."

They got out of the car and opened the front door. The fluorescent lights cast harsh shadows on the deserted waiting area. Fletch stood in the middle of the waiting room, blinking, looking lost. McVie pulled his phone out and called a number.

He waited a moment, then said, "We're here, Michi."

He clicked off.

"She'll be right up."

Fenway stifled a yawn—it was almost eleven.

Dr. Yasuda opened the door. "Mr. Jenkins," she said, shaking his hand. "I'm so sorry we had to meet under these conditions." She shook her head. "Follow me, please." She turned and quickly walked through the door she had just come out of. Fenway and

McVie started to follow her; Fletch rocked back on his heels, caught a bit off guard.

"She walks fast," McVie said. "Let's go."

Through the corridors, they walked past the morgue's double doors into an observation room that had a large window with a curtain pulled over it on the other side.

"We need to determine if the deceased is your mother, Alice Yeardley Jenkins," said Dr. Yasuda. "I'm sorry, but we will need a verbal affirmative or negative from you when you see the body."

Fletch nodded.

Dr. Yasuda tapped on the window. A man in scrubs, a medical hat and mask—probably Kav, Fenway thought—pulled back the curtain then stepped toward the table. A body lay under a sheet on the metal table in the middle of the small room. He lifted the sheet and drew it down, uncovering the mayor's face.

Fletch's face crumpled and his hand covered his mouth. "Oh, God," he said. "Yes, that's her. That's my mamma." He turned from the window, keeping his hand over his mouth, and wrapped his other arm around himself.

"I'm so sorry, Mr. Jenkins," Fenway said.

"Listen," McVie said, "let's go back upstairs. I'll get you a cup of coffee, Fletch. We've got a couple of things for you to take back with you."

Fenway nodded goodbye to Dr. Yasuda. McVie and Fenway walked back upstairs, with Fletch dragging behind them.

"Where do you want to do this?" McVie said. "Do you want to use the break room? Or would you prefer a little privacy?"

"Uh," Fletcher said, "whatever, I guess."

"Let's go into one of these side rooms," McVie said. "It'll be good for us not to be in the break room, where everyone can see and hear everything." It was an excuse, Fenway knew; the break room was deserted. But Fletch didn't pay close attention.

They walked into a room, about eight feet by ten, with barely enough room for a small table in the middle and two chairs on either side. Fletch staggered into a chair on one side, and McVie and Fenway took the two chairs facing him. Fletch stared at the table, eyes unfocused.

"I'm having some of the literature brought in," McVie said. "It's not much, but it might help you with the next steps. And we partner with several grief counseling services in the area. You know, if you, or maybe the girls, need to talk to anyone."

"Thanks, Craig," Fletch said, seeming to snap out of his state. "So I probably need to tell you... there were some things that my mom and I found out. I think they might have to do with why she was killed." His eyes, bags under them in spite of his nap in the car, were alert.

McVie straightened up. "Okay, Fletch, just, really quickly, just as a formality, I need you to know your rights. You have the right to remain silent. Anything you say can and—"

"You reading me my Miranda rights, Craig? After I just told you I might have some information about why my mother was murdered?"

"Just a formality, Fletch. I swear I'd rather I didn't have to. But I can't skip any steps investigating your mom's death. You don't want her murderer to go free just because I didn't go by the book, do you?"

Fletch leaned back, a confused look on his face.

"Okay, anything you say can and will be used against you in a court of law. You have the right to an attorney. If you cannot afford an attorney, one will be provided for you free of charge. Do you understand the rights I've read to you?"

Fletch's eyes were tired but wary. "Yeah, I understand."

There was a knock at the door.

"Not right now," McVie said, but the door already swung open.

"Sorry," Melissa said, holding the pill bottle in a clear evidence bag.

"Never mind," said McVie. "Just give it to me later."

Melissa nodded, then backed out of the room, closing the door behind her.

"What's going on here?" said Fletch. "Is that a bottle of buprenodone?"

McVie looked uncomfortable. "That's just a piece of evidence."

Fletch was quiet for a moment. The look on his face changed from open to closed, like window blinds. "What does that bottle have to do with my mom's death?"

McVie paused. "It's for a different case. Now, weren't you ready to give us some information?"

Fletch's mouth went into a thin line. "Are you guys trying to railroad me?"

McVie cocked his head to the side and looked at Fletch. "We're not trying to railroad you, Fletch," McVie said. "Why would you think that?"

"Because I knew you in high school, Craig."

McVie shook his head. "That was a long time ago."

"Where did you find that bottle of buprenodone?"

McVie paused. "I told you, Fletch, it's for another case. It doesn't have to do with your mother's death. Why? Do you know something about that bottle?"

Fletch screwed up his mouth and tapped his foot. "I think I better come back later with my lawyer."

"You sure you don't want to tell us now? Not even if it can help us find your mom's killer?"

Fletch rubbed his eyes, as if he couldn't believe what was happening. "Am I under arrest, Sheriff?" Not *Craig* anymore, Fenway noted.

McVie paused and leaned back. "Of course not, Fletch."

Fletch stood up. "Then I'll be headed back home. I'll come back in on Monday with my lawyer."

"Okay," McVie agreed.

"We can give you a ride," Fenway offered, hoping that he'd open up in the car on the way back.

"I'll take an Uber, thanks."

"It's gotta be fifty miles back to Vista Del Rincón," McVie said. "Let us drive you."

Fletch's voice was measured and calm. "I don't care if it costs a thousand dollars. I don't care if I have to hitchhike back. I don't want a ride from you tonight. And I'd appreciate it if you left me and my family alone until I come to see you on Monday."

He walked out, gently closing the door behind him.

McVie and Fenway sat at the table in silence for a moment.

The sheriff sighed. "Dammit."

"What do you think about his alibi?"

"I don't know," McVie said carefully. "That could have been Tracey's receipt, I guess."

"Yeah, but he seemed pretty confident that the cashier would recognize him."

McVie tapped his fingers on the table, lost in thought. "I suppose we could get video footage," he mused. "Drake's has cameras. Easy enough to ask for."

"And more useful than a greasy shoe store receipt."

Another knock. Melissa opened the door and spoke from the threshold. "Hey, I just wanted to let you know—"

"Dammit, Melissa," McVie said. "He clammed up after you brought that bottle in."

"You said you wanted—"

"I know what I said!" McVie shouted. He looked down at the table.

Melissa looked over at Fenway and raised her eyebows. Fenway pursed her lips and didn't say anything.

"Sorry, Melissa," McVie said. "I apologize. Not your fault. I know I told you to bring the bottle to me."

"No problem, Sheriff," Melissa said, although the tone in her voice suggested otherwise. "I came in here to say that we're going to have to run the fingerprints in the morning."

"In the morning?" McVie asked. "This is the mayor's murder we're talking about."

"I know that, Sheriff, but the fingerprint database server has a maintenance window tonight. It's going offline in thirty minutes."

McVie screwed up his mouth, annoyed.

"Everyone's going home for the night. We're going to start on this fresh in the morning."

McVie nodded.

"Do you two need anything else from me?"

"Nope," McVie said. "Have a good night, Melissa."

Fenway started to say something about enjoying her evening with Officer Huke but decided against it. Melissa closed the door.

McVie looked at Fenway. "What were we talking about?"

"Video footage from Drake's. And then you were going to drive me home so I can go to bed."

McVie smiled sadly. "I guess we need to pack it in for the day."

They left the small room and walked downstairs. McVie turned and pushed open the doors to the morgue.

"Hi, Michi," he said. "I think we'll be heading back to Estancia unless you've got anything else."

Glumly, the M.E. said, "No, go ahead. I'm going to do the autopsy on the mayor tomorrow morning."

"I'm sorry," McVie said softly, walking over to Dr. Yasuda. "I wish you didn't have to."

She leaned against him, and they shared an awkward side-hug for a moment. A tear went down Yasuda's cheek. "She was a really good person," she whispered.

McVie nodded. They broke apart.

Dr. Yasuda cleared her throat. "Are you going to be here too, Fenway?" she asked.

"I was planning on it," Fenway said, "but I just realized I don't have a way to get here. My car is in Seattle."

"Seattle?"

"I drove it up there to get some of my mom's things out of storage. Flew back when Dez called about the mayor."

"Maybe Dez would be willing to drive you back here," Dr. Yasuda said.

"I can ask her," Fenway said. "Or I could rent a car."

"Or take an Uber like our friend Fletch," McVie mumbled.

"I'll figure something out. What time will you be starting?"

"It's late," Dr. Yasuda said. "I want to be well rested. I don't think I'll get here before nine. Call me when you arrive; we don't usually staff the front on Sunday mornings."

They said their goodbyes and walked up the stairs and out to the parking lot.

Fenway's mobile phone dinged. She pulled it out of her purse and looked at the screen. A text from her father read, *I heard you're back in town. Breakfast tomorrow?*

She knew she didn't have a lot to eat at her apartment, and thought she might get a decent breakfast before her trip. She might have to endure the over-engineered brunch concoctions at Mimosa's instead of the blue-collar bacon and eggs she preferred. But the mayor's death and Rachel's poisoning had rattled her. Some family time—even with her father—might settle her down.

Can you do it early? she texted back. *I have to leave for San Miguelito at 8:15.* She got the affirmative response before she even got into McVie's cruiser.

As McVie waited at the stoplight to get them on the highway back to Estancia, Fenway thought about her Accord. And Akeel.

She looked over at McVie.

"I like working with you, Craig," she said simply.

He looked her in the eyes. "I like working with you too, Fenway. I wish it didn't have to be in such a shitty situation."

She gave him a sad smile before he turned back to the road.

Fenway looked out the window. The palpable darkness outside cloaked the canyon, with its fast-moving creek below. Past the next curve, she saw the lights of San Miguelito's hotel district, the famous Spanish architecture, the railroad yards, then finally the slow climb up to Cuesta Pass.

She wished she were still in Seattle. She wished that she and Akeel were wrapped up together, intertwining their fingers as they kissed, their legs entangled. She wished her mother's painting was safely boxed up in her trunk, waiting for a trip back to its spiritual home, waiting to again hang on a wall, waiting to be appreciated.

PART III

SUNDAY

CHAPTER SIX

———◆———

WHEN HER DOORBELL RANG AT SEVEN, FENWAY EXPECTED HER father. She pulled the door open and Nathaniel Ferris stood there, but so did a tall man in a light gray chambray suit and a crisp white shirt. His tanned skin, square jaw, and bright blue eyes made Fenway think her father had brought along a movie star who had one of the beachfront mansions in Estancia Estates.

"Hi, Dad," Fenway said, a little unsure of herself. "I didn't expect a guest."

Nathaniel Ferris looked disapprovingly at his daughter's blue jeans and simple cream blouse, with navy blue flats.

"Good morning, Fenway," he said, a bit formally. "I guess I should have mentioned that Everett Michaels would be joining us for breakfast this morning."

Fenway nodded. She was not going to apologize for dressing somewhat casually.

"Nice to meet you," Fenway said.

"The pleasure is all mine," Everett Michaels said. He reached out and shook her hand and flashed a crooked smile with beautiful, straight, white teeth. "You've certainly done a fantastic job as coroner, and in such a difficult situation, if I may say."

Fenway nodded, a little off guard. "Thank you. That's always nice to hear." She turned to her father. "I think I mentioned that I had to head out for the medical examiner's office after break-fast," she said. "It won't be a problem to drop me at the airport car rental, will it? I had to leave my car in Seattle."

"Oh," Nathaniel Ferris said. "You're still on the mayor's case?"

"It just happened yesterday," Fenway said. "I'll be working on it for a while."

"Right," her father said. "Of course we can drop you off there. I guess we better get going—we don't have a lot of time."

Everett Michaels insisted on taking the back seat of the Mer-cedes. True to Fenway's expectations, her father took them to Mimosa's. His driver having Sundays off, Ferris drove, and opened up the S500 on the freeway, despite the short distance.

Fenway knew that Mimosa's positioned itself for the weekend brunch crowd: post-church socialites in their Sunday best, or post-hike outdoors types laughing too loudly over Bloody Marys. At 7:15, the three of them walked into a mostly empty restaurant. The hostess greeted them sleepily and sat them unnecessarily far away from the kitchen, at a booth in a corner window.

Fenway sat next to Everett Michaels and caught a whiff of his cologne for the first time. It didn't smell overpowering, but the spice and sweetness intermingled wonderfully. She looked at him, and he gave her a smile suggesting he knew how good he looked.

Her father looked happy and effervescent. After they gave their coffee order to the server, he clapped his hands together.

"Fenway, I'm really glad you agreed to come to brunch with Everett and me."

Fenway held her tongue, as she had agreed to a meal with her father, not a stranger. Also, she thought, isn't 7:15 too early to call it brunch?

"As you know, Everett's the vice president of innovation at Carpetti Pharmaceuticals, and the candidate I'm backing for coroner."

Of course, Fenway thought. *Eggs with a side of ambush.*

"I know," Ferris continued, "that you're not comfortable introducing Everett at his campaign announcement event on Monday without knowing the man." He clapped Michaels on the shoulder. "And I shouldn't have assumed that you would. I've known Everett for almost twenty years. He served as a grooms-man when I married Charlotte."

Fenway gritted her teeth. She hadn't been invited to the wedding. He hadn't shown up for her high school graduation; three weeks later, he married a twenty-five-year-old and jetted off to his honeymoon in Rome.

"But I thought if the two of you were able to chat for a bit, get to know each other, well, Fenway, you might reconsider. If you read some of Everett's articles, maybe some of the reports he's submitted, you'd see what a great scientific mind he has."

Everett Michaels broke in. "And Carpetti's obtained FDA approval for the first pain reliever with the effectiveness of oxycontin without the addictive side effects." Michaels leaned forward, eyes bright. "Not only is it non-opioidal, it also causes significantly less stress to the renal system than acetaminophen, or even ibuprofen."

"I'm going to pretend I understood that," laughed Ferris, then his face grew serious. "Don't you want a coroner who actually cares about medicine?" He looked directly at Fenway. "I know you're no fan of Dr. Klein. You don't want to see Klein in position to tear down everything you've built here."

Fenway, nonplussed, wondered what exactly she had built. The team hadn't changed since she started, except for Rachel's promotion to public information officer. Unlike her predeces-sor, she never second-guessed the staff or overstepped boundaries, but Fenway didn't think that counted toward *building* anything.

But she didn't want to argue, and she really wanted to be in San Miguelito in time for the autopsy to start. She took a deep breath and girded herself.

She reached out across the table and took her father's hand, and felt her voice pitch up slightly. "Dad," she said, shaking her head, "I'm so glad that you know me well enough to know why I don't feel comfortable with this." She turned her head toward Michaels and again breathed in his scent. "Nothing against you, Mr. Michaels. If you've done half the things my dad says you have, and if your new medicine works like you say it does, you obviously have a wonderful scientific mind." *Or at least employ some top-notch scientists and take the credit,* she thought, pulling her hand back from her father's. "But I'm afraid I'm going to be far too busy with the investigation into Mayor Jenkins' murder to commit to anything else."

The server brought their coffees, handing the latte to Fenway. She took a sip and set the large cup back in its saucer. "And frankly, Dad, I think Monday would be far too soon to announce. It will look disrespectful to the memory of Mayor Jenkins. If you're worried about Dr. Klein getting a jump on you, let *him* announce on Monday. That way, *he's* the one who looks bad in front of the press."

Michaels smiled and leaned back. "Your daughter has a point, Nate," he said. Fenway didn't think she had heard her father called *Nate* since her parents were still together. "We've been focused so much on the boxing match with Klein that we've forgotten the optics."

"That's my girl," Ferris said, smiling, but his lips were tight. "Doing what's best even when it isn't what I want."

Fenway bristled, but kept the smile on her face. "Well, then, you'll love this, Dad." She turned to Michaels. "If you want to have any chance at the election, Mr. Michaels, you're going to have to actually grieve for the mayor."

Michaels looked confused. "But I didn't even know her. We met no more than two or three times. Likely at some committee meetings."

"Sure," Fenway said, "but you've got to understand, *everyone* loved Alice Jenkins. The most stoic, hard-assed, emotionless people I've met in town are crying over her death. This is not going to be an easy thing for Estancia. For the county. And if you, Mr. Michaels, come out and look like you just want to sweep her memory under the rug, you're going to lose in a landslide."

Michaels rubbed his square jaw thoughtfully. Fenway thought Michaels hadn't heard pushback like that before; his good looks and powerful position usually discouraged people from disagreeing with him so directly. But she had to get to the autopsy, and she hoped getting to the point would move the conversation along. It's not like she needed Michaels on her side—in fact, he wanted her on *his*.

"You're very straightforward, aren't you, Miss Stevenson?" he asked, although it sounded like more of a statement. Fenway noticed that he didn't call her *Miss Ferris*, an error that almost all of her father's friends and business colleagues made. Michaels must need her on his side more than she thought.

"Our time is valuable, Mr. Michaels," she said. "I don't think you want me blowing sunshine up your dress."

Her father visibly winced, but Michaels smiled widely. "I certainly don't," he said. "Enough business talk. Let's get some breakfast."

After the server took their order—Ferris and Michaels ordering omelettes with French sheep's-milk cheese and herbs that Fenway couldn't pronounce, and Fenway keeping to a simple egg breakfast that she had to order a la carte—Michaels started to probe Fenway about her master's program in forensics. He seemed especially interested in trace evidence. Unless Fenway imagined it, Everett subtly flirted with her; just enough for her to notice, but not enough for her father to pick up on it. A brief touch of the hand, a look that lingered a little longer than it might have ordinarily.

After the food came, Fenway talked about the new acid treatment they had in San Miguelito that could raise filed-off identification numbers from guns, car parts, and other metal objects.

Michaels talked about the new pain reliever at length: the drug interactions that almost derailed FDA approval, and about the rigors of drug testing and clinical trials.

"We were fortunate that the process for Nozithrapham went as quickly as it did," he said. He smiled at Fenway and she felt her heart flutter. "Sometimes drugs like this take years to go through approvals. But we have the best clinical trial manager in the business." He laughed. "I hired him away from one of the big European companies. Moved him here from Austria. That's how seriously we take it."

"That's why Everett couldn't take the coroner position in May," Ferris interjected. "They were still testing, and without Everett's guiding hand to navigate the bureaucracy, it might have been delayed for months."

"Years," Michaels corrected, touching Fenway's forearm lightly. "And I can't take all the credit—I couldn't have done it without Gottfried."

"It takes a village," Ferris said. Fenway stopped herself from rolling her eyes.

"And I'm sure you've heard all the concern over opiate addiction and pill-popping," Michaels continued. "It's all over the news, and the regulators are getting more and more involved. It's bad for our reputation, and frankly it's bad for business."

"But then you have this miracle drug," Fenway prodded.

Michaels shook his head. "I don't like that term," he said. "But that doesn't mean I'm not bullish on the prospects of what this can do."

"It's not often you get to do something good for society *and* make a lot of money from it," observed Fenway.

"That's exactly what I told the board of directors," Michaels said, slapping the table for emphasis. "This is why I got involved in the development of medicine to begin with. Sometimes, with the investors screaming about quarterly earnings and expecting double-digit growth every year, I feel like I'm up against the ropes."

She could feel her pulse quicken with this conversation, and, even knowing that he was trying to play her to get within her good graces, she couldn't help but be intrigued.

"One thing that I don't get," Fenway said. "You're in a great position at Carpetti. You must be making a lot of money. You're helping people. Why give it all up to run for coroner?"

Everett leaned on the table and looked down. "My mother taught me that serving your community is one of the most important things you can do," he said softly. "Estancia has been very good to me. I haven't found the right woman." He paused and looked up into Fenway's eyes. "I don't have children. My legacy is going to be how I helped our patients and customers, and how I helped the community." He sat up straight. "And, truth be told, I've had critics who say I'm a selfish bastard, that I only think about myself, and that I only care about money." A smug smile came over his face. "I can't wait to prove them wrong."

Fenway leaned back. "I guess there's some nobility in that," she said.

As they continued to talk about medicine, Fenway found herself engaged and interested in spite of herself, and the man certainly was easy on the eyes—and the nose. Her father looked both lost and bored by the conversation, which Fenway relished, though she tried not to show it.

"All right, gentlemen," she finally said, "I need to get to San Miguelito. I've got the most important autopsy of my career starting in an hour, and I've got to rent a car."

Ferris held his hand up. "Hold on, Fenway. Everett, you didn't leave anything in the Mercedes, did you?"

"No, I don't think so."

"In that case, I'll let Fenway borrow the Merc. We're enjoying our breakfast and our tee time isn't until ten. I can have Charlotte come out in the Range Rover and meet us here when we're done."

"You'd let me drive your Mercedes?" Fenway said.

"Don't get a ticket," Ferris said, holding the keys out for her. "You think you're doing 65, then you look down and you're going 90. That car craves the autobahn."

Fenway again tried very hard not to roll her eyes, and mostly succeeded.

———————◆———————

Fenway got into the Mercedes, prepared to be unimpressed by the s500's pomp and circumstance. She had forgotten about the buttery-soft leather, and, turning the car on, she felt everything in easy reach, like the car had been created just to cater to her whims.

"Ah," she breathed. "*This* is why my father can't understand why I'm okay with a Honda."

The car, though large, handled crisply, and she opened it up on the highway to San Miguelito. The low, throaty growl of the engine as she downshifted and sped past an RV on the Cuesta grade pleased her on a visceral level.

But the strangeness of Mayor Jenkins' death and Rachel's attempted murder weighed down her thoughts. She turned over much of the interview with Fletcher Jenkins in her head. She couldn't imagine that the two crimes wouldn't be related some-how—especially with Fletcher's relationship with the mayor and the pill bottle, possibly his, found next to Rachel. It might not be his, of course—she hoped the report on the fingerprints would be available by the time the autopsy finished—but it just seemed too coincidental. And she knew enough from her two months on the job not to like coincidence when it came to dead bodies.

She turned off the highway and drove through the streets of San Miguelito until she turned into the parking lot of the M.E.'s office, a few minutes early. Kav and Melissa greeted her in the waiting room.

"The advance crew is here, I see," she said wryly, but their faces were sullen.

"Dr. Yasuda isn't doing well," Kav said. "She's normally so calm and reserved around cadavers. But she's having a problem with this one."

"She really liked Mayor Jenkins," Fenway said, nodding. "And I get the feeling she doesn't really like a whole lot of people."

"You may have to perform more of the autopsy than you might have thought," Melissa said, as they exited the waiting room and walked down to the morgue. "Dr. Yasuda waited till you got here to start, but I get the feeling that she doesn't really want to start at all. I'll go pull the mayor out of the fridge and get her prepped." She hesitated. "I hope you don't mind, but, uh, I'm not going to sit in on this one."

Fenway turned into the lab room and grabbed a set of scrubs. She put them on, tucked her black curls into a medical cap, and pulled on gloves. Then she took a deep breath and walked out into the examination room.

The supine body of Alice Jenkins lay on a table in the middle of the room, with the sheet turned down to reveal her face. Dr. Yasuda's laptop rested on a counter slightly above where she sat on a stool, facing slightly away from the body, shoulders slumped. Fenway had never seen her like that before. Dr. Yasuda looked up, her face creased with pain.

"I'm really sorry," Fenway said. "I know a lot of people are having trouble with the mayor's death. I didn't know her very well, but I know that she touched a lot of people's lives."

Dr. Yasuda nodded, lips a thin line. She started to speak, then stopped, then took a deep breath.

"I may ask you to make the Y incision," she said. "I'm not sure I can do it."

Fenway nodded.

"I did the CT scans last night before I left," she said. "Melissa helped. They're on the computer."

Fenway walked over to the laptop and clicked through a few of the images. "Did you see anything?"

"Four stab wounds. Each wound measures between seven and fifteen centimeters deep." She cleared her throat. "The wound up here, by her heart, went in nine point three centimeters and appears to be the source of most of the bleeding. The other stab wounds are in her abdomen."

"Have you started a tox screen?"

Dr. Yasuda nodded. "Yes. I mean, I can't fathom any drugs or illicit material in the mayor's system. But you never know. I see a lot of things as the M.E. that I can't explain, for sure. I drew the blood samples yesterday and sent them in for review this morning. We actually have a full staff today."

"Okay," Fenway said. "Are we ready for the incision?"

Dr. Yasuda looked down and nodded.

Fenway took a scalpel off the tray, closed her eyes, and took a deep breath. She had done this several times in her lab classes in both her nursing and forensic programs, and had cut open two cadavers in the last month, both victims of drug overdoses. Dr. Yasuda had to perform the autopsy of the suicide victim; Fenway hadn't been sure she could do it without messing up the evidence of the suicide.

She pulled the sheet down and saw the four stab wounds in Alice Jenkins' torso. The wounds had been cleaned from the blood, and their sharp lines looked sterile, almost academic.

"The fork of the Y might disturb the aortic wound," Fenway said. "Is that okay?"

"We're going to examine the heart and remove it," said Dr. Yasuda. "We've taken pictures and x-rays. Everything has been marked into evidence. You're okay."

Fenway hesitated to make the initial incision. She looked at Dr. Yasuda's face; the medical examiner had her eyes closed.

Fenway turned back and cut, as confidently and cleanly as she could. It seemed to take hours to make the incisions, although it must have been only a minute, maybe less. She noticed she hadn't cut one of the forks of the Y far up enough on the shoulder. "Rookie mistake," she said under her breath, and she extended the cut.

When she finished, she placed the scalpel back on the tray. "Thank you," Dr. Yasuda said, and a heavy burden seemed to lift off the M.E.'s shoulders. Fenway noticed it; perhaps once Dr. Yasuda focused on the body parts—and not the person—she could relax and gather herself back into the cool, professional demeanor that characterized her interactions with Fenway.

They weighed the internal organs. Of particular interest to Fenway were the contents of the stomach. "This is probably poultry of some kind," Dr. Yasuda said. "We can check if it's chicken or turkey, but I've seen enough digested chicken to know that there's something different about this. We'll give it to the lab to analyze. Kav should be able to make quick work of it."

"Notice the color of the liver and the kidneys," Dr. Yasuda said. "This isn't the liver of an addict or an alcoholic. If she does have some sort of drug in her system, it's not a regular occurrence."

Dr. Yasuda worked efficiently, pointing out minor anomalies to Fenway, who assisted. Fenway had started to anticipate Dr.

Yasuda's needs on the last couple of autopsies, and felt especially connected to her as they worked. After two hours, Dr. Yasuda set down her tools.

"We've worked quickly, Fenway. Thank you for helping me through this." She cleared her throat, and Fenway saw the doctor come back to herself.

"When can we get the contents of her stomach?" Fenway said. "If there's a clue to where she ate, we might be able to trace her steps on Friday night."

"Sheriff McVie will want to start with that for sure," Dr. Yasuda said. "If you don't mind, I'd like to take a little more time with the stitches. I don't want her to look like a softball when we're done. You don't have to stay for this."

"Thank you," Fenway said. "I really should get to the hospital and see how Rachel's doing."

Dr. Yasuda nodded.

Fenway reached out and took Dr. Yasuda's hand, gloves and blood and isopropyl alcohol and bile and all, and gave her a reassuring squeeze.

Dr. Yasuda squeezed back. Fenway started to let go, but Dr. Yasuda held on for a second longer. She whispered, "Will you tell Dez I'm sorry?"

Fenway was taken aback. She hoped it didn't show, either in her face or in her hand, still holding the doctor's.

"Of course," Fenway said. "Will she know what you mean?"

Dr. Yasuda studied Fenway's face for a moment. She started to speak, then closed her mouth. Finally, she said, "Yes. Dez will know what I mean. I don't know if it'll do any good. But she'll know what I mean."

Fenway let go of Dr. Yasuda's hand, gave her a wan smile, and walked out of the suite, throwing away her gloves, and into the prep room, where she took her scrubs off and put them in the laundry, then scrubbed her hands, face, and arms thoroughly. The gloves and the scrubs had protected her skin, but she still felt in need of cleaning.

She went to say goodbye to Dr. Yasuda and Melissa, then went back upstairs and outside and stood blinking in the brightness.

"Sunshine is the best disinfectant," she muttered to herself, and pulled her father's car key out of her purse.

Fenway drove back to Estancia still dazed a little bit, no longer enjoying the experience of the Mercedes. Despite her scrubbing, she felt—and perhaps smelled—death and antiseptic on her skin, and it gave her goosebumps.

She turned off at the hospital exit. She didn't know where to find the ICU, so she followed the signs to the main entrance of the hospital. She saw Dez's red Impala in the lot and figured she was in the right place.

Cars jammed the parking lot, and Fenway had to park in the rapidly filling overflow lot. Annoyed at first, she got out of the car and realized how much she needed the fresh air and a decent walk to get the stress of the autopsy off her. She looked forward to seeing Rachel, but just anticipating the beeping and sickness and injury in the ICU made her blood pressure rise. She closed her eyes and breathed in, a deep, long breath, that nevertheless caught a couple of times. She exhaled the same way, long and slow.

She wondered if Rachel would ever regain consciousness, then pushed the thought out of her mind.

Fenway walked up to the hospital entrance and stopped. She wondered if Dez still held vigil over Rachel.

She remembered doing the same for her mother in her last days, how quickly the pancreatic cancer had knocked her mother from a healthy, vibrant woman to a morphine-hazed shell of herself. It had been three weeks from diagnosis to death. Her mother had told her a story about how she figured out a recipe when Fenway was little. She had been fighting sleep, and in the middle of the sentence, gave in. She never woke back up.

Fenway shook her head, trying to slough off that memory, or at least bury it back in the box.

She heard her phone ding in her purse. She fished it out, wanting to switch it to silent mode before she went into the hospital.

The notification was a text from Dez.

Rachel's awake.

CHAPTER SEVEN

FENWAY FOUND THE ICU AND RUSHED INTO ROOM 9. DEZ SAT AT Rachel's bedside. Rachel slowly blinked, her bed raised halfway to a seated position. She didn't acknowledge Fenway.

"Have you asked her anything yet?" Fenway whispered to Dez.

"Just asked her how she was feeling. She shook her head at me, then whispered that she wanted some water. I just informed the nurse."

Fenway walked out to the nurse's station and came back to Rachel's bed with a cup of water and straw, which Rachel leaned forward to take in her mouth and drank gratefully. It took some energy out of her, and she leaned back to her half-seated position.

"What happened?" she whispered.

"What do you remember?"

Rachel shook her head, trying to clear out the cobwebs. "It's all kind of a blur. I went to the gym in the morning and I remember wondering what I wanted for lunch."

"I found some containers from Dos Milagros in your trash," Fenway prodded.

"Oh, that's right. Yeah, I stopped there. I ate the tacos in the car on the way home. I remember I spilled some hot sauce on the seat."

"What did you do when you got home?" Dez asked.

"Uh... I think I started watching TV."

"Did you have a drink at the *taquería*? A Coke or something?"

"Oh, no. I remember now. I had just been at the gym so I thought I should have Gatorade. I threw the trash from the tacos away, and I went to the fridge to get some Gatorade. And *then* I sat down to watch TV. And... then I woke up here."

"Did you see a note on the table when you got home?" Dez said.

"The kitchen table?"

"Yes."

"I don't know. I didn't notice anything there. Did you find a note in my apartment? On the kitchen table?"

"Yes."

"What did it say? Did it threaten me? What do they want from me?"

Dez shifted uncomfortably.

"What is it?" Rachel had more color in her face now, eyes going from Dez to Fenway.

"It was a suicide note," Fenway said.

"A suicide note? From who?"

"From you," Dez murmured.

Rachel's eyes widened. Her mouth opened and closed, and finally she spoke. "I swear to you, Fenway, I didn't try to commit suicide. I didn't write that note. I don't know who's doing this to me or why."

Fenway nodded. "I believe you. We all believe you. Whoever wrote that note didn't spell your sister's name right. It's an obvious forgery."

"But who would do something like that?"

"That's what we're trying to find out. And we think it's got to do with another murder."

"Another murder?"

"Yes," Fenway said.

"I'm not sure we should talk about this, Fenway," Dez said sharply.

Fenway looked at Dez. "I don't see how we move forward without it. Whoever tried to kill Rachel will figure out pretty soon that she's not dead. And if it's tied to the murder, the faster we catch who did it, the sooner Rachel will be safe."

"You think someone tried to kill me?"

"I do."

"And—" Rachel paused, and swallowed, her mouth dry, "they'll try to kill me again?"

"I don't know." Fenway shook her head. "The police are all over this case now, so maybe not. But if whoever it is thinks you know something you shouldn't, and if it's dangerous enough to them, sure, they might try again."

Rachel looked horrified.

"I'm sorry, Rachel. It's tough to hear, I know."

"Especially after just waking up from being unconscious for who knows how long," Dez said pointedly, looking at Fenway.

Rachel was silent for a moment. "I don't think I know anything I shouldn't," she said. "Who was murdered?"

Fenway hesitated. "Mayor Jenkins."

Rachel's eyes widened. "No."

"I'm afraid so," Dez said softly.

"And I think that whoever tried to kill you," Fenway said, "also had a hand in the mayor's murder."

"What?" Dez's head turned to Fenway. "You haven't told me anything about that."

"It's not anyone's theory but mine," Fenway said to Dez. "I just think there are too many coincidences for them not to be connected." She turned to Rachel. "Did you uncover something about the mayor, or about any of the mayor's enemies, or, um, family members, anything like that?"

Rachel was quiet.

"Think back over the last week, Rachel. Maybe two weeks. Did anyone tell you anything off the record? You're the public information officer now. People are coming to you for all kinds of official announcements, but did anyone come to you for anything unusual?"

Rachel hesitated. "Lots of people come to me with stuff that's off the record."

"Anyone in particular? Anything to do with the mayor?"

"You know there are a couple of councilmembers that are the worst. Dr. Klein especially. He hates everyone on the board, he thinks the police are out to get him." Rachel laughed ruefully, if a little weakly. "He thinks *everyone* is out to get him. He's constantly trying to put out misinformation about Ferris Energy."

Fenway had a strange feeling that Rachel purposely evaded her questions. She opened her mouth, but Dez spoke first.

"What do you do about that?"

"Maisie warned me about Dr. Klein before she left," Rachel said. "She would throw him a bone every once in a while to calm him down. You know, so that he wouldn't completely go off on her either. She played sympathetic, but insisted that Klein release *factual* information, not innuendo. She told me she could get away with it because she appealed to Klein's need to, well, cover his ass. She told him if he based his attacks on innuendo and not facts, his 'enemies' would turn it against him." Rachel paused. "Plus, honestly, I think Klein had a big crush on Maisie. He followed her around the office like a puppy when he came in."

"Did he try the same tactics with you?" Dez asked.

"He didn't know what to make of me," Rachel said. "He knew you and I were friends, I guess. But he's only approached me a couple of times."

"With what?"

"Uh... once about the new park opening on the east side."

"Anything else?"

"No, I don't think—oh, right, the new open space off 326."

"Did Alice Jenkins bring anything to you in the last couple of weeks?" Dez asked.

Fenway leaned forward.

"The last couple of weeks," Rachel said, choosing her words carefully. "The mayor's office sends over meeting minutes. I release those pretty much verbatim into the public record and on the website." She paused. "I don't remember anything interesting."

"Maybe it doesn't look interesting to you," Fenway said, "but maybe someone else thinks it's very interesting."

"Worth going through," Dez said.

"I got the meeting minutes on Friday," Rachel said. "I always post the minutes on Monday morning. Guess I won't make it for this week."

"Can't Natalie do it?" Fenway asked. "Kind of what an assistant is there for, right?"

Rachel hesitated for a split second; Fenway didn't think Dez caught it. "Sure," Rachel said. "Sure, Natalie can do it, of course."

Fenway looked at Rachel's face. Rachel was holding back something important.

"Anything else about the mayor, Rachel?"

Rachel shook her head. "I don't think so."

"Are you sure?"

"Come on," Dez interrupted. "Girl's been through hell and back the last twenty-four hours. What's with the third degree?"

Fenway looked from Dez to Rachel. "Sorry," she said quietly. "I just want to make sure we're being thorough."

"I get it," Rachel said. "Not a problem."

"Okay, thanks," Fenway said, nodding. "Oh—and Rachel, one last thing. Do you have a prescription for buprenodone?"

"For what?"

"Buprenodone. It's an anti-anxiety med. But lots of people use it for a sleeping pill." She paused. "It's what you overdosed on."

"No," Rachel said firmly. "I've never even heard of that. I'm not on prescription anything. Well, birth control. Not that I need it right now."

"Okay," Fenway said. "I'm sorry to bring this up, but what about Dylan? Did he take medication?"

Rachel paused. "He, um, he wasn't prescribed anything. But he would take Norco sometimes. When he felt depressed. When he got a bad review at work, or something like that."

Dez nodded. "Do you know his contact?"

"Contact?"

"Who got him the Norco?"

"Oh," Rachel said. "Dylan's brother."

"That's Parker, right?"

"Yeah. Well—Parker didn't actually get Dylan the Norco, he just knew a guy at the restaurant who had a connection."

"Maybe the dealer knows someone who can get buprenodone," Dez said.

"It's a generic now," Fenway said. "Every pharmaceutical company produces some version of it. All the major ones, anyway. It's not hard to get."

Dez nodded again, thoughtfully. "Still worth a shot to talk to Parker's contact, though."

"Probably makes sense to talk to the sheriff's office about local prescription drug rings too."

The nurse came in and Fenway and Dez were quiet while the nurse took Rachel's vitals.

"You gave us quite a scare, Miss Richards," the nurse said to Rachel. "It looks like you're not going to have any permanent liver or kidney damage. And it looks like you're getting your strength back."

"When can I go home?" Rachel said.

"First things first," the nurse said. "Let's get you transferred out of the ICU and into a regular room. We'll keep you for observation tonight for sure. Then let's see how you're doing."

Rachel nodded, her eyes drooping.

"All right, ladies," the nurse said. "Rachel is too polite to tell you to get out, but I'm not. So get out." She smiled, but Fenway knew she was serious. "She needs her rest. She wants to go home tomorrow, and she won't get to do that if you're interviewing her like she's on some damn awards show."

Fenway and Dez both went over and hugged Rachel before they said goodbye. They exited the hospital into the warm, still air.

"Who do you suppose is around to talk to?" Fenway said. "And where do you want to start?"

"I think we start with Parker's co-worker at the restaurant," Dez said. "That buprenodone didn't appear out of thin air."

Fenway and Dez stopped at the Impala. "I actually think we've got a good idea where the buprenodone came from," Fenway said. "Did McVie tell you that we dragged Fletcher Jenkins to San Miguelito yesterday to question him?"

"Yeah, McVie told me," Dez said. "The William Matisse connection. But I couldn't talk for very long. Did he have a connection with Rachel, too?"

Fenway said, "He's got a prescription for buprenodone. And he couldn't find his brand-new prescription bottle. So there's that."

"You know," Dez said, "I hate to get all conspiracy-theory on you, Fenway, but doesn't it seem awfully convenient that the murder victim's son just happens to have a prescription for a seemingly unrelated crime?"

Fenway nodded. Her phone rang and she pulled her phone out of her purse, glancing at the screen. "Oh, it's the M.E."

"I'm not here," Dez said.

Fenway looked at Dez quizzically, and picked up. "Hi, Dr. Yasuda."

"Hi, Fenway. We got a hit on the fingerprints on the prescription bottle. Fletcher Jenkins."

"I wondered about that. Were his fingerprints on the suicide note too?"

"Strangely, no," Dr. Yasuda said. "No fingerprints at all. Like the person who wrote it wore gloves."

Fenway paused. "Why would Fletcher use gloves when writing the note but not on the pill bottle?"

"I don't want to speculate on that," Dr. Yasuda said. "But the fingerprint evidence on the pill bottle strongly suggests that Fletcher Jenkins' buprenodone was used to poison Rachel."

"Does it suggest that he's the one who poisoned her?"

"That's less suggestive, Fenway; you know that. The fingerprints don't have a time stamp on them."

"Yeah, you're right, of course. Thanks, doctor. Oh—Melissa said she suspected the Gatorade had the buprenodone in it. Have you tested that yet?"

"Yes. It tested positive. A high concentration, too. Certainly enough to kill her. It's a good thing she didn't drink any more of it than she did."

"That sure looks like attempted murder to me."

"That's a theory that certainly fits the available evidence," Dr. Yasuda agreed. "Okay—I've got another autopsy to do—not a murder victim, thank goodness."

They said their goodbyes and hung up.

Dez looked at Fenway. "Fletcher's fingerprints were on the pill bottle, but not on the suicide note?"

"Right."

"The conspiracy theory doesn't sound so crazy now, does it?"

Fenway crinkled her nose up. It didn't sound crazy at all.

"All right," Dez said, "I'm going to head home. I'm beat."

"Oh—before I forget, Dez." She paused, and then decided to just say it directly. "Dr. Yasuda told me to tell you that she's sorry. She said that you'd know what she means."

Dez narrowed her eyes. "Okay. Thanks for letting me know."

Fenway opened her mouth to say something, but then clamped it shut. Dez turned, got in her car, and started it. Fenway walked through the parking lot toward the Mercedes, figuring she'd mind her own business.

She opened the door of the Mercedes and sat for a moment, basking in the warmth of the sun reflecting off the black leather. But after just a few seconds, the leather seats radiated too much heat and the stifling air made her feel claustrophobic. She turned the car on and turned the air conditioning to high. She pulled her phone out again and called her father.

"Nathaniel Ferris."

"It's Fenway, Dad."

"Hi, sweetie. You still in San Miguelito?"

"No, I'm back. I just saw Rachel. She regained consciousness."

"Oh, I'm glad to hear it." She heard him take the phone away from his ear. "Everett, that PR officer I told you about? The one they found poisoned? She's regained consciousness." She heard the phone being muffled, then some conversation in the background, then a sound like a hand sliding over the mouthpiece, then her father came back on. "I'm putting you on speaker, Fenway." The background noise got suddenly louder. "Fenway, I'm going to tell Charlotte. She'll probably want to send flowers or something. I bet she remembers Rachel at our wedding—just a teenager at the time, of course, but not one of those sullen teens. She was polite and engaging; Rob told me how proud he was of her."

An awkward silence fell over them; Ferris had brought up the wedding again, as well as the previous coroner's killer, currently awaiting trial.

Ferris cleared his throat. "Anyway, I'm really glad she's okay."

"Give her my best, too," Everett said.

"Sure," Fenway replied.

Everett's voice lowered slightly; he spoke directly to Ferris. "Did you get the name of the hospital so Charlotte can send flowers?"

"Oh—no, I didn't. Say, Fenway, what hospital is Rachel at?"

"She's at St. Vincent—but, Dad, she's in the ICU. They don't allow flowers in there."

"Of course," Ferris said. "I'm sure we'll think of something."

Fenway heard rustling as Ferris moved the phone. "Thanks for telling us about Rachel, sweetie."

"Sure, Dad." Fenway paused. "So, listen, I'm finished with the car."

"But you don't have the Accord back, do you?"

"No—but I'm not driving the Mercedes all around town."

The sound changed again; Ferris had taken Fenway off speakerphone. "Why not? I've got plenty of other cars."

"Because, Dad, it wouldn't look right. And you already gave me the Accord."

"Fenway, come on, don't be like that. Let me help you out."

"You've already been a big help today, Dad."

"Listen, if you would just—"

"Dad! I'm done talking about this. You can pick the car up whenever you like."

"How about you come up to the house for dinner? You can drop the car off."

"Then I wouldn't have any way to get home."

"I think we can give you a ride home. Or take an Uber if you're all high and mighty about me helping you."

Fenway sighed. "All right, Dad. What time? Seven?"

"That's perfect. See you then."

CHAPTER EIGHT

———— ✦ ————

THE MERCEDES' ENGINE PURRED AS SHE EXITED THE PARKING LOT, a pleading note telling Fenway not to stop driving. She needed to go by the sheriff's office, though, and see if McVie had returned so she could give him the M.E.'s information. The more Fenway thought about it, the less she liked that Alice Jenkins and Rachel had gotten attacked in the same twenty-four-hour period. And it may have been the medication talking, but Rachel dodged questions about talking to the mayor, and Fenway tried to work out why in the world she would do that.

Fenway decided to stop by Rachel's office and see if anything on her desk or in her notes would ring any bells. Maybe Fenway could take anything suspicious over to the hospital for Rachel to see; that might actually force her hand. It might have been grasping at straws, but she didn't really have any other leads.

She pulled into the parking structure and parked far away from the other cars there. She killed the engine and walked across the street to the sheriff's office.

She greeted Officer Huke at reception. He smiled but not his usual jovial grin. This city was grieving for Alice Jenkins.

Fenway saw McVie in his office, working on paperwork, head down, concentrating. Fenway watched him for a moment; his square jaw, his intelligent, kind eyes soaking in the information on the page. Fenway mentally kicked herself for feeling this way about someone so much older—and married to boot. She closed her eyes and willed herself to think of Akeel—those abdominal muscles, the electricity between them when they touched. She opened her eyes and knocked on McVie's door.

He looked up from his paperwork, and the flash of recognition landed on his face with a smile that put Akeel's abs to shame. He motioned her in. She opened the door and took the seat across from him.

"Hi, Fenway," McVie said. "Any news?"

"Rachel's awake."

His head popped up. "Oh, thank God. That's great news. Does she remember anything?"

Fenway shook her head. "We think someone slipped the buprenodone in that big bottle of Gatorade in her refrigerator while she went to the gym yesterday morning. Probably after Mayor Jenkins' murder."

"So that's a different time than the alibi that Fletch gave."

"True," Fenway said. "But we didn't ask for an alibi for 10 or 11 that morning. We asked for the early afternoon. Because that's when we thought she drank it. Or at least when we thought the bottle had been dropped to make it look like a suicide."

"What do you think of Fletch for the attempted murder?"

"I don't know, Sheriff. I just found out the pill bottle had a ton of fingerprints from Fletch on it."

McVie nodded. "And with the empty box at his house, I think we can assume the bottle is his. That's pretty damning."

"Right," Fenway said, "but the suicide note didn't have any fingerprints on it at all—not Fletch's, not Rachel's, not anyone."

McVie stroked his chin thoughtfully. "That certainly under-scores that Rachel didn't write the note, but it doesn't let Fletch off the hook. Fletch could have put gloves on before going into Rachel's apartment, but forgot that he had handled the pill bottle many times before."

"True."

McVie paused. "When we talked to Fletch last night, though, it sure seemed like he was shocked that his bottle of meds went missing."

Fenway nodded. "But maybe he's a good liar."

"His wife seemed pretty convincing too, though. What are the odds they're both good liars?"

"Maybe she didn't know what he was up to."

McVie shrugged. "The evidence all points at Fletch right now, though. I usually trust my gut, but I don't have any other explanation."

"What do you think about the mayor's murder? Do you think Fletch is involved in that too?"

McVie shook his head. "All we have to connect him is the name *William Matisse* on the hotel room reservation."

"And he doesn't have an alibi. Not a good one, anyway."

"It was one in the morning," McVie pointed out. "No one has a good alibi at one in the morning."

"But isn't it a little too coincidental that both Rachel and Mayor Jenkins were both attacked within twenty-four hours of each other?" Fenway thought about adding that she thought Rachel evaded her questions, but without anything more than a hunch to go on, she decided not to mention it. "So I'm headed over to Rachel's office. I thought I could take a look in there and see if anything gives me a clue where to look next. Want to join me? Maybe get some lunch?"

McVie stretched his arms above his head and smiled. The muscles in his arms flexed, and Fenway saw the cute crooked front tooth he had. Fenway mentally kicked herself—again.

"That sounds great," he said. "I could use a change of scenery. I've been working on the M.E.'s report that Yasuda sent over on the mayor, trying to see anything that would point me toward the murderer. There's nothing—no fibers, no DNA." He stood up and came around the desk. "Or I should say, there's *plenty* of fibers and fingerprints and DNA in that motel room—but nothing that stands out. So far, I've got print matches on about thirty people who are in the system, but none of them seem to be attached to Mayor Jenkins. I'll start interviewing them if I don't get any promising leads."

"Have you looked to see if any of those thirty people are attached to Rachel?"

"No. I suppose that would be the next item on the agenda."

They walked out, past the front desk, across the plaza. The sun pounded the sidewalk—it was shaping up to be one of the few truly hot days in Estancia. McVie put on his sunglasses; they were a classic design that looked good on his face.

Rachel's office was in the City Hall building next door. They took the long way, through the plaza, enjoying the shade of the elms, and walked down the sidewalk, past an ice cream vendor— good day for it, Fenway thought—and walked through the glass doors of the City Hall building and into the blast of air conditioning. They walked past the County Clerk's office and down a hallway on the ground floor. They stopped at a mahogany door with "Public Information Officer" etched into the smoked glass. McVie tried the door; it swung open easily.

A Filipino woman in her early forties sat behind the desk and a young black woman, who looked about twenty-five, stood on the other side of the desk; they looked to be deep in conversation. "Oh, good afternoon, Sheriff, Fenway," the woman behind the desk said. "I didn't expect anyone here on a Sunday."

"Hi, Natalie," McVie said. "A lot of people are putting in extra time with everything that's happened this weekend." He looked expectantly at the young black woman.

"Hi, I'm Sascha Abrams with the Estancia Courier," she said, holding her hand out to McVie.

The sheriff shook her hand warily.

"I've been assigned to the story about Mrs. Richards," Sascha explained. Fenway found herself distracted by the *Mrs.*—she knew that's what widows were called, but Rachel seemed far too young to be married, much less a widow.

"From the reports I've seen, it looked like an attempted suicide," Sascha continued. "I hoped you could help me figure out—"

"I'm sorry, Miss Abrams," McVie said firmly, "but the reports you've seen don't provide a final conclusion. We're still investigating what happened, and right now, I'm not at liberty to disclose where we are in the investigation." He took a couple of steps forward, inserting his muscular six-foot-two frame in between the reporter and Natalie. "Now, Ms. Andrada might think we'll get a bad story written about us if she kicks you out of this office, but as some of your colleagues at the *Courier* can attest, I don't have a problem appearing rude and risking bad press in order to protect an investigation."

Sascha looked at Natalie, but Natalie averted her eyes.

"Okay," she said. "I'll be contacting you later today, Sheriff. I hope you have something you can give me. I have other sources, but I'd love to get the *official* word on what happened to Mrs. Richards."

McVie nodded curtly. Sascha stepped behind Fenway and out the door, closing it behind her.

McVie turned to Natalie. She had a round face and prominent cheekbones, with a shock of hair, short at the back but partially over her forehead and eyes, dyed a bold shade of violet, an almost garish hue that nevertheless complemented her mocha skin. She looked strong, with biceps that almost rivaled McVie's. She had several spreadsheets printed out in front of her, and a meeting planner spread open to Monday's date. A table clock sat on the desk, about a foot high with an American flag on one side and a Marine flag on the other, and a globe with an eagle, wings spread, on top. Etched in a gold band on the bottom was *Cpl Natalie Andrada.*

"Hope you didn't mind that, Natalie," McVie said.

"Yes, thank you, Sheriff," Natalie said. "I cleared Miss Richards' calendar, to see what could be rescheduled for later in the week. I came back from church, and I was sitting at my house with everything that's happened running through my head, and I just had to do something. I got here in the early afternoon, and then that reporter came in a few minutes ago, trying to get information about Rachel. She tried to dig for background on why Rachel wanted to commit suicide."

"Maybe we should have mentioned to the reporter that someone staged the scene," Fenway said.

McVie shook his head. "I don't want whoever staged it thinking that we're onto them."

"I don't want Rachel's reputation dragged down if the public thinks she can't handle being the youngest public information officer in California."

McVie gave Fenway a look that said, *Not here.* Fenway knew McVie disagreed, but it dawned on her that he respected her too much to escalate this and make the department look bad in front of the public—and that included people like Natalie.

"But I understand that catching whoever did this is probably the priority," Fenway said lamely.

"Oh, that reminds me," Natalie said, "Rachel called me about ten minutes before that reporter showed up. She said the doctors weren't letting her go until Monday."

"At least," Fenway responded.

"I know what it's like to be stuck in the hospital, not being able to get anything done," Natalie said. "So I came here to try to get a jump on tomorrow."

"Rachel said she usually sends out meeting minutes."

Natalie nodded. "Seemed like I needed to do *something* besides think about who would do that to Rachel."

"Rachel told you about the forged note?" Fenway said.

Natalie nodded again.

"Listen, Natalie," McVie said, leaning casually against her desk. "We're trying to figure out who poisoned Rachel and staged it to look like a suicide attempt. We wondered if she had appointments with anyone last week, or maybe the week before, with anyone who might be tied to some of the people of interest."

Natalie pushed the meeting planner in front of McVie. "You're free to look if you'd like."

"You have Rachel's planner?" Fenway asked.

"No, this is mine. Miss Richards keeps hers on the computer. I still like the feel of pen and paper."

Fenway nodded. "Do you have a visitors' sign-in log?"

Natalie hesitated. "We keep it out here during business hours, but I put it in Rachel's office after we close up for the day. I don't like to keep it out in the open, even if we do lock that first door."

"Can we see it?" asked McVie.

Natalie paused, drumming her fingers on the desk. "I'm not sure it's a hundred percent accurate," she said. "Sometimes people sign in on the wrong day, or don't sign in at all."

"It'll still be helpful," McVie said.

Natalie hesitated, the wheels spinning in her head.

McVie kept up his relaxed posture. "You're not breaking any confidentiality rules showing it to us."

"No, I don't suppose I am," she finally said. She got her keys off the desk and backed her wheelchair out from behind her desk. She was missing both her lower legs. She wheeled over to Rachel's office door, and unlocked it.

"There you go," she said, pushing it open. "Let me know if you need anything else."

"Thanks, Natalie," McVie said. "I don't want to interrupt you any more than I already have."

"It's no trouble, Sheriff," Natalie said firmly, wheeling back to her desk. "If I could catch whoever did this to Rachel myself, you know I'd do it."

Fenway looked at Natalie's muscular arms and envisioned her pummeling the criminal with her fists.

McVie pushed the door open further, and Fenway walked through ahead of him. On Rachel's desk lay a guest book and pen set. The book was leather-bound, attached to a matching base, and a gold pen stuck out of a holder on the right side. Open to Friday, July 14, the entries had a few names that Fenway didn't recognize, but represented local businesses that Fenway *did* recognize. She flipped back to Thursday. More names, including a reporter named James Monroe—like the doctrine, Fenway thought—from the *Estancia Courier*.

"Another reporter from the *Courier* came here on Thursday," Fenway called to Natalie. "Do you know what they talked about?"

"No," Natalie called back. "Rachel had her door closed."

"Does she usually close her door during meetings?"

"Not usually."

Fenway kept looking. She flipped back a page, but nothing caught her eye on Wednesday. She flipped back again to Tuesday. She saw Alice Jenkins' neat, flowing cursive writing, with nothing under the representing column. And below that another name.

Fletcher Jenkins.

"Are you kidding me?" Fenway said. McVie, who had been taking a look around the office—Rachel's desk items, picking up her stapler and turning it over in his hands—came over to see. Fenway pointed her finger underneath it.

"Oh," McVie said.

"Why do you suppose he didn't mention this during his interview?" Fenway asked.

McVie shook his head. "I honestly don't have any idea."

"And why do you suppose *Rachel* didn't mention this when Dez and I talked with her earlier today?" Fenway took her phone out and took a picture of the sign-in log with all the names listed.

McVie shook his head. He stared at the sign-in book with a furrowed brow.

"I mean, we asked her directly if she discussed anything with the mayor in the last couple of weeks, and she flatly denied it."

"She *denied* it?"

"Yes—well, no. She responded with some minor stuff. But she wasn't forthcoming."

"I guess we can go back to the hospital and ask her," said McVie. "Did anyone else here come in that day?"

"There were a few people here," Fenway said, scanning the sheet. "But the mayor and Fletcher came in at 2 P.M. and Rachel didn't see anyone else for the rest of the day."

"Let's bag that and get it fingerprinted," McVie said. "I know there are going to be hundreds of prints on it, but let's see if there are any surprises."

Fenway pulled out an evidence bag from her purse and slipped the sign-in book into it. "That's my last bag," she muttered to McVie. "I'm going to have to stock up tomorrow."

Fenway walked around behind the desk. She moved the mouse on Rachel's computer and the monitor went on, asking for the username and password.

"We might have to get onto this computer in the next couple of days," Fenway said. McVie nodded. Fenway looked at the monitor; Rachel had put several sticky notes around the edge of the computer. One said *Parks* PR *date – 8/11.* Another said *Lunch Tina Tues 11:30.* Another said *Jenkins –* SRB.

"Look at this," Fenway said to McVie. He leaned over the desk.

"Hmm, SRB," he repeated. "You have any idea what that means?"

"No."

"Natalie?" McVie called.

She wheeled over to the threshold of Rachel's office door. "What is it?"

"There's a note here on Rachel's monitor that says *Jenkins—SRB*. You know what SRB means?"

Natalie frowned and shook her head. "No. SRB—I mean, we have a million acronyms in county government, but I'm not familiar with that one. Maybe the State Recording Board. That's a PR thing that Rachel got invited to last month."

McVie nodded. "Thanks, Natalie—oh, one more thing. How long did Rachel meet with the mayor and her son?"

"Not for very long. I think they were just talking about meeting notes."

"Meeting notes?"

"Yes," Natalie said.

"With Fletcher in the room?"

Natalie shrugged. "I just deal with the calendar, Sheriff."

McVie smiled. "Sure. What time did they leave?"

Natalie shook her head. "I don't remember exactly, but it wasn't long. Half-hour tops."

"What time did Rachel go home?"

"That evening? Five-fifteen, maybe five-thirty."

"You were still here at five-thirty?"

"That's right. I normally stay till Rachel leaves, even if she tells me to go home."

Fenway looked at McVie. "I don't know what's going on, Sheriff," she said, "but I think it's time we talk to Fletcher Jenkins again."

"Do we want to talk to Rachel first? See what they talked about in their meeting? Ask what SRB means?"

"That's a much better idea," Fenway said. "Natalie, do you have the number of the hospital?"

"Way ahead of you," Natalie said, wheeling back to her desk and picking up the phone.

"What do you think it was about? Do you think the meeting might have been on the mayor's calendar?"

"I honestly don't have any idea," McVie said. "I don't get how Fletcher could be visiting the county public information officer with his mother one day, and then two days later be on a bender at the Cactus Lake Motel and stab her four times."

"Maybe something happened in that meeting that sent him over the edge," Fenway suggested. "Maybe he got mad at something. Maybe he felt ganged up on."

McVie shrugged. "It's possible. That just doesn't sound like the Fletch I know."

Natalie hung up the phone. "Rachel's asleep. She's still quite weak."

Fenway said, "Do we wait to find out about the meeting from Rachel, or do we ask Fletcher ourselves?"

"I don't know," he said. "I don't want to spook him. It sure seems like he's ready to run."

"If he's a flight risk, all the more reason to go now," Fenway said. "You should at least send some uniforms over there to pick him up."

"The uniforms would *really* spook him," McVie said. "Maybe if I went over. Maybe in plain clothes. Maybe not in my cruiser. Maybe in my regular car. Maybe he'd talk to me."

"That might work."

"You want to come?"

"What for?"

"You were good with his wife," he said.

"You need to bring me because you have woman trouble?" Fenway said.

McVie looked a little sheepish, but sadness flashed in his eyes.

Fenway thought a moment. "All right, Sheriff. You want to go right now? All I have going on today is dinner with my father, my horrible stepmother, and my father's handpicked candidate for coroner."

McVie paused. "That guy from the pharma company?"

"Yep."

"What's his name? Michael something?"

"Everett Michaels."

"Ah, yes."

"We had breakfast at Mimosa's this morning."

"Good ol' Mimosa's. I'd expect nothing less from your father. What did he want?"

"He wanted me to endorse Michaels for coroner."

"What did you say?"

"I told him no. Nicely. But no."

"Why not? You don't want Klein to be coroner, do you?"

"No, but it's not like I trust Everett Michaels, either."

"Oh," McVie said. "Is that why your dad wanted you to go to breakfast with them? So Everett Michaels could win you over?"

"I guess."

"But he *didn't* win you over."

"I don't know. He sure turned on the charm." Fenway remembered his classically handsome features, and how intoxicating his cologne was. "And he's smart. And he knows a lot about medications and the pharmaceutical process."

"Is he good-looking?"

Fenway looked at McVie. He seemed a little bit on edge, as if he just realized Everett Michaels might make a play for Fenway's affections.

"Yes," Fenway said carefully. "He's quite handsome."

Fenway saw McVie tense up, but he visibly made an effort to stay calm. "Is there a 'but' in there?"

Fenway shrugged. "I don't think he's really that interested in figuring out how people died."

McVie nodded. "I guess that's pretty important for a coroner."

Fenway paused. "You know, I *assume* that's pretty important for a coroner. It's pretty important for *me*."

McVie hesitated, then spoke quickly. "That's one of the reasons I like you so much. I mean, I like *working* with you so much. You're actually interested in this stuff."

"Of course I am," Fenway said.

"Did you tell your dad that it's important that the next coroner cares about the job?"

Fenway laughed. "No, that wouldn't have mattered to him. I just made him think it behooved him not to have me endorse Mr. Michaels. And I made him think he came up with the idea to wait."

"Hmm," said McVie, and Fenway saw a smirk playing at the corners of his lips, "that's probably for the best."

"It probably is," Fenway said.

"Tell me again why you aren't running?" McVie asked.

"Got my nursing boards in three weeks. Can't take my eye off the ball now."

"Okay," McVie said, although he looked like he didn't quite believe her. "Let me go back to the office; I'll change there, get that sign-in book couriered over to Michi, and then we can head down to Vista Del Rincón."

"And lunch," Fenway reminded him.

"And lunch."

"And not at a crappy fast food place. Real lunch. Like Dos Milagros."

"Is that your favorite *taquería* over on Third?"

Fenway grinned. "Maybe."

And with that grin, Fenway realized she hadn't really smiled since getting back into town. Granted, there wasn't much to smile about. But being with McVie—especially after the rocky first week, and after Stotsky's arrest—satisfied something in her soul. It gave her both comfort and excitement, a sense of both ease and engagement. If only she could figure out how to stop thinking about him like this.

They walked back to the sheriff's office, Fenway keenly aware of how much distance came between them, how their fingers accidentally brushed together when they both reached to open the door; she noticed her own breathing and she tried to judge it: was she breathing too hard, too shallow? He looked at her as they walked through the door of the office, and he smiled at her, a little awkwardly. She thought she saw some of the same longing in his eyes that she felt toward him. She supposed she could be imagining it, just seeing what she wanted to see.

While McVie went to the locker room to change, she waited in his office, trying not to look at the photographs of him with Amy, looking happy and in love.

CHAPTER NINE

MCVIE DIDN'T WANT TO EAT IN THE CAR WHILE THEY WERE driving, so they wolfed down their tacos at Dos Milagros. Fenway ordered the special, which she loved, but it had a lot of raw onions on it. She surreptitiously sneaked a piece of gum on her way to the car. Fenway knew she was being ridiculous, but couldn't help herself; nothing would happen in the car requiring Fenway to have fresh breath.

They arrived at the sheriff's personal car, an unassuming Toyota Highlander with a beige interior. Fenway thought about making fun of him for such an out-of-character car, but she remembered she had been driving an old Nissan with a rusted floor less than three months before.

They arrived forty-five minutes later at Fletcher Jenkins' house in Vista Del Rincón. They pulled into the driveway; both the Jeep and the Toyota were parked in front of the garage.

Fletcher warily stepped out of his door onto his front porch. He looked exhausted. He wore the same clothes he had had on the night before during the interrogation.

"What do you want now?" he said.

"I just want to talk," McVie said. "I'm not here as the sheriff. I'm just here as a guy. A friend."

Fletcher chuckled mirthlessly. "You and I weren't friends back in high school, and we sure aren't friends now, Sheriff," he said. "But sure. Let's talk. Let's talk like we're old pals from back in the day."

McVie came up to the porch and sat down. Fenway stood in the driveway, watching the house. She thought that Tracey would have come out by now, if only to yell at them, or simply to see what had happened. But Fenway saw no movement at the front door, nor through any of the windows that she could see. She must have had the second car, maybe to go into Estancia to discuss funeral arrangements for her mother-in-law, although that didn't seem quite right. Maybe the girls had gone to a birthday party, or a soccer game.

"I'm not going to lie, Fletch," McVie said. "There's a lot of evidence that points to you, not only for your mother's death, but for the attempted murder of one of our own."

Fletcher's eyes seemed to sink deeper.

"You didn't tell me that you and your mom went to go see Rachel Richards earlier this week," McVie said. "We asked if you knew her, and you said you didn't."

Fenway switched her gum to the other side of her mouth.

"No," Fletcher said. "You asked *Tracey* if we knew her. Tracey doesn't know her. She told you the truth. And I looked for those pills. I planned to tell you when I came out, but we started talking about other stuff and I forgot."

"We had a really long drive to San Miguelito," Fenway said. "You didn't think to mention it then?"

"No," Fletcher said, a hint of anger in his voice. "I started to tell you that I had some information that me and my mom found out. But you wouldn't listen. You just read me my rights and assumed I had done it."

McVie nodded. "Okay. Maybe I'm wrong. In fact, Fletch, I'd love nothing in the world more than being one hundred percent wrong about this." He took a step closer. "But I'll tell you, it looks bad. Your fingerprints were found on the pill bottle next to Ms. Richards. Someone left a phony suicide note on her kitchen table. And you didn't tell us about the meeting."

"I guess that looks pretty bad," Fletcher admitted.

McVie nodded.

"So if you have something to tell us about the information you and your mom found, now's the time."

Fletch looked down at the ground.

"Does it have anything to do with why you and your mom went to see Rachel Richards—and spent all afternoon with her?"

Fletcher thought for a moment. He looked back at the front door. He scratched his head, then his beard, then he ran his hand over his face and exhaled.

"I did it," he said. "I'm the one."

Fenway's mouth fell open in disbelief.

"What exactly did you do, Fletch?" McVie asked. "Are you confessing to the murder of your mother? Or the attempted murder of Rachel Richards?"

"It was me," Fletch said.

McVie set his mouth in a line; Fenway could see he wasn't pleased. "Both?" he said.

Fletch didn't say anything else.

"Fletcher Jenkins, you have the right to remain silent," McVie started, and Fenway tuned him out as he finished the Miranda warning and Fletcher agreed to it. McVie got on his phone right afterward, talking to the sheriff's office, dispatching a unit to the small, unassuming mint green house in Vista Del Rincón.

"Ten minutes," McVie said.

Fenway nodded.

He put his phone back in his pocket and turned back to Fletcher. "So when you say you did it, that it was you, what did you mean?"

Fletcher looked out past his front yard. Fenway followed his gaze. From the porch, she could see the ocean on the other side of the freeway. "This beautiful sea," he murmured. "I'm going to miss it."

"You going to answer my question, Fletch?"

Fletcher shook his head. He hadn't moved. "No, after you read me my rights, I thought about it, and it makes sense to remain silent."

"Sure," McVie said.

There was silence for a few more minutes.

Fletcher shuffled his feet. "Craig, you mind if I sit?"

"I don't mind," McVie said. "I'm sorry it has to be like this."

"You do what you have to do," Fletcher said. "I understand."

"Mr. Jenkins," Fenway said, "should you tell Tracey what's happening? Do you want to say goodbye to your girls?"

He shook his head. "I knew why you were here," he said sadly. "I said my goodbyes right when you pulled up."

"We've got time."

Fletcher looked up at Fenway but couldn't look her in the eye. "Tracey just wants the girls to be safe," he said. "I put them in danger. That's all there is to it."

Fenway nodded. Her gum had lost its flavor long ago. Something didn't sit right with her, but she couldn't identify it. Fletch had put them in an awkward position, sounding like he confessed to one of the two crimes, but without his confirmation, it would be challenging to arrest him for the *correct* crime.

She stepped to the front door. "Since we have to wait for the cruiser, do you mind if I use the bathroom?"

"Sure," Fletcher said, miserably.

Fenway opened the door and stepped inside. She didn't walk into the bathroom; she went into the living room, which looked messier than the night before, but about the same. "Tracey?" she called.

She listened but got no answer. She walked into the small but tidy kitchen. A large red faux-leather purse hung over the back of a kitchen stool.

"Tracey?" she called again. She paced around the kitchen and found the trash can. She opened the lid and almost spit her gum in it when a white three-by-five index card, half under a few pieces of junk mail and a paper towel roll in the trash, caught her eye.

Fenway could see neat block printing, written in black pen, that said:

IF YOU'RE GUILTY

The rest of the card hid under the other trash.

Fenway looked around. She didn't hear any movement in the house.

She reached down and pulled the index card out from under the other trash.

IF YOU'RE GUILTY, THEN SHE LIVES
NO COPS

Fenway thought for a second and weighed her options. For a moment, she thought about searching the kitchen drawers until she found a zip-lock bag and pair of tongs. But she didn't know how soon it would be before Tracey came in. And Tracey would certainly notice a pair of tongs in Fenway's hand.

She looked on the counter. There were several plastic grocery bags. She hesitated for a brief second, then decided she needed to take action. She took one of the plastic grocery bags off the counter, but it made a noticeable loud rustling noise—she couldn't sneak the note out inside that.

She scanned the counter for any other options, but found none. She dropped the index card in her purse. It was far less than ideal—they probably wouldn't be able to get any usable prints off it—but Fenway figured the value of having it, even without prints, outweighed the idea of letting it stay in the trash.

She heard a noise in the next room. Fenway looked down to her purse to see if the index card stuck out. Fenway put her wallet on top of it, and she thought she could get away with it if she kept Tracey's attention on other things.

Tracey walked in and jumped a little when she saw Fenway. Her face, red and puffy, was devoid of makeup and her hair stuck up crazily.

"Sorry, Tracey," Fenway said. "I just—I don't know, I felt bad, I thought he should say goodbye to you and the girls."

"He already said goodbye," she said, in a rough voice, like she hadn't slept. She stopped and covered her face with her hands. "Did he tell you he did it?"

"Yes," Fenway said. "I'm so sorry."

Tracey looked like she wanted to say something, but she stopped. "I think you better leave," she finally said, not looking at Fenway.

"I'm so sorry," Fenway said again, and started to walk out of the kitchen. Tracey reached out and grabbed Fenway's arm.

"He's innocent," she whispered. "He'd never hurt his mother."

Fenway looked in Tracey's eyes. They were desperate, pleading. Then, suddenly, they went back to sullen and dark.

"Forget I said that," she said. "I just don't want to believe it. He told me himself that he did it." She looked for a moment like she might cry, but she held it together.

Fenway squeezed her arm, trying to imbue it with meaning. *I know something else is going on,* she wanted to say. But Tracey didn't try to take meaning from Fenway. Fenway hesitated a moment, not sure she should take the index card without telling her.

"How are the girls taking it?" she asked, as gently as she could.

Tracey shook her head and looked down at the floor.

Fenway opened her mouth to say something else, but then she heard the police cruiser pull up into the driveway. She didn't know if she did the right thing, taking the threatening handwritten note from the trash, but she couldn't figure out a better course of action. She tried to run through scenarios in her head. Could they use this as evidence, or was it too tainted? Could they get fingerprints from it besides Fletcher's and Tracey's?

She let herself out the front door. The police cruiser had arrived, and Fenway saw the sheriff put Fletcher in the back. He looked out the window, toward the west, where the blue-green ocean could be seen between the houses and trees.

———◄►———

Fenway was silent as they had turned out of Vista Del Rincón onto the ocean highway.

"You're quiet, Fenway," McVie said, keeping his eyes on the road.

"Yes," she said. The ideas and scenarios were playing ping-pong in her head. Finally, she opened her mouth, then shut it again.

But McVie had noticed. "What is it?"

Fenway finally spoke. "I found something that, uh, really worries me at Fletch's house."

"What did you find?"

"That's the thing; I'm not sure I should tell you. Quite frankly, I'm not sure that I'm *allowed* to tell you. It's dangerous. It *could* be dangerous. I don't know. I don't know what it is. I don't know if I did the right thing. I *think* I did the right thing."

"Okay," McVie said, "now you're worrying me. Out with it."

"I went in the house," Fenway said. "And I opened up the trash can to spit my gum out. And I found this." She took the index card carefully by the edges from her purse.

McVie glanced over. "What is that? A paper?"

"An index card," Fenway said. "And it says, 'If you're guilty, then she lives.'"

"What?" McVie exclaimed. "And you didn't think to tell me?"

"No, I didn't," Fenway said, raising her voice, "because under that it says, 'No cops.'"

McVie quickly swerved into the right lane and took the next exit at Puerto Avila. The exit ramp split two sand dunes, ending at a stop sign; to the left stood the Puerto Avila state beach, to the right, a road winding up behind the granite rock face that buttressed Vista Del Rincón. He turned left toward the beach.

The parking lot was crowded, but he pulled his car into a fire lane and put his hazard lights on, engine and air conditioning still going. "Whoa, hold on, you've touched it?

"Of course I touched it. I had to get it out of the trash."

"Your fingerprints will be all over it."

"Yeah, maybe. I tried to be careful with it. But even if mine *are* on it, hopefully we can get other fingerprints off it too."

McVie shook his head. "I don't know if that will stand up to chain of custody rules," he grumbled.

"Okay, Sheriff, what would *you* have done?"

He considered this for a moment. "I don't know that I would have done anything different. Sorry." He reached behind Fenway's seat. "There's a black plastic case on the floor back here. I've got an evidence bag in there." Fenway heard the snap of plastic tabs and McVie straightened back up with the bag. He opened the top and Fenway eased the index card inside.

McVie took the evidence bag with the card in it and turned it over, seeing the blank back.

"They sell these index cards at every office supply store in the U.S.," he said. "That probably won't help us."

"You never know. We might get lucky. With that, or maybe the ink."

McVie rubbed his temples. "This is really tricky," he said. "I'm not sure how we do this. I've never been involved with a kidnapping. Or a hostage situation. Who do you think it is? Who's the 'she' on the card?"

"I suppose it could be talking about Alice. Maybe this *was* a threat to Fletcher, and he didn't follow the directions, and they killed his mother."

"I think it's more likely that it's one of his daughters," McVie said.

"Me too. Especially since Fletch gave himself up so quickly. Last night it seemed like he had convinced himself to fight it tooth and nail."

"I don't know. He might have slept on it and realized he couldn't get away with it."

"Does that seem right to you?"

McVie paused. "My gut's not *always* right."

"But it's saying that it's more likely that something's happened to Fletch's daughter, right?"

McVie paused. "Even if we're right, Fenway, I'm not sure what to do about it."

"You're going to search the house, right?"

"That's part of the current plan," McVie said. "I wanted to make sure we had a signed warrant."

"You don't have probable cause after he confessed?"

"There's a case before the appellate court right now about this very issue. With a murder as high-profile as the mayor's, I want to make sure that a judge's signature is on *everything* before we search the house."

Fenway nodded. "If that's the case, then we can't make it known to anyone that we know about this note."

"Fletch *did* give you permission to enter the house. Although I don't think it can be argued that the note was in plain sight."

Fenway shook her head. "No, I mean that *if* one of those little girls is kidnapped, we can't jeopardize her by showing this to the cops."

McVie rubbed his chin. "Let's think about this, Fenway. All we have is this note. And the strange way Fletch acted. We don't have enough evidence to conclude that one of the daughters has been kidnapped."

"No, of course not," Fenway said. "This could never go to a jury. But this isn't about going to a jury. This is about doing the right thing. And my gut tells me we have to assume one of their girls is kidnapped, and that the cops can't know. The risk is too high *not* to assume that."

"This is barely enough to get the police to do a welfare check," McVie said.

Fenway exhaled, exasperated. "Stop thinking like a cop for just one second and start thinking about what you and I should do with the information we have. There's a threatening note. There's a chance one of the girls is kidnapped. And you know as well as I do that in kidnappings, every second that the victim isn't found means there's a lower chance of survival."

McVie thought for a moment. "Okay. We're going to have to do some stuff in secret." He sighed. "And because the girl hasn't been reported missing, we're going to have to go slower than I'd like."

"Slower?"

"I don't think there's any way around it," McVie said. "And I'm going to need to call in that favor your father owes me." He put the car in gear and exited the parking lot, getting back on the freeway. "You said you were going to your father's house tonight?"

"Yeah. I'm meeting him there at seven. We're having a fancy dinner."

"Is your father up for one more guest?"

"Tonight? For dinner?"

"Yes."

Fenway cleared her throat. "I don't see why not. What favor are you going to call in?"

"We're going to need to do some digging without police resources. And that costs money."

"Ah," Fenway responded. "You think he'll say yes?"

"He will if I call in the favor he owes me."

Fenway gave McVie a tired smile. "And with you there, I probably won't have to make as much polite small talk with Charlotte."

"I'm glad I can help," McVie put his hand on Fenway's knee. She felt a spark of electricity between them and closed her eyes. He must have felt it too, because he moved his hand quickly.

Fenway tried to act as if she hadn't felt anything. "Does it seem weird to you that the motel room was under the name *William Matisse*?"

"What do you mean by *weird*?"

"Well—that doesn't seem like something Fletch would do. It seems like something that someone *trying* to frame Fletch would do."

McVie nodded. His radio buzzed.

"All units, ten-thirty-two in progress in the ICU at St. Vincent's hospital. Repeat, ten-thirty-two in progress. All units available, proceed to St. Vincent's hospital. Repeat, ten-thirty-two in progress."

"Holy shit," McVie said, rolling down the window, reaching under his seat, and grabbing the siren ball. He floored it while putting the ball on his roof and Fenway was thrown back in her seat. The siren began to blare.

"That's where Rachel is."

"I know."

"What's a ten-thirty-two?" Fenway raised her voice over the roar of the engine.

"Man with gun."

Fenway felt the color drain from her face.

McVie weaved among the cars—even with his siren, not all of the cars pulled over to let him pass. But he kept the accelerator down, and the old Highlander's engine complained but kept going. Fenway sneaked a glance at the speedometer; they were doing 95. She felt a sinking feeling in her stomach.

"Hang on, Fenway," McVie said, and slid onto the left shoulder to pass stopped traffic in the left lane. The shoulder was bumpy and Fenway felt her teeth chatter in her head. A big rig had stalled out in the fast lane, and McVie swooped from the shoulder onto the roadway after passing it.

They were in the southern part of Estancia now, coming up onto the exit to Vincente Boulevard. They passed a blue sign with a white H with NEXT EXIT under it in smaller letters.

"Is a SWAT team coming?" she said.

"I sure hope so." He ran a red light at the bottom of the Vincente Boulevard exit, narrowly missing a minivan driving through the green light the other direction. He accelerated through the next green light, and Fenway saw the sign for the hospital parking lot on the next block. He turned into the lot at forty-five miles per hour, coming to a hard stop just before the hospital entrance.

"You're staying here," he barked at her. She had started to open the door.

"But—" she said.

"No!" he shouted. "There's a guy shooting in there. You won't help. Stay here!"

He pulled his gun out—Fenway hadn't even seen him get it— and checked it before running into the building.

Fenway realized McVie's car, right in front of the entrance, was a sitting target—not just for her, but as a possible getaway car for the shooter. She slid over to the driver's seat—McVie hadn't even turned the car off—and drove across the parking lot.

She parked behind a Chevy Suburban and killed the engine. She got out of the car and ducked down, shuttling around to the other side, putting the Highlander between her and the hospital entrance.

She heard three shots from inside—a single report, followed by two more shots.

About twenty people ran out of the entrance, making a beeline for the parking lot.

Another shot.

And then silence.

The air was deathly still for about forty-five seconds—although it seemed like an hour. Then Fenway heard more sirens, then heard the sirens turn off. She turned around to see two additional cruisers come into the parking lot, although they weren't speeding or driving like they were in a hurry. Both cruisers stopped in front of the entrance, and all four officers got out of the cars, and walked quickly—but didn't run—into the hospital.

It must be over, Fenway thought. *Whatever happened, it must be over.* She tried to move, tried to walk over to the entrance, but her legs wouldn't cooperate. She tried not to think about Rachel, or Craig, or Dez. Dez had gone home, hadn't she? She wouldn't have come back to the hospital—Rachel had gone back to sleep.

After ten minutes more, she saw some movement at the front entrance. McVie walked out. He looked at where the cruisers were and stared in disbelief for a few seconds, then looked up and scanned the parking lot. Fenway's knees felt like they were about to give out, but she stepped out from behind the car and waved at him. He nodded and started walking toward her.

She smiled weakly, and then she started feeling the same tightness in her chest that she had felt at Rachel's before she walked home. She pushed the feeling down. McVie walked up to her.

"You made it," she managed to say.

"I, uh," McVie said, his voice breaking. He coughed. "I got him."

"You got him?"

"Yes," McVie said. "He shot a nurse and a security guard in the ICU. I got him."

"The gunman's dead?"

McVie nodded.

Questions flooded Fenway's mind. Why did the gunman come to the hospital? Who was he? Had McVie ever shot anyone before?

"You're okay?" she said.

He nodded.

And she took another step forward and wrapped her arms around him. Inhaled his scent, mingled with sweat from the stress and the faintest hint of gunpowder. "I'm glad you're okay," she said, whispering in his ear. He shook a little. Almost imperceptible.

He hugged her back. He wrapped his arms around her, squeezed her. "Me too," he said softly, his mouth near her ear. The embrace was too close to be a co-worker hug. She held him, breathing him in, not wanting to let go.

A van from the local Estancia television station raced into the hospital driveway. McVie broke the embrace. "Thanks, Fenway."

She cleared her throat and took a step back. "He didn't go after Rachel?"

He ran his hand through his hair. "Uh, yes," McVie said. "Yes, he did. Rachel had woken up and had just called the nurse when a man dressed in dark slacks and a dress shirt came into her room and pulled a gun out."

"How did he get in?"

"Callahan and Salvador are sorting that out," he said. "I don't know how Rachel got away. The ICU nurse has a bullet in her shoulder. It doesn't look life-threatening. At least that's what the doctor said."

"I guess if you're going to get shot, it helps to already be in the hospital."

McVie managed a tired smile. "I'm not sure about the security guard. He was shot in the abdomen. They're trying to stabilize him now." He looked over Fenway's shoulder at the news van. "The media is here. I'll probably have to go say something, since our public information officer isn't here."

"Oh—how is Rachel doing? She must be scared out of her mind."

McVie hesitated. "That's the thing. She escaped."

"Right, you said that—you didn't know how she got away from the gunman."

McVie shook his head. "That's not what I mean, Fenway. I mean, she escaped from the hospital. Tore the IVs out of her arm. We can't find her."

CHAPTER TEN

———◆———

IT TOOK THEM THREE HOURS TO PROCESS THE SCENE AT THE hospital enough to let McVie leave. The press corps were still hanging around. A reporter from the *Los Angeles Times* interviewed a few people on the scene; the local news channel spoke with McVie for a few minutes before another officer stepped in and began speaking in nonspecific platitudes, saying the investigation was ongoing and the police could provide no additional information at this time. A few of the reporters got bored and packed up.

Amy arrived about forty-five minutes after the shooting stopped, and she wrapped her arms around McVie the same way Fenway had. Fenway caught McVie's eye during the hug, and McVie had a look that Fenway couldn't read; the jumble of emotions on his face made it hard for Fenway to pick up any particular one.

McVie and Amy spoke for a few minutes; she looked worried. A woman in a State Police uniform came up to talk to McVie. He didn't look pleased, but he nodded. He spoke with Amy again; she nodded, squeezed his hand, and then walked back to her car and drove away.

"I've been placed on administrative leave," McVie said to Fenway. "I'm not going to be a sheriff for the next week, at least."

"On leave? But the timing is horrible!"

"It's an automatic thing, Fenway. Officer-involved shooting."

A burst of panic popped in Fenway's head. "I really need you in this case, Sheriff," she said. "That index card—ransom note—whatever you call it—that throws everything up in the air. We need to figure out what happened to their daughter. *If* anything happened to their daughter." She set her jaw. "And we need to find Rachel. She's not well enough to be running around—they were going to move her from the ICU today."

"Look," McVie said, lowering his voice, "I agree with you. But we don't know who's behind any of this. We don't know if Rachel's still in danger." He rubbed his chin thoughtfully. "We don't know for sure what 'if you're guilty, she lives' means—whether it refers to Fletch's mother or daughter. Or even someone else."

"Come on, Sheriff, even I can figure out what 'no cops' means."

"Exactly, Fenway. We can't have the police involved." He hesitated before continuing. "And I don't know if we have a mole in the department."

Fenway cocked an eyebrow. "A mole?"

"I still think someone was paid off at the jail a couple of months ago, the night Dylan was murdered," McVie said. "And if they were paid off for that, they could be paid off for tipping the kidnappers when anyone at the sheriff's office talks about anything."

Fenway pursed her lips.

"I think this actually might be a blessing in disguise," McVie continued. "I can be more involved, since I won't have a job to go to for a week or so, and I can coordinate things with you a little better if there's no official visibility with what I'm doing."

"What do you propose?"

"So—that favor I need from your dad? I think he needs to hire a private investigator to find out what's going on," McVie said. "I know he's had to look into people stealing from him, who's selling his intellectual property to the competition, stuff like that. I bet he knows more than a few investigators who'd be good. Figuring out if someone kidnapped Fletch's daughter is going to feel like a walk in the park to him."

"And what makes you think he'll pay for it?"

"Besides that he owes me a favor?"

"Yeah."

"Because he feels guilty about what happened to Rachel a few months ago," he said. "He'll want whoever is behind this to be stopped."

"How do you know *he* isn't behind this?"

McVie gaped. "Jeez, such strong words coming from his own daughter."

"I'm just saying, look what happened with Stotsky."

"Ferris didn't have anything to do with that."

Fenway shook her head. "No, he had a *lot* to do with it. He just didn't cross the line. But he looked the other way. He enabled the bad behavior."

McVie nodded, choosing to ignore Fenway's tone. "Be that as it may, we need his money for a private investigator. Unless you've got a thousand bucks a day plus expenses."

Fenway shook her head.

"Right. Listen, I'm going to give my statement to the state police—they're sending someone in from the Santa Barbara field office. You go to your dad's and tell him I'm coming over too. We've got to figure out where to go next with this."

"Well," Fenway said, "I'm probably one of the people that Rachel trusts, so she might wind up at my apartment. I should head there and wait—at least until I have to leave for Dad's."

McVie looked at his phone. "Okay. It's almost five. I think I'll be able to meet you by seven-thirty."

Fenway nodded.

"Come on, I'll give you a ride," McVie said.

"I've got my dad's Mercedes back at the station," Fenway said. "I think the walk could do me good. It'll clear my head. Make me more useful tonight."

"You sure?"

"Yes. Go ahead. I know you have stuff to do."

"It's really no trouble. I'm going to right where your car is."

Fenway shook her head. "It'll be good for me."

McVie got into his car and drove off. The local news camera crew looked up as he backed up from the parking space, but didn't move.

Fenway stood silently, watching McVie drive through the maze of cars in the hospital parking lot, make a left turn onto Vincente Boulevard, and then disappear from view. She closed her eyes, not relishing the prospect of trying to find Rachel on the street.

And who was the gunman? Who was the man who had shot two people, and tried to shoot Rachel in her hospital bed, and who had ended up dead on the floor of the ICU? Fenway wanted to be at the autopsy of that man, when they tried to identify him through fingerprints or dental records. Or maybe they would find identification on him.

She saw Sergeant Mark Trevino walk out of the hospital. He went to his car, and Fenway, on impulse, ran up to him to try to catch him before he drove off.

"Mark!" she called.

He looked up. "Fenway? Were you here when the shooting happened?"

"McVie and I were down in Vista Del Rincón when we got the message," she said. "The sheriff raced here, siren going and everything."

"So you weren't inside?"

"No."

"You were lucky. Active shooter. Shot the security guard and a nurse."

"I heard Rachel got away."

"Yes. We don't think she was hurt. But we can't find her."

"Do you have anyone looking for her?"

"Honestly, no," Mark said. "The sheriff's office doesn't have the manpower for that right now."

"She's still in danger," Fenway said. "She's had two attempts on her life in the last twenty-four hours."

"I heard they've got a team of people working on setting up a protective detail," Mark assured Fenway. "But we need to actually find her before we can put the plan into place."

Fenway nodded. "So do you have any idea where she went? Security footage? Did anyone see her?"

Mark shook his head. "We haven't done that yet, no, but we're planning to go over the security footage pretty soon. We're interviewing the nurse, and the doctors are stabilizing the security guard as best they can."

"Okay," Fenway said. "What about the shooter?"

"Died at the scene," Mark said. "The ER staff tried to resuscitate him but no luck. It would have been nice to be able to ask him a few questions." He paused and shook his head. "Not that he would have answered them."

"Do you think he's the one who killed Mayor Jenkins?"

Mark put his hands on his hips. "I don't know. There's no sign of any connection I can see yet. This hospital shooting actually has some marks of a murder-for-hire."

"Did the shooter have ID?"

"No. That's one reason why we think it might've been a hit."

"How did he get here?"

"I assume he drove."

"Then his car is probably still in the lot." Fenway thought for a moment. "Did he have any keys? Maybe he had one of those remote-controlled door locks. We could go out and see which car beeps."

"No, he didn't have any keys on him." Mark shook his head. "Fenway, come on, let the investigators do their jobs. They've followed all the protocols correctly so far, but give them some time."

"When are they going to check the security footage?"

"Fenway," he said, "I know I report to you, but go home. Do something worthwhile. This is still an active crime scene. I'm not looking for you to get in trouble."

Fenway nodded. "Sorry for being so, I don't know, in your face about it. Rachel's my friend. I'm worried about her. I want to find her, and I don't want to leave any stone unturned."

Mark took Fenway's hand. "I get that. I'm not bothered. She's my friend too. I liked working with her a lot. We all want to keep her safe."

Fenway smiled, a little sadly. "Is Randy upset you had to work on a Sunday?"

Mark shook his head. "He had rehearsals this afternoon."

"He has rehearsals a lot."

"And I have to put in a lot of overtime. That's what makes our relationship work. Conflicting schedules." He smiled and clapped Fenway on the shoulder. "I'll see you later, kid."

Fenway smiled back, then turned and walked through the parking lot. She didn't recognize any of the cars save the cruisers that Mark and the other officers had driven. All of the cars looked lived in, some with bumper stickers, many with mileage markers or high school letter stickers on the back windows. Many with custom license plate frames. Family members visiting patients; it made sense.

There was a white Buick Verano backed into one of the visitor parking spaces, perfectly straight. It gave Fenway pause. Recent California plates, but a thoroughly nondescript car otherwise—a car that screamed *rental*.

"Lots of reasons a rental car could be in a hospital parking lot," Fenway mumbled to herself. She walked over the car and looked at it. Stock tires, no custom paint. She looked inside. Cloth seats.

But the backed-in car bothered her. Backing into the parking space would have given the shooter a quick getaway. She thought about the state of mind of people coming to the hospital, visiting loved ones or worried about treatment. They often wanted to get into the hospital quickly, not take the time to back in.

She walked around the parking lot, looking at the remaining cars. Not a single other car had backed into a visitor space. A couple of the staff cars. But no visitors.

There were a couple other nondescript cars in the parking lot that could have passed for rentals, but upon closer examination through the windows, she saw at least some semblance of personalization—a rosary hanging from a mirror, a child safety seat in the rear.

She walked back to the Buick. If the shooter had driven here but didn't want the keys found on him, she reasoned, he would have left the keys in the ignition. She looked closely at the side of the steering wheel and in the cupholders. She didn't see any keys, but she saw the pushbutton start ignition; the keys could have been under the seat or in the center console, and the car would have still started up right away.

And if the killer *had* left the keys in the car, he would have also left the door open.

Her hand moved to the door handle. The door opened with a satisfying click.

She almost let herself in when she remembered she had no gloves and she didn't want to mess up the car with fingerprints.

She looked back at the cruisers. Mark sat in his car, writing something on a clipboard. Fenway ran over.

"Mark," she said, "that white Buick right there?" She pointed to the Verano. "I think that's the shooter's car."

"What?"

"It's the only car in this whole lot that's backed in. You know, so he can make a quick getaway. And I'm almost positive it's a rental."

"There are all kinds of reasons why people back their cars in. And in all your years of working as a nurse, you never had family members visit from out of state who needed a rental car?"

"It's not just that. The door's unlocked, too. I bet if you look in there, you'll find the keys hidden so he could make a quick getaway, and maybe you'll find who rented it, and maybe even some permanent ID in the center console or glove box."

Mark shook his head and smiled. "Always having to stick your nose in," he said. "Okay, Fenway, thanks for the tip. I'll get one of the officers to check it out. But, you know, it could have been a bereaved family member of someone else here. People get worried about their sister or mother or cousin. They could have just left the keys."

Fenway thought for a moment. "So why don't you have the hospital make an announcement over the intercom? Say they left their lights on. If no one comes, maybe check inside then."

"Fenway—" Mark began, then stopped. "You're not letting this go, are you?"

"I guess I'm not," Fenway admitted. "Look, that Verano looks like a rental. You can get the name on the rental with a couple of calls. Or there might be ID in the car. Can you just check?"

Mark looked at Fenway and nodded solemnly. He opened his door and got out. Fenway took out her smartphone, then turned and took a picture of the license plate of the Buick, then followed Mark through the entrance of the hospital. Behind the reception desk, four people in hospital scrubs talked in hushed, worried tones.

"I'm sorry," Mark said to the woman nearest the front, "but I noticed there's a white Buick Verano in the parking lot with its lights on."

Fenway recited the license plate number.

The woman picked up the phone. She pushed three buttons, and her voice, repeating the notice and the license number, sounded throughout the hospital. She hung up.

"That doesn't go into the ICU or the ER, by the way, or in the patients' rooms," she said. "But if the owner of the car is anywhere else in the hospital, or if they're in a room with the door open, they should hear it."

"Thank you," Fenway said.

Mark and Fenway went back outside, and Mark leaned against the cruiser. "Stand on that side of me and chat," he said. "That way if someone comes out we can see who it is."

"I don't think anyone's going to come out," Fenway said. "I wish I had my kit here. I'd get my evidence bags and my gloves and we could see if it's the right car and we could get the ID."

"Fourth amendment, Fenway," Mark said, his tone gently scolding.

"The guy is dead," Fenway said. "If it's not the dead guy's car, we'll know in a couple of minutes."

"And if it points to a murder-for-hire, or the person who killed the mayor," Mark said, "you know it needs to stand up in court."

Fenway was quiet.

"You know I'm right," Mark said. "Honestly, I don't even think we have enough for probable cause."

Fenway pursed her lips but didn't say anything.

Mark thought for a moment. "But..." He stopped and sighed. "I think your instincts deserve to be followed. I'm going to get them to run the plates." He leaned into his car and picked up her radio. "If it's a rental, we should be able to get an ID. Or if it belongs to someone, as soon as we see a photo, we'll know if it's the same guy."

"I never saw him," Fenway said.

"I saw him enough for both of us," Mark said. He clicked through to dispatch and soon ran the license plate. The answer came back almost instantly: a rental from the Estancia airport.

Mark put his radio back, and took his cell phone out of his pocket. He talked on the phone for a minute, asking about the license plate. He hung up.

"Rental agency?"

"Yes," Mark said. "They're sending me a copy of the driver's license."

His phone dinged. He tapped the screen a couple of times.

"Okay, Fenway." Mark opened his trunk and got out an evidence kit. "Christmas in July." He opened the kit and pulled out a pair of blue nitrile gloves and several clear plastic evidence bags.

"You saw the ID for the guy who rented the Verano?"

"Yes. Definitely the shooter. Texas ID, Allen Evan Patrick. We've got probable cause that the car aided in the commission of a crime. Knock yourself out."

Fenway walked over to the Verano and opened the door again. She looked inside a center area under the climate control system and in front of the gearshift, but it was empty. She reached over and opened the glove compartment; there were a few papers from the rental agency and a manual for the car, but no ID.

Between the two front seats, behind the cupholder, there was a fabric-covered raised surface, slightly rounded on top. Fenway felt along the line where the fabric met the plastic, and found a release button. The fabric top eased open. She found a wallet inside, with the Buick's key on top.

Fenway pulled the wallet out and opened it. A California driver's license—Alan Patrick Scorrelli. The picture was of a balding, clean-shaven white man with a crew cut, a sharp nose, a mole high on his left cheek, and a cleft chin.

She looked through the wallet; there were a few credit cards, also in the Scorrelli name. In a pouch behind the main card section on the right, however, she found a Texas license with the name Allen Evan Patrick, and a Visa in the Patrick name.

She put the Texas license in one evidence bag and the wallet in the second, got out of the car, and walked back to Mark.

"Found the ID in the car," she said, holding out the license for Mark to see.

Mark looked at the driver's license. "That's him," he said. "Mole on his cheek and everything."

Fenway breathed out. "All right," she said. "He's got a California license in the wallet too. Alan Patrick Scorrelli is the name on it, different spelling of *Allen.*"

"We should call Kav," Mark said. "Dust the car for fingerprints, look in the trunk. And we need to look at the airlines, see where he flew in from. See what connections he has to Estancia."

Fenway nodded.

Mark paused. "You're not going to hang around and look over Kav's shoulder too, are you?"

"Sorry, Mark, I know I got all up in your business," Fenway said. "But we know more now than we did fifteen minutes ago, right?"

"Like I said, you deserve to follow your instincts."

"Okay," Fenway said. "Give Kav my best. I need to clear my head. Especially after this. I'm walking back to the station."

CHAPTER ELEVEN

BY THE TIME FENWAY GOT BACK TO THE OFFICE, IT WAS PAST FIVE. She opened the door to the outer office and saw two young white men in the beige plastic desk chairs. She recognized one of them.

"Hey," she said, "you're Dylan's brother. Parker, right?"

Parker had a family resemblance to Rachel's late husband, and wore board shorts, flip-flops, and a surf company tee shirt. The other guest dressed similarly—his flip-flops were leather instead of canvas—and his straight, long, sun-bleached hair fell to his shoulders.

"Yeah," Parker said, looking Fenway up and down. "Damn, girl, you clean up good."

"Okay," said Fenway sharply, "you didn't come here to creep on me. What can I do for you and your friend?"

"It's just that you were in sweats and a Red Sox cap last time I saw you. Just saying you look nice."

"Parker, I just came from the shooting at the hospital. I don't have time for this crap."

"Jeez, fine," Parker said. "Maybe there's a place we can talk?"

Fenway narrowed her eyes at Parker. "Sure. Come with me."

She walked past Migs—who had, bless him, come in on a Sunday to help out—and went to her private office, with Parker and his friend following her. She stepped aside as soon as she crossed the threshold to let Parker and his friend take the two guest chairs in front of her desk.

"So," she said, closing the door and going around her desk to sit behind it, "what brings you two in on a Sunday evening?"

Parker looked at his friend, who looked too stunned to speak. "Okay, so my boy Zoso got a call from the police earlier today. They wanted to know about some, uh, business dealings that he may have had."

"You're Zoso?" she said to Parker's friend.

He hesitated, then nodded.

"You know, the sheriff's office is across—"

"Dude, I know," Parker said. "But when all that shit happened a few months ago with Dylan, you listened to me. Like, that parking ticket stuff that I told you might work? You actually listened to me."

Fenway was quiet.

"The point is, Zoso isn't a big fan of the cops. Especially when it comes to giving them information about his business dealings."

"Ah," Fenway said. "He might have some information about some customers who take some painkillers." She looked at Zoso; panic splayed across his face. "I mean hypothetically, of course."

"Come on, Zoso," Parker said. "I told you she's cool. She just wants to know stuff that will help Rachel." Then he looked up at Fenway. "Right? You want to know stuff that can catch that guy who almost killed Rachel?"

"Right," Fenway said.

"Okay," Zoso said slowly. "So I start hearing some things on the street. Like, there's some new shit coming, and it's going to make those other pills look like they don't even do anything."

Fenway had to bite her tongue from asking about the other pills. "So did you try to get some?"

"It ain't out yet," Zoso replied. "But there's only one source for this new pill, and the other pills are already getting squeezed out. The distributor for this new shit, he's got some sort of corner on the market. I mean, it better be as good as he says it is. He can threaten me all he wants, but if the product sucks, then no one's going to want it."

"What's the stuff called on the street?"

"Red Skies," Zoso said.

"Red Skies?"

"Like, 'red skies at night, sailor's delight.'"

"Is this particularly delightful to sailors?"

Zoso shrugged. "I'll let you know when I get my yacht. The one I want is on back order." He cracked a smile, pleasantly surprised at his own cleverness.

"All right," Fenway said. "And Zoso, you ever have, uh, business dealings with Fletcher Jenkins?"

"Who?"

"He goes by Fletch." Fenway pulled out her phone and brought up Fletch's picture. "This guy. He one of your customers? Buprenodone, maybe?"

"Buprenodone? I never heard of that. That some good shit?"

"If you've got a problem with anxiety," Fenway said.

"This Fletcher dude got a problem with anxiety?"

Fenway raised her phone so he could see the picture better. "Look again. Is this one of your customers or business partners?"

Zoso shook his head. "I've never seen him before. But it's kind of, you know, uh, segregated. Black guys go to black dealers, white guys go to white dealers."

"I'm disappointed. That's not very progressive."

Zoso shrugged.

Fenway sighed. "All right, Zoso. Thanks."

"That stuff about Red Skies is helpful, right?"

Fenway nodded. "Sure. I'll keep my eyes peeled."

Parker and Zoso got up and left the office. Fenway started picking up a few files, then looked at the clock. It was almost five-thirty; she needed to get ready for dinner.

She drove home in her father's Mercedes and took another quick shower, taking care to cover her hair. After a three-mile walk from the hospital to the office, she felt she needed to clean up. She looked at herself in the mirror. If she and McVie were going to be asking her father for a favor, she needed to dress up a little bit; she knew he didn't care for the casual look.

She got out the shower and pulled off her hair wrap. Dez had recommended a hairstylist in Estancia who actually knew what to do with her curls. She remembered her undergrad days at Western Washington; she had never found a decent hairstylist in Bellingham, and she and her ancient Nissan Sentra would make the trek to Seattle every six weeks to see her mother's hairstylist, the one she'd been going to ever since she and her mother had arrived in Seattle.

She dressed in a fitted casual dress with black-and-white flowers that reminded her of her mother's charcoal drawings. She looked at herself in the mirror; the dress showed a hint of cleavage, but probably nothing that her father would criticize. It certainly didn't compare to Charlotte's revealing outfits.

She did her makeup carefully, putting on more than she usually wore, but not too much. She looked in the mirror when she was done and felt a little disgusted with her preening. She slipped on low black heels and left the apartment.

She looked at the clock in the Mercedes as she accelerated onto Estancia Canyon Drive; she'd be a little late, but the sheriff knew her father well, so it shouldn't be an issue.

She felt a twinge. She had forgotten to tell her father that she had invited McVie. Part of her simply shrugged at that—he had neglected to mention that he had brought along his preferred coroner candidate for breakfast that morning—but she didn't need Charlotte giving her grief. She pulled her phone out of her purse and called her father's cell, putting it on speaker.

"Nathaniel Ferris."

"Hi, Dad."

"Fenway! Calling to tell me you'll be late?"

"I'm in the car, but yeah, I had to shower after what happened at the hospital. Did you hear?"

"I saw it on the news—wait, you were there?"

"Yes." Fenway turned onto the freeway onramp. "And the sheriff was too—and we have some things we need to discuss with you."

"About the shooting?"

"About our investigation," Fenway said.

"The shooting at the hospital is because of your investigation?"

"Let's talk about it when I get there, Dad. And I should have called earlier to tell you the sheriff is coming too."

"Ah. I suppose it would have been nice to know more than ten minutes before dinner, but we should have plenty of food. We'll just set another place."

"Sorry."

"Don't worry about it."

"Okay. Craig—Sheriff McVie—might beat me there." She grimaced, but her father hadn't noticed her calling the sheriff *Craig*. "Just so you know."

They said goodbye and Fenway ended the call, just as she turned off the freeway onto Las Manzanitas Drive.

The road narrowed, then zigzagged toward the cliffs. With a granite wall on her left side and a guard rail between her and a dropoff to the ocean below, she made a hairpin turn onto a side road that rose steeply for about a hundred feet, and emptied out onto a plateau, where her father's mansion overlooked the Pacific.

The mansion, designed in the Mediterranean style, was enormous. The focal point of the house was two floors of large central rooms with six archways in front—a set of three on the ground floor and an identical set of three on the second floor, all with white stucco columns. The windows behind the columns were grandiose, showcasing the interiors.

From these central rooms and archways, several rooms symmetrically flared out, set back a few feet from the archways, giving the whole mansion a larger-than-life feel. And bookending the house were two sets of low marble staircases. A long wall fountain was set below all the rooms, spanning the entire length of the house, from staircase to staircase. A red tile roof topped the house, and two small towers jutted up on either side above the central rooms.

The whole house exuded an ostentatious extravagance that Fenway hadn't noticed as a child, but now brought on a pang of agitation as she thought about her college loans.

McVie's beige Highlander stood in the parking area in front of the separate six-car garage, but behind the large circular driveway. The lawn spanned at least an acre in front of the driveway, and looked as precisely maintained as a golf course.

Fenway pulled the Mercedes up to the garage, and pushed a button in the ceiling-mounted console. The fourth garage door opened, revealing an empty space, and Fenway pulled in. She got out and walked quickly to the mansion, wishing she had brought a jacket; even in July, the ocean breeze made it so much cooler than at her apartment, just a couple of miles inland. She hurried up one of the low marble staircases, and turned toward the middle archway on the ground floor.

Through the window, she could see McVie and her father, sitting on opposite sides of the coffee table. McVie, still in his street clothes from earlier, had his muscular arm on the back of the sofa; her father leaned forward in an exotic-looking chair, elbows on his knees, engaged in conversation. Both of them were holding what looked like a glass of reddish-brown liquid—knowing her father, most likely scotch. Everett Michaels stood at the head of the coffee table, holding a highball glass of the same with a single large ice cube in it, his smoky eyes on her father, paying close attention to Ferris' words and gesticulations.

Fenway rapped on the glass with her knuckles, and suddenly became acutely aware that she hadn't brought anything, not so much as a bottle of wine or a dessert.

Her father sat straight up at the sound of the knocking and he turned his head to look at Fenway. He smiled easily and motioned for her to come in.

She pushed open the door, and suddenly she felt eight years old again. Miles Davis played on the sound system. Two Red Sox jerseys—Wade Boggs and Dustin Pedroia, autographed and framed—hung above the short curio cabinet against the far wall. She remembered that curio cabinet and the Boggs jersey; the Pedroia jersey must have been a more recent acquisition.

"Hey!" McVie said. "You made it." He stood up and crossed over to her. His face smiled, but his eyes were tired. He embraced her, which she didn't expect in front of her father, and she embraced him back, if a little late.

"Yeah," she said, lamely, taking a seat on the sofa. "Did you hear that we found the ID of the gunman?"

"You did?" Everett Michaels said, sitting down next to Fenway. His eyes raked down and back up her body, taking in the low-cut dress, the cinched waist, her legs, the heels, back up and looking in her eyes. It almost took her breath away, even though she felt almost shamefully exposed. His cologne, subtle but still noticeable even this far into the day, mixed with the mild scent wafting up from his glass of scotch. Fenway got distracted—she had never been so affected by a man's scent before. Although perhaps Akeel came a close second, based on pheromones alone.

She blinked hard a few times, trying to get back her concentration.

Michaels continued, "Did you figure out who he worked for?"

McVie shook his head and shot a glance at Fenway, not missing the once-over Michaels had given her. "Not yet, Everett. I just heard about it myself. Sergeant Trevino texted me when I was leaving the sheriff's office."

Fenway nodded. "Mark and I found the Buick after you left."

"How long is your administrative leave?" Michaels asked.

"Until they've completed the investigation," McVie said. "Probably about a week. They've assured me it's routine."

"Wait, did you say you're on administrative leave?" Nathaniel Ferris said, setting down his scotch. "Why are you on leave?"

"I took down the gunman," McVie said.

"You shot him?"

McVie nodded. Fenway saw his eyes turn down.

"How about that," Ferris said, a note of admiration in his voice. He rubbed his chin. "Sheriff, I'm sure glad you were there. The news said that a couple of people were shot, but not killed."

"The nurse will be okay," said McVie. "The security officer, I'm not sure. He was in critical condition last time I checked."

"Still, it could have been a lot worse, right, Everett?"

Everett Michaels looked lost in thought. He didn't respond for a moment, and then seemed to snap back to reality. "Right, Nate," he said.

Charlotte walked into the room, wearing a short black dress with a plunging neckline, and holding a glass of white wine. "Hello, Fenway. I didn't hear you come in."

"Good evening, Charlotte." Fenway fought an urge to curtsy and an equally strong urge to sneer. Charlotte turned her head so her earrings caught the light. They were unusual—a line of five small diamonds and then a large hexagonal-shaped diamond, easily two carats, hanging below that. Platinum rivets held all the diamonds in place. Fenway found herself staring.

Out of the corner of her eye, she noticed that Everett Michaels still had his attention on her; Charlotte's entrance, low-cut dress, unusual earrings and all, hadn't even ruffled him.

"Sandrita tells me dinner is almost ready," she said. "Just about five more minutes. You're not still talking shop, are you?"

"Sorry, Charlotte," McVie said, "but whenever there's a public shooting like this, it's going to be what we talk about."

Charlotte examined her nails.

"Anyway, I'm sure you're going to keep hearing it on the news," McVie said. "The press was all over it today. They're probably camped out on my front lawn."

"Those are quite unusual earrings, Charlotte," Fenway said before she could stop herself.

Charlotte fondled her earlobes and briefly smiled. "I found a wonderful custom jewelry designer down in Santa Barbara," she said. "Your father gave these to me for our anniversary last month."

Sandrita came out to announce dinner. They walked through the open archway into the formal dining room, five places set at the large table. Her father took the head of the table, and Charlotte took the other end. Fenway quickly maneuvered to the single place setting on the long side, leaving Everett and McVie to sit next to each other across from her.

It was a full four-course meal, with a salad, soup, entrée—a fancy pheasant dish—and dessert.

"I haven't had pheasant since you took me to Maxime's," Fenway said to her father.

"I couldn't get the recipe from Ernesto, and that's the only place on the Central Coast you can get pheasant," Ferris said.

"The only place? What about down in Santa Barbara?"

"There's a great French restaurant there that did a wonderful pheasant Normandy with Calvados and apples, but they replaced it with a thoroughly mediocre game hen dish last year," said Charlotte. "But Sandrita just does a masterful job with this."

"Did you say a calvado?" McVie said. "Is that like an avocado?"

Everett chuckled. "Calvados is an apple brandy," he said, his tone a little condescending. "It's made in Normandy."

McVie looked a little embarrassed. Fenway found Everett Michaels a little less attractive after that comment. Although she was glad she hadn't asked the same question.

"So who's Ernesto?" asked Fenway.

"The owner and head chef," Ferris explained.

"At Maxime's?" asked McVie.

"He can charge more for dinner at a place called Maxime's than a place called Ernesto's," Charlotte said. She poured herself another glass of wine.

Charlotte looked bored and annoyed. Fenway wondered, a little too eagerly, if trouble loomed in her father's marriage.

They finished up dinner and moved back into the great room. Ferris offered another round of scotch to McVie and Everett. Fenway would have said yes to a nice scotch on the rocks, but Ferris didn't ask her.

"I better not," McVie said. "I'm driving, and that road out of here isn't an easy one. And all I need is to get pulled over after I—" He cut himself off and looked at Charlotte. "After what happened today," he finished.

"As a matter of fact, Dad, we needed to talk with you about the investigation," Fenway said. "With some of the things that happened today, we—well, we need your help."

"I'm listening," Ferris said. He sipped his scotch, picked up the remote, and started scanning through his jazz collection.

"I'm sorry, Mr. Michaels," Fenway said, "but I think this needs to be a private conversation."

"Nonsense," Ferris said. "If Everett's going to be the next coroner, he's going to have to learn about the investigation process. Now's as good a time as any. Right, Craig?"

McVie looked uncomfortable. "Normally I'd agree with you, Mr. Ferris." He rubbed his chin. "But we're talking about a life and death situation here." He looked at Michaels. "Not that we don't trust you, Mr. Michaels. But we have to be very careful about the information we have."

"I understand," Everett Michaels said. "Don't worry about me. I'll go into the kitchen. Charlotte could use the company, I'm sure. Someone who won't talk about work." He got up, winked at Fenway, and walked into the kitchen.

The mansion's open floor plan, with a large, grandiose archway heading into the kitchen, made it hard to keep conversations private. Fenway was a little concerned that Michaels could still hear, but she supposed she was worried about nothing.

"Okay," McVie said, lowering his voice. "We've been looking at both the murder of Mayor Jenkins and the attempted murder of Rachel. And all the evidence so far—especially for Rachel—points to the mayor's son."

"Fletcher?" Ferris said. "I don't believe it. I mean, I know he had his troubles with cocaine, but that was years ago."

"Fifteen years," McVie replied. "But even so, we have a lot on him. Fingerprints. Motive. His wife gave him an alibi, but really nothing that could be independently confirmed."

"So are you watching him?"

"We arrested him," McVie said.

"He confessed," Fenway interrupted.

"He confessed?" Ferris exclaimed.

"Shh!" Fenway admonished. "Not so loud, Dad."

"Fenway, you really don't have to worry about Everett. If this were six months in the future, he'd be here instead of you."

Fenway shot McVie a look. He returned her look with a softer gaze. Fenway sighed and continued in a quiet voice. "Okay, but here's the thing. At their house, I went to spit out my gum, and a note sort of halfway buried in their trash can said, 'If you're guilty, then she lives. No cops.'"

In spite of defending Everett, Ferris kept his voice down. "Wait, say that again."

"'If you're guilty, she lives, no cops,'" McVie repeated.

Ferris paused. "What does that mean?"

McVie set his jaw. "We don't know for sure what it means."

"But," Fenway cut in, "It might mean that the real murderers have framed Fletcher for his mother's murder, and they've kidnapped one of his daughters so that he'll take the fall. I think they're holding his daughter hostage until Fletcher is found guilty."

"Holding her hostage? How old is she?"

"We don't know which daughter it is. One girl is five. The other is about a year and a half."

A look of horror struck her father's face.

"See, Dad," Fenway continued, "this is where it gets complicated. Because we're not supposed to know. The kidnappers—or whoever—never intended for me to find that note. And the police *can't* find out, either—or at least, the kidnappers can't ever think the police know."

"But surely," Ferris said, "if there's a missing girl, that's a matter for the police. Or the FBI or somebody like that."

McVie shook his head. "Neither Fletcher nor his wife will confirm that one of their daughters is missing. The police won't do anything until there's confirmation of a missing child—or until a report is filed. And if you'll remember, I'm on administrative leave. I don't even have the standing to do *anything* as a police representative right now."

"So there might not be a kidnapping at all?"

"That's correct," McVie said, choosing his words carefully. "But given what Fenway found, and given the way Fletch acted, kidnapping is a very real possibility. One that I don't think the police can act on, but one that I don't think I can ignore."

"So if we're right," said Fenway, "if one of Fletcher's daughters *has* been kidnapped, we need to figure out who took her—and get her back."

Ferris held up his hands, palms out. "Hang on. Why are you telling me this? How am I supposed to figure that out?"

"Not you, Mr. Ferris," said McVie. "People you know."

"You know some of the best private investigators in the business," Fenway said. "You've dealt with stolen intellectual property. You've dealt with executives who were skimming money. And you haven't done it yourself. You've had investigators do it."

"Rob always did that kind of stuff for me," Ferris protested.

Fenway shook her head. "Stotsky didn't do that stuff alone, Dad. You can't tell me you don't have those contacts. When you had to deal with stuff that hit your business interests, you must have known the details."

Ferris sighed. "Yes, you're right." He paused and pursed his lips. "I have a guy who's dug into some computer records on K and R stuff in Latin America."

"K and R?" Fenway asked.

"Kidnap and ransom," McVie said. "But, Mr. Ferris, this isn't financial motivation. This isn't negotiating ransom down into the six figures from ten million. This is something different."

Nathaniel Ferris thought a moment. "In that case, there's another contact I have." He tapped his chin in thought. "He's expensive, but he's really good—a former Russian hacker who works for the good guys now. But I don't think the county can afford him."

"*You* can afford him, Dad," Fenway said.

"Me? Why am I footing the bill for this?"

"Because, Dad, a little girl's life is at stake."

"*Might* be at stake."

"Yes, Dad. *Might* be at stake."

Ferris paused. "You're asking me for charity."

"Is that the way you look at it?" Fenway snapped. "As *charity*? There's a little girl, probably scared out of her mind, being held against her will, and her father is willing to go to jail for the rest of his life for a crime he didn't commit—just to keep her safe. That little girl not only deserves to be rescued, she deserves her dad back—her dad, who is willing to lose *everything*." She looked hard at her father. "Don't you think a father who is willing to sacrifice his freedom, his life, his future, deserves his daughter back?"

Ferris dropped his eyes.

"And if you won't do it because it's the right thing to do, then do it because of Stotsky. Because whoever is behind this has tried to kill Rachel twice in the last two days, and if they succeed, Dad, you're up shit creek."

Ferris opened his mouth—probably to deny what Fenway implied, and then thought better of it. He looked down and pinched the bridge of his nose. "Fine," he said. "I'll set up a meeting. I'll foot the bill for it." He coughed. "But I better not get any speeding tickets in Dominguez County for the next year."

After McVie dropped her off at home, Fenway opened her front door and half-expected Rachel to greet her. Instead, the apartment was dark and empty. Fenway set her purse on the coffee table.

She paced around the apartment for a few minutes, thinking about the jealous glances from McVie, the admiring looks from Everett Michaels. She looked at the empty spot on the living room wall, where the painting of the cypress tree and the ocean should be. She pulled out her phone from her purse; not quite ten o'clock.

After a moment of internal debate, she called Akeel. He picked up on the second ring.

"Hey, Akeel."

"Hey, Fenway," he said. "You make it home okay?"

"Sure."

"You coming back any time soon?"

"You *interested* in me coming back any time soon?"

Akeel paused. Fenway heard some noise in the background. "Hang on a sec." After the sound of a door closing, the background noise got quiet. "Sorry. Hanging with the boys tonight, but I'm going to leave soon. Got work tomorrow."

"Yeah, unfortunately, me too."

"Still working that murder that called you away?"

"Yes. Just barely scratching the surface, actually."

"Oh, man. They really couldn't have done without you on Saturday night?"

"No," Fenway said, abruptly.

"All right," Akeel said. "I didn't mean nothing by that."

Fenway thought Akeel wanted an apology. She gritted her teeth; she didn't want to tell him she was sorry—because she wasn't.

"Hey," Akeel said, "I found a key under the coffee table after you left. I think it's yours."

"Really?" Fenway asked. "I don't think so. I've got all my keys; apartment, car—I had to drive to the airport."

"It's a big silver key with a red plastic insert in the, what do you call it, the part you hold onto."

"Oh no," Fenway said. "That's the storage unit key. Crap. It must have fallen out of my purse."

"When we were doing some interesting stuff," Akeel said, trying to crank up the sexiness in his voice, but Fenway didn't take the bait.

"Yeah," she said. "Thanks for letting me know. I would have gone crazy looking for it."

"Sure," he said, and Fenway could hear his disappointment that she didn't want to flirt on the phone.

They talked for another ten minutes, but the disappointment in Akeel's voice faded into disinterest. She promised to call as soon as she made plans to return to Seattle.

She hung up even more frustrated than before. She paced around her apartment restlessly, even though she could barely keep her eyes open. She tried doing some research online about Alan Scorrelli, or Allen Patrick, but came up empty. She suspected that Dez or Mark would have more luck using an actual police database rather than just normal web search tools.

When she finally decided to try and get some sleep, it was midnight, and her brain wouldn't turn off. She went back and forth on who the mystery man in the Buick might be, and how he was connected to Rachel, and Alice Jenkins, and Fletcher.

She started drifting off after tossing and turning for another hour—when suddenly Barry Klein popped into her head. Barry Klein, running for coroner, with an optometry business to sell or close up if he did. He had a medical background. She thought for a moment. Could optometrists order medication? She thought they could. Anyone might have been able to break into Fletcher's house.

Klein was also an angry man—she found that out in the County Board of Supervisors meeting. And she had seen him at City Hall a couple of times since then. He acted just as passive-aggressive and nasty to the other county supervisors as he had been to her.

She swung her legs out of bed and got back up. She padded to her computer in her bare feet and started to search for Barry Klein and anything she could find on Alice Jenkins, Rachel Stotsky Richards, or Fletcher Jenkins.

Klein had attended St. Benedictine's in Paso Querido, the private high school, and had graduated about five years after Fletcher.

No articles or web sites listed the two of them together, although she did find an article from two years previous in the *Estancia Courier*, announcing Tracey Jenkins as one of the Teacher of the Year finalists for Dominguez County.

Fenway found nothing on the combination of Klein and Rachel. A search for Klein and the mayor came up with hundreds of hits on the county websites, most of which were transcripts of meetings, or news clippings of both of them at public events. She was nowhere.

On a whim, she typed in *Tracey Jenkins and Barry Klein* and hit the search button.

The search returned the LinkedIn profile of Tracey Klein from Garrison, Florida; a couple of open database files which looked like DMV records from Pennsylvania; and a set of odd character strings from a long URL that started with HikeUpMeetUp.com.

Fenway yawned and thought maybe she had distracted her brain enough and she could go to bed. Thinking that she'd probably unearth the hiking trail history of the stranger from Florida, Fenway clicked on the HikeUpMeetUp link, fully ready to close the window and put her PC to sleep.

The browser window turned to black, then a new page came up with the HikeUpMeetUp logo on the top.

A text conversation, dated three weeks prior, popped up on screen between *eyeguy805* and *crazygrrl10*. At first, Fenway couldn't tell if she was reading a hiking site conversation or a cheating-spouses site—but it definitely piqued her interest.

> *eyeguy805: hi pretty girl nice to see you again*
> *crazygrrl10: thanx for PMing me*
> *eyeguy805: you lonely tonight?*
> *crazygrrl10: lonely every night*
> *eyeguy805: yr profile says your married*
> *crazygrrl10: doesn't make a difference*

eyeguy805: no problem
crazygrrl10: you into stuff other than hiking?
eyeguy805: yeah I like to meet new friends and play.
eyeguy805: Nothing too serious.
crazygrrl10: I like ur photos
eyeguy805: thx
crazygrrl10: you have some great abs in your profile pic
eyeguy805: you like hiking too?
crazygrrl10: yes beach or mountains?
eyeguy805: either
crazygrrl10: you live in 805 area code?
eyeguy805: y
crazygrrl10: me too. near Sand harbor. great hiking
eyeguy805: i just live a few mi away from sand harbor i love it ther
crazygrrl10: we should go
eyeguy805: and just hike?
crazygrrl10: maybe more
eyeguy805: wife is out of town till Friday
crazygrrl10: husband doesn't give a shit ever. so I'm down
eyeguy805: coffee bean on estancia cyn? 3pm
crazygrrl10: yes bring hiking shoes and lots of water
crazygrrl10: you might need to stay hydrated haha

Fenway read the passage through twice. Barry Klein and Tracey Jenkins had arranged a tryst in Sand Harbor Regional Park—meeting at the same coffee place not two blocks away from her apartment less than a month ago.

She opened the *eyeguy805* user profile in a new tab. Barry Klein, in hiking shorts but shirtless—and with ripped abs—stared back at her. Fenway had no idea that such a muscular frame hid under his sport coat and oxford shirt. He had seemed skinny to her before. And opening *crazygrrl10*'s profile in another new tab brought up a picture of Tracey, but instead of hiking clothes, she had on a black sparkly top with a pretty generous amount of cleavage showing. The background looked exactly like the kitchen in which she had found a suspicious note in the garbage, not twenty-four hours earlier.

Fenway took screenshots of the conversation and the user profiles and sent them to her work email. Then she did another search on what medications optometrists could prescribe, and discovered each state differed. In a report titled *California Medication Jurisprudence for Optometrists*, she read that they could prescribe "all oral analgesics that are not controlled substances." Another search revealed that buprenodone was not classified as a controlled substance in the United States.

"Interesting," she said out loud. "Very interesting."

PART IV

MONDAY

CHAPTER TWELVE

FENWAY ARRIVED AT WORK JUST BEFORE SEVEN ON MONDAY morning. She had gotten a few hours of sleep, although she had been so excited about her discovery that she had trouble settling down. If Fletcher Jenkins had told his mother about the affair, and if they had contacted the county's public information officer—Rachel—to figure out how best to go public with the accusations, then Klein might have very well been behind everything: the murder of the mayor, the staging of Rachel's "suicide," and the attempt on Rachel's life in the hospital. Given the dead shooter's multiple identities, it made sense that he was a professional hitman.

As usual, Dez had beaten Fenway into the office.

"I thought for sure I'd get here before you today," Fenway said.

Dez shook her head. "Not a chance. Not after I missed all the action yesterday."

"You all caught up?"

"I read the sheets. Not looking forward to doing this without McVie for the next week or two, I'll tell you that much."

Fenway debated telling Dez about the possible kidnapping of one of Fletcher's daughters, as well as the note they found, but decided that they were already pushing their luck with McVie knowing about it.

"You got a delivery first thing this morning too," Dez said.

"Me? What did I get? Someone send my car back from Sea-Tac?"

Dez smirked. "It's just flowers from a mysterious stranger."

"Seriously?"

"Seriously. They're on your desk."

Fenway stepped into her office. A large bouquet of multi-colored lilies, in shades of pink, white, and orange—a summer selection, Fenway supposed—bloomed on her desk in a glass vase with a square bottom that flared wider at the neck.

"Who are these from?" Fenway mused.

"I'm not as nosy as you are; I didn't go snooping," Dez said.

Fenway shot her a look.

Dez laughed. "Okay, fine. They're from Everett Michaels. He was thrilled to meet you in person and he's hoping he can convince you to endorse him for coroner."

Fenway rolled her eyes. "The way to my heart isn't flowers, it's coffee," she said. "But I guess I appreciate the gesture."

"He's hoping he can continue to convince you by taking you to dinner on Friday," Dez said.

"Oh, really." Fenway put her hands on her hips. "I think he wants me to give him more than just an endorsement."

Dez cackled.

"Speaking of inappropriate relationships, I found out something yesterday," said Fenway. "Barry Klein and Fletcher's wife had an affair. Maybe they're still having one."

Dez looked at her sideways. "How'd you find that out?"

"HikeUpMeetUp.com needs to secure their servers better," Fenway said. "I bet they've locked it back down now, but I got the screenshots."

Dez paused. "Didn't Fletcher confess already?"

"Well, yes." Fenway narrowed her eyes. "But, uh, I don't believe him."

"He confessed, but you don't believe him?"

"Rachel got shot at in the hospital at the exact same time we were arresting Fletcher," Fenway said. "It doesn't make sense."

"Not if Fletcher hired the gunman." Dez cleared her throat. "Look, Fenway, I know I pushed the conspiracy theory earlier, but it's really tough to deny a confession."

"I think Fletcher was coerced into it."

"*Was* coerced? Who coerced him?"

"Uh..." Fenway tapped her foot and scrunched up her face. "I don't know. Not yet."

Dez searched Fenway's face. She squinted and tilted her head to the side. "And why do you think some unknown person coerced him?"

"I'm sorry, Dez," Fenway replied, "but I don't think I can tell you that."

"Who else knows about this supposed coercion?"

"Sheriff McVie."

Dez pursed her lips. "And he agrees with you that Fletcher's innocent?"

Fenway paused. "I think so. I don't know he'd say that definitively. But there's certainly a lot of doubt."

Dez pushed her chair back from the desk. "Okay, rookie," she said, "I'll lay off about it for now. Let me see your cheating husband thing."

Fenway pulled out her laptop—the county had yet to replace the Acer notebook with the broken Escape key—and showed Dez her email with the screenshots of the conversation between Tracey Jenkins and Barry Klein.

"Okay," Dez admitted, "this is pretty damning evidence that two people are going to cheat on their spouses. But how do you know that *eyeguy805* is Klein and *crazygrrl10* is Fletcher's wife?"

"They've got profile information with their photos. This is a hiking meetup site, not some cheating spouses site. I mean, it looks like that's what the two of them used it for, but it had their real names and photos in their profiles."

Dez sat back in her chair and thought for a moment. "All right," she said. "Let's go pay Dr. Feelgood a visit."

———◆———

With her ancient laptop, it took Fenway five minutes to print out the conversation and the photos. Klein Optometry didn't open until nine, so Dez thought they could catch the optometrist at home. Klein lived in a large rambler on the north side of Estancia off Cypress Grove Avenue. It took Dez about ten minutes to drive there.

"This is just like when you first started and didn't have a car, rookie," she said. "And I drove your sorry ass around all the time."

"I'll remember that when I'm paying two hundred bucks to get my car out of long-term parking, en route to a sixteen-hour drive back here," Fenway said.

Dez pulled into the driveway and they got out. "It's only seven-thirty," Fenway said. "Do you think it's too early?"

"Not on a Monday morning in this neighborhood," Dez said. "All the good little mommies and daddies are awake and getting their rugrats ready for the day. If they're not already at preschool."

"Okay, Dez. You going to lead this one?"

"Hell, no. This man might be my boss in six months. I'd wait in the car if I didn't think you'd screw this up if I weren't here."

Fenway rapped on the door. A girl of about four pulled the door open, and a man's voice—Klein's—shouted behind her, "Emily, don't open—oh come on, Em—"

He stopped when he saw Fenway.

"Miss Stevenson," he said coldly. "What are you doing here?"

"I'm sorry to bother you at home," Fenway said, although she'd really only be sorry if Klein's wife weren't there. "But as you probably know, we're investigating the mayor's murder."

"I don't see how I have anything to do with it," Klein said.

"Last week, the mayor and her son met the county public information officer for several hours. And less than seventy-two hours later, someone murders the mayor, and someone tried to kill Rachel Richards as well. We believe that they discussed something that put them all in danger."

"Are you suggesting that they discussed *me*?"

"It's possible," Fenway said. "Would you like to step outside so we can have this conversation more privately?"

"No, I wouldn't," Klein said. "I'm not putting myself out just to make things easier on you."

"Very well," Fenway said. "It looks like you've been having an affair with Tracey Jenkins."

"Tracey who?"

"You might know her better as *crazygrrl10*?"

Klein was silent, narrowing his eyes.

"Are you denying the affair, Dr. Klein?"

He gritted his teeth and clenched and unclenched his fists. "Yes," he said. "I *am* denying the affair. And after November, you better run for the hills, Miss Stevenson. I'm coming for you."

"Is Emily having an unscheduled play date with Tracey's little girl?" she blurted out.

Klein looked at her sideways. "What the hell are you talking about?"

Fenway kicked herself for tipping her hand—and for not getting anything for it. For his part, Klein seemed truly confused—but he might have just been acting quite well. She couldn't do much about it now, however, so she pressed on with the same line of questioning. "I'm talking about you having an affair with Tracey Jenkins. I'm talking about your affair going public, and you doing some things to try to keep it secret."

Klein narrowed his eyes. "I am *not* having an affair with Tracey Jenkins," Klein said, "and any further unsubstantiated conjecture and you're risking a slander suit." He started to close the door.

"You're *eyeguy805*, right?"

The door stopped closing.

"What do you want?" Klein said softly.

"I want you to tell me where you were Friday night and Saturday morning," Fenway said. "I want you to tell me if we're going to find anything to connect you and the murder of Alice Jenkins—or the attempt on Rachel's life."

"This is a witch hunt," Klein said. "There's no hint of murder, and you know. You're just trying to derail my campaign before it even gets started."

"Hey, Dr. Klein," Fenway said, pulling the folder with the conversation and photos out, "if this *isn't* your photo with these washboard abs, and if you're not *eyeguy805*, and if you didn't arrange a meeting at the coffee place right next to my apartment to go cheat on your wife, then just tell me. Maybe your photo has been used by some Russian hackers who really want Tracey Jenkins to show up at The Coffee Bean all by herself."

Dez piped up. "Don't be silly, Coroner. We can just get their security tapes. The Coffee Bean keeps 'em for two years or so. We got plenty of time to review."

Klein pressed his lips together, then stepped out onto the porch and closed the door. "Fine," he hissed. "Tracey and I met at the Coffee Bean a few weeks ago. But who cares? It's two adults having coffee."

"For one, I think the voters will care if you're having an affair," Fenway said. "And the police will care if the mayor threatened to expose your affair and you killed her because of it."

"I did nothing of the sort, and you know it," Klein sneered. "This is a smear campaign. You know I'm planning to run for coroner and you're such a daddy's girl you're doing his bidding, so *his* candidate will win."

"Oh, Dez, Dr. Klein just called me a daddy's girl," Fenway said, sticking out her bottom lip. "That hurts my feelings."

"Yeah, how about this?" Klein snarled, opening his front door and stepping back inside. "Get off my property. You're trespassing. And I bet you didn't obtain those private messages legally. I'll deny everything, and my lawyer will get those charges dismissed faster than you can run crying to daddy."

He slammed the door in their faces.

They were both quiet for a minute.

"What do you think, Dez?"

"What I think is that you need to tell me where Fletcher's daughters are," Dez said.

Fenway jumped, as if Dez had startled her. "I—uh—"

"Now see here, Fenway, you made some nonsense comment about a playdate with Fletch's daughter."

"That—uh—"

"That was highly suspicious, is what that was," said Dez.

Fenway paused. "I'm not supposed to tell you, Dez. The cops can't know."

Dez narrowed her eyes at Fenway. "Why can't the cops know?"

"Ah, crap," Fenway said. She couldn't see a way around without telling Dez the whole story. They stepped off the porch and moved onto the driveway. "I found a note in the Jenkins' kitchen trash when we were there taking Fletcher in. I made an excuse to go inside, but I wanted to talk to Tracey. And I stepped on the trash can thing to open the lid, and this index card in there. The note said, 'If you're guilty, then she'll live. No cops.'"

"Oh. I see." Dez stopped for a minute. "Did you talk to Tracey?"

"Yes."

"Did she tell you someone kidnapped her daughter?"

"No, but she acted strange. I mean, her husband had just been arrested for murder, but she kept going back and forth, like she had something to tell me but couldn't."

"Did you *ask* her where her daughter was?"

Fenway shook her head. "I guess I didn't want to put her in a worse situation."

Dez tapped her foot. "Does McVie know about this?"

"Yes."

"And he doesn't want to involve anyone else in law enforcement?"

"Right after I told him about the note, the shooting broke out at the hospital, and McVie shot the gunman and got taken off duty."

"That doesn't matter, Fenway. You and he are both mandatory reporters. When a child's life is in danger, you've got to report it."

"I thought that was only for abuse or neglect."

"You seriously don't think kidnapping falls under that?"

Fenway nodded. "But it hasn't been reported to us. All we have is this index card I found in their trash. They might not even be talking about one of the daughters. Maybe they're talking about the mayor, and Fletch didn't think they'd kill her and they did."

Dez put her hands on her hips. "I hope you have your story straight when this whole thing comes out and you're explaining yourself to a judge."

"Also, Dez," Fenway said, lowering her voice and pulling her further down the driveway, "McVie thinks we have a mole in the sheriff's office somewhere. He thinks someone purposely let in Stotsky to kill Dylan Richards in his cell, and we haven't caught him yet. So we don't want this to go to the sheriff's office where someone we don't trust could send that information to the kidnappers."

"Oh, man," Dez said softly. "Okay, I get why you haven't let the cops know. But they have a lot more resources, they've dealt with hostage situations before. I mean, we oughta be able to keep it to a few people we trust."

"Maybe." Fenway thought for a minute. "But we don't want to put a girl's life in danger. Plus, remember, Fletcher and Tracey haven't even reported their daughter missing yet. We don't even know which daughter it is."

"There's one way to find out. We can go talk to Tracey."

"But what if they're watching the house?"

"Talking to the wife after the husband's been arrested for murder is par for the course, Fenway. No one would suspect anything if we showed up."

"Or what if they've bugged the house?"

"Then we have a different problem." Dez thought for a moment. "We might be able to borrow a bug detector. I don't like it much, but I could do it."

"That's great news. Who's got the bug detector?"

"San Miguelito County. The detectives who run vice. Got it with some Homeland Security grant money a couple of years ago."

"Good. I have to go there anyway. I need Kav or Melissa to run the note for prints without entering it into the system."

"You actually *have* the note?"

"Sure I do. I took it out of their trash and put it in my purse."

Dez shook her head. "I'll give you one thing, Fenway, you've got guts."

"What do you mean?"

"I mean, you go into someone's house and take a ransom note out of the trash can."

"I had to, Dez. It was evidence. And I couldn't let Tracey know I took it."

"I know, I'm just saying, you've got guts."

They stood in silence for a moment.

"You do know," Dez said, "how ironic it is that you don't want cops to be involved, but you're okay getting Kav and Melissa involved."

Fenway paused, turning it over in her mind. "They're not technically cops, and neither am I. And since he's on administrative leave, McVie isn't really a cop for the next week or two either."

"You think the kidnappers are going to care about technicalities?"

Fenway was silent.

"Listen," Dez said, "you trust Mark, too, right?"

"Yes," Fenway said.

"Then let's tell him about this. He's better in the field than I am. He can go root some stuff out that doesn't even occur to me."

They started to walk back down the driveway toward Dez's cruiser.

"Do you need to get read in on this officially?" Fenway said. "I really don't want anything to get back to the kidnappers. If there are, in fact, kidnappers."

"Read in on what?" Dez said.

"Read in on this whole—"

Dez shot Fenway a look.

"Oh. Right."

"It's not by the book, but I think we need to keep this hushed up until we know what we're dealing with." She paused. "I might be able to get the names of a couple of private investigators who could work on this. Not sure how we work payment out with them, but we can cross that bridge when we come to it."

"We're way ahead of you, Dez. McVie and I stopped by my father's house last night. He's agreed to foot the bill for a P.I. He says he knows a great one. He's setting up a meeting with us, hopefully for later today, assuming she's not on a job already."

"Wait—your father knows all about this?"

Fenway grimaced. "Well, yes. And I had some reservations about it. But I think my father has changed a lot after what happened with Stotsky. He knows he can't be involved with shady stuff anymore. He knows how lucky he is that Stotsky hasn't turned on him."

"Yet."

"Right, yet. But still."

Dez shook her head as they got to the car. "Who do you think coordinated Rachel's promotion?" she said. "You think Rachel, with her can-do attitude and thirty seconds of experience, just magically ascended to public information officer?"

Fenway blinked.

"Oh mercy me. You *do* think that. You *do* think Rachel got the promotion because she's so fantastic." Dez put her hands on her hips. "Look, Rachel's capable. The county did the right thing to hire her. But your father talked to a couple of the county supervisors, maybe strong-armed the acting HR director a little, and made the promotion happen in exchange for Stotsky's silence."

"How do you know that?"

"Because he offered Rachel a PR position at Ferris Energy right after Stotsky's arraignment."

"Really? She didn't tell me any of that!"

"Well, no, she knows you have a complicated relationship with your father. She told *me*, though, and she already knew enough to figure out your father had something up his sleeve. So she declined. She told him her dream of one day being White House press secretary, and that she wanted to stay in public service. I've gotta give your dad credit for being resourceful. He gave the public information officer the PR job at Ferris Energy instead, and then basically pushed Rachel's name through. Without calling attention to himself. And by the time I realized all the strings your dad pulled, Rachel had already said yes to the job. I didn't have the heart to tell her that Ferris had tricked her."

Fenway opened her mouth to respond and found she couldn't.

"Look, Fenway, I know you're a little bit jaded already, but you're not jaded enough when it comes to your dad. He already knows, so there's nothing we can do but hope he's not involved. I sure hope he's not. And it would be idiotic for him to be involved, because if anything happens to Rachel, your dad's deal with Stotsky goes out the window."

Fenway nodded.

"Okay," Dez said. "Let's go get that ransom note and bring it to San Miguelito. I can't put off seeing Michi face to face much longer anyway."

They opened the doors and got in the cruiser. Dez started the car up and started back to Fenway's apartment.

"Dez, can I ask you something?" Fenway said.

Dez looked over at Fenway and read the question on her face. "I'm surprised it's taken you this long."

"Look, I know it's none of my business, but, you and Dr. Yasuda?"

Dez sighed. "Yes, Fenway. Me and Dr. Yasuda. She's my ex."

"You keep that pretty hush-hush."

"Yeah, I do. I'm not out at work."

"Why not? Mark's out. Even when Walker ran things, it didn't seem to be a big deal."

"Heh. Spoken like a straight person."

Fenway cringed. "Sorry."

Dez sighed. "It's easier for Mark, he doesn't have to be gay *and* black."

"Yeah, okay." Fenway leaned back in the seat. "So when Dr. Yasuda says she's sorry..."

"Michi couldn't—" Dez started, then faltered and looked down. "I know we're not out at work, Fenway. But she didn't want *anyone* to know. She and I couldn't go out as a couple. She made us stay in separate rooms when her parents visited." She paused. "I'd had enough. We both probably said some things we didn't mean. But it broke us."

Fenway turned back onto the freeway. "I'm sorry, Dez."

"Yeah, well. Shit happens." Dez looked over her shoulder and changed lanes and took a deep breath. "I'm just so *angry* with her. I can't even talk to her on the phone without yelling."

Fenway didn't know what to say.

"Listen," Dez continued, "I know it's a two-way street. Long commute for me, long hours for both of us, both of us dealing with dead bodies all the time. Me not being the best, maybe, at telling her how I felt."

"You said you were living together?"

Dez looked out of the corner of her eye at Fenway. "No, we weren't just living together. We were married."

"Married? And you kept it a secret?"

"Yep. Alice Jenkins was the officiant at our wedding," Dez said. "And she made sure both of us got taken seriously in our jobs."

"The mayor held sway in San Miguelito?"

"You better believe it. She's very influential, all up and down the coast. She broke the damn glass ceiling for every woman and every minority who's come after her. And she didn't compromise. And she proved to me that you could have principles and stand up for yourself and still have people love and respect you." Dez cleared her throat. "I miss the hell outta her."

Dez turned off on Broadway and made a right on Estancia Canyon. "And there's the famous Coffee Bean where Barry and Tracey met to start their affair."

Dez left the car running when she pulled into the parking lot of Fenway's apartment complex. Fenway jumped out and took the stairs two at a time up to the second floor. She looked quickly around for signs that Rachel had been there, but there didn't seem to be any.

She unlocked her door and went into her bedroom, where she dug the card in the evidence bag out from the bottom of her lower nightstand drawer. She looked again for any signs of Rachel. If she were just wearing her hospital gown, Rachel probably didn't have the key that Fenway had given her. But Rachel might be resourceful enough to get in anyway. She looked wistfully around the room, but nothing had changed since she had left.

She locked up and got back in the Impala. "Okay," Fenway said. "Next stop, San Miguelito."

CHAPTER THIRTEEN

They stopped at the Coffee Bean on the way out of town, deciding to put pictures of both Klein and Tracey in front of the baristas. Neither one of them remembered those faces, but one of the baristas had only been working there for a couple of months, and the other one didn't work weekday mornings during the school year. Fenway and Dez looked at each other and shrugged, then ordered coffee and got on the road to San Miguelito.

Fenway called Kav ahead of time; Kav had come into work a little on the late side, having worked into the night all weekend, and Melissa, who had worked even more hours than Kav over the weekend, wasn't coming in till noon.

"Kav, I need a big favor," Fenway said. "And it's got to be kind of hush-hush."

"Hush-hush how?" Kav said. "Like, I can't tell Dr. Yasuda about it?"

"Exactly."

"What do you need?"

"I have a piece of evidence from a possible crime scene. But it's sensitive. I need to know what I have before I involve the police in any kind of official capacity."

"Does this have to do with the mayor's death?"

"Maybe. And maybe the attempts on Rachel's life. And maybe with some other stuff. But I won't know until I see for sure what this evidence says. If it even says anything at all."

There was silence on the other end of the line.

"Kav? You still there?"

"I'm still here, Fenway. I'm thinking."

"The attempts on Rachel's life, Kav. It's important."

He sighed. "Come see me when you get here. Don't let Yasuda see you come down. If she catches me doing anything off-book, I'm taking you down with me."

"Deal."

"Where are you now?"

"We just passed the turnoff for the highway to Fresno."

"Okay, you're about twenty minutes out. I should be in the lab by the time you get there."

Fenway hung up. Dez had a determined look on her face and Fenway didn't want to disturb her train of thought. She looked out the window at the trees going by.

Finally, Fenway said, "Kav is okay with this, but he said not to have Dr. Yasuda involved."

"Yeah," Dez said, "Michi is kind of a by-the-book kind of M.E. Even with her morbid sense of humor and everything."

"So I guess you might need to distract her."

"We've gotta get the results of all the tests from the hospital shooting," Dez said. "I'm hopeful that they were able to finish yesterday."

"Kav and Melissa were both there pretty late," Fenway said. "They put the gun into the acid bath so they can raise the letters on the serial number. But that usually takes longer than twelve hours, give or take."

"But they've run fingerprints on our mystery shooter?"

"I didn't ask. Sorry. I got into asking Kav about doing a fingerprint analysis of the note."

"Okay," Dez said, steeling herself. "I think I can give you about fifteen minutes when you and Kav can do whatever you need to. After that, I think Michi will insist on coming to the lab to go over the details with you. And if I have to delay her any longer, I'm going to have to use some tool in my emotional arsenal that I'd rather keep to myself for now."

Fenway nodded. "I'm sorry. And thank you. I know this is a lot."

"I'm not doing it for you, rookie. I'm doing it for Mayor Jenkins," Dez sighed. "And because it's time."

Fenway looked at the trees outside the window. Fenway wondered if this was the right thing to do. Though not technically a police officer, she knew analyzing it outside of the rules of police procedure was tricky, if not outright dangerous. The longer it stayed out of the official evidence from the case, the less value it might have at trial.

Of course, turning it in would raise a lot of the same questions. She had found the note in the trash, without a search warrant. And involving the police might endanger the little girl's life.

She hadn't been confident in the right thing to do when she picked up that paper from out of the trash. Now she felt even less sure of herself.

And Rachel was still missing.

"Dez," she said, "I'm worried about Rachel. I thought she might come to my house. I know the police are looking for her, but it just doesn't seem like they're doing enough. I heard she hasn't contacted her sister. You haven't heard from her, have you?"

"No," Dez said. "I'm worried about her too."

"You don't think she's in danger, do you?"

Dez frowned. "I don't know; aren't you a nurse? I mean, she was out of the woods—they were transferring her out of the ICU—but she needs to be in the hospital, doesn't she?"

"She needs to rest," Fenway said. "I think she's past the worst of it, medically speaking. I mean, from everything I know about buprenodone, it just has to work itself out of your system. But I didn't mean if she was *medically* in danger. I meant if the people who want her killed will still look for her."

"Your guess is as good as mine. You've seen all the evidence that I've seen, too."

"I really wish she'd just contact us," Fenway said. "If we find out what she talked about with Alice and Fletcher, it might blow the whole thing open. It might mean we catch the people who are trying to kill her."

"You're absolutely right," Dez said.

They were silent the rest of the way to the M.E.'s office in San Miguelito.

———————————

They arrived at the M.E.'s office just after nine-thirty. Fenway took the hallway to the left and went into the lab as Dez took the staircase down into the basement to the morgue. Fenway looked back at Dez; Dez took a deep breath just as she opened the door to the stairs.

When she entered the lab, she saw Melissa at her desk, working on some paperwork. Fenway nodded to her and Melissa smiled back. Fenway saw Kav across the room, rooting through a drawer.

"Hey," she said. "Thanks for doing this for me. I really appreciate it."

"Let's just hope I can get the fingerprint analysis done on this without raising too many flags," Kav said quietly. "I'm not too keen on being the new guy here and flouting the rules."

"You said you'd blame it on me."

"You know pointing fingers doesn't fly with Dr. Yasuda," Kav said. "Okay—what else do you have for me?"

Fenway gave Kav the evidence bag with the note inside it.

"A ransom note?" Kav said, incredulous.

"I told you it was important."

"And it says 'No cops.' That's why you want this all hush-hush." Fenway nodded.

Kav took a closer look at the note. "Block lettering. Not a lot of help in a handwriting analysis."

"No," Fenway said. "I took a course in my forensics program last year, but I don't see anything I can go on here."

Kav nodded. "A fairly thick nib, I see," he said. "It looks like high-quality ink, too. We might be able to get something off the chemicals—maybe if it's an unusual ink, we can get a clue where the pen might have been purchased."

He picked up a pair of tweezers and pulled it out of the bag, then placed it on the fingerprint tray and dusted it with powder.

"Okay," he said. "There are a bunch of fingerprints on this. Partials and full prints. If these prints are in the system, we'll know soon enough."

"You can enter these into the system without Dr. Yasuda finding out?" Fenway asked.

"I can try," Kav said. "There won't be a ping on her desktop saying that I've ordered a fingerprint analysis. And I'll process this with the stuff from the house that we got after Fletcher's arrest. If she looks closely, she'll see it, but I might be able to get away with it."

"If it comes back as a hit," Fenway said, "there might not be any need to hide it from her."

"And we all live happily ever after," Kav chuckled. "Oh—listen, the sign-in book from Rachel's office?"

"Oh, right. The sheriff had that couriered over."

"So—lots of fingerprints, as you'd expect. Rachel's mostly, but also Alice Jenkins, Fletcher Jenkins, a couple of hits from reporters, the rep from the newswire company, yours, and then a few unknowns."

"Mostly what you'd expect."

"Right. But there are two sets of prints here that are quite unusual."

"Two sets?"

"Right. One belongs to a captain in the Marines, name of Elena Valenzuela."

Fenway thought for a minute. "Rachel's admin was a former Marine. Maybe Ms. Valenzuela is a friend from the old days, and she came in to visit Natalie. Maybe they went to lunch."

"I'd agree to that as a reasonable explanation, but Ms. Valenzuela's name isn't in the guest book. But her fingerprints are all over the book—on a lot of the pages, on the pen, and all over the cover."

"Maybe Rachel had already gone to lunch and Natalie showed her friend around, and she picked up the book. Maybe she hoped to find a celebrity signature."

"I suppose," Kav said skeptically. "Okay, what did you say the admin's name is?"

"Natalie Andrada."

"And you said a former Marine?"

"Rank of Corporal, if I remember right. She's missing her legs—I assume from a war injury."

Kav looked through the list of names. "She doesn't show up."

"Maybe she's one of the unknowns."

"Marines all get fingerprinted. She should be in the system."

"Maybe she didn't ever touch the book. Maybe Rachel managed it."

"I don't know," Kav said. "Without seeing the rest of what's in that office, I can't tell for sure."

"Was that the second red flag?"

"No," Kav said. "One of the sets of fingerprints came back classified."

"Classified?"

"Yes—the system recognized it, but we don't have the security clearance to see who it is."

Fenway paused. "That's pretty strange. Maybe *that's* Natalie."

"I suppose. Maybe she got assigned to some secret military mission and they classified her fingerprints."

"So nothing definitive—two unusual sets that are there, one set that's unusual because it *isn't* there."

"Unless Natalie Andrada is the second unusual set."

Fenway exhaled and stretched her hands over her head. "All right, Kav," she said. "Can you send those results over to Piper Patten in the sheriff's office? Maybe she can dig something up on those."

"Is she the hotshot cybercrime whiz kid I've been hearing about?"

"Yeah. Piper Patten. She is crazy good with cybersecurity,"

"Sure."

Fenway leaned forward. "I heard that there are a bunch of results from the hospital that we need to go over. Especially regarding the dead gunman, and his weapon. And I'm wondering if you found any evidence in the car besides the ID and the wallet, stuff like that."

Kav nodded and went to his desk to get a folder. Fenway followed him. "We got a hit on the fingerprints of our deceased," he said, opening the folder. "And a pretty good-sized criminal record, but mostly small-time stuff. First of all—his real name is Alan Patrick Scorrelli. He's got a list of about ten known aliases, and the two IDs you found are apparently his real ID and one of his aliases." Kav flipped the page. "He's mostly into embezzlement and fraud. He's gotten involved in some insurance schemes. Arrested about eight times, from what I see here. Only convicted twice, both misdemeanors. The first time he pled down from insurance fraud to a lesser charge of filing a false report."

"What about the second time?"

"Originally charged with fraud, conspiracy to commit fraud, and making false identification papers," Kav said. "Only the false papers stuck, also charged as a misdemeanor. The judge in the case sentenced him to 60 days and served 30 of them before his release."

"What about a history of violence? Anything with weapons, or assault, or maybe domestic disputes?"

Kav shook his head. "Nothing like that. His name doesn't even turn up on any of the gun registries. Mr. Scorrelli may be a thief and a con artist, but nothing in the file suggests that he'd shoot up an ICU ward."

Fenway nodded.

"Sorry," Kav said, "that's my personal opinion. I'm not a detective or anything. But I sure don't see it."

"So what's the story with the gun?" Fenway said.

"The serial number had been filed off, surprise, surprise," Kav replied. "I heard you guys had a gun for another case before I started here. An old CHP gun where the numbers had been filed off, right?"

"Right. My first week here," Fenway said.

"If I remember the story right, those numbers got raised pretty quickly because the number wasn't filed off very well. Anyway, these numbers look like they were filed off by someone who really knew what they were doing—not the amateur job from that other case. It's pretty professional."

"Hmm." Fenway scratched her temple. "That doesn't follow, since this guy doesn't have a history of violence. Whatever he was doing there, it looks like he might have been in over his head. But getting the serial number professionally obfuscated?"

"Yeah, the guy is pretty far from being a professional hitman, but Mr. Scorrelli might have gone to a true professional to get his hands on that gun."

"All right, Kav, what do you have from the rental car?"

"First of all, Mr. Scorrelli didn't pay for the car. It was paid for by a company called SRB Investment Holdings. They have a mailbox in one of those shopping centers in suburban New Jersey. I did a little digging last night, and it looks like it belongs to a shell corporation in the Cayman Islands. Not sure how far down the rabbit hole you want to go, but when I think of Cayman Islands shell companies, I think of dead ends when it comes to forensic accounting."

"Did you say SRB?"

Kav looked at his notes. "Yes, SRB Investment Holdings."

"I saw that somewhere," Fenway said, closing her eyes. "That's right—Rachel had a Post-It on her monitor that said *Jenkins—SRB*." She tapped her chin. "I don't suppose they list any contact information."

"Not in their public filings. Maybe that Piper girl could find something?"

"Yeah. I can call her and see what she can dig up."

"Okay. All the fingerprints from the car came back as Allen's." Kav paused. "We won't mention some fingerprints under the driver's door handle."

Fenway looked down and blushed.

"Now when it comes to the tox screen—well, see for yourself," Kav continued. "We tested for a couple of different opioids and they came back negative. But taking a look at his lungs and heart, he's got all the symptoms of an opioid addict."

"Could those symptoms be from buprenodone?" said Fenway.

"No, this is definitely different than buprenodone effects."

"Maybe it's another type of drug? Maybe it's something that's being dealt at the Cactus Lake Motel and Alice Jenkins got in the middle of it."

"Melissa suggested there might be a new designer drug on the market," Kav said. "I've put a call into my contacts in L.A. If there's a new designer drug on the streets, they'll know about it."

He raised his head. "Hey, Melissa, can you come over here for a second?"

Melissa walked over.

"You had a couple of ideas on the tox screen that didn't show any known opiates."

"Yeah," Melissa said. "I thought it might be something new. Some sort of designer drug that just came out, maybe. I've heard there's a new pill. Some new opioid is my guess."

Fenway nodded. "I've heard something new is coming out too. I just talked with one of Parker's friends."

"One of whose friends?" Melissa asked.

"Dylan Richards' brother, Parker."

"Oh," Melissa said quietly, a shadow falling over her face.

"This friend of his is a dealer—pills, I think, mostly Oxy and Norco from what I hear. And he said that there are rumors that there's a new drug coming up that's going to put the Oxy and Norco dealers out of business. Or make them work with a new distributor."

"Hmm," Melissa said. "That kind of reminds me when *El Magnate* used to run the pill trade on the West Coast."

"*El Magnate*?"

"Yeah," Melissa said. "You probably remember a few years back—that big Silicon Valley CEO was arrested for something like a hundred counts of drug dealing and murder for hire."

Fenway nodded. "Yeah, I remember that—some white guy from Harvard, not a Colombian drug lord or anything, though, right?"

Melissa laughed. "I think he had his people call him *El Magnate* for street cred."

"The Magnet?" Kav asked.

"Literally translates to 'The Mogul,'" Melissa replied. "Anyway, *El Magnate* had control of most of the Oxy and Norco distribution in California. I wonder if whoever controls the supply of this new drug is trying to become *El Magnate Nuevo*."

Fenway tapped her temple. "I wish I could remember the name of the drug."

"You know the name of the drug?"

"I heard the street name. It's something with a color, like Blue Water or Black Friday."

"Yellow Submarine?" Kav suggested.

"Red Skies!" Fenway said. "That's it. Red Skies."

"Ah," Melissa said, "not The Beatles, The Fixx."

"When are you going to hear back from the lab in L.A.?"

"I hope they'll be running the tests this week."

This week?

"It's the biggest city in North America, Fenway," Kav said. "We have to get in line. They're sometimes backed up for weeks. We actually got lucky. Donny knows a guy down there."

Fenway sighed. *Donny knows a guy.* "Okay. We got the aliases from the gunman?"

"Yes, we sent them over to Mark and you a few minutes before you got here. Along with his mug shots and driver's license photos. In situations like this, we usually take a picture of his face, but, well, there's not much of it left. McVie shot him right under the eye and it pretty much destroyed his face."

"Lovely."

"Yeah. Anyway, Mark said he'd be running reports on all the aliases. He thought he might be able to piece together a work history."

"Thanks, Kav. Anything else?"

"Dr. Yasuda has Mr. Scorrelli opened up in the suite downstairs," Kav said. "We'll let you know if she finds anything. Kidney or liver function that's been compromised, maybe. That might narrow down the drug. That will take two or three days, though."

"Good to know. Thanks."

"And I'll let you know about the fingerprints as soon as I can. Hopefully some time this afternoon."

"Anything else on your side?"

Fenway paused. "Just want your reaction on this, Kav. So, let's say, hypothetically speaking, you want Rachel dead. You've created some complex fake suicide thing, but Rachel doesn't die. So you hire someone to shoot her in the hospital, but the guy you send is a drug addict who misses twice and doesn't look like he's ever held a gun before."

"This is hypothetical?"

Fenway plowed ahead. "There's no disputing that he couldn't hit a stationary target from ten feet. Does that make any sense to you?"

"Maybe the criminal is resourceful and smart, but maybe the operation is stretched a little thin," Kav said. "When *he's* the one trying to push the plan, almost everything goes well. But when he needs to hire someone, he has to make do with the people he has working for him."

Fenway nodded thoughtfully. "Or, if he's trying to take over as *El Magnate*, maybe he knows a lot of stuff about how to make the pills but nothing about how to do the wet work."

Kav grimaced at the term. "Hey, and you know something weird?"

"What?"

"In most of the shooting situations like this, the gunmen are wearing athletic shoes. Like running shoes. So they can get away quickly, I guess, or that they feel comfortable in. But not Scorrelli. He had on loafers. Loafers with tassels on them."

"Like he went on a business trip and only brought one pair of shoes."

"Yes, exactly," Kav said. "Very impractical for a shootout." He paused for a moment. "But didn't Fletcher confess? Isn't he the one who tried to kill Rachel?"

"He confessed," Fenway said. "To which crime, I'm not exactly sure. So I guess we need to look into connections between Scorrelli and Fletcher."

"Yep, that's certainly where I would start."

"All right, Kav. Have a good rest of your day."

Fenway walked out of the lab and backtracked through the waiting room. She opened the doors into the parking lot and stepped out into the bright sunshine. San Miguelito, forty miles inland and on the other side of the coastal hills, was often much warmer than Estancia. In the summer, San Miguelito would get into the nineties even when Estancia struggled to break seventy.

She took her phone out of her purse and dialed.

"IT and Cyber, this is Piper."

"Hey, Piper, it's Fenway."

"Oh, Fenway! Good. Celeste gave me a few names to work on earlier. Aliases of the gunman from yesterday, right?"

"Right."

"Okay. I'm running them this morning."

"I've got another couple of things for you to look into," Fenway said.

"Okay, hang on, let me take some notes." Fenway could hear a few clicks on Piper's keyboard. "All right, I'm ready."

"See if you can find any names or contacts—or anything at all, really—on a company called SRB Investment Holdings."

"S as in Sam?"

"Yes. R as in Robert, B as in, uh, Bob."

"Sounds like an overseas thing."

"Cayman Islands, with a mailbox in New Jersey."

"Okay," Piper said. "This is related to Rachel or the mayor?"

"Maybe both," Fenway said. "Rachel had it on a Post-It along with Jenkins' name, stuck to her monitor. Now we find out that SRB paid for the dead gunman's rental car too."

"Gotcha. Which do you want first?"

Fenway paused. "I guess SRB. It might help us find whoever's trying to kill Rachel."

"The aliases of the dead guy won't?"

"I don't know, Piper. I have a feeling about SRB, but my gut's been wrong before."

"Not that often."

"And mostly about the men I date," Fenway said. "Speaking of which, how are you and Migs doing?"

"Good," Piper said. "A lot better once he finally got up the nerve to ask me out."

"How is it being taller than him?"

"Oh. I guess I don't really notice. Honestly, Fenway, I've never dated a man taller than me. I guess I like short guys." She paused. "You usually date guys taller than you?"

Fenway shrugged. "Mostly. Not always. I've dated shorter guys who say they're okay with it, but secretly they're pissed off that I'm taller than they are." She thought of Akeel and the heat between them. "But not always. Sometimes it's, uh, pretty good."

"Was Seattle 'pretty good'?" Piper said. Fenway could hear the smirk in her voice.

"It had the potential to be pretty good," Fenway said, thinking that one day she'd laugh about it. "But I had to fly back down as soon as I got there. And I miss my car."

"Sure."

Piper waited, probably hoping to hear about Akeel. Fenway didn't feel like talking about it.

"Okay, I'll let you know what I find. I'll do the SRB thing first. Anything else?"

Fenway paused. "Actually, yes. I have to figure out who else could have a motive. I mean, I know Fletcher Jenkins confessed, but with the other attempt on Rachel's life, it just doesn't feel right." Fenway winced at how weak that sounded, but didn't want to tell anyone else about the possible kidnapping.

"I guess."

Fenway soldiered on. "So I thought about political enemies of Alice Jenkins, and I thought of Barry Klein."

"Dr. Klein? I suppose so. He hates everyone."

"Right. So I did a web search for him and Alice Jenkins, then Rachel, then Fletch, and I then did a search for Klein and Fletcher Jenkins' wife, and I came across a whole conversation on Hike-UpMeetUp.com." She paused for dramatic effect. "They had an affair."

"An affair?"

"Yeah, apparently they private-messaged each other. Got a little steamy."

"How did you get access to that conversation?"

"It just came up in the web search," said Fenway. "Maybe it was a security hiccup. Maybe they were updating their servers and forgot to close a firewall port or something."

"All that stuff should be encrypted," said Piper.

"Maybe we'll tell their security team *after* you do a more thorough search for whatever you can on Barry Klein and Tracey Jenkins."

"Jenkins, like Mayor Jenkins?"

"Yes."

"Tracey with a Y or an I?"

"With an E-Y at the end," Fenway said.

"Got it. Consider their love lives breached."

"Thanks, Piper."

"Oh—we've also got traces on all Rachel's credit cards and ATM cards, and we've got officers at her apartment and her sister's place too."

"Any luck yet?"

"No," Piper said. "We don't have her on camera leaving the hospital, but the parking lot camera picked something up that could be Rachel. Just moving toward Vincente Boulevard, though. Nothing helpful."

"You're not sure it's her?"

"The video is too grainy at that distance. Too hard to see."

"All right," Fenway said, disappointed.

"See you later, Fenway."

Fenway hung up and turned back toward the entrance. The door opened and Dez came out. She wore sunglasses and had her keys in her hand.

"I hope your fingerprint shit was worth it," she spat. "You're going to drive back, and you're not going to ask me about anything that bitch said to me in there. If you hurt my Impala I will *kill* you."

Dez held out the keys. Fenway took them.

CHAPTER FOURTEEN

———— ◆ ————

Dez, silent behind her sunglasses all the way back to Estancia, had set her mouth in a thin line of blue-hot anger. Fenway didn't speak until they were almost at the Broadway exit. "Should we go see Tracey down in Vista Del Rincón?"

Dez shrugged.

"Okay," Fenway said. "I think we better go see her, so that's where I'm going."

Dez turned and looked out the window.

"Um," Fenway said, "did you happen to go by vice and see if they had a bug detector?"

Dez sighed. "Shit."

Fenway cleared her throat. "That's okay. I'll figure something else out."

They got to the little green house by eleven. The house looked closed up, though both cars were in the driveway. Fenway thought a minute, then asked Dez for her notebook and a pen. Dez pulled her purse up to the seat and let Fenway go through it until she found them.

Fenway opened the door. "You coming?" she said to Dez.

Dez shook her head.

Fenway walked up and rang the doorbell. She had to ring it three times before Tracey answered.

Tracey looked awful, her face red and puffy, dressed in a stained t-shirt and pajama bottoms. "What do you want?"

"Hi, Tracey," Fenway said. She took out the notebook and wrote "I think your house is bugged" and showed it to her.

"I thought maybe I could ask you a few questions about Fletcher and his whereabouts on Friday night," she said. "But it's such a beautiful day, I thought maybe we could go for a walk. I'll buy your kids an ice cream down at the store."

Tracey gaped at Fenway.

"Sure," she said. "But, uh, Olivia is at her aunt's house today. This whole week, actually. But I've got Isla here, and I bet she'd love some ice cream. You'll have to wait a minute, I need to get the stroller."

"No problem," Fenway said. "I'll wait here on the porch."

The full shade in their front yard and the ocean breeze kept everything cool—a good twenty-five degrees cooler in Vista Del Rincón than it had been in San Miguelito. Fenway pulled out her phone and texted McVie.

Olivia is missing

Tracey came out with Isla in the stroller. Isla had a big mop of curly black hair, and the russet color of her skin almost matched Fenway's. She looked up at Fenway with big, dark eyes, pointed. Fenway had rarely thought about children before, but Isla looked like a baby Fenway might have had. She wondered if Olivia looked the same way.

Isla said a string of unintelligible syllables.

"Yes, she is a nice lady," said Tracey.

They walked past Dez in the Impala and down the narrow streets toward the general store in the little town.

"When did they take Olivia?" Fenway said in a low voice to Tracey.

Tracey looked at Fenway. "I told you, Olivia is at my mom's house. She's fine."

Fenway kept walking. "You know you said she was at her aunt's house earlier."

Tracey looked down at the handles on the stroller, mouth clamped shut.

"I swear I'll keep this away from the police as long as I can."

"Aren't *you* the police?"

Fenway shrugged. "I just want you to get your daughter back."

Tracey rubbed her temples. "Fletch wasn't supposed to tell you."

"He didn't. I saw the note in the trash the last time I came over. When I threw my gum away."

Tracey hesitated, worry and shame and fear in a tangled mess of emotions on her face. Then she seemed to give up, and began to talk, her voice shaky.

"There were two men that came into the house the night you and the sheriff came to talk with us the first time," Tracey said, a tear running down her cheek.

"Before or after we were there?"

"After." Tracey fought to keep control of her emotions. "We didn't know what was going on. They were in a black van. One of those cargo vans, not like a minivan. They just broke through the door. We were all asleep—Olivia in her bed, and Isla in her crib. Fletch and I both ran out of our bedroom when we heard Olivia screaming. The skinny one had her and ran down the hall. They were back out the door and out of the driveway before we even knew what happened. We got a call about two minutes later, saying if we called the cops, they'd kill her." Tracey stifled a sob. "I don't know what I'm going to do."

"I think I can help."

"You're not getting the cops involved," Tracey said flatly. "If Fletch confesses and goes to jail, they'll let her live. They'll bring her back. Once they arraign him and he pleads guilty, right? Then they'll bring her back?"

"I don't know," Fenway said. "I've never been in a situation like this before. We're not getting the cops involved until we know for sure Olivia will be safe. You know who my father is, don't you?"

Tracey nodded. "He owns Ferris Energy."

"Right. He's pretty much the most powerful man in the county. He's hiring a private investigator to find out where they're holding her. No cops, like the note said. I'm supposed to be meeting him this afternoon."

They got to the shop and Fenway bought a chocolate ice cream in a cup for Isla. She made sure to ask if Tracey was sure that Fletcher was in bed all night on Friday. Tracey confirmed that she was positive.

They sat outside in the sunshine. The patio had a great view of the ocean, and they watched a few surfers and body boarders, little specks on the water, go in and out.

"What did the men look like?" Fenway asked.

"The two of them had ski masks on." Tracey said. "But I could see a little bit of their necks and eyes. The white, skinny one was about medium height. The other one had muscles, like he worked out a lot. He had darker skin. Not white. Asian maybe, or Latino. I guess it could have been Middle Eastern. Dressed all in black. The muscular one wore a black track suit. Adidas, I remember that. And I remember the skinny white one had on black loafers with tassels, which was kind of weird."

Fenway took her phone out and went to her email. She pulled up a photo of Alan Patrick Scorrelli and showed it to Tracey.

"Did you hear about the shooting at St. Vincent's yesterday?"

"No," Tracey said. "I haven't been paying attention to a whole lot of stuff."

"This guy came into the ICU and shot a nurse and a security guard. He tried to kill the woman we asked about the other day, Rachel Richards. He had on black loafers with tassels too. Kind of an odd choice for a shooter."

"I don't know if that's the same guy. I didn't see his face. He had a ski mask on." She paused. "Get me a photo of the shoes and I can tell you. He had a big scuff mark on the top of the left one, just above the tassels. I don't know why I noticed that. I'd recognize the stitching pattern too. And the shoes had a raised edge around the toe."

"Right," Fenway said, texting a message to Kav. "And the one in the track suit—what kind of shoes did he have on?"

"I didn't see. It happened really fast."

"Okay." Fenway paused.

Tracey spooned another bite of ice cream into Isla's waiting mouth.

Fenway cleared her throat. "So, Tracey, I've been asking myself who has the motive for this. To kill your mother-in-law. To kill Rachel. To get Fletch out of the way."

"I don't know," Tracey said. "Fletch did say he had to take his mother to City Hall last week."

"Yeah, I found out that he spent all afternoon with Rachel and his mother. Four hours. Do you have any idea what the topic of the conversation might have been?"

Tracey shook his head. "He said some kind of work stuff."

"Where does he work?"

"Aperture Consulting," she said. "He's an auditor there. He reviews mergers and acquisitions, annual 10-Ks, that kind of thing."

"You think it had to do with one of his audits? That he'd take his mother into an appointment with the county public information officer?"

"I don't know," Tracey said. Her eyes were starting to lose focus.

"See, one thing that makes sense to me is that they could be talking about one of the upcoming candidates for coroner." Fenway watched Tracey's face closely. "Maybe about something that could derail a campaign before it even started. Somebody who cheated on his wife, maybe."

Tracey looked down.

"So what do you think, Tracey? Does that make sense to you too?"

Isla reached for the spoon and started to fuss. Tracey put another bite of ice cream in her mouth.

"We found evidence of your affair with Barry Klein," Fenway said softly. "Maybe Barry didn't like that Fletcher and Mayor Jenkins found out about the affair. Maybe he tried to hush it up."

"No," Tracey whispered. Tears were welling in her eyes and starting to fall down her cheeks.

"Are you still seeing Barry? Or did you break it off with him? Maybe he didn't like that you broke it off. Maybe you broke it off and confessed everything to your husband."

"No," Tracey repeated, wiping her cheeks with the back of her hand. "No, Barry and I weren't having an affair. I don't know how you found out, but he and I *did* make plans to meet up. I thought it might get, um, physical." She shook her head, like she could prevent herself from seeing the past. "Fletch has been really distracted lately. I started playing around online. I found Barry there and we flirted." Tracey laughed, but it caught in her throat. "Honestly, I liked getting noticed. Getting some attention."

"I saw your private messages."

"Huh." Tracey looked at the ground. "I guess they're not so private."

"And you met him at the Coffee Bean. The one over on Estancia Canyon."

Tracey didn't say anything.

"You going to deny that you met him there? I'm sure the Coffee Bean has security footage."

"No, I'm not going to deny it," Tracey said softly. "But when I saw him—when I saw a real live person, and not just a guy showing off his abs on the computer—I don't know, I just couldn't go through with it." Tracey picked at the pinkie fingernail on her left hand. "I had gotten dressed up, too, I mean, not fancy, but in a low-cut top. His eyes went right to my boobs. I mean, of course they did. But I just couldn't do it. We made small talk for a little while and he kept trying to turn the conversation into something dirty."

Fenway looked at Tracey's face, but Tracey avoided eye contact.

"I just couldn't do it," she repeated.

"How did Barry react?"

Tracey shrugged. "Not well. He called me a prick-tease. He had trouble keeping his voice down. I left pretty quickly. He followed me out and apologized, but by then I realized what a bad decision that had been."

Fenway nodded. "Did he think you'd tell anyone? Maybe wreck his political career?"

"I don't know," Tracey snapped. "I don't really care what he thinks I'd do."

"Well," Fenway said carefully, "if he thought you might tell your husband and your mother-in-law, he might be afraid of losing the election in November, and getting kicked off the board of supervisors."

Tracey looked up at Fenway.

"And," Fenway continued, "he might be desperate enough to try to get rid of anyone who might have been able to do anything."

"You think he's behind Olivia's kidnapping?"

"I don't know," Fenway said. "I can't think of anyone else at this point. Can you?"

Tracey spooned another bite of ice cream into Isla's mouth.

Fenway continued to press. "But if Fletch found out, and if the mayor found out, it could end his political career. Might even hurt his optometry business. People might not want a cheating husband to be two inches from their face, looking them in the eyes with a flashlight."

"I guess. I don't know. A political candidate cheating on his wife doesn't mean what it used to."

Fenway paused. "That's true enough. Especially in a town like Estancia."

Tracey paused. "And he didn't even cheat. I didn't go through with it."

Fenway's phone dinged. She looked at it; Kav had sent a photo of the dead shooter's left loafer. It had a big scuff mark on the top, just above the tassels, as Tracey had said. She held it up to Tracey. "Is this the loafer the kidnapper had on?"

Tracey looked at it. "Yes. That's the exact one. There's the scuff. And that's the raised edge I told you about."

Fenway nodded and put her phone back in her purse.

"But you don't think Klein had any idea that Fletch knew about the two of you meeting?"

"Fletch didn't know. Doesn't know. Or if he does, he's hiding it really well."

"Okay," Fenway said. "Do you know Barry's whereabouts on Friday night and Saturday morning?"

"No," Tracey said. "I told you, Fletch and I never left the house. I don't keep track of Barry ever. He and I only met that one time."

"Okay."

Tracey gave the last spoonful to Isla. She gurgled happily, ice cream all over her mouth. Tracey took a couple of napkins and cleaned her face as Isla's gurgles became mild protests.

"When will you know anything about where Olivia is?" Tracey whispered, trying not to cry.

"I don't know yet," Fenway replied. "We're meeting the private investigator soon. But we haven't started yet."

"Barry's got a daughter about Olivia's age, doesn't he?"

"Yes," she said. "Oh no—you don't think—"

"I don't think anything yet, Tracey. I don't think your husband killed his mom, or tried to kill Rachel. I'm just trying to think of who'd have a motive to do all of that plus kidnap your daughter."

"I mean, I don't know Barry that well. But Barry's wiry, not muscular—neither of the kidnappers looked like Barry at all."

Fenway opened her mouth to mention different scenarios, especially the one where Barry hired people to do his dirty work, but realized that wouldn't be helpful to the mother going out of her mind with worry. "If you think of anything else, please let me know. But tell it to me when you're out of the house."

"So you're keeping the cops out of it."

"I'm doing my best."

"Okay." Tracey stood up, threw away the napkins, and pulled the stroller away from the patio table. "I'm kind of going crazy, Fenway. Please get Olivia back."

"I'll do everything I can," Fenway said.

———◆◆———

Dez had taken her sunglasses off and had moved behind the wheel when Fenway and Tracey got back. Tracey had calmed down, although she still looked worn out and anxious.

"I'm going to head out," Fenway said. "I appreciate your time today."

"Say thank you for the ice cream, Isla," Tracey said.

"Ankee keem," said Isla.

"You're welcome," Fenway cooed to her.

Fenway got in the passenger side. "Okay, Dez. Anything you want to ask her before we go?"

"Nope," Dez said. "Thanks for taking that on. And thanks for driving."

"Don't mention it."

Dez started up the car and they were driving through Vista Del Rincón's narrow streets.

"It's Olivia, their five-year-old," Fenway said. "She's the one who's missing."

Dez straightened up in her seat. "Okay, well, now that we know for sure, I'm definitely getting Mark involved in this," she said. "Did she give you any idea about what the kidnappers want or who they are?"

Fenway shook her head. "Not much. Fletch was so distracted at work that Tracey considered having a fling with Barry Klein. I guess she decided not to."

"How did Barry take that?"

"Not well," Fenway said. "But you saw him at his house. I think he's a horrible husband, but I don't think he'd kidnap a little girl. I don't think he would go that low."

"Are there any other possibilities?"

"Yeah," Fenway said. "The mayor and Fletch met with Rachel last week. Rachel's assistant said the meeting didn't last long, but all three of those people are involved in this—they killed the mayor, they tried to kill Rachel, and they're trying to frame Fletch for everything."

"We just don't know who 'they' are."

"Right."

They had just pulled onto the highway back to Estancia when Fenway's phone rang. She looked at the screen and picked up.

"Hi, Dad."

"Okay," Nathaniel Ferris said, "we're going to meet the P.I. tonight. Grafton & Gale's, six o'clock. He's driving up from L.A. right now. He'll get settled in at his hotel and come meet us."

"Six o'clock, Grafton and Gale's," Fenway repeated. "Got it."

"Can you make sure Craig comes too?"

"Um, I can call him," Fenway said. "But I haven't seen him all day." She missed the camaraderie she had with McVie. She missed it with Dez too; she had been just getting out of her bad mood from the mayor's death, and talking to Dr. Yasuda had sunk her lower than Fenway had ever seen her. Fenway hoped Dez would come out of it soon.

"Okay," Ferris said. "Let me know if you can't get in touch with him." He hung up.

Fenway sighed and started to text McVie about going to Grafton & Gale's to meet the private investigator, but then thought better of it and called him instead.

"McVie."

"Hi, Craig. It's Fenway." She stopped at the sound of her own voice—she hardly ever called him *Craig*—although she kept catching herself slipping up recently. Maybe his administrative leave made Fenway think of him without his sheriff title. Or, she thought, maybe her subconscious was somehow trying to get closer to him. She made a mental note to stay professional and go back to calling him *McVie*.

"Hey, great, Fenway. Listen, I didn't get a chance to thank you at dinner, but I really appreciate you talking your father into hiring that P.I. without me needing to call in my favor."

"Right," Fenway said. "To be honest, I kind of forgot he owed you the favor. It's just something he should have done because it's the right thing to do."

"True," McVie said, "But I still appreciate it. Anyway, I need to talk to you about what our next steps are."

"Good. You got my text earlier?"

"Yeah. You're sure it's Olivia?"

"Tracey told me all about the, uh, incident. So I've got some stuff to discuss with you too. We can meet tonight."

"Okay, I've got a concert to go to with Amy, but I can meet late. Maybe ten-thirty or eleven, if that's not too late for you."

"Actually, the guy my father hired is going to meet us tonight at six o'clock at Grafton & Gale's. You might want to be at that."

McVie exhaled. "Okay. I know this is more important."

"I'm sorry, Craig." She said his first name before she could stop it. She plowed on. "I know you're trying to get some alone time with Amy."

"We're trying to work on it," he said, through what sounded like gritted teeth. "But I'm just so *angry* she had the affair with Dylan. Sometimes it's okay, and I forget about it, and she's the woman I married. And then sometimes, when she's mad about me cancelling on her, it's all I can do not to throw Dylan in her face."

Fenway was quiet.

"And of course, he's dead, which I think she still blames me for."

"Yeah."

"Sorry. I shouldn't be unloading on you."

"That's okay, Craig. Oh—uh, I need to tell you—I had to bring Dez in on this. She came with me to Vista Del Rincón when I talked to Tracey."

McVie was silent for a moment. "Okay, Fenway. I'm pretty sure that whoever the mole is isn't in the coroner's office."

"So does that mean you're okay bringing Mark in on it too?"

McVie sighed. "The more people who know, the higher the chance that the kidnappers are going to find out that we didn't keep it out of the cops' hands."

"Dez says Mark is really good at missing person cases."

"He is."

"So you're okay with it?"

"Now that we've confirmed that Olivia is actually missing, we better do everything we can. So, yes, I'm okay with it."

Fenway mouthed, "McVie's okay bringing Mark in." Dez nodded.

"So do you need me to pick you up?" McVie continued.

"I guess so. Will a quarter to six give us enough time to get there?"

"Yeah, that should be fine. See you then."

They said goodbye and hung up.

Dez said, "So I take it you're meeting the private investigator tonight."

"Yeah."

Dez tapped the steering wheel. "Seriously, watch yourselves. They've already killed one person, and anyone who would kidnap a little girl isn't playing around."

Fenway pursed her lips and nodded.

"And I'll get Mark working this as soon as he can," Dez said. "And we'll keep it quiet. He'll keep it to himself."

"I know."

They drove in silence for a minute.

"And, girl, since when have you called that man *Craig*? You backsliding? Do I have to kick your ass again?"

Fenway laughed, but she could tell Dez sensed her nervousness. "Probably just because he's on leave. Calling him *Sheriff* seems weird."

Dez looked at Fenway out of the corner of her eye and didn't say anything.

They got back to the station in another ten minutes and walked into the office. Fenway saw Migs behind the desk and he looked horrified. "Hey," he started, "I tried to stop him but—"

Dr. Barry Klein stood on the other side of the door.

"See how you like it, Miss Stevenson," Klein growled. He had a manila folder in his hand. He angrily slammed the folder on the table next to Migs and opened it up.

Fenway looked—they were photos.

Photos of her.

She panicked at first—had he found her old boyfriend from college? Or the one-night stand she had on her trip to Miami to celebrate her graduation?

But she looked closer, and the top photo showed Fenway on her back, a man on top of her, her blouse torn, her face turned away from his.

Books—Dostoevsky, Tolstoy, Gogol, Turgenev littered the desk in the clean but untidy office. The nameplate on the desk read *S. Delacroix*.

The photo showed her Russian Lit professor raping her.

She staggered.

"Still think the people of this county will love you when they see you having sex with your professor for grades, Fenway?" Klein sneered. "Do they know you cheated your way to your valedictorian honors?"

Dez gaped. "What the hell is this?"

Fenway couldn't catch her breath. The room spun. "It's my lit professor raping me," she gasped. "I don't know how he got those."

Klein's face fell. "What? No! He's not—" And then he looked closer at the picture, and he saw Fenway's face in the photos, and it dawned on him just what the photos were showing.

"Oh shit," he said. "Oh shit. I didn't—I'm so—"

Dez pushed him into the table. He tripped and fell. Dez landed on top of him, her knee in his ribs. He groaned as the air completely went out of him. Dez got down low, right against his ear.

"How dare you." Her voice dripped with contempt. "How dare you come in here with those pictures. Pictures that are *illegal* for you to possess. You don't come into someone's office and confront them with pictures of them getting raped, you sociopath. Just because you thought you could get away with screwing someone else's wife."

"No!" Klein gasped. "I didn't know—I couldn't tell—"

"Barry Klein, you are under arrest for possession of obscene matter under penal code three-twelve point three." Dez seethed with anger. "Migs, call an officer before I do something to Dr. Klein's face that I'd really enjoy but probably regret."

Migs picked up the phone and dialed.

"What do you think, Fenway?" Dez said. "Think he's behind Rachel's attempted murder too, or is he just another entitled prick?"

The room kept spinning.

"Fenway?"

The walls started closing in.

"I have to get out of here," Fenway said.

She backed out of the office and almost knocked over a bookcase next to the door. She couldn't breathe. Her vision blurred. She felt her chest tighten and knew that she would start crying soon and didn't want to give Klein the satisfaction.

She ran to the ladies' room, pulling the door open even though it seemed to weigh a thousand pounds. She found her way into one of the stalls and her stomach did a flip and she vomited into the toilet, sinking down to her knees. Then she vomited again. The retching tightened all her muscles from her stomach up through her face. Her eyes pinched shut and tears flooded out between her lids. She couldn't close her mouth and her stomach kept heaving, trying to get everything out. She couldn't catch her breath. She tasted bile on her tongue.

Her stomach finally relaxed and she wheezed. And then sobbed.

A tentative voice called from the next stall.

"Are you all right?"

"No," she gasped. "I thought I was all right but I'm not."

"Can I get you something?"

"Dez," she said. "Get Dez."

She heard a flush, the sound of the stall door opening and closing, and heels on the tile going out of the bathroom.

That woman didn't wash her hands, Fenway thought, and then laughed miserably.

Her sobs died away.

Fenway waited a few more minutes. Her stomach had settled down. It seemed to her like it had passed. She took a couple of deep breaths, her inhalations still catching from the remnants of the sobs. She stood up, a little cautiously. She looked at her blouse and her pants. There were a couple of flecks near the top of her blouse. She had, perhaps miraculously, kept the vomit off her pants and out of her hair, at least from first appearances.

She walked slowly over to the paper towel dispenser and got six paper towels, wet them under the automatic faucet, and dabbed at her eyes and her ruined mascara, and at the spots on her blouse. She blotted her cheeks and looked at herself in the mirror. She shook her head, cupped her hands under the faucet, and splashed water on her face for a couple of minutes.

The room had stopped spinning, at least.

Dez walked into the bathroom.

"Hey, Fenway," she murmured. "I'm sorry. I'm really sorry."

Fenway nodded.

"I don't know what to do with him. I want to push him down a flight of stairs with his hands cuffed behind his back."

"Thanks, Dez," Fenway said.

Dez stood there in silence for a minute.

"What did you arrest him for?"

"I told him child pornography," Dez said. "I told him you weren't eighteen at the time."

"Yes, I was."

"*He* doesn't know that."

Fenway didn't say anything.

"Don't worry, Fenway," Dez said, "I filled out the paperwork for cyber exploitation, not child pornography."

Fenway nodded.

"Dr. Klein is going to have a rough night in holding," Dez continued. "It's possible that Migs has accidentally misplaced his paperwork." She cleared her throat. "How about if I take you back to your apartment? Why don't I go meet the P.I. your daddy hired? You can decompress. You've had enough for one day."

"You can take me home," Fenway said, "but I'm going to meet the private investigator. I owe that to Olivia. I owe that to Fletch and Tracey."

She looked in the mirror, at the wet splotches on her blouse, the tightness in her face, the tangled mess of her hair.

"And if it turns out that Barry Klein *is* behind the kidnapping, I'm going to cut his balls off."

CHAPTER FIFTEEN

———◆———

Dez drove Fenway home, and she had a couple of hours before she had to meet the private investigator. She walked through the door to her apartment in a daze.

She set her purse down on the kitchen table and kicked off her clothes as she went into her bathroom. She turned on the shower as hot as she could stand it and stood underneath the pulsing spray, feeling the water's fingers drum against the top of her head. She had done the same thing in the dorm in Bellingham after the attack. After the rape. Trying to wash it all away.

Her hair had gotten wet—she'd have to have a wrap or something tonight, or flatiron it later. But she tried to think about other things. She tried to think about Dr. Barry Klein, terrified, in a holding cell with drunks and fighters and thieves, a long, hellish night ahead of him. She tried to think of him shouting through the bars, trying to pull rank with the police—*Don't you know who I am? I'm on the board of supervisors!* But she knew that Dez held more sway with the officers than Barry did.

Yet the thought of him spending a cold, frightened, miserable night didn't make her feel any better. So she turned the water all the way to the cold side. It felt like ice on her skin. It felt like walking through the freezing sleet on her way to class in Bellingham the morning after it happened, thinking how she would get an A in the class just to spite him, and how she would change her major from English literature to nursing.

She changed the water again, this time to a comfortable temperature. She got the soap and scrubbed her body, her thighs, her shoulders, her chest, her neck. She felt it all again, like it had happened yesterday: the shame, the fear, the worry. But this time, it didn't stick; like an imprint, a ghost of the emotion, like she had vomited all the shame and fear out and only flecks on her heart remained. And she wanted it to all disappear down the drain with the soap.

She rinsed herself clean, turned off the shower, then got out and dried herself carefully and thoroughly. She walked into her bedroom and looked at the clock; she still had an hour and a half. She blow-dried her hair and took forty minutes to flat-iron the unruly curls out of it; when she finished, it hung at her shoulders, slightly curling in toward her chin at the bottom, framing her face nicely.

She looked in the mirror and set her jaw. She hated that Barry Klein could do this to her with a short series of nine-year-old photographs from the worst day of her life. But she took a deep breath and put those memories in a box in her mind, and got dressed.

She knew her father would want to see her in a dress, and not the jeans and cap-sleeve V-neck she pulled on, but she made the decision to be comfortable in her own skin. She did minimal makeup, then got her purse off the kitchen table and walked out the door.

After she walked down the stairs, McVie had pulled in the lot in his Highlander. For a brief instant, even after the horror of the last two hours, Fenway had butterflies in her stomach, like she did in high school when the boy she had a crush on came to pick her up. She shook her head to get the image out.

"Hi, Craig," Fenway said. He wore a black tee shirt and dark blue jeans with black European-style loafers. The shirt snugly fit his muscular frame.

She didn't seem to be able to call him *Sheriff* although she thought she gave it effort. "Is Amy okay with the change of plans for the evening?"

"She'll get over it," McVie said, somewhat gruffly.

They arrived at Grafton & Gale's just before six, and were seated at the end of the bar, looking almost directly at the front door. Fenway ordered a Diet Coke; McVie a ginger ale.

Nathaniel Ferris joined them about five minutes later, still in his charcoal grey suit, white dress shirt, and a blue-and-orange tie. "Sorry I'm late," he said. "Work meeting ran long. It doesn't look like Vasily is here yet."

"I'm sorry—who?"

"Vasily. He's Russian. Haven't I told you the story?"

"The story about Vasily? No."

Ferris nodded, excited to have an adventure to tell. "He's an interesting character. Loved computers when he was growing up around the Russian mob. He fell in with them as a teenager, stealing credit card information, stuff like that. Then when he turned eighteen, he came to New York and worked for the mob there. I heard he hacked into that big New York bank a few years ago. But then he broke away from the mob—apparently he hacked his own identity to escape them—somehow made it to L.A., probably on someone else's credit card. But he had a change of heart. Wanted to start hacking for the good guys. He started finding missing persons for families and for a few police forces up and down the coast. You hear of people going off the radar, but no one can completely get away from their digital footprint. Not for long anyway, and not when Vasily is trying to find you."

"And he's good?"

"The best. I had an accountant go missing with about three hundred thousand dollars a few years ago. He had moved a lot of money around for payments for crude oil from Venezuela—this is when we were still importing oil from there—and we had to do a few complicated hops. He falsified the exchange rate in the books and pocketed the difference. By the time our auditors found it, he vanished from the company—from the country, in fact. I hired Vasily to find him."

"I take it Vasily succeeded," said McVie.

"Oh, of course," said Ferris, nodding. "I had hired another P.I. first who didn't get anywhere. Vasily found the accountant on a beach in Nicaragua. He had bought a fishing boat and found a little *señorita*" —Fenway cringed at this— "and he thought he'd live out his days fishing and snorkeling. We couldn't extradite him, unfortunately, and he could only give us back some of our money. But we found him. Vasily can work miracles."

The three of them sat in silence at the bar for several minutes. Ferris got his phone out and made a phone call, but hung up after about half a minute. He tapped his phone on the bar, then got up and walked over to the bartender, discussing bourbons with him, and ordered an old fashioned made with a rye whiskey Fenway had never heard of.

"You know this place?" Ferris asked McVie.

"I've been once or twice. Not really my speed, but decent enough food. Amy liked it. How about you?" he said to Fenway.

Fenway shook her head. She still looked at the door. She started to get up when it opened, but a couple walked in, laughing and smiling.

"Is Vasily usually on time?" she asked.

The bartender slid the old fashioned in front of Ferris, who nodded before picking up his drink. "It's possible that his plane got delayed. He didn't answer his phone just now."

They chatted awkwardly for a few minutes. McVie kept looking at his watch.

"You still have time to catch the concert if you leave now?"

"I should," McVie said. "It says 7:30 on the tickets, and there's an opening act. I could leave now and even pick Amy up before we head over."

Fenway lightly touched her father's arm. "Call the airline, Dad."

Ferris looked a little distracted. "I don't know where he could be." He had a little trouble getting his phone out of his pocket, but managed to retrieve it, and called, pressing the phone to his head.

"If I've cancelled on Amy for nothing, I'm going to be a little pissed off," McVie said in a low voice.

"Remember that I found out about four hours ago that Olivia is really the one who's missing," Fenway said, raising her voice slightly, "and she's now been gone for almost forty-eight hours. We've gotta get the P.I. going on this right now. If he's another half-hour late, or hell, even an hour or two, that's still closer than we'll get to finding Olivia if we cut bait tonight."

"You might be right, but this isn't even official police business," McVie said.

"Like that makes a difference? What if it was Megan?" Fenway pointed out. "What if the person in charge said to you, 'Oh, I'd love to find your daughter before they kill her, but I've got a date with my wife, so can we start tomorrow?'"

McVie didn't say anything.

Fenway turned back to her diet Coke, clenching and unclenching her fists.

Ferris hung up. "Flight landed in Estancia at three-thirty," he said. "That should be more than enough time to go to the hotel and head here."

"Let's have dinner," Fenway suggested, "and if he doesn't show up by the time we're done, let's go to his hotel and figure this out. Maybe he thought we were meeting tomorrow, or maybe he had the wrong bar."

"He picked it," said Ferris.

"Maybe *we* have the wrong bar."

"I guess," Ferris said. He pulled his phone out and called again; but again no one answered.

McVie stood up and stretched. "Maybe his phone is powered off or maybe he left it at home. I'm going to head over to his hotel now. If he's still there, I'll bring him back. And if he's not there, I better get to that concert," he said. "If he shows up while I'm gone, let me know. I'll leave the concert if I have to, but if this guy just flaked on us, I'm not going to miss out on this evening if I can help it." He paused. "Plus, we have Mark working on this in secret, right?"

Fenway was glum. "Yes."

"That might be just as good as a P.I. anyway. Someone who knows how to access police resources without setting off any alarm bells."

"Okay. Let me know if Vasily's at his hotel."

"All right. Fenway, you can get a ride home?"

"Sure."

Fenway nodded and stood up from the stool. Without thinking, she opened her arms for a hug and McVie hesitated before awkwardly embracing her. She could feel the stress in his back, probably from the conflict between his promise to his wife and his duty to the job—even though he had been placed on leave. But then, she felt him relax, and he held her for a moment longer than he needed to. The embrace mellowed into an embrace like the one in the hospital parking lot. Fenway broke from the hug first, and McVie turned and shook hands with Ferris, and walked out the door.

Ferris watched him go, then sipped his old fashioned. "Okay, Fenway, what do you want to do?"

"I think it's kind of weird, don't you?"

"That Vasily is so late?"

"Yes."

"It's certainly not like him. Especially for the first day on the job. I guess I could call around, see if he actually got on the plane in Los Angeles."

"I mean, it's a thirty-minute flight. It's not like he wouldn't have called, right?"

Ferris thought a moment. "It's definitely not like him."

Fenway tapped her fingers on the bar. "Is he the kind of person who might not take something like this seriously?"

Ferris shook his head. "No. He'd take something like this *very* seriously. His sister disappeared in Moscow when Vasily was little."

"We can't call Missing Persons yet. Maybe he's just late. Maybe he got lost on the way here."

Ferris was silent.

Fenway walked over to where the bartender stood, washing glassware, and ordered a beer. She went back over and sat with her father.

"Dinner?" she asked.

"I suppose," he replied.

"We've gotta eat, right?"

Ferris nodded.

The bartender brought Fenway her beer and she asked for two menus. She knew as soon as she looked at the menu that her father wouldn't like it. They may have had a bourbon that met with his exacting standards, but a man used to eating pheasant and sheep's-milk cheese omelettes wouldn't want to waste his palate on cheeseburgers and fried chicken.

Ferris didn't say anything about the lack of finesse on the menu, however, and they ordered. Ferris didn't even special order anything. It was clear to Fenway that Vasily weighed heavily on his mind.

She tried to distract him by talking about the rye whiskey he had ordered. He talked for a few minutes about the small batch rye in Utah that he had found after a trip to Zion, which became a story about taking a helicopter tour of some of the monuments there. In the middle of talking about the delicate hike of Angel's Landing, he stopped.

"I can have Justin check this out," he said. "He's good at it."

"Justin?"

"My new head of security," he said. "Used to work for a cybersecurity firm up in Silicon Valley. Likes the surfing down here better."

"Okay."

Ferris pulled his phone out again and called a number. He spoke in hushed tones for about five minutes. Fenway watched the bartender clean the glasses as she sipped her beer.

"Justin's going to look into it," Ferris said, hanging up.

They sat in silence for a few minutes, Ferris finishing his drink, Fenway drinking her beer, trying not to think about what Barry Klein had done to her that afternoon.

"I have to tell you something, Dad," Fenway finally said.

"Sure," he said. "Sorry I'm quiet tonight. It's just not like Vasily to be this late."

"I was raped in college."

Ferris stared at his glass for a minute. "Did I hear that right?"

"Yes."

He paused. "I'm sorry," he said. "I'm really sorry. Are you okay?"

Fenway sighed. "I thought I was. It happened a long time ago. He was my Russian Lit professor."

Ferris looked at Fenway. "He was your *professor*?"

"Yes, my Russian Lit professor. At Western Washington. I came in during office hours. He locked the door behind me."

Ferris cleared his throat. "What—uh, why..." His voice faded away.

"Barry Klein came into the office this afternoon with pictures of me."

"Pictures of you?"

"Of me with my professor while it was happening. Apparently, my professor had a hidden camera in his office."

"What?" Ferris said sharply. "Why the hell would he bring in pictures of that?"

"It's complicated," Fenway said. "He thought I had traded sex for grades."

"Where the hell did he even get them?"

Fenway shrugged. "Probably online. The dark web or something. I don't know. I don't think it matters."

"I'm going to kill him," Ferris seethed. He stood up from his barstool.

"Dez took care of it, Dad," she said. "He's cooling his heels in jail tonight."

"I'll kill him when you release him in the morning." Ferris paused. "Why the hell are you telling me this now?"

"Because it's out there. If Klein—who is an absolute idiot—could find them, then it's for sure out there. I wanted you to hear it from me. I didn't want you to find out from the internet, or someone forwarding it to you asking if you knew."

"I hated that guy before," Ferris snarled. "I'm going to drive a stake through his heart."

"Dad," Fenway said gently.

Ferris breathed heavily but turned his face back to Fenway.

"I thought I could just push it down and forget it ever happened," Fenway continued. "But I guess I can't. I didn't know he recorded it. Or took pictures. And I definitely didn't know you could find those pictures on the internet. So it's out there. I'm out there. And," she finished, "I wanted you to hear it from me."

Ferris put his head in his hands. His shoulders started to shake.

"I really screwed up, didn't I?" he said, his voice cracking. "I was so angry at Joanne that I totally forgot everything about you. About how all of this would affect you."

"This isn't about that, Dad," she said, her tone curt.

"I'm sorry," Ferris said. "I don't know what to do." He got up from the bar and started toward the door.

"You're not going to stay for dinner? You just ordered."

"I'm not hungry," he said. Ferris stepped back, pulled out his wallet, and threw a pair of hundred-dollar bills on the bar. "I'm sorry, Fenway. I just—I don't know. It's a lot. I'm really sorry."

And he, like McVie before him, exited Grafton & Gale's.

Fenway turned back toward the bar. Her breaths were slow and even. She felt a little bit like she had just been talking about someone else. Like it happened to a woman she knew a lifetime ago. She felt something in her brain, a little chaotic, a little like screaming. But she kept her attention on her breathing.

She picked up her beer glass and drained it.

The bartender came back over. "Can I get you another?"

Fenway's phone dinged. She looked at it; it was a message from McVie.

Vasily isn't at the hotel. Checked in but not answering door or calls.
Let me know if he shows.

Fenway thought back to junior high, growing up poor, not only without her father's wealth but without the man himself. It had been tough on her mother, and as much as she'd turned out all right, she knew she had gaps in her emotional maturity, in the way she dealt with people. Especially men.

And this little girl, Olivia, had a father who cared about her so much he was willing to go to jail so she would be safe. A father who would attend all the school plays and volleyball games and junior proms and graduation ceremonies. This little girl deserved to get home safely, and more than that, she deserved to get her father back.

But Fenway found herself at a dead end with nothing more to do. She had hoped the private investigator would start right away, not be a no-show for their first meeting. She had hoped she'd already have found Olivia, safe, back with her mother, and be in the process of getting Fletch out of police custody. But instead, she found herself exhausted and out of ideas.

It was seven-fifteen, making Vasily officially over an hour late. The bartender was still waiting for her answer.

"Can you make that food order to go?" she asked.

PART V

TUESDAY

CHAPTER SIXTEEN

FENWAY TOOK AN UBER BACK TO HER APARTMENT, THE smell of her meatloaf and of her father's turkey sandwich wafting through the back seat. She put the sandwich in the fridge and ate her meatloaf without tasting it, watching the previous week's episode of *Hold Your Horses* to catch up with Rachel.

She went to bed early, but didn't sleep well, tossing and turning through most of the night. She had a weird dream about Craig in the trunk of a car, tape stretched tight over his mouth. She awoke, sweaty, and looked at the clock. It was four-thirty and she knew from the way her heart pounded in her chest that she wouldn't be going back to sleep.

She padded barefoot from her bedroom to the kitchen, opened the refrigerator door, and stared into it for a few minutes. Restless, she felt like she treaded water everywhere she went: the police thought they had the mayor's killer, but she knew the confession was fake. And all the missing people: Fletch's daughter, the man who had been hired to find her, and Rachel. Fenway didn't even know where to start.

Well—she could think of one person who might know something.

And the buses started running at five.

She pulled on a pair of loose black trousers and a shapeless long-sleeved gray tee shirt. She forced herself to eat a bowl of cereal, then finished getting ready. She dug in her change jar and picked out twelve quarters.

She walked down to the bus stop and stood in the darkness. She wanted some coffee but the Coffee Bean next to the stop didn't open until six. She didn't have to wait long; she could see the headlights of the bus down Estancia Canyon a couple of blocks.

The bus was empty except for a tired-looking Latina woman in the third row. Fenway thought she recognized her face from the bakery downtown, a couple of blocks down from her work. Fenway made a mental note to visit the bakery.

She put her two dollars and fifty cents in quarters in the machine next to the driver and got her all-day pass. She tried not to think about her Accord in Seattle or her father's jet.

She got out at the City Hall stop, and walked to the jail behind the sheriff's office. She went through the metal detector, and then stopped at the table behind it to sign her name. She waited patiently for the guard to arrive and let her in.

The room felt clinical and sinister: painted an antiseptic white color, the fluorescent lights dropped harsh shadows. A door at the far end of the room had a tall, rectangular, wire-reinforced window, about eight inches wide, spanning from doorknob height to just below the top of the door. Another door behind the table, solid with no window, opened, and the guard walked through. He brightened when he saw Fenway.

"Hey, Miss Stevenson! Kind of early for you. No one drove another truck through your office, I hope."

"Oh, hi, Quincy," Fenway said. "Come on, you know you can call me Fenway. When did you transfer over here?"

"About a month ago," he said. "After the truck incident, the county moved us around. We're almost all in different spots now."

"You still have graveyard?" Fenway asked, pulling out her county identification badge.

"I wouldn't have it any other way." Quincy glanced at the sheet and at the badge. "Who are you here to see?"

"An overnight guest. Dr. Barry Klein."

"Oh, yes, Dr. Klein. Evidently, he thinks I don't know who he is. Threatened to take my job for not letting him out."

"That makes me even sadder that the paperwork hasn't made it here yet." She paused. "How's he doing?"

"Scared out of his mind."

"Anyone mess with him?"

"We picked up a couple of guys for fighting last night at O'Grady's Pub. They started messing with Dr. Klein at about midnight. I separated them before any blood was spilled, but he got a punch to the gut. Dr. Klein didn't put up much of a fight."

"Did you give him his phone call?"

"Sure did. He called his wife. She's been calling for the sheriff incessantly, but he's on leave, so she can't get through."

"That's a shame." Fenway paused. "It is actually too bad we're putting her through this. She probably didn't have anything to do with it. At least—I hope she didn't."

"What did Dr. Klein do, if you don't mind my asking?"

Fenway paused. "He had nonconsensual sexual images of a county employee that he tried to use for purposes of extortion."

Quincy's eyes widened. "Seriously?"

"Seriously."

"Anybody I know?"

Fenway looked Quincy in the eye, her mouth a thin line.

Quincy set his jaw. "Now I wish I hadn't separated them."

Fenway patted Quincy on the shoulder. "No, you did the right thing. I think he's gotten the message. I mean, I still want to kick him in the face, but I won't." She paused. "Probably not, anyway."

Quincy pushed a button on the wall and a buzz and a loud click came from the door with the window in it.

"Want an escort?" he said.

"Actually, I need a more private conversation. Would you please get him and bring him to one of the rooms down in the other wing?"

"Sure thing. All the rooms are open. You okay with room two?"

"Sounds great."

Fenway opened the door and turned left down the first corridor. She had been into a couple of these rooms before; they were looking at a heroin overdose death, and they had interviewed a couple of the small-time dealers in one of the rooms.

She opened the third door on the right, labeled with an overly large "2" in black paint on the white door. A cheap table with fake oak laminate took up the middle of the room. The room also contained three mismatched chairs. One of them, a wooden chair with a chunk out of the seat, looked like it could hurt if the person sat down wrong. Fenway pushed it to the far side of the table and pulled the other two to her side. She sat down in the cleanest of the remaining two chairs.

After a couple of minutes, Quincy opened the door, with Dr. Barry Klein in front of him. Handcuffed, his hair matted and sticking up, and wearing smudged glasses, he looked exhausted. He saw Fenway and winced.

"What I did was unforgivable," he whined. "I'm so sorry. I know I deserved what I got. Please, you have to believe me. I didn't know what that was until you said it."

Fenway held up her hand. "Dr. Klein, I'm not here about that."

He gaped at her. "Well, *I'm* here about that! When am I going home?"

Quincy sat Klein down in the broken chair opposite Fenway. "Do you need me to stay, Fenway?"

"No, that's okay. He and I need to talk privately."

"Okay. Just push that button and I'll come right in." He glared at Dr. Klein.

"Thanks, Quincy."

Quincy left and shut the door behind him.

"So, Dr. Klein," Fenway began, "the reason why I'm here is very sensitive. I'm not exaggerating when I say it's a matter of life and death. I know you and I have had a very rocky relationship, but I need your word that you won't repeat any of what I'm about to tell you."

He looked at her. "You need my help?"

"I don't know," Fenway said. "I need to ask you these questions anyway, and I need your word that you will keep silent."

Klein shifted nervously in his seat. "Suppose I say no."

"I'll be disappointed, but I'll understand. You go back to your holding cell with your friends from the Irish pub, and I'll try to find another way to answer my questions. Your wife might know the answers, for example."

He set his jaw and narrowed his eyes. "Fine," he said. "I promise to keep my mouth shut."

"Terrific," she said. "You know Tracey and Fletch's kids, right?"

"Not really," he said. "I haven't met them. Alice talks about them all the time in meetings. Two girls. Five and one, if I remember correctly."

"Olivia and Isla."

"If you say so."

"Two people kidnapped Olivia the day after the mayor's murder."

Klein paused. "What?"

"Olivia was kidnapped. Tracey and Fletch were told to keep it from the cops or Olivia would be killed."

"Why would anyone do that?"

"I'm in this room with the only person I know with a motive."

Klein's jaw dropped open. "Me? Why would I do it?"

"To save your political career," Fenway said. "You're about to run for coroner. The way I see it, Fletch found out, and he went with the mayor to go see the county public information officer. Now the mayor's dead, the public information officer has had two attempts on her life and is now missing, and Fletch's daughter is kidnapped."

Klein swallowed hard. "And you think I did all of that?"

Fenway shrugged. "Like I said, you're the only person I know with a motive for all that."

"What proof do you have?"

"The investigators are digging into it and they told me they found something they wanted to show me this morning," Fenway lied. "But I couldn't sleep after what you did to me yesterday afternoon. So I figured I might as well come wake you up."

Klein didn't say anything.

"Am I wrong, Doctor? Do you not have a motive for this?"

Klein looked away. "I didn't kidnap anyone, I didn't try to kill the PR woman, and I sure as hell didn't kill the mayor."

"Do you have an alibi for late Friday night and Saturday morning?" Fenway asked. "And when we dig through your financial records, are we going to find a large cash payment to a gentleman with one of about a dozen aliases who just shot up St. Vincent's hospital trying to kill the public information officer?"

Klein closed his eyes. "I'm telling you right now, I didn't do any of that, so I'd encourage you to keep looking. But I'm going to invoke my right to see a lawyer before I answer any more of these questions."

"Okay," Fenway said. "I know I shouldn't be asking this since you've invoked your right to counsel, but if you answer this question—and it's correct—I'll drop all of the charges on the, uh, incident yesterday. You can go home."

"Okay, what's the question?" He sat forward.

"Where's Olivia?"

Klein deflated. "I don't have any idea. I didn't kidnap her. I don't know who did."

Fenway sighed, got up from her chair, and pushed the intercom. "Hi, Quincy. Dr. Klein is ready to return to the holding cell now."

The two of them sat, staring at each other until Quincy came in. Dr. Klein stood, catching the back of his trousers on the broken wood of the chair. He grimaced in pain and Fenway heard the fabric tear slightly. Quincy led Klein out, closing the door behind them.

Fenway sat in the silent room for a moment, considering her options. As much as she hated Dr. Klein, she didn't think he knew anything more. To put the puzzle together, she needed a big missing piece.

She thought about Rachel's disappearance, and strongly believed that whatever Rachel, Fletch, and Alice Jenkins had discussed that afternoon in Rachel's office held the key to all of this. But she didn't have any way of knowing what they talked about.

Except.

Except for that Post-It note on Rachel's monitor.

Fenway pulled her phone out of her purse and checked the time. Not quite six-fifteen. She could go to Java Jim's and get a latte. She could dig a little bit on her own. She could check with her father about what his new head of security found out about Vasily's whereabouts. There were still avenues to go down.

Fenway let herself out. She said goodbye to Quincy at the front desk and walked down the street to get her first latte of the day.

She got nowhere on the SRB research. No website, no board of directors listed, not even a mailing address besides the New

Jersey address in the public filing information. Her phone dinged just as she finished typing in a new web search.

She picked it up; a text from her father read:

Call me I have info on Vasily

She took a drink of her latte and called her father.

"Nathaniel Ferris."

"Hi, Dad."

"Oh, I didn't expect you to call me back so quickly."

"I couldn't sleep. Came into work early."

"I couldn't sleep either." He hesitated for a moment before he spoke. "I know it was hard for you to tell me what you told me last night, Fenway. A father never wants to hear that. I don't think I reacted very well."

Fenway agreed, but stayed silent.

"Listen—I just want to say that, uh, I wish it hadn't happened to you. I wish I could do something about it. I don't know how to react, though. I just—I just don't know what to say. I want to say something that will make it go away, I guess. But I can't."

"No, Dad, you can't. I don't really expect you to say anything. I just didn't want you to hear it from someone else. Because it's probably going to come out pretty soon."

He cleared his throat. "Anyway, Justin looked into Vasily yesterday. He picked up the rental car, a Ford Fusion. I have the license plate. You have a pen?"

Fenway got a pen and pulled her notepad toward herself. "Yes."

"Okay, Eight-One-Tango-Hotel-Yankee-Juliet-Four-Five."

Fenway repeated what she wrote down. "California plates?"

"Yes. And he checked into the Coast Harbor Marriott at 4:45 P.M. Room 428."

"Did your guy go by the hotel?"

"Yes. The car's not there. And no one answered his door."

"Okay, thanks. Any other leads on him?"

"Not yet. Justin is still on it."

"All right. Let me know if he finds anything else."

She hung up and tapped her fingers on the table. She couldn't put a BOLO out on the car; Vasily hadn't been missing for forty-eight hours. She thought about going to the hotel and talking her way into his room; maybe pretend to be his girlfriend, or a one-night-stand who left a cell phone or tampon case in the room. She thought of a million ways that it could go wrong. And this was a Marriott, not the Cactus Lake Motel; they could spot grifters a mile away, and so could probably also spot a law enforcement officer trying to sneak into a room.

And what did she think she'd find in the room anyway? A dead body? Probably not the best place to be, sneaking into a hotel room when there's a dead person in it, especially since she had been trying to avoid informing the police.

She exhaled and stood up. Without probable cause, without having Vasily go missing for forty-eight hours, she didn't think she could do anything anyway, even if she did call the cops.

She picked up the phone and called McVie.

As soon as she hit the button to call him, she panicked—it wasn't yet seven o'clock, and if Craig and Amy had had a date night planned, it might not be pretty. She decided to hang up if it rang more than twice.

McVie picked up on the second ring.

"Hello?" he sounded awful—his voice croaking and scratchy.

"Craig?"

"Ugh. Hi, Fenway. What time is it?"

"It's early," she said. "It's not quite seven." She paused and closed her eyes. "Did you make it to the concert?"

"Mmm," he grunted. "Yes. Stayed up too late."

"Did I wake Amy?"

"No, she slept upstairs."

Fenway paused, fairly certain that McVie didn't realize he had just given that piece of information out. Were they sleeping in separate rooms? Had they slept apart since they started seeing the therapist a couple of months before? Fenway had many questions—but could not ask any of them.

"Um," McVie said, "did the private investigator ever show up?"

"No," Fenway said. "That's why I'm calling you. Because his rental car isn't at his hotel. He checked in last night, but it doesn't look like he ever came back to the room after six o'clock."

"He's not a missing person yet."

"No," Fenway said, "but we need to do something."

"I'm not sure what we *can* do," said McVie. "The right thing to do would be to put out a BOLO on his rental car, but that would mean involving the police in an official capacity."

"Right."

McVie thought for a moment. Fenway heard the sound of a coffee grinder.

"You ever think about the night we spent together, Craig?"

McVie paused. Fenway wished she hadn't said it.

"Yes," he said. "I probably shouldn't, but I do."

"I do, too."

McVie was quiet for a minute.

"I'm sorry," Fenway said. "I know I shouldn't be saying stuff like this when we work together."

"And we *like* working together," McVie said.

"Yeah." She wanted to say more, she wanted to talk about what might happen if Craig and Amy couldn't make it work. She thought maybe she could be the reason that Craig and Amy wouldn't make it work. But she kept her mouth shut. The silence stretched out.

"You know," he said, "I know the local captain over at the CHP. I can ask them to keep an eye out. They can keep it hushed up a little better than we can."

"Okay. Do you want the info?"

"Yes. Let me get a pen—okay, ready."

"It's a Ford Fusion, white. California plates, Eight-One-Thomas-Hotel-Yankee-Juliet-Four-Five."

"Tango," McVie said.

"Not *Thomas*?"

"Nope."

"Dammit, I almost had it. I'll get it one of these days."

There was silence on the other end of the line.

"Sheriff? You still there?"

He cleared his throat. "A white Ford Fusion?"

"Yes."

"It's parked in front of my house."

CHAPTER SEVENTEEN

FENWAY RAN OUT TO THE PARKING GARAGE BEFORE SHE REALIZED that her Accord was still back in Seattle. She pulled her phone out and requested an Uber—and fortunately one arrived in just a couple of minutes. She got to McVie's house about ten minutes later. His daughter's Jeep was parked on the side of the driveway, the Highlander across the street. Amy's car must be in the garage, she figured.

McVie stood in the driveway, in black sweatpants and a dri-fit workout shirt. Fenway knew he'd had a rough night, and it showed. She got out of the Uber, thanking the driver, and made her way over to the white Ford Fusion parked at the curb next to the front lawn. The license plate matched.

Fenway nodded in greeting.

"Do you want to get Amy and Megan out of here?" she asked McVie. "I don't think they should be here if there's a dead body in the car."

"They're already gone," McVie said in a gravelly voice. "Amy took Megan to a friend's house, and then she went to work."

"Everything okay?" Fenway said, hoping for some clues about the night before—if Craig had slept on the sofa, what had happened? She tried to sound concerned, pushing down as much enthusiasm as possible.

"No," he said, "but I don't want to get into it right now. We've got a problem in front of my house, and I want to figure out what to do."

"I think we try the door and see if it's open."

"You're not concerned that it might be rigged? Some sort of bomb?"

Fenway paused. "Well, *now* I am."

McVie considered for a moment. "I don't think it's rigged. I think whoever did this is trying to send a message to me. I don't think they're trying to kill me."

"Still, though, it's not like losing a twenty-dollar bet. If it's rigged with a bomb, you'll die."

"Yeah," McVie said. "With the week I'm having, that might be an improvement." He started to walk over to the driver's side door.

"Wait!" cried Fenway.

"What?"

"If you're going to be an idiot and open the door, at least put gloves on. Don't ruin the fingerprints." She pulled two pairs of blue nitrile gloves out of her purse.

"What size are those?"

"Mediums," she said. "You'll just have to squeeze your big mitts into these."

He pulled them on with difficulty as he walked over to the car, then tried the handle. It clicked.

Nothing exploded.

McVie pulled the door open. He bent down and popped the trunk.

Nothing exploded.

The trunk lid raised about two inches. Fenway walked over, pulling her pair of gloves on as well, and opened the trunk the rest of the way.

A skinny white man of about forty-five lay supine in the trunk. He had a white oxford shirt on, with a huge bloodstain on the left side of his chest. He had grey slacks on, without shoes or socks, his legs bent at an awkward angle. His eyes were covered with a white index card, just like the one Fenway had found in the trash can in Vista Del Rincón.

McVie came around the back of the trunk and looked at the body. Fenway reached out and picked up the index card. She flipped it over. The handwriting matched the first index card.

I SAID NO COPS

Fenway pursed her lips.

"I take it that we're looking at Vasily," McVie said.

"I would assume."

McVie sighed. "And now is when I'm going to get in some real trouble," he said. "There's no way I can't call this in. And now you and I are going to have to answer a ton of questions about who this guy is. I guess I know what I'm doing the rest of the day."

Fenway pulled out her phone.

"Not from out here," McVie said. "Let's go inside to the kitchen table."

Fenway grabbed his wrist. She felt the electricity between them again. "No," she said. "I don't trust any of this. The killer's got eyes in places where we think it's safe. I don't know if they've bugged your house, or my apartment, or what."

"You don't have to talk to me about being paranoid, Fenway. I'm the one who thinks there's a mole in the office. We never found out how Stotsky got into the jail cell to kill Dylan that night." McVie shook his head. "You know I think he paid off one of the guards to look the other way. And we don't know who that guard is."

"But you want to do something to make it obvious to the kidnappers that we're letting the police in on it?" Fenway asked, exasperation thick in her voice.

"They obviously found out that we hired a private investigator."

"Right, which is why I don't want to talk about this inside your house or at my apartment. Because those places might be bugged."

"Where do you suggest we go?"

"I think we should go pick up Dez and then we should go talk at Rachel's apartment. The CSI team has been all over that place. If that apartment had been bugged, they would have found it."

"Dez gets in early."

Fenway looked at her phone. "I'll call her. She hasn't left yet." She dialed. "Dez!" she said. "Hey—if I come to your place, can you give me a ride to work?"

"I'm starting to regret not letting you drive your precious new car back," Dez replied. "Fine. I was getting ready to leave, but I can wait. Are you walking here?"

"I'm getting a ride."

"Girl, you better not have woken up over at the sheriff's. I thought you learned your lesson last time."

"No, Dez," Fenway said, glancing up at McVie. "I can be there in ten minutes. Thanks. You're a lifesaver."

Fenway hung up. They closed the trunk of the Fusion and made sure the door closed all the way, and after discussing it, took Megan's Jeep over to Dez's apartment.

Dez opened the door in her uniform, with her purse over her shoulder and her keys in her hand.

"Oh—Sheriff," she said, surprised. She cast a suspicious glance at Fenway. Fenway gave Dez a subtle side-to-side shake of her head.

"Let's go somewhere we can talk," McVie said. "Fenway and I don't trust that our places aren't bugged."

They were in Rachel's townhouse a few minutes later; Dez used her key to get in. All three of them went to Rachel's kitchen table and sat down. Dez spun Rachel's keychain around on her finger.

McVie started talking. "Okay, Dez," he said. "I'm afraid I've got some bad news."

"Is it about that P.I. you and Fenway were being really cagey about yesterday?"

McVie hesitated. "Yeah, unfortunately, it *is* about the private investigator. He went missing. And this morning, his rental car was parked in front of my house."

"Wait, slow down," Dez put her hands up. "What happened?"

"The P.I. never showed up for our meeting last night," Fenway said. "I had a tough time sleeping, so I went in early this morning and I talked to my father on the phone." Fenway skipped the part about visiting Klein in jail, but recounted the conversation with her father, the new head of security finding the license plate, and Fenway calling McVie with the information.

"Okay," Dez said. She put Rachel's key down on the table.

"And I took an Uber over to McVie's house, and he and I opened up the car. It looks like the private investigator was stabbed in the chest, close to the heart, then dumped in the trunk. And there's an index card, just like the one I found in Fletch's trash, and it says, 'I said no cops.'"

Dez closed her eyes and breathed in deeply. She thought for a moment. "So what do you want to do?"

"I'm not sure," Fenway said. "We pretty much have to call this in. There's a dead guy in a trunk."

"What about the missing girl?" Dez said.

"They didn't mention Olivia."

"Then she's still gotta be the first priority. It obviously means something that she's not in the trunk with the private investigator."

McVie nodded agreement.

Fenway paused for a moment. "Yes, I suppose that's true. Has Mark found anything yet, Dez?"

"I talked to him just before you called. He's heading down to Aperture Consulting. He thinks it might have something to do with the audits Fletch did."

"That sounds like a pretty long road."

"If it's the *right* road, it doesn't matter how long it is," McVie interjected.

"This is obviously not a person—or, I guess, it could be a group of people—who are shy about murder," Dez continued. "And I bet they don't give a rat's ass about whether this little girl lives or dies. So why are they keeping her alive?"

"Because they want to be sure that Fletcher is convicted of the murder of his mother—" Fenway began.

McVie cut in. "But why in the world would they want that?" He tapped his fingers on the table. "That just doesn't make any sense at all. If they wanted to get rid of him, shouldn't they just kill him?"

"I think someone on the other side thought this would be a neatly wrapped package for the police," Dez said. "That's why they don't want any cops involved."

"Come on, they must know that I'd have to report this to the police," McVie said, amazed.

Dez clicked her tongue. "I would wager that they don't know what a Boy Scout you are when it comes to your job," she said. "I know how far out of your comfort zone you went just hiring the private investigator, Sheriff. But when you did that, I think that it looked to this outside observer—to this murderer—like you were a civil servant with a price for your silence."

McVie shook his head.

"So—what are our options, if we don't go through the official police channels?" Fenway asked.

"Let me think," said Dez. "If you were the killer, and you did this, what would you expect a regular civil servant who bent the rules to do?"

"Panic, I guess," said Fenway. "And if you panic, then you close the trunk and drive the car somewhere it can't be found."

McVie bristled. "I wouldn't panic. No one in the sheriff's office would panic."

"Right," said Dez. "But this isn't about what *you* would or wouldn't do. The kidnappers know you've been hiding the kidnapping from the cops. And I think they're counting on you *continuing* to hide it from the cops. So I think that's exactly what you should look like you're doing."

"Do you think someone is watching us?"

"I have no idea," said Dez, "but I'd at least behave like it."

"Then I guess we shouldn't use our phones to coordinate any of this," McVie said.

"I don't know," said Dez. "That may be the wrong thing to do. I don't want to mess up the crime scene."

"I think it'll be more valuable if we can try to get fingerprints off the car, or try to find some other type of evidence. Let's check for skin under Vasily's nails. If our killer was careless with the evidence, we might catch a break."

"But if we do that," reasoned Fenway, "won't that put Olivia in danger?"

"They obviously think we've already gone to the cops," said McVie. "Well—I mean, since I *am* the sheriff of this county, and they left the car in front of my house, *they've* already involved the cops. But they didn't kill Olivia."

"Not that we know of," Fenway said.

"If they've already done that, we don't have anything to lose anyway," McVie said. "Either they draw the line at killing children, or they want to keep Olivia alive to motivate Fletch to plead guilty to something he didn't do."

"I still don't think it's worth the risk," said Fenway.

"It doesn't have to be," said Dez. "We can make it look like the cops aren't being brought into this. Do it so that an outside observer won't know."

"How would we do that?" Fenway asked.

"We could just leave it," Dez suggested. "That actually might be what the kidnappers are counting on you doing. No one knows there's a body in the trunk but the three of us."

McVie shook his head. "I think you're right, Dez, but I can't do that. Every minute that we waste figuring out what to do about it means there's evidence we're not gathering. We've got to go through proper channels."

Dez pursed her lips. "But that puts the little girl at risk. There's got to be a way to do this without letting the kidnappers know the cops are involved."

Fenway thought for a moment. "Look," she said, "the body needs to go to CSI. We're talking about a crime scene in front of the house. I suppose we could stage something so that it looks like we didn't mean to tell the police, but that's just as risky. We'll call the police out. The CSI team will run what they need to run. That's not what the killers would expect. Maybe that'll put them on their heels."

McVie sighed and looked at Dez. "I don't really have a better idea."

Dez was lost in thought for a moment, then said, "No. I don't have a better idea either."

"Do we want to involve any other agencies?" McVie asked.

"I don't think so. The girl hasn't even been reported missing yet." Fenway's voice was firm.

"Do we want to give away what we're doing to the police?" Dez asked.

"I guess it depends on what questions they ask," Fenway said.

"I'm going to come clean," McVie said. "I've got to lead by

example. It's what I'd want my people to do if the shoe was on the other foot."

"Okay," Dez said. "Fenway, this is your dad's P.I., right? Do you want to tell him what happened?"

Fenway paused. "Not right now. Let's keep this as buttoned-up as possible until CSI arrives."

Dez nodded. "Call it in from here?"

"From there," Fenway said. "Keep everything on the up and up."

McVie nodded. "Okay, shall we all go back there, then?"

"Let me go to the bathroom first," Fenway said.

Dez got up from the table. "See you over there," she said, her face grim and determined, as she pushed Rachel's key on the table over to Fenway. "Lock up when you leave."

"Okay." Fenway got up as Dez went to the door. "Don't forget to get the key back from me."

McVie and Fenway drove Megan's Jeep back to the house. They were looking out for people who were following them, or anyone who hung out around the neighborhood in a car they didn't recognize or on a park bench pretending to read a paper. But they saw nothing.

They gathered in the driveway and used McVie's phone to call it in. Less than five minutes later, Celeste Salvador showed up on the scene. She asked the three of them several rounds of questions, all while following the procedures on securing the scene—police tape and everything. The CSI van arrived about thirty minutes after Celeste, and they watched Kav and Melissa get out of the car with their kits, walk over to the car, open the trunk, and get to work. Kav stayed back with the body, and Melissa dealt with the interior of the car itself.

By the end of the discussion, McVie had told the team everything: Fletch's missing daughter, the desire to keep it out of the police's hands until confirmation could be made, and how the shooting at the hospital had put a huge monkey wrench in the middle of everything.

———◆———

Fenway rode in silence back to the coroner's office with Dez. McVie stayed back at his house with Celeste, who had a few follow-up questions. The body in the trunk—no one had been able to identify it, although everyone's money was on Vasily—rode in the van to San Miguelito and Dr. Yasuda.

While Celeste took their statements, Fenway got a message from Dr. Yasuda to give her a call, but she wanted to settle in back at the office first. She tried to block out Dr. Klein and the pictures he had brought in the day before. The dead body in the trunk did a pretty decent job of keeping it out of her head.

She walked in the door after Dez, and Migs popped his head up.

"Hi, Fenway," he said. "Piper found out some stuff while you were dealing with—whatever you were dealing with this morning. She's at her desk."

"Okay," she said. "Just give me a second."

Fenway went into her office and shut the door. It had only been her office for a short time: after the truck had gone through her office wall a couple of months before, the construction to repair the wall had been fast—especially for public works—but had only been completed two weeks ago. The workers definitely piecemealed the wall together—a visible line where the paint changed colors slightly, a small bulge evident to the left of the window in the drywall—but Fenway had never had an office all her own before.

She put her purse on the chair and walked back out.

"Maybe I should come with you," said Migs.

Fenway smirked. "Oh, yes, I definitely think it's important for you to come with me to see Piper. You never know what legal ramifications it might have."

"Okay, fine, Fenway."

"I'm just busting your chops. You can see your girlfriend."

"She's not my—"

"You don't want to finish that sentence," Fenway said. "You've been following her around like a puppy, and unless you want me to kick your ass—and you know I can—you'll stop right there."

Migs looked down and didn't say anything else. He followed Fenway out the door.

They walked down the hall to the Information Technology and Cybercrimes division. They walked past the propped-open door and saw Piper at her desk, dressed a green dress with cap sleeves, her red hair in a simple French braid.

"Hi, Piper," Fenway said.

"Oh, hey, Fenway." Piper looked at Migs and smiled. "Hey, Migs."

Fenway wanted to roll her eyes—the honeymoon phase of their relationship made her crazy—but she got down to business. "I heard you have some new information for me?"

"Yes," Piper said, breaking out of Migs's gaze. "So, I looked into SRB, and it's very interesting. They don't seem to be as well-concealed as some of the other organizations that I've heard about."

"Great," Fenway said.

"Come around so I can show you the papers I found."

Fenway walked around behind her and pulled over a side chair so she could see Piper's screen.

"So," Piper said, clicking on a window, "SRB Investment Holdings is registered in the Cayman Islands. It's difficult to get any information on the ownership—which you would expect of your typical shell corporation. But I can run a reverse search on some of the payments made with their routing numbers. A lot of the information is obfuscated, but I've still been able to find some payments and who they were made to."

"Don't you need a warrant for that?" asked Migs.

"I didn't say you could use this in court," Piper said.

"But foreign entities don't necessarily have the same expectations of privacy," Fenway said. "Even I know that, Migs."

"True. If there's reasonable suspicion that a crime has been committed, you should be okay," Migs said. "Plus, there are some payments that are a matter of public record."

"And, as you can see," Piper said, clicking on another window that showed the photo of a cancelled check, "we would have found out about some payments by looking into certain payees— who were next on my list."

The screen showed a cancelled check dated July 15, three years prior, for the amount of $150,000.

Made out to Alan Scorrelli.

Fenway stared at it for a moment. "So, I've kind of been working off the assumption that Scorrelli was *hired* to kill Rachel," she said. "Are you telling me that SRB paid a hit man a hundred and fifty grand three years ago?"

"Yes," Piper said. "Although we don't have direct evidence what the payment was for." She clicked off the application and opened another screen. "But I think I have a pretty good idea. See, I looked into Scorrelli's whereabouts during the time of the payment. He lived over in San Miguelito at the time, but his mother—Lilith Scorrelli—she lived here in Estancia. In January, three years ago, a car crash injured her pretty badly. There are payments to three different doctors in late January, and Alan Scorrelli paid each of them from his credit cards. Now, I can see the purchase of a wheelchair, a medical bed, oxygen tanks. I can also see payments at pharmacies— some of these are hundreds of dollars. See these payments here? I went through the Medicare co-payment database, and someone on the Medicare schedule would have to pay this amount of money for a month's supply of Oxycontin—that's the eighty milligram tablets. I searched the medical database, and there isn't a single other medication that would result in this exact amount. I know that's no guarantee that it *was* Oxycontin, but I think it's, uh..."

"Suggestive?" said Fenway.

"Sure," Piper said, smiling. "Especially since I see payments listed every month from February through May." She clicked again, and a form with hospital information in Monterey appeared on the screen. "Now, no one paid for that medication in June or July. And Mrs. Scorrelli transferred to Diego-Riley Medical down in Santa Monica on May 17. That would have been three years ago."

"Diego-Riley? That's quite a change from home care," Fenway said. "So that payment allowed Scorrelli to move his mom to a better facility?"

"I don't think so," Piper said. "Lilith Scorrelli moved two months *before* her son got the payment. I'm still looking into it. The medical records are sealed, of course, but I'm searching start and end dates for other accidents, anything like that."

"Diego-Riley's a research hospital, isn't it?" said Migs. "Maybe they were studying her in exchange for free care."

"Maybe," Piper said. "I'll see what I can find."

"So where does SRB fit into all of this?" Fenway said.

"I'm getting to that," Piper answered. "So, as you'll see, on July thirteenth, there was an episode in the hospital involving Lilith." Piper brought up a form from Diego-Riley entitled *Report of Workplace Violence*. "According to this report, Mrs. Scorrelli pulled her IV out, hit nurses in the face, kicked a security guard. The staff finally got her under control. They sedated her, but she went into cardiac arrest and died."

"I didn't hear about that," Migs said.

"It happened before your time in the coroner's office," Piper said. "Dez and Mark might not even have heard about it. The death didn't happen in Dominguez County."

"Did they determine the cause of death?" Fenway said.

Piper shook her head. "They never did an autopsy."

"They never did an autopsy?"

"No," Piper said. She clicked another window. "The report says that the next of kin refused an autopsy on religious grounds. And the judge ruled that the state didn't make a compelling enough case to justify overturning the wishes of the family."

"I can't really believe the judge would rule that way," said Fenway. "An old woman going crazy and attacking nurses? Don't they pretty much make you do an autopsy when something like that happens? I figure they'd make the family agree to open you up to figure out why you died."

"I downloaded the judge's decision," Piper said. "I don't understand it, but that's what it is."

Fenway looked at her crowded monitor. "Holy crap, Piper, how many windows do you have open?"

Piper blushed. "I like to be thorough."

"Okay, so they issued the payment—what date? The fifteenth?"

Piper nodded.

"Two days after Mrs. Scorrelli died."

"Yes. And the same day before the lawsuit got filed that stopped the autopsy."

"And let me guess," Fenway said, "it was filed by Alan Scorrelli."

Migs looked adoringly at Piper. "You're awesome," he said.

Fenway rolled her eyes. "You know, guys, I thought the disgusting level of hormonal attraction would stop when you two got together for real. If anything, you two have gotten more gross. Especially for those of us who are going through summer without a summer fling."

Piper blushed. "Sorry. But one more thing," she said. "I haven't been able to find any money changing hands between Fletcher Jenkins and Alan Scorrelli. It's possible that Scorrelli used one of his many aliases, but I would think I would have found it by now. It's not like he used any brand-new aliases in the last couple of months. Otherwise he would have shown up with the new IDs, right?"

"Probably," Fenway said, scrunching up her face, "but not necessarily. He might have had his bank account under a name he kept totally clean."

Piper shrugged. "At any rate, I haven't found anything that looks even remotely suspicious."

"Okay," Fenway said, "any other strange payments?"

"There are several," Piper said. "I've flagged about thirty-five payments so far. There are some that I don't think I'm going to be able to get to the bottom of, though. This is some first-class financial obfuscation."

"All right," Fenway said. "Let me know if any of those payments come through, Piper. Excellent work."

"And Fenway," said Piper, "let me know if any of that information leads to anything else you want me to look up. This is sure a lot more interesting than fixing Officer Callahan's blue screen of death."

"Yeah," Fenway said, "the bad guys always keep it interesting."

Fenway and Migs walked out.

"What do you suppose that hundred and fifty thousand was for?" asked Migs.

Fenway shook her head. "Probably hush money," she mused. "Although I don't know why. Maybe SRB holdings is a front for some insurance company for off-the-books payments."

"Maybe the mayor found out what they were doing," Migs said.

Fenway stopped. "Of course," she said. "I don't know why I didn't see it earlier. Fletch is an accountant. I wonder if he uncovered something. Maybe he audited a company that tied to SRB holdings and he ticked off the wrong person."

"I heard they're still holding Fletch," Migs said. "They've got to let him go soon, don't they?"

"Well," Fenway said, 'it's not that easy. He's got some issues—his confession, first of all. The police really don't like letting someone go who's already confessed. Especially if they haven't recanted."

"But they can't think that he hired—"

"That's exactly what they think," Fenway replied.

When they walked back into the coroner's office, Fenway's phone rang. She looked in her purse; the phone screen illuminated Rachel's key. Fenway had forgotten to give it back to Dez.

She pulled the phone out and looked at the screen; it was the medical examiner's office.

"Hi, Dr. Yasuda," Fenway said.

"Good afternoon, Fenway," Dr. Yasuda said, sounding jittery.

"Did you find something, Doctor?"

"You'll have to excuse my excitement, but it's not often there's a first in my line of work."

"A first?"

"Yes. The first time I've ever found *pheasant* in someone's stomach."

"Whose?"

"The mayor's," Dr. Yasuda said. "I haven't yet started work on that unfortunate man you found in the trunk. Hard to specify time of death on that one with all the temperature fluctuations, though. Did you see Kavish's initial report at the scene?"

"No, I was busy answering questions."

"Fair enough," Dr. Yasuda said. "Kavish puts the time of death sometime yesterday evening, between five and seven P.M."

"Well—hold on, Doctor, tell me about the mayor's stomach contents."

"Sure, I'm sorry I got distracted. The mayor's last meal consisted of pheasant, sweet potatoes, zucchini and yellow squash. Some red wine too. Traces of figs and honey, lots of butter."

"Maxime's," Fenway said.

"What?"

"Maxime's," Fenway repeated. "It's a fancy restaurant here in Estancia. Apparently, it's the only place on the whole Central Coast that you can get pheasant."

"Oh, I don't think that's true," Dr. Yasuda said. "I had a wonderful pheasant Normandy down in Santa Barbara last year." She sighed. "In better times."

"Yes—I know what you're talking about. It's a French place, but they took the pheasant off the menu a few months ago," Fenway said. "My father is a huge fan of pheasant. I just had this conversation with him a couple of days ago—apparently it's prepared with some sort of avocado brandy."

Dr. Yasuda was silent on the other end of the line.

"Anyway, thanks for the call, Doctor. Now I at least have a place to start looking to piece together the mayor's timeline that night."

CHAPTER EIGHTEEN

DEZ DROVE FENWAY TO MAXIME'S. THE RESTAURANT WAS CLOSED, it being too early for dinner, but they walked around back and found the door open and the chefs preparing for the evening's dinner service.

"Mademoiselle!" said a familiar face. "Good to see you again! Tell me how brilliant I am—that infused pale ale paired deliciously with the corn soup, did it not?"

Fenway blinked as the name came back to her: Eric The Sommelier. He had served her and Nathaniel Ferris during their first meal out together when Fenway arrived in town. "Eric!" she said. "It's good to see you again."

"You're not with your father," Eric said, "so I assume you're not here to make reservations."

"No," Fenway said.

Dez pulled her badge out. "I'm afraid to say we're here on official business."

The look on Eric's face stuck halfway between dismay and curiosity. "I'm not sure what we can do here, Officer," Eric The Sommelier said, "but of course I'll do everything I can to help."

"We appreciate that," said Dez drily. Eric The Sommelier's charms didn't affect her. "So let's get to it. Your name is Eric?"

"Right. Eric Dreyfuss. Eric with a 'c.'"

"Were you working here on Friday night?"

"Certainly," Eric said. "Friday and Saturday nights are my best tip nights—I'm here every chance I get."

Dez opened her notebook. "Did the mayor eat here that night?"

"Oh—yes. I was so sad to hear what happened to her. I saw the article online on Monday. I don't normally keep up with current events on the weekends—too busy with work. But we're closed on Mondays, and I finally got to it then."

Dez's pen moved quickly. "Did she eat with anyone?"

"Oh, yes. A well-dressed, very handsome man, probably in his mid-forties. Very sharp dresser. Grey suit with fine black pin-stripes, a white dress shirt, and a purple floral tie."

"White guy?" Fenway asked.

"Yes," Eric replied. "I guess I should have said."

"I probably don't have to ask you if you'd recognize him if you saw him again."

"Or smell him," Eric said.

"What, did the guy have B.O.?"

"Just the opposite," Eric said. "I don't usually notice cologne or perfume, but man, this guy just smelled fantastic."

"Wait," Fenway said. "I wonder..." She took out her phone and brought up her web browser. She went to the Carpetti Pharmaceuticals website and loaded their management page. "Sorry—it's loading."

"Can I continue, Zuckerberg?" Dez said.

"Almost have it—there!" Fenway turned her phone around to Eric. A picture of Everett Michaels appeared onscreen.

"Oh yes, that's him," Eric The Sommelier said.

"You're sure?" Fenway said.

"Of course I'm sure."

"So you dealt with their table?" Dez said.

"Eric's the sommelier," Fenway said. "Who was the server?"

Eric blinked. "That's a good question." He rubbed his chin. "Both Malik and Nyla were working that night. I honestly don't remember which one served them."

"Are either of them here?" Dez asked

"No," Eric said, "I think Malik is working the dinner shift tonight. Nyla only works the weekend. I *do* remember that Mr. Smellsgood there ordered one of our most expensive bottles—a Lokoya Cabernet, which I tried to encourage against. Not a good wine to pair with the pheasant that the mayor ordered. But good enough for the bone-in filet that *he* ordered. We have a lovely Syrah that pairs with both dishes. But the mayor waved me off."

"Waved you off?" Dez kept scribbling.

"Their conversation turned heated pretty quickly. It's not like they screamed at each other, but they definitely disagreed. I remember at one point, Mr. Smellsgood excused himself to make a call. When he came back, I walked up to pour him another glass and top off the mayor. As I reached their table, she told him that he needed to make something right."

"What does that mean?"

"I'm sure I don't know. But I heard the mayor clearly. 'You're going to make it right.' He didn't answer her. Or maybe he waited to answer until I left their table. I had the feeling I shouldn't stick around."

"Does the mayor eat here often?" Dez folded over a page and continued writing.

"Enough so that I recognize her," Eric said. "But maybe only a few times a year. She's usually with business leaders. She's been here on her birthday. She and Demetrius used to come on their anniversary before he passed away."

"How about Mr. Smellsgood?" Fenway said. "Does he eat here often?"

"I don't remember seeing him here before," Eric said. "And I would think that I'd have recognized him."

Dez nodded. "Did you happen to catch any more of their conversation?"

"No," Eric said. "But about halfway through dinner, the mayor's phone rings. She took the call, got upset, talked to Mr. Smellsgood, and left the restaurant."

"How about Mr. Smellsgood?"

"He finished his steak, called for the check, and left."

"No dessert? No after-dinner whiskey?"

"No," Eric said, "but he did make a stink about our pen."

"Your pen?"

"It apparently didn't work right, and he made a stink about it. We offered to get him a new one, but he made a big show of signing it with his own special pen."

"Special? One of those four-color ballpoint pens? Those are cool."

Eric laughed. "He waved around some solid gold million-dollar fountain pen given to him in person by the Royal Duchess of Bullshit. He's one of these guys who thinks it's impressive to throw money around. And I'll tell you what else, he left half the bottle of Lokoya. That's a six-hundred dollar bottle."

"What did you do with the bottle?"

He looked around. No one paid any attention to their conversation. He lowered his voice. "What do you think? I corked it and took it home."

"Are you not supposed to do that?" Fenway asked.

"I'm not sure that it's expressly forbidden," Eric said, "but it is rather, well, *gauche*. But a Lokoya is a Lokoya. And we're talking about the Mt. Veeder, not the Howell Mountain. A much better match with steak."

"Oh, of course," Fenway deadpanned. "Not the Howell Mountain."

Eric smiled enthusiastically, mistaking her sarcasm for interest. "The Mt. Veeder is one of those special cabernets that actually has notes of steak—some say grilled, some say tartare. It's outstanding with a good cut of beef. The Howell Mountain is more herbal, notes of leather and chocolate. Don't get me wrong, it's a great wine, but—"

Dez put up her hand. "While Miss Stevenson here might be hanging on every word of your tasting master class, Eric, I'd like to get back to the events of that night."

"Right. Sorry."

"How did she leave? Did she have a car here?"

"That I don't know," Eric said. "It's possible that the hostess or the valets might know. But she left in a hurry, that's for sure."

"How about Mr. Smellsgood?" asked Fenway.

"I don't know that either," Eric said. "And you'll have to wait for the valets until tonight. I think Ashley hosted that night, though, and she's in the back."

"All right," Dez said. She looked over at Fenway, who gave her a face shrug. "I really appreciate you talking with us. Can you point us in Ashley's direction?"

"I'll have her come out," said Eric. "We're prepping for dinner so it'd be better if you two weren't in the kitchen. I don't want Ernesto to start getting too upset."

Eric The Sommelier stepped back into the food preparation area.

"What do you think, Fenway?" Dez asked.

"I think it's weird that Everett Michaels didn't say anything about having dinner with Alice Jenkins on the night she was killed," Fenway whispered. "I had brunch with him Sunday morning. If you have dinner the night someone is killed, don't you mention it to, well, everyone? Especially if it's a famous person?"

"The mayor's not a movie star," Dez said.

"Close enough for a town like Estancia."

"Even for a rich guy like Everett Michaels?"

"Sure," Fenway said. "Come on, you know as well as I do that most people see someone on the street who's found dead the next day and they're like, 'So sad what happened, I just saw him the day he died.' In fact, most people exaggerate and say they had lunch or played a game of Monopoly."

"Monopoly?"

Fenway rolled her eyes. "You know what I mean."

A smile touched Dez's lips.

"Hi," said a voice behind them. They turned around. An Asian woman, about five-foot-four and in her late twenties, looked at them. She had a round face, auburn streaks in her long black hair, a crisp white long-sleeved oxford shirt, and tight black trousers that Fenway thought were trying too hard to look like leggings. "I'm Ashley Park. Eric said you had some questions for me?"

"Right," Dez said. She cleared her throat. "Eric told us you worked the hostess stand on Friday night?"

Ashley tilted her head to the side. "That's right," she said, looking earnestly in Dez's face. "I worked that night. Is this about the mayor?"

"Yes," Dez said. Dez looked a little off kilter.

"Did the mayor come here that night?" Fenway asked.

"Yes," Ashley said breathily, nodding quickly. "I seated her and her dinner companion at table twenty-six. That's over by the fireplace. But she left early. I noticed that she got a phone call and then left in an awful hurry."

"Why do you think she rushed out?" Dez asked. She took a step forward and to the left, boxing Fenway off to the side.

"I don't know," Ashley said. "I didn't even have time to ask her if she needed anything. She just left. I saw her stand on the sidewalk, and then she took out her phone. I thought she probably got an Uber. Turns out the mayor is old-school—a taxi came up and took her away."

"Do you remember which taxi service? Yellow Cab, Lucky, Checker?"

Ashley frowned. "I didn't see the name on it. The cab was yellow, though."

They're all yellow, Fenway thought.

"That's okay," Dez said soothingly. "Did you see which way the taxi went?"

"They went off to the right, but I didn't see which way they went after that."

"Did she seem angry?"

"Not angry," Ashley said. "But, you know" —she lifted her hand and touched Dez on the arm— "she got agitated, and she seemed really distracted. I worried about her a little bit, if I can say so. She seemed in a hurry. I would have asked her if I could call someone, but once I saw her pull her phone out, I figured she had it under control."

"Can you remember anything else?" Dez asked gently. She didn't take her arm away from Ashley touching her. Fenway looked at Dez's arm, then looked at her face. It had an expression on it that Fenway didn't recognize. "What about the man she had dinner with?"

"*That* man, ugh," Ashley groaned. "He came in with the mayor, and while they were waiting for their table, he kept making small talk with me, hitting on me. He told me I had gorgeous eyes, and asked where I went to college." She shook her head. "I used to get that all the time at other restaurants. Usually it's not a problem here. Every so often there's a rich man who thinks I'll be all impressed with him." She lowered her voice conspiratorially to Dez. "Sometimes I get the feeling they'd get mad if they found out they're not even the right gender."

Dez nodded. "I hear you, girl," she said. "I got that in my younger days too."

"You don't get that now?" Ashley said, looking up at Dez with large, coquettish eyes.

Fenway turned away. She figured Dez could use the ego boost. She walked outside. The empty valet station on her right had a lectern that would have been right at home in a hotel banquet room.

She looked to her left at a coffee shop a couple of doors down. She thought perhaps she might have time to get a latte and be back before Ashley and Dez were done making googly eyes. She stood there for a moment in the late afternoon sun, like a cat that unexpectedly walked into a sunbeam.

She couldn't figure out why Everett Michaels wouldn't have told her or her father about having dinner with Alice Jenkins.

Dez came out behind her. "Okay, rookie?" she asked.

"You have a date later?" Fenway said, surprised to hear a touch of rancor in her own voice.

"Oh, now, just because you had your booty call broken up a few days ago doesn't mean you need to be all angry with me."

"You seriously asked her out?"

Dez clapped Fenway on the shoulder, almost jovially. "She asked *me* out. Me being a worldly mature woman and all. Plus I'm still hot."

Fenway thought about mentioning the age difference between Dez and Ashley, and then realized it was probably about the same as the difference between herself and McVie. Besides, Fenway reasoned, Ashley had asked Dez out, so she kept her mouth shut.

Dez was in a much better mood on the way back.

Fenway and Dez arrived back at the coroner's office just before four o'clock. They walked in and saw Piper talking to Migs at his desk. She looked up as soon as they walked in.

"Fenway," Piper said, "I'm glad you're here. I wanted to give you this as soon as possible."

"Sure, Piper," Fenway said. "Come on into my office."

"I'm going to ask Mark to get ahold of the taxi companies," Dez said. "See if we can figure out where they dropped her off."

Fenway nodded.

Piper picked up a folder and followed Fenway into her office and shut the door behind her. "Okay," she said excitedly, "I've found out some really interesting stuff."

"Lay it on me, sister," Fenway said.

"Okay. So first of all, I found an ad for clinical trial patients at Diego-Riley during the June and July time frame."

"A clinical trial for what?"

"A new pain reliever. I found an opinion article in a medical journal that called it 'oxycontin without the addictive properties.' It's got a long name that begins with N." She looked through the folder. "Nozith—uh, *Nozithrapham*."

Fenway paused. "Let me see that." Piper handed her folder to Fenway. "Huh. Nozithrapham. I've heard of that somewhere before." Then she snapped her fingers. "Of course—that's the new Carpetti drug. Everett Michaels talked my ear off about all the politics with clinical trials."

"Let me tell you what else I uncovered. This is about SRB. And, I think, it might relate to Nozithrapham too."

"Really?" Fenway said. "Okay, what did you find?"

"Do you remember in the news about a month ago, those two senators who were found to have overseas shell corporations?"

"Um, I guess so," Fenway said. "They weren't from California, were they?"

"No, Virginia and Oklahoma. So the Virginia guy had one called Delmarva Holdings. The one from Oklahoma had a shell company called Exterior Imports."

"Okay. I didn't remember that."

"Honestly, I didn't either, I just looked it up." Piper pulled a few sheets out of her folder. "So here are few transactional statements."

Fenway sat down at her desk. She laid the papers out in front of her. "All right," she said. "What am I looking for?"

"Look at the highlighted payments."

Fenway saw two scratches of bright yellow marker on the spreadsheet: one payment for $75,000, with the payee listed as Delmarva Holdings; the other payment also for $75,000, paid to Exterior Imports.

"So SRB paid off a couple of senators," Fenway said.

"Exactly," Piper said. "Now let's see what those two senators did around the time of the payments."

She pulled out two more papers. "Just about the only thing these two senators have in common is that they both sat in on an FDA panel last month. Now, I've got another $75,000 payment to an unidentified bank number. I traced the number to a Swiss bank account. But I ran into a brick wall there."

"I bet the FDA approved a new drug that week, right?"

"Yep. And I bet you can't guess which one."

"Nozithrapham."

Piper nodded.

"So what you're saying is that we've got two illicit payments to senators to grease the wheels for a new type of high-effectiveness pain reliever."

Piper nodded. "And we've got jurisdiction. The company that ran the clinical trial is local."

"Carpetti Pharmaceuticals."

"Right. And the manager of the clinical trial is some Austrian guy—Gottfried Ebner."

Fenway pinched her eyes shut. "Oh, dammit, Dad," she muttered to herself. "You're waking up with fleas again."

"What?"

"Everett Michaels," Fenway said. "The guy who talked to me about Nozithrapham. He and my father took me to breakfast on Sunday and we talked about drug testing and FDA approvals. And Gottfried Ebner. And Nozithrapham. It's the big release that is supposedly making a ton of money for Carpetti and allowed Michaels to quit so he could run for coroner."

"Do you think someone at Carpetti is behind the murder of the mayor?"

Fenway thought for a moment. "I guess the motive fits," she said. "But I don't have any proof that anyone at Carpetti committed that crime—or Rachel's attempted murder."

"And you don't have a murder weapon," Migs interrupted. "And—don't forget—you've got someone else who admitted to the crime."

"True," said Piper. "But someone at Carpetti could have paid Fletcher Jenkins to kill the mayor."

"I'm going to have to think more on this," said Fenway. "I just don't know yet." She sighed. "If Rachel would just come out of hiding, this could all go away."

"Do you think Rachel is even out there?" Piper said. "What if the murderer got to her first?"

"I can't think like that," Fenway said. She shook her head. "I can't believe she's in this much danger. And I can't believe she's still in hiding."

"Now that I've found out all this stuff about SRB," said Piper, "do you want me to try to figure out Rachel's whereabouts?"

"You think you can find Rachel?" Fenway said. "Do you have some sort of magic GPS? Hasn't she just been off the grid completely since yesterday?"

"No one's off the grid completely," said Piper. "I bet I can find some trail somewhere."

Fenway nodded. "Sure, if you think you can find her, then absolutely."

"I'm on it." Piper turned and left the office. Fenway hoped that Piper would be as good at finding Rachel as she had been at finding the payments to Alan Scorrelli from SRB.

Dez walked into to Fenway's office. "So, boss, I got something to tell you."

"What is it?"

"I think it's time for us to lose Barry Klein's paperwork and let him go."

Fenway paused. "Why would you do that?"

Dez said, "Part of it is political. I don't want you to get in any trouble for keeping one of your political enemies locked in jail for too long."

"Klein isn't my political enemy."

Dez looked out of the corner of her eye at Fenway. "If you don't think Klein is your enemy, you're more naïve than I thought," she said. "Klein has been itching to get you out of this position ever since you entered it."

"The sheriff was ready to appoint him," Fenway pointed out. "I'm just here to babysit it."

"Now you and I both know that isn't the whole truth," Dez said. "Come on, Fenway, you're not talking to the *Estancia Courier*, you're talking to me."

"Fine, he's my political enemy. Through no fault of my own. Is he getting arraigned, or are you just releasing him?"

"We're just releasing him—on one condition," Dez said.

"What's that?"

"He tells us where he got those photos."

Fenway blinked. "Yes. That's probably the best solution. I don't want anyone else to go through what I went through yesterday." Fenway paused. "Dez, I told my father. The two people I didn't want to know what I went through were my mother and my father. Well, my mom's dead, and my father knows now."

Dez paused. "How did your dad take it?"

Fenway looked down at her desk, not focusing on anything in particular. "Not well. Not well at all. And of course, he made it all about himself. How *he* couldn't handle it." She paused. "Not like I'd expect anything different."

Dez's face filled with compassion and concern.

"Don't look at me like that, Dez," Fenway said. "I can't even tell you how much I hate the fact that I had to tell him."

"I can only imagine," Dez said softly.

"Anyway, you have your date with Ashley to worry about. Do I need to deal with any paperwork for Klein?"

"Nope," Dez said. "Like I said, we seem to have lost the paperwork. But we should definitely remind him that we can find it all the way up to the statute of limitations. Which is ten years. And might even be longer after these California legislators get done with it."

"Wait—you want *me* to go over and release him?"

"Who better, really," Dez said. "And I want you to put the fear of God into him. He's an entitled sonofabitch and the county will be better off if he's taken down a rung or two."

"I can't say I disagree with that," Fenway said. "So—I've never gotten anyone out of jail before. Do I just go over there and get him out?"

"Sometimes I forget what a newbie you are," Dez said. "All right, I'll go with you. You need the right form." She stood up and went to the open office area where she opened one of the file drawers. She pulled a piece of paper out of one of the folders and came back into Fenway's office.

"Here it is, Form 378B, release of detained individual." Dez put the form down on the desk between them, reached across the desk, and took one of Fenway's pens. Under "Detainee's name," she scrawled "KLEIN BARRY," not taking care to stay within the boxes for each of the letters. She ignored much of the rest of the form, only checking "Lost Paperwork" under "reason for release."

"Okay," she said. "Let's head over."

"That's all you're going to fill out?" Fenway asked, incredulous.

"You think Dr. Klein's going to complain?" Dez said. "Come on, let's see if we can get him home in time for dinner."

They walked across the street to the jail behind the sheriff's office. Quincy was working at the front table again, and he buzzed them both in.

"Hey, Aunt Dez," Quincy said.

"Hey, Big Q," Dez said.

"You making it over for Sunday dinner?"

Dez shook her head. "Not unless we catch who did Mayor Alice. Tell your momma I'll be working this weekend."

"You work too much, Aunt Dez."

"Aw, now, don't be like that," Dez said. "You're gonna break my heart."

Quincy raised his head in greeting. "Hey, Fenway. What can I do for you two lovely ladies this afternoon?"

"We're here for the release of Dr. Barry Klein," Dez said.

"Oh, and he's been having so much fun in here," Quincy said. "You sure he has to check out?"

"I'm all torn up about it," Fenway said drily. "But yes. It seems like it's probably the right thing to do."

Quincy took the paper from Dez and looked at it. "All right," he said. "Looks like everything is in order. I'll bring him out."

"Great," Fenway said. "We should accompany him back to his vehicle."

"Oh, I forgot to tell you, Fenway," Dez said. "There's no overnight parking in the structure. They towed his car last night. It's in impound."

Fenway nodded. Klein deserved it—he probably deserved worse.

"It's too bad that the impound lot closes at five," Dez said. "He won't be able to get it until tomorrow, and he'll have to pay storage fees for another day."

"What a shame," Fenway said.

They waited for a few minutes in the pale blue fluorescent light of the room. Only the faint buzz of the lights augmented the silence with Dez.

After several minutes, the door opened and Klein came out. He wore his day-old clothes and he rubbed his wrists. Quincy followed him and closed the door behind them. Klein's eyes, rimmed with dark circles, raised to look at Dez and Fenway. He had a cut on one cheek and his mouth turned down. His feet shuffled forward. Quincy had him stop in front of Dez.

Dez screwed up her mouth and clicked her tongue against her teeth.

"Barry Jacob Klein," Quincy recited, unlocking Klein's handcuffs, "I hereby release you into the custody of Sergeant Desirée Roubideaux."

"Thanks, Quincy," Dez said quietly.

"You're welcome," Quincy said, retreating back behind the door.

Dez looked at Klein. He dropped his eyes and started rubbing his wrists. "Am I free to go?" he asked. His voice had lost its earlier chiding, churlish tone.

Dez closed her eyes for just a moment, then opened them. "If it were up to me, Dr. Klein," she said softly, "you'd be in here a long time. It's absolutely disgusting what you did."

"I know," Dr. Klein said. "I just—" and then he thought better of it and shut his mouth.

Dez pretended not to hear the last part. "Miss Stevenson didn't think it was right to keep you locked up," she said. "Even though possessing pictures like that of a seventeen-year-old is punishable by a long jail term, a permanent sex offender status on your record, and, I hope, reason for your wife to take away your children and never speak to you again." She tapped her foot. "Plus, they don't treat people who are convicted of that kind of stuff too well in the prison system."

"I know," Klein said again.

"As much as it pains me to do it," Dez said, "I'm releasing you. But on one condition."

"What's that?"

"You tell us where you got those pictures."

Klein's lips drew into a snarl, but then he dropped his eyes. "Oppo research."

"What?" Fenway asked.

"Opposition research. I hired a firm out of L.A. to dig up dirt on Fenway. I thought for sure she'd throw her hat in the ring."

"And who found it?" Dez questioned.

"One of their data analysts, I guess."

"Is that a euphemism for *hacker*?"

Klein shrugged.

"Okay, Dr. Klein," Dez said, "You're going to send us the contact information of the opposition research firm you engaged. I want you to tell them to share what they know with us. Currently, we seem to have accidentally lost your paperwork before your arraignment. Which means no charges filed. Nothing on your record."

Klein nodded. "Thank you," he said.

"But if we don't get that contact information in forty-eight hours," Fenway said, "I'm pretty sure we'll be able to find that paperwork again. We were looking all over this morning for it. Maybe it's in somebody's desk drawer."

Klein swallowed. "I understand."

"Would you like to call someone to come pick you up?" asked Dez.

Klein nodded. "My wife."

Fenway handed her cell phone to Klein, who dialed. He walked over to the corner and spoke in low tones, and then hung up, walked back over and sheepishly handed the phone to Fenway.

"Thanks," he murmured.

"Shall we wait outside?" Dez suggested. "It's such a beautiful day."

Fenway and Dez led Klein outside. They stood on the sidewalk and Klein took a few steps forward, into an empty parking space. They waited in silence for ten minutes. She could see Klein shift his weight uncomfortably from foot to foot, and steal awkward glances over his shoulder to Fenway from time to time. He started forward when a silver Toyota Camry pulled into the lot, but he soon recognized that it wasn't his wife's car.

Finally, he took a couple of steps back, next to Fenway. "I'm sorry," he said. "I know saying that isn't enough, and I know you probably think I'm just sorry I had to spend the night in jail. But please know that I'm truly sorry."

"You're right, Dr. Klein," Fenway said, "that isn't enough."

Dr. Klein stepped forward again, and another awkward silence ensued.

Finally, another silver Camry pulled into the lot, and this time, Fenway saw Dr. Klein's wife behind the wheel.

"But I suppose it's better than nothing," Fenway said.

Dr. Klein swallowed hard and nodded.

The Camry pulled up next to him and he went forward, opened the door, and got in. Fenway looked at his wife, who wouldn't look at her or at Klein. He didn't even have time to reach back for his seatbelt before she pulled away.

CHAPTER NINETEEN

PIPER STARED AT THE SCREEN. "SO, FENWAY, I THINK I'VE uncovered something interesting. Maybe a little disturbing."

Fenway blinked. "What are we looking at?"

"Rachel's email," Piper replied.

"Are we allowed to do this?"

"I've got admin access—*I'm* allowed to do this," Piper said, "and since you're investigating the attempts on her life, I hereby give you permission to review Rachel Richards' email."

"Jeez, Migs is rubbing off on you."

Piper looked at her sideways.

"Oh, gross, Piper. You know what I mean."

Piper giggled. "Okay, here's Rachel's emails the week before the fake suicide attempt."

Fenway scanned through the first couple of pages. "I'm not seeing anything relevant in here at all."

"Right," Piper said, nodding. "There's nothing in here that pertains to SRB Holdings, or Rachel's meeting with the mayor and her son."

"Yeah. So we're out of luck?"

"Look what *is* here. Lots of communications back and forth on all of Rachel's other to-dos. The concert in the park series. The symphony funding drive. The communications to reporters, everything. It's obvious that Rachel's preferred form of work communication is email."

"It's not that surprising. She's new in her job and she is interested in documenting everything, to make sure everything's on the up and up."

"Sure," Piper said, "that's what I thought too. And you see who's copied on every single work email."

"Sure, Natalie Andrada. Rachel's admin. That makes total sense. She'd want to be copied on everything. Did you know she's a former Marine?"

Piper nodded. "Yes. I met her on Rachel's first day. She's really quite fantastic. Ruthlessly efficient. Way overqualified for that job."

"Sure," Fenway agreed. "So why are alarm bells going off for you?"

"Does it strike you as odd that there isn't anything at all on the meeting with Alice Jenkins and her son?"

"Not if she tried to keep it quiet."

"But there's nothing. Nothing to hold her calls. Nothing to ask Natalie to cancel her other appointments that night. Nothing to even say to go home at five as usual, or to stay late, or anything."

"Maybe—" Fenway said, and stopped.

"Why would there be no communication with the guardian of your schedule when you have a big stick of dynamite exploding your whole afternoon like this?" Piper asked.

"Because Natalie sat in the meeting too," Fenway said.

"Right," Piper said. "That's the only thing I can think of."

"But," Fenway protested, "Natalie didn't say anything about..." Then her voice trailed off.

"So why didn't Natalie say anything about the meeting?" Piper said. "We've been pulling our hair out because we can't talk to

Rachel about what went on in that meeting. But Natalie was in it and didn't say anything?"

"I can't for the life of me think why she wouldn't say anything."

"It's certainly suspicious," Piper said, "so I did a little digging into Natalie Andrada."

"Oh no," Fenway said.

Piper shook her head. "Whatever you're thinking, this isn't it." She clicked a few windows and took a deep breath.

"Okay."

"So you know how you had Kav send over those finger-print sets—that classified one, and that one from the other Marine?"

"Sure. Elena something."

"Valenzuela," Piper replied, clicking on the screen. Natalie Andrada's face appeared—a decade younger, and with short, cropped hair.

"Did Natalie serve in Elena's unit?"

"No," Piper said. "You're looking at a picture of Elena Valenzuela."

Fenway gaped.

"Elena Valenzuela is a native of San Marcos, Texas."

"Not local to California?"

"No," Piper replied. "She's on the GI Bill. Goes to UT San Antonio, studies mechanical engineering. Then goes through basic training, gets a year at Fort Davis up in Tacoma, then gets shipped to Afghanistan. On her second tour, a roadside IED gets her a Purple Heart and an honorable discharge."

"So why did she change her name and take an administrative position for the county here?"

"Exactly my question," Piper said. "And after she got out of the hospital, with a few weeks' less of rehab than expected, she pretty much vanishes."

"Really?"

"Yes. Nothing. We don't get her applying for jobs, or postgrad programs, or VA assistance. No record of where she's living. No record of any of her movements."

"No clues at all to what she did when she got out?"

Piper tapped the screen. "Except for this, three years after her release."

Fenway blinked and looked at the screen. The photo showed a table in a fancy restaurant with a couple, dressed to the nines, smiling for the camera. "I don't get it. Who are these people?"

"You remember a news story about *El Magnate*?"

Fenway squinted at the picture. "Sure. Well—I don't remember it, but Kav and Melissa were telling me about him. About seven or eight years ago, right?"

"Close enough."

"They arrested some big-shot tech CEO as the kingpin of some major drug cartel."

"Right," Piper said. "But not for cocaine or heroin or meth—opioids. Oxycontin, Norco, all that stuff. He had a huge network of doctors to skim just a few bottles each. But on a massive scale."

"Is this *El Magnate*?"

"Yes. This is a picture taken of him and his wife—not twenty-four hours before his arrest." Piper tapped the face of a woman who was sitting behind the couple. "Now look closer at the picture."

Fenway leaned over Piper's shoulder. At first she struggled to arrange the slightly out-of-focus features in her head, the woman's light brown hair, the elegant evening gown. Then she saw the handle of a wheelchair behind her shoulder and recognized the face, despite the heavy application of makeup. "Oh. That's Natalie."

Piper nodded.

Fenway stood up. "Was Natalie—or Elena, or whoever she is—part of their opioid cartel?"

Piper paused. "It could be a coincidence, the photo of her in that restaurant. But that's a big coincidence."

"She doesn't look like herself."

"You probably looked different nine years ago, too."

Fenway nodded. "Do you think she used the opioids for pain after her injury? Maybe they realized she'd be valuable with her military background?"

Piper hesitated. "I don't know. I guess that's how she could have gotten involved. I mean, *if* she got involved."

"And now, with Nozithrapham coming onto the market, she's aligning everything so she can be the new kingpin, now that *El Magnate* is taken down?"

"That theory fits," Piper said glumly.

"But you're not convinced."

"I mean, it's a photograph in a restaurant." Piper pursed her lips. "There could be a hundred reasons why she's there. Maybe it's a friend's birthday, maybe her boyfriend took her to a fancy dinner."

"Where's the restaurant?"

"It's in a rich little suburb of San Jose, where that tech CEO had his above-board company. Little town called Los Gatos. Apparently, the high school there is next to a Ferrari dealership."

Fenway nodded. "So how did she get there without leaving a financial footprint?"

Piper tapped her fingers on the desk. "I have some ideas, but no evidence. She might have been able to live under an alias for a few years, for instance. She obviously changed her name here— and convincingly enough to get a government job. I'm sure she left a trail of aliases, which would have left a financial footprint somewhere I'm not looking."

Fenway thought back to her conversation with Natalie. "She tried to get me and McVie to ignore 'SRB' when we found it on the Post-It on Rachel's monitor," she mused. "She said it must stand for one of Rachel's PR things—State Research Board or something like that."

"Well," Piper said, "if that is the case—if Natalie really is the kingpin behind some new white-collar painkiller drug organization, then she's probably got all kinds of backup. People willing to do her dirty work for her."

"Yes," Fenway agreed. "Including hiring someone to shoot up a hospital and try to kill her boss." *And including hiring the man in the track suit to kidnap the mayor's granddaughter, and stab the mayor*, Fenway thought. Although who knew what she hired out and what she did herself. Fenway suspected that Natalie had more physical strength and agility than most people who still had their legs. She wouldn't put it past her to have killed the mayor and the private investigator herself. The wheelchair, an old-lady crocheted blanket over her shoulders to hide her chiseled upper-body muscles, and maybe even a gray wig would have given the impression of a weak, infirm person—not a kick-ass former Marine on the wrong side of the law.

"What do you think we should do?" Fenway said. If a rogue with military knowledge wanted to take over a prescription-based drug organization in her county, she could barely wait to get started on the case.

Piper shook her head. "I have absolutely no idea. We don't have any evidence—just some stuff that looks shady, and a suspect with an empty space where her past should be."

Fenway felt a familiar surge of adrenaline—she hadn't felt like this since she found out that Robert Stotsky was Rachel's father. She hadn't had evidence then either—but she pushed forward, manipulated the situation, and got Stotsky to reveal himself as the murderer that night.

"We should definitely talk to Miss Andrada—or Valenzuela," Fenway said. "She's been caught in a lie to the sheriff, at least. That might shake something loose."

Piper frowned.

"What is it?" Fenway asked.

"If you're not sure of her involvement—and you're not," she said sharply when Fenway tried to interrupt, "then you're not going to be able to get backup from the sheriff's department—or the DEA, or the SWAT team, or whatever you need to make sure this woman isn't going to pull you inside and cut your throat."

"I don't think—"

"Let me finish, Fenway." Piper stood up. "You were lucky Rachel came for you when Stotsky went after you. You were lucky she brought a gun. And you were *really* lucky she was willing to shoot her own father to protect you." She put her hands on her hips. "If Natalie Andrada is as dangerous as her dossier would leave me to believe, you're not going to go in there with McVie and ride out with Rachel."

I'm more worried about Olivia, Fenway thought.

So Fenway pressed forward. "But she doesn't know we know," she said. "She won't be able to tell that we think she's got Rachel. She won't be on her guard."

"How many Marines have you met?" Piper said. "My ex's older brother served in Iraq as a Marine. He's always on guard. He's *always* going to think that people are after him. He says he can relax, but you just look at him—especially if you knew him before—and he's changed. He's never going relax again in his life." Piper shook her head. "I don't think Natalie's ever going to be the same either. Especially since she lost both legs over there. It's a constant reminder that one second—*one second*—off your guard can ruin your life forever. Every morning when she swings her legs out of bed and her feet don't touch the floor."

Fenway didn't say anything.

"You think you're going to go in there with your clever questions and my list of stuff that 'doesn't quite add up' and *rattle* her?

That woman's been through hell, Fenway. You and your questions won't even rate as a blip on her radar. She could stab you in the neck and be a different person in another state tomorrow. Don't forget that."

"*If* she's the one who did it," Fenway said weakly.

"You're not going to find out anything going to her house," Piper said. "It's just five o'clock now. You might be able to go over to Rachel's office, see if Natalie is still there. Pretend you need to go through her desk one more time. Really casually ask a few questions. That might be worth it. But you need to be careful. You have a good win under your belt, but you can't let on why you're there. You're still new at this."

"I'm not *that* new at this," Fenway protested.

"Oh, come on, Fenway. I'm only twenty-four and I've been at this for a year longer than you. If it were me, I'd take Dez or Mark along."

Fenway nodded. "I guess that would be a good idea."

Piper sat back down. "I know you trust your gut, especially after last time, but just be careful," she said softly.

Fenway rushed back to the coroner's office. Migs had just packed up for the day, and Mark was on the phone.

"How's everything going?" Fenway asked.

"Dez called it quits at five," Migs said. "She said she had a pretty rough day." He thought for a second. "Although she was in a *really* good mood when she left."

"Did Mark get any information on the taxi that picked up Mayor Jenkins from the restaurant?"

"He's been on the phone for over an hour," Migs said. "I think he wants to talk with you, so don't leave yet."

"Gotcha."

"I've been on the phone trying to figure out if we could get a warrant for any of Carpetti Pharmaceuticals' financials."

Fenway nodded. "I guess that's a pretty good idea," she admitted.

"Isn't that still the main theory of the crime?" Migs said.

"I have a slightly different take on it," Fenway said. "It has to do with the black market for their new painkiller."

"Okay," Migs said. "Should I call off the dogs?"

Fenway thought a moment. In spite of what her gut was telling her, she had to admit that she should still get financials for Carpetti Pharmaceuticals. "No, don't call them off just yet. Are you having any luck?"

"I tried Martinez and Wainwright first," Migs said. "Thought they'd be most likely to weigh the interest of the state heavily. It might be a long shot, but all the other judges are longer shots. Neither of them were in—Martinez is in probate court until five-thirty. I'm hoping to get a call back then—I left my cell number with the clerk."

"Okay, good work, Migs," Fenway said. "I've got to head over to Rachel's office. Try to see if there's any paperwork that we missed or anything like that."

"Need anything else before I go?" Migs said.

"Just give me a call if the warrant for Carpetti's financials comes through," Fenway said, opening the office door. "I want to get on that as soon as we can. Wake up a financial forensics specialist if we need to."

"Good night, Fenway."

"Good luck, Migs."

Migs walked out just as Mark hung up the phone.

"You have some information for me, Sergeant?"

Mark nodded. "I do, but it's not about the taxi. I haven't been able to locate it yet—I think I might have to go down to the cab companies to look at their log books. But I did finally get the phone records back. Mayor Jenkins did get a call that night, but we traced it to a burner phone."

Fenway thought for a minute. "That doesn't really tell us much. Did you get any information about the burner?"

Mark said, "It was purchased in Texas."

Fenway paused. "Bought in Texas?" She thought of Elena Valenzuela of San Marcos, Texas. "Does it say when?"

"Two weeks ago," Mark said.

"That doesn't make sense."

"It does if Alan Patrick Scorrelli bought it," Mark said. "He had a Texas driver's license. We're still running down where he flew in from, but my money is on Dallas. The phone was purchased from a convenience store in McKinney."

"Is that near Dallas?"

"More or less."

Fenway wondered if Natalie had known Scorrelli in Texas—an awfully big state, however.

"Do you know where San Marcos is?" Fenway said, trying to sound as casual as possible.

"Between Austin and San Antonio. Hundreds of miles from McKinney. Why? You got a person of interest in San Marcos?"

"No, I just don't know Texas geography as well as I should." Fenway thanked Mark and walked across the street to City Hall, lost in thought. She wondered what she would use for a cover story if she walked into Rachel's office and found Natalie working late. What would she need to uncover in Rachel's office? Maybe she could get in there with the idea that Fletch might have been acting threatening in the meeting. As far as anyone knew, besides her office mates and McVie, Fletch was still the guilty party. Gathering evidence of his whereabouts that day would be standard procedure. And she didn't think Kav or Melissa had dusted for fingerprints in Rachel's office. It gave her a great excuse to do it herself.

She got to the City Hall building and decided to take a sharp right and go to the sheriff's office instead. She opened the door and found herself face to face with Officer Donald Huke.

"Officer Huke," she said.

"Miss Stevenson."

"I need a favor, Don—Officer."

"What do you need? Car won't start or something?"

"No, Officer Huke, I need a fingerprint kit and gloves right now. It's time sensitive."

Officer Huke hesitated. "I don't know, Miss Stevenson. You've usually got to fill out a form. You can take some from your office, can't you?"

"I've got to get into Rachel's office right now," Fenway said, "and it just dawned on me that no one has dusted her keyboard or her desk for fingerprints, even though the mayor met with Rachel on Wednesday afternoon."

"That doesn't necessarily mean anything," Officer Huke said.

"Of course not," Fenway said, growing impatient. "But are you going to follow the rules to the exact letter, or are you going to follow the spirit of the rules and help me get those fingerprints lifted tonight?"

"It can't wait till tomorrow?"

"The cleaning crew comes in tonight," Fenway said, although she had no idea if that was true. "Tonight's their night to do a full wipe-down of the office. If we don't do it tonight, any evidence we could've collected will be lost."

Officer Huke nodded. "Okay, give me just a second." He turned and sprinted to another office. In that moment, Fenway could see what Melissa saw in him.

He returned less than a minute later. "I'll go back and fill out the paperwork," he said. "Go."

"Thank you," Fenway said, feeling a little guilty for her lie. "I won't forget this."

"Just make sure Fletcher Jenkins doesn't walk," he said. "The more evidence against him, the better. You'd be surprised how many confessions get thrown out of court."

She nodded and ran back to City Hall. She sprinted upstairs and opened the door to the communication director's office.

Natalie looked up from behind the desk. "Oh, Miss Stevenson," she said. "I didn't expect you—I was just about to pack up and leave."

"Yes," Fenway said, a little out of breath, "that's why I rushed over. I wanted to catch you before you left. I wanted to look at a few other things in Rachel's office. See if I could find anything I missed the first time."

"I hate to do this," Natalie said, "but I really should get home. This can't wait until tomorrow? I'm already a little late getting out of here."

"I hope I won't be too long," Fenway said.

"Isn't that a fingerprint kit?" Natalie pointed out. "Won't that take you at least an hour?"

"Well, maybe I can lock up."

Natalie shook her head and winced. "After what happened with Rachel, I don't really trust anyone else to do that."

"Of course. I understand. Maybe I don't have to do the fingerprint kit tonight. Maybe I can just check the drawers and the desk one more time."

Natalie sighed. "Listen, Miss Stevenson, I appreciate that Rachel's your friend, and she's missing and you're trying to be thorough. But I bet you've been going through the wringer. Get a good night's sleep. I'll come in early tomorrow if you want—seven-thirty, maybe? And I'll open up the office and you can spend all morning in there if you want. Honestly, I've had a tough day, and when I'm stressed out I start feeling pain in limbs I don't have anymore."

Fenway hesitated, turning it over in her mind, then nodded. "Right. You're right. I have been going crazy with this investigation—first Mayor Jenkins' death, then the attempt on Rachel's life, then her disappearing after the shooting in the hospital. I just want to get this solved before anyone else is in danger."

"Look," Natalie said, leaning forward on her desk, and lowering her voice, "I get it. I served in Afghanistan. I know what it's like when you need to do a job, and just feel powerless, like you can't get your job done, and there's nothing you can do about it. You think you're not worthy of Valhalla. Everything you try feels like running in quicksand."

Fenway nodded.

"You're going to look back on this time, and you're going to realize you were working your *ass* off," Natalie continued. "You're going to wonder where you got the energy to press forward when it looked like there weren't any more stones to turn over, like there were no clues left, and I don't doubt that you will find her. And, Fenway, you *will* be worthy of Valhalla."

Fenway turned Natalie's words over in her head. This conversation had started out the way she had been expecting—trying to get Fenway out of the office—but she didn't expect these words of encouragement.

"But just like I needed in Afghanistan," Natalie said, "you've got to give yourself a break. You've got to slow yourself down. Your brain will thank you. You'll see everything from a different angle in the morning. You might even find the breakthrough you need."

Fenway swallowed hard. "Thanks, Natalie," she said. "That's just what I needed to hear." Fenway meant it—although she didn't trust the messenger. She said goodbye to Natalie, who grabbed her purse and briefcase, and rolled out the door right behind her.

CHAPTER TWENTY

FENWAY AND NATALIE TOOK THE ELEVATOR DOWN TO THE ground floor together. Fenway felt the awkward silence and thought that she should say something, but after the advice that Natalie had given her, she couldn't think what to say. Fenway didn't know what to make of the ex-Marine—she knew that Natalie had a fake identity and had at least some involvement in the murder and the attempt on Rachel's life. But no evidence linked her to the recent goings-on. She didn't even act cagey.

Fenway could see that Natalie felt the awkward silence too, but she could tell it didn't bother her. Fenway felt relief when the elevator dinged to signal their arrival on the ground floor. As the doors opened, she saw motion through the front windows of City Hall in the half-circle of steps that formed the small amphitheater area.

"Is there a play going on there tonight?" Fenway asked Natalie. "I didn't think the Shakespeare in the Park people started until eight."

"It's not them," Natalie said. "There are cameras out there. Looks like a press conference."

Fenway looked at the bowl of the amphitheater and balked. Barry Klein.

He had cleaned up and looked a million times better than he had that afternoon when he had been released. "What's he doing?" Fenway murmured.

She walked outside, holding the door open for Natalie, who turned toward the parking structure. "You're not going to stay for this?" Fenway asked.

"Not on your life," Natalie laughed. "This smacks of political theater. And if you haven't noticed, I tend to lose parts of my body when politics are involved." She wheeled herself away from the amphitheater. Fenway watched her go, and then saw Migs standing on the top step of the amphitheater, all the way on the right-hand side. Barry Klein, dressed in a black suit with a red and blue striped tie standing out against a white dress shirt—subtle, Fenway thought—tested his microphone, and the babble of the small crowd started to die down. His wife stood by his side, in a soft gray blazer and matching skirt that went to mid-calf. Fenway walked over to where Migs leaned against a concrete pillar.

"I thought you went home," she said quietly.

"Piper just had to finish up a couple of things," Migs whispered back. "And I saw this and got curious. So I stuck around." He looked at Fenway and searched her face. "Did you get what you needed?"

Fenway closed her hand around the fingerprint kit in her purse. "Not yet. Tomorrow morning." She squinted at Klein. "What do you think he's doing? Do you think he's announcing his run for coroner?"

"I hope not," Migs said. "I kind of thought that after what happened to him, he'd resign from the board of supervisors."

Fenway pursed her lips. She had a bad feeling about this.

Klein's wife stepped up to the podium microphone. "Ladies and gentlemen, we're ready to get started," she said in a clear, strong voice. "I'd like to introduce you to a member of the county board of supervisors, an experienced doctor, a business owner, and a pillar of our community—and my husband for the last ten years. Dr. Barry Klein." She took a few steps back as her husband walked forward and took his place at the microphone.

Fenway looked around during the polite applause from the small crowd. She counted only two photographers, and she recognized them from the *Estancia Courier* and the *Independent Voice*. There were a couple of reporters there too. One of them, an older heavyset man with a white mustache, scribbled on a notepad. She also saw the young *Courier* reporter she had met in Rachel's office. The reporter held out a recording device. Fenway struggled to remember her name.

"Thank you, Catherine," Barry Klein said, as she sat down on her folding chair. "I've had the pleasure to serve as a member of the board of supervisors for a couple of very rewarding terms now. I've stood up for small business owners, and I've accomplished a lot to attract high-growth industries to the area."

He started going through a list of local tax incentives and pet projects that he spun in his favor. Fenway stifled a yawn, and looked around—a few people in the small crowd were looking around or were staring at their phones.

"Now many of you," Klein continued, "know that I ran for county coroner last year—but unfortunately, the rich and powerful in this county outspent and outmanned my grassroots campaign." Fenway rolled her eyes. Klein went on. "I've kept going with the board of supervisors, though, never wavering in my commitment to the residents of this county." He cleared his throat. "The tragic murder of Alice Jenkins has shaken me to my core, and I don't mind admitting that." He looked around; people were looking up and starting to pay closer attention. "And so close to the murder of another public servant, Harrison Walker, this great county's previous coroner. I don't think I need to remind anyone here that the killer turned out to be the handpicked head of security for Ferris Energy. The same energy company responsible for that monstrosity of a refinery we have just over the grade. The same energy company that's filling our beaches with black tar. The same energy company whose owner likes to think he can do whatever he wants in this county."

Klein found Fenway in the crowd, looked right at her, and narrowed his eyes.

"When I think of Alice Jenkins, I think of a brave woman who put this community above herself. Not for a year. Not for a decade. But over her whole life of public service. As a mayor, as a judge, as a civil rights lawyer before that," he said, looking out over the crowd and raising his right hand in front of his face in a fist; it looked awkward, but the crowd seemed to like it. "Whoever the next mayor of Estancia is, they need to remember Alice Jenkins' commitment to the people, to the values of fairness and justice, and to this community."

Catherine Klein stood and started to applaud, and soon a few scattered members of the crowd joined her. People walking by on the sidewalk stopped to listen. A few of them walked toward the amphitheater and stood at the sides, watching.

"Alice Jenkins and I often disagreed on what needed to be done," Klein said. "I'm not going to deny that. But we both wanted the best way forward for the county—the best way forward for Estancia. And while I can never fill Alice Jenkins' shoes, I would be honored if you, the voters, would let me do my best to try."

Migs and Fenway looked at each other. "He's not announcing his candidacy for *coroner*," Migs said.

Catherine Klein stepped forward and leaned around her husband to get to the microphone. "Ladies and gentlemen," she said, clearly and distinctly, "the next mayor of Estancia, Dr. Barry Klein." She began to applaud, as several people in the front row rolled out red, white, and blue canvas signs they were holding that said, "Klein for Mayor." The people nearest the front clapped along with Klein's wife. The photographers clicked away.

"I'm not sure that went as well as he hoped it would," Migs said into Fenway's ear. "Kind of a tepid reception."

"A little too soon, I think," Fenway agreed. "But he's got name recognition, and he'll own the local news for a week or two."

The young female reporter jumped up and down, trying to ask a question.

"No questions," Catherine Klein said.

Fenway could just make out the last part of the reporter's question, "...in jail overnight for?"

Dr. Klein and his wife clasped hands, raised them above their heads, and walked off to the side, away from the reporter still gamely trying to get their attention.

Fenway ran over to the reporter. The couple went into the City Hall building, flanked by a few other people holding "Klein for Mayor" signs. Fenway supposed that they were going in there to symbolically turn in their paperwork to the county clerk to make it official.

The reporter, disappointed, turned away just as Fenway reached her. "Excuse me," Fenway said, "but how did you know that Dr. Klein had spent the—"

"You're the coroner I met in Rachel's office a couple of days ago," the reporter interrupted. She switched the recorder back on. Fenway's eyes widened. "Miss Stevenson, there was much speculation that Dr. Klein would be running for coroner," she began.

"I'm sorry," Fenway cut in. "I can't remember your name."

"Oh, of course," the woman said. "Sascha Abrams. I'm on the political beat."

"The *Courier* has a political beat? I thought you were writing about the attempted murder of Rachel Richards."

Sascha laughed. "That was two deadlines ago. So, Miss Stevenson, with Dr. Klein announcing for the mayor's race instead, how does that affect *your* decision to become a candidate in November?"

Fenway stared at Sascha. "What?"

"I asked how it affected your decision to become a candidate."

"For coroner?"

"So you *are* considering it," Sascha said.

"I'm sorry," Fenway said, "but I, uh, disagree with the premise of your question."

"That Dr. Klein just announced his candidacy for mayor? I think we just saw that pretty clearly."

"No," Fenway said, "that there's any decision to be made about running for coroner."

"But no other candidates have announced," Sascha said.

"It's early," Fenway replied. "The deadline to file isn't for another few weeks."

"So you *have* looked into it." She raised the recorder again. "And maybe you know this, Miss Stevenson," she said in a rush. "Why did Dr. Klein spend last night in the Dominguez County jail?"

"Oh, I think we might have to wait for the paperwork on that one," said Fenway. "It's probably all detailed in there."

Sascha clicked the recorder off; Fenway saw the red light flicker and fade. "Just so you know, Miss Stevenson, I thought you handled the whole Harrison Walker case really well. I've been covering the political races since my college days and I don't want Barry Klein anywhere near the politics of this county. You sure you're not thinking about running?"

Fenway shook her head. "My father has already picked the horse in this race," she said. "And I'm a nurse, not a politician. I want to save lives in an ER, not be worried about re-election every four years."

"I think that's exactly why so many people I've talked to think you're the best coroner we've had in a long time," Sascha said.

Fenway averted her eyes and tried to ignore the compliment. "Hey—one question. The *Courier* has a reporter who visited Alice Jenkins the day before she was killed. I wanted to talk to him, see if anything there would help the investigation."

"Who is it?"

"James Monroe."

"Ha," Sascha said. "Reporters give names of presidents when we don't want to divulge our real names. Kind of an in-joke."

"Really?"

"Really."

"Are *you* James Monroe?"

Sascha smirked. "Now what would be the fun in telling you that?" She clicked her recorder back on at her side, hoping Fenway wouldn't notice. "And one more question for you, Miss Stevenson. Which horse did your father pick?"

"He told me never bet against American Pharoah," Fenway said with a wink, then turned to go back to Migs. She almost ran into a photographer who immediately snapped her picture.

"I appreciate the time," Sascha called after her. "And that James Monroe wrote one hell of a doctrine."

She found her way back to Migs, who offered her a ride home.

"Thanks, Migs. I'll take you up on that."

"No problem." Migs paused. "Everything okay?"

"I guess. No. I'm kind of annoyed. Dr. Klein, announcing his run. It seems, I don't know, really disrespectful, so soon after the mayor's death. And dealing with that reporter, too."

"You've dealt with reporters before."

"I know. Maybe I'm just in a lousy mood."

Migs nodded. "Anything I can do?"

Fenway smiled. "Yes. You can stop for tacos on the way home."

Migs laughed. "Dos Milagros, right?"

"Do you even have to ask?"

Migs tried making some small talk during dinner, but Fenway found herself thinking about how Natalie could be the king-pin—*El Magnate Nuevo*—from the administrative assistant's desk outside Rachel's office. Although, Fenway reasoned, remembering her high school Spanish, it should be *La Magnate Nueva*. She shook her head to clear it.

Fenway snapped back from her own little world about half-way through the meal. She raised her head and asked Migs about how things were going with Piper. Migs' family still hadn't met Piper, and he worried about how the family would feel about him dating a white woman.

"I mean, my brothers are totally cool with her," he said. "Sure, they're dicks about it—they call me 'Latino Lover' in front of her, and they call her *guera*—but they do it in front of her face, so I know she passed the test with them. But *mi litta*—that's a different story." He shuddered.

Fenway paused halfway through a bite of her carne asada taco. She still hadn't worked up the nerve to try the *lengua*. "Your what?"

"*Litta*. My grandma. She's a tiny little woman—I think even Rachel's taller than her—but she's mean. And there's a girl from back in Alcaraces that I think she's picked for me."

Fenway nodded through the next bite of her taco.

When they were done, Migs drove Fenway back to her complex. It was just past eight o'clock, and the sun scattered reds and purples across the buildings on either side of Estancia Canyon Boulevard.

Migs turned into the driveway of Fenway's apartment com-plex, and Fenway's attention snapped to the black Mercedes S500 in one of the visitors' spaces.

"Oh no," she said, half to herself. "What's my father doing here?"

Then she saw her new Honda Accord in her assigned parking space. "Oh, you've *got* to be kidding me."

Fenway opened the car door before Migs fully drove into the visitors' space. "Dad!" she yelled.

The door of the Mercedes opened and Nathaniel Ferris got out. "Fenway!" he said, his arms open wide. "I knew how much you needed your car back, so I decided—"

"You flew up in your private jet to get my car and drive it back?"

Ferris looked taken aback by Fenway's aggressive tone. "Not me, but yes, one of my drivers. He was happy to do it."

"Why in the world would you spend that kind of money?" Fenway walked over to her father, purpose in her stride.

A confused look came over Ferris's face. "Spend what kind of money?"

"I know it takes twenty-five thousand dollars just for you to take off and land," she said, seething. She pointed straight at her father's chest. "On the other hand, it's three hundred bucks, tops, for me to take a commercial flight up there, take an Uber to where my car is parked, and then drive home."

"You're busy with this homicide investigation," Ferris said. "Which I think is more important to the community."

"Going round trip to Seattle in your jet costs more than the car does, Dad," she said, more quietly, but still just as angry.

"So what?" Ferris said, and now anger crept into his voice too. "It's my money, I can spend it how I like."

"Do you have any idea what fifty thousand dollars would mean to me?" Fenway said, her voice cracking. "Do you know how much that forensics program at Seattle University cost? How much debt I'm in from that, and Western, and all the room and board?"

Ferris didn't say anything.

"And you spend it like it's nothing. Just to get my car back home." She tapped her foot. "I'm sure you worked your magic to get it out of long-term parking without the ticket, and I'm sure you worked your magic at the dealership to get an extra key—"

"I had one made when I bought it," Ferris offered lamely.

"So did you at least work your magic at the storage facility to get Mom's paintings?"

Ferris was quiet.

"So when all of this is done, I *still* have to drive two days up there and two days back?"

Ferris shuffled his feet. "I thought you'd be happy to have your car back," he said quietly. "It wasn't easy to get a driver to agree to do it. He didn't want anything to happen to the boss's daughter's car and him get blamed for it."

"You didn't *think*, Dad!" Fenway shouted. "You didn't think what *I* would want, you just thought about how it would make you look!"

Ferris set his jaw. "I can tell this is just going to be unproductive. I spend fifty thousand dollars to do something nice for you and this is the thanks I get."

"Maybe next time you can do something that actually *helps* me," Fenway said. "Maybe do something yourself. Don't just throw money at a problem and make it go away. Maybe *be there* for me."

"I didn't think you wanted me around," Ferris said.

"After you didn't show up for my high school graduation, or my prom, yeah, you better believe I didn't want you around," she said, her voice rising. "I didn't bother inviting you to my valedictory ceremony because I didn't want to be disappointed that you were choosing something else besides me. Again."

"We've been over this, Fenway," Ferris murmured.

"We may have been over this, but that doesn't mean it went away." Fenway raised her voice even higher. "You've got to do more than just say you're sorry and listen to my favorite Coltrane album and tell pretty stories about the Red Sox in the back of your Mercedes. You've got to follow it up with some actual time. Some actual repair. You've got to be there for me. And you've *never* been there for me." Fenway was almost shouting now. "Are you embarrassed of me? You ashamed of me? Maybe you don't want all your rich white friends to know you have a black daughter?" She got right in his face and lowered her voice. "Or maybe you're ashamed that I was raped. Maybe you think I'm not a good girl anymore."

Ferris took a step back as if she had punched him in the chest. "That's not true," he stammered.

"Give me your keys," Fenway snarled, a tear escaping her eye and running down her cheek. She took a step back. "I don't want you screwing with my stuff anymore."

Ferris stared at his daughter for a moment, then fished a Honda key out of his pocket and handed it over.

Fenway clenched and unclenched her fist around the key. "Thank you for getting my car back to me," she said through gritted teeth. She turned on her heel and walked upstairs to her apartment.

She heard the sound of a car starting, and it didn't sound like the Mercedes. She vaguely remembered that she had left Migs in the parking lot, caught between helping his boss and minding his own business. She fumbled with the key to the door as more tears ran down her face, rushed inside, closed the door behind her and threw herself face-first on the sofa, trying to keep control of herself. She grabbed a throw pillow that her mom used to like and buried her face in it as she screamed as loud as she could.

She thought she had gotten over this. She thought she had left it all behind her, that seeing the photos—enough of a gut punch in itself—and confronting Barry Klein had moved her past it. But the room spun and she couldn't breathe. And not just because the pillow still covered her mouth.

She got up and paced around the room restlessly. She couldn't stay in her apartment tonight.

Getting out of her apartment sounded good. Something that would make her forget everything that overwhelmed her thoughts—something that would drive out the bad images, the rash of shame, the crash of guilt for keeping her father out of the loop, the horrible feeling in the pit of her stomach.

She went to her mirror. In spite of everything that had happened, miraculously, she was having a good hair day. The flat iron's effects were gone from her hair, but her loose curls were behaving, framing her face and her high cheekbones. A touch up on her makeup—or maybe modifying it like she did when she was going to see Akeel—and she could really turn heads tonight. Lose herself in loud music. Get a few drinks. Maybe even meet someone who looked like Akeel. It would be salve for her wounds.

She found the black dress in her closet, the one she'd thought about wearing the day after she spent the night with Craig, the day of the previous coroner's funeral. As she changed into it, she remembered everything about the dress, a great purchase that really flattered her body. It showed off her curves in all the right places, or at least she thought that's how Akeel would see it. And Craig. And whatever guy might be on the dance floor, looking for her that evening. She looked in the mirror again and saw her body in the dress, all slink and slither. She stood up on tiptoe and turned her head down, just to imagine how good those strappy black heels would make her calves look, how she'd walk into that dance club and knock back a whiskey sour and just let her body move to the music and let Craig's hands go all over her, starting at her hips and working their way up until she went crazy. Or Akeel's hands. Or whoever.

She looked down at the floor of her closet and saw the strappy black heels lying on the floor. She started to retrieve them and then she remembered.

The cleaners had been able, after three tries, to get Stotsky's blood off them. Some of the black on the back of the heel had faded in the cleaning process, but she could barely even see it. If she hadn't hit Stotsky in the face with that sharp heel, slicing his cheek, she might not be alive.

And she might not be trying to go out dancing tonight. To meet someone. To maybe forget that Akeel was a thousand miles away and Craig was still very married.

She took her shoes to the bedroom. She pulled a small black clutch off the top shelf in the closet and put just her wallet, keys, phone, and compact in it.

Crap. She had never given Rachel's key back to Dez. She'd have to do that tomorrow.

She did her makeup carefully, and added a bit more eyeliner and mascara than her usual clean look, and dug in her drawer to look for the lipstick she wanted. Then she remembered it was still in the makeup bag in her suitcase. She had used the red shade when she had seen Akeel on Saturday afternoon. She found the lipstick in the bag, and did her lips in the mirror. She took a step back and looked at herself. She liked her outfit, flattering and sexy, perfect for the club. She liked the way she felt in it, and how she carried herself in it.

She walked in her bare feet out to the kitchen. She poured herself a glass of water, realized she'd have to redo her lipstick, but drank it anyway. It was only nine o'clock; the clubs had barely opened their dance floors. If she wanted to meet someone, she'd be waiting awhile. Although, she supposed, dancing away her frustrations wouldn't be the worst thing to do before she needed to turn her charm on.

CHAPTER TWENTY-ONE

SHE MANAGED TO KILL ANOTHER HOUR, READING A NEW BOOK she had purchased that won some big literary prize, although she only halfway paid attention to it. She argued with herself over driving to the club or taking an Uber, but she knew she wanted at least a couple of whiskey sours. And she didn't want to have to count how many drinks she had to figure out if she could still drive or not.

The Uber took ten minutes to pick her up. When she walked outside, the fog had started to roll in, making the night dark. The driver greeted her nicely enough, but slid his eyes all over her as she got in the back seat. Fenway could feel his eyes on her through the rear-view mirror. He tried to make small talk, and Fenway faked a phone call so she didn't have to answer his increasingly probing questions.

But when she got to the club, she felt almost relaxed. The glassy-eyed doorman let her in without paying the cover charge— on a weeknight, it didn't cost much to get in, and there weren't very many people in the club, but it still made her feel good to get in for free. And only about five or six brave souls were scattered on the dance floor. There were about twenty people in the club altogether.

The music had a powerful, electronic beat to it; she didn't recognize the song. She walked alone to the bar and figured she should start on her first whiskey sour. She saw several men swivel their heads to watch her travel from the door to the bar, and for the first time she wondered whether it was a good idea to arrive alone.

She noticed the bartender, with dark wavy hair, and dark eyes that were also looking her up and down. She made eye contact with him, and he walked from his spot in front of the register to meet her.

"What can I get you?" the bartender asked in a deep baritone. The music hadn't been turned up to overwhelm conversation—though Fenway thought the volume would get cranked up soon enough.

"Whiskey sour."

"Make it two," said the man sitting on the stool next to her, holding out his credit card.

The bartender glanced at Fenway. She took a quick look at the man on the stool; he was young and white and fairly cute, but was dressed too casually for a night out dancing, in faded blue jeans and a wrinkled two-tone blue short-sleeved button-down shirt. He was looking at her the way Akeel looked at her, though, and she turned back to the bartender and shrugged. The bartender nodded and took his card.

"Thanks," she said, sitting on the stool next to him.

"You're welcome," he said. "I don't think I've seen you in here before."

"I don't usually come here," she said. "Especially on a work night."

He held out his hand. "I'm Zach."

"Nice to meet you, Zach. You here often on a work night?"

"Never on a work night." Zach grinned. "Often on a school night, though. Good thing it's summer break."

Fenway smirked. "Yeah, I figured you were a college boy. You over at PQ, or are you strictly private school?"

Zach's grin faltered a bit, but he recovered. "Private. I'm a senior at Nidever. How about you? Where do you work?"

"At the county," Fenway said, evasively.

"Ah," Zach said. "So, county girl, you got a name?"

"Joanne," Fenway said.

"Nice to meet you, Joanne."

The bartender brought their drinks. "Keep it open?" he said, holding up Zach's card. Zach nodded, not taking his eyes off Fenway.

Fenway started to take a drink and then noticed Zach awkwardly held his up to toast. She pulled the drink away from her mouth.

"To the prettiest girl in here," he said, and he made an effort to pull his mouth into a genuine smile.

Fenway nodded, trying to save him from an even more awkward moment, clinked his glass, then took a drink. The cheap bourbon tasted like rubbing alcohol and burned going down; not even the lemon juice and syrup could adequately cover it up.

"Yeesh," Fenway said.

"A little strong for you?"

Fenway shook her head. "It's not that. I should have asked for a better bourbon."

They talked a little more; Fenway quickly determined that they had absolutely nothing in common. He liked rock climbing and sailing. Fenway got the idea he'd been born into an incredibly rich family. In fact, he may have gone to the same private elementary school as Fenway before she and her mother had left for Seattle. He would have been about six years behind her.

"So, Joanne, why did you come out on a Tuesday night? Rough day at work?"

"Rough *week* at work," Fenway replied. "And my father is being a dick." She drained the last of her drink.

"Join the club," Zach said, a little sadly. "Can I get you another?"

"Actually," Fenway said, "I came here to dance."

"Oh." Zach nodded, but looked wary, like he didn't really want to dance.

The music changed to an old R&B hit from the eighties, but with a modern house beat behind it. Fenway recognized the song, but couldn't quite place it. A few people who had been hanging around the edges of the dance floor started to move to the music and slowly made their way toward the center of the floor.

"Oh, I love this song," Fenway fibbed. "I've got to get out there. Thanks for the drink."

Fenway got up from the stool and went out onto the dance floor. She started to sway her hips to the rhythm as soon as she got up, and she noticed out of the corner of her eye that Zach slammed the rest of his drink, put the empty glass on the bar, and followed her out to the dance floor.

Fenway knew she danced well, and the whiskey sour, even with the rotgut bourbon, erased most of the self-consciousness she'd felt when she walked in. She danced, paying attention mostly to the music, and Zach stepped closer to her, beat by beat, song by song.

Zach's rhythm faltered, and he looked uncomfortable as he realized how good of a dancer Fenway was. He tried to make eye contact, smiling as he attempted to mirror some of the steps Fenway made. She smiled back at him, mostly to try to get him to feel more comfortable. Although she had come dancing to rid herself of *her* discomfort.

She closed her eyes for a moment and lost herself in the rhythm of the music, feeling the booming bass in her chest. The music frenetically crescendoed, building, building, like she was slowly ascending a tall track on a roller coaster, feeling the clicks as the ground got farther and farther away.

Then just at the peak of the crescendo—all the instruments went silent.

Fenway felt the lurch of the music almost as strongly as if the coaster plummeted toward the earth.

It only took a quarter of a second, but it was brilliant. She opened her eyes again as the music restarted, the chorus triumphant.

Zach had moved closer to her.

He was starting to relax, even if he couldn't stay in rhythm. And he *was* cute, if almost certainly too young to have anything more than a fling with. Which, she reminded herself, was exactly what she wanted tonight.

She took a step closer to him, too, and leaned forward. He met her halfway and their lips met, tentatively. She, at over six feet tall in her heels, had a good three inches on him, and had to lower her face slightly to kiss him. She tasted lemon juice and cheap bourbon. He smiled and leaned in again.

She put her arms on his shoulders and they kissed again, this time with more feeling, more effort. She opened her mouth slightly; so did Zach. She stepped into his body in time with the beat of the music.

"Wow," Zach breathed.

Fenway smiled again and pulled him closer again for another kiss.

They broke apart slightly, and Zach visibly caught his breath. "Damn, Joanne," he said, "you are super hot for a black girl."

Fenway felt like she had just been punched in the stomach.

For a black girl.

She kept a smile on her face. Zach reached his right arm forward from his side and put his hand on her left hip and started to pull her into him again.

Fenway, laughing without feeling any joy, spun out of his reach, masquerading it as a dance move. He looked a little confused, though he tried to hide it, and she smiled at him and started to step away.

"Bathroom," she mouthed to him.

She stepped off the dance floor and into the corridor that led to the restrooms. She exhaled, exasperated, and swore at herself as she walked into the women's room. Both stalls were taken, but she didn't really have to go anyway.

She looked at herself in the mirror and she saw the hurt and the loneliness in her eyes and wondered if everyone else could see it too.

Two women came in, breathless, talking about the men they had left on the dance floor. Fenway maneuvered around them, stuck her foot out to prevent the door from closing, and pushed it open with her hip.

The empty corridor greeted her, and Fenway sighed. This hadn't worked out like she hoped. The promise of a night with Zach had been dashed, and with the way she had acted with him on the dance floor, kissing him, grinding up against him, it would be difficult to change dance partners.

A skinny man, looking more like a surfer than a club kid, shuffled into the corridor, up to Fenway. "Hey, girl, you looking for anything?" he mumbled. "I got Red Skies if you're down."

Fenway looked at the man. It was Zoso.

"Hey, Zoso," she said quietly.

He looked up at her, shocked. "Oh, hey—you're, uh, Parker's friend."

"Yep," Fenway said.

"I didn't recognize you." He looked her up and down, taking her in through his half-lidded eyes. "You don't look like no coroner *I've* ever seen," he drawled. "How you doing? You good?"

"I didn't know you were dealing at clubs, Zoso. The establishment cool with that?"

"Uh," Zoso said, realizing that this exchange was less social than he'd thought. "We haven't had any trouble yet. Lot of rich kids with money in here. Everyone's looking for a good time."

Fenway suddenly realized why the doorman had been glassy-eyed.

"I thought you said the pill trade was segregated," Fenway said. "Why you trying to sell to me?"

"Maybe I'm trying to be more open-minded."

Fenway chuckled.

"Listen," Zoso continued, "are we cool?"

Fenway looked at Zoso out of the corner of her eye. "You know I *shouldn't* be cool with this, right?"

Zoso shifted uncomfortably.

"I thought you said you didn't know the Red Skies distributor guy," Fenway said.

"Naw," Zoso said. "I just couldn't get none before."

"Something change?"

"I figured I'd go with the lower percentage he offered me. A little percent of a lot is bigger than a big percent of jack shit."

"That sounds like a rational business decision."

Zoso held up his hands in front of him, palms out. "Hey, listen, you don't need to make fun of me."

"I'm not making fun of you, Zoso. I'm saying you make good business decisions. A lot of people in your line of work have some trouble with that."

He looked at her with suspicion.

"And another good business decision would be for you to tell me what you know about the distributor."

Zoso shook his head. "No way. I'm not getting in trouble with those guys."

"Those guys?"

"Yeah, I heard they do some bad shit. And it's not the guy I've met, it's his boss."

"His boss, huh? You got a name?"

Zoso shook his head.

"You know if it's a him or her?"

Zoso looked at Fenway quizzically.

"A her?" He laughed. "Man, I never heard of a boss who was a her. You must not know the game."

Fenway pulled her phone out of her purse and brought up a picture of Natalie. "What about her?"

"As the boss? Are you serious? This chick is spakka."

"She's what?"

"You know. In a wheelchair and shit. Big-ass muscles, though. She could rip my shit up."

"How do you know her?"

"How do I know her? She's one of my best customers. She gave me some sob story about getting blown up in Iraq or Iran or some shithole like that. She's been after me for Red Skies forever. She asked about them before I even knew what they were." He ran a hand through his hair and looked around. "These vets are the best. They get money like clockwork from the government and spend all of it trying to forget they only have half their body."

Fenway felt queasy from the conversation. "You ever see her with the distributor guy?"

Zoso shook his head.

"So tell me about this distributor guy you've been talking to."

"You mean here?"

"Sure."

"Oh. I thought you meant like at the station. I can't be seen at the station again."

"Because of your relationship with your new distributor?"

"You know it."

"So spill it, Zoso."

He paused. "And you won't take me in for dealing?"

"If you tell me about him. You get a get-out-of-jail-free card tonight."

"Okay," Zoso said. "So I get a call on my cell, and I don't really know how he got my number, but he did. And he says he wants me to be the first dealer to get Red Skies in my territory, which I know is bullshit, because I know Tommy G got some last week, but I don't say anything, because if I don't get his shit, I might be out on my ass in a couple of months."

Fenway nodded.

"And he gives me an address out on 28th, near La Crescenta."

"The warehouse district."

"Yeah, a warehouse space. A bitch to find, too. Behind a couple of other buildings, and the numbers don't make any sense there."

"So did you see him?"

"Yeah. A short guy, maybe five-five or five-six, but stocky, really muscular." He paused. "I'd pay money to see him fight the handicapped chick, though. That'd be a good fight."

"What else about him? White? Black?"

"Some sort of Asian," Zoso said. "I don't know, Japanese, Chinese, Thai, something."

"Maybe Filipino?" Fenway thought of Natalie—maybe she had a brother or cousin, and maybe the vet-looking-for-a-fix was a front to see how her potential dealers fared in unusual situations.

Zoso shrugged. "He always wore track suits, though. Like he was in an eighties nerds-versus-jocks movie. Pretentious little prick, too. Like he thought I'd give him ebola if he touched me."

"Like the shiny Adidas-type of track suits?"

Zoso nodded.

"Okay," Fenway said. "Sure you don't want to come down to the station and sit with a sketch artist?"

"Yeah, I think I'll pass on that."

"Okay, Zoso," Fenway said. "Thanks anyway. This is a big help. This guy might be behind the mayor's murder."

Zoso looked puzzled. "But I thought they caught the guy."

"Yeah," Fenway said, the wheels turning in her head about how Natalie might be running the show while at the same time be posing as a user. "If you believe the guy's confession."

Zoso looked at Fenway. "You don't?"

Fenway shrugged. "I guess I've said too much. Thanks again for your help."

Fenway started to walk past Zoso toward the dance floor. Zoso grabbed her arm.

"One more thing," he said. "I thought the guy would want to impress me with the amount of shit he had in the warehouse. But he wouldn't let me get near it."

"Really?"

"Yeah. I heard some sort of crying or something. I figured the guy had his girlfriend there and maybe she had brought her kid."

"Her kid? The crying sounded like a little girl?"

"Shit, I don't know. How am I supposed to know what a little girl sounds like?"

"Did you see a child when you were over there? A girl, about five? Maybe one with my skin color?"

Zoso shook his head.

"Okay. Can you give me that address?"

"No, come on, Fenway, I don't want to get this guy into trouble. It'll get back to him that I gave it to you and then I'm a dead man."

"Did you hear what I asked you? Whether it sounded like a little girl? Whether you saw a little girl?"

Zoso paused. "You think this guy kidnapped a little girl?"

Fenway looked at Zoso. "I know *someone* kidnapped a little girl, and I'm trying to find her."

"Shit," Zoso said. "These assholes can't ever just stick to pills. They gotta be all up in everyone's shit too." He set his jaw and pulled out his phone. "Yeah, fine. Eleven fifty-seven 28th Street.

It's the building behind eleven ten, which makes no sense, but whatever."

"Thanks, Zoso," Fenway said, typing the address into her phone. "You might have saved a little girl's life."

"Aw, shit, girl, don't try that with me. Don't pretend I'm gonna get religion and join the academy."

"Wouldn't dream of it. Okay, I gotta go say goodbye to my, uh, dance partner." She took a couple of steps to the end of the corridor and looked around the dance floor. Zach wasn't there. She looked at the bar. He had sat back down on the stool, two more whiskey sours in front of him.

"I guess I didn't scare him off," Fenway murmured.

Zoso turned to look. "That guy?"

"Yeah." Fenway smirked. "Don't get all jealous, Zoso, it's not working out between us."

Zoso hesitated.

"What?" Fenway asked.

"Uh—maybe you don't want to have that drink with that guy."

She gaped at him. "What the hell, Zoso? Did you sell him something to put in my drink?"

"I ain't saying I sold this guy anything, all right?"

Fenway frowned and looked Zoso in the face. He wouldn't meet her eyes.

"I'm just saying, get out of here. And don't drink that."

Fenway narrowed her eyes. "It's not just me, Zoso. If I don't drink that, another girl might," she said.

Zoso looked uncomfortable. "Maybe you can talk to the bouncer."

"Maybe *you* can talk to the bouncer, Zoso."

"No way. I don't want him to—"

"All you have to do is tell him you saw that guy put something in my drink. You don't have to admit to selling it to him."

"They'll know it was me, though."

Fenway crossed her arms. "That get-out-of-jail-free card still look good to you? I might change my mind."

Zoso shuffled his feet. "Fine. I'll take care of it," he said miserably.

"You're lucky you gave me the address of that warehouse," Fenway said through gritted teeth. "If I ever hear you're selling roofies, you're never getting another get-out-of-jail-free card from the department again."

"Okay," Zoso said softly, looking down at the floor. He started to walk toward the front of the club where the glassy-eyed bouncer was manning the door. Fenway followed him, hoping Zach wouldn't notice her leave.

Zoso stopped to say something in the bouncer's ear as Fenway went past them. When she got to the exit, she looked behind her. The bouncer was walking purposefully toward Zach at the bar. Zach started to look up and Fenway ducked around the door out of sight.

CHAPTER TWENTY-TWO

SHE GOT OUT TO THE STREET AND STARTED TO WALK TO THE downtown parking garage when she realized she didn't have her car. She was glad she had only had the one drink. She stopped under a light, in front of brightly lit restaurant that was just starting to close up.

Fenway pulled her phone out of her clutch and called Dez. It rang twice.

"Roubideaux," Dez answered, her voice tired.

"It's Fenway."

"You okay, Fenway? It's late."

"I know where Olivia Jenkins is being held."

"What?" All the fatigue went out of Dez's voice. "How did you figure that out?"

"I got an address from a dealer," Fenway said. "In the warehouse district. 28th and La Crescenta. Behind a bunch of other buildings."

"You got this from a dealer?"

"I promise you it's a fascinating story, Dez, but don't you want to get over there with some officers right away?"

"Hang on, Fenway," Dez said. "How do you know the girl's there?"

"My dealer went to get some supply from the warehouse. They wouldn't let him in, and there was a little kid crying in there."

Dez exhaled. "That's not enough for a warrant, never mind exigent circumstances."

"I know for sure there are black market drugs in there. That's gotta be enough for probable cause, right?"

Dez considered for a moment. "Yeah," she said. "That's enough for probable cause. All right. I'll call Mark. We'll see how we want to play this. You have the address?"

"I can text it to you."

"Okay. I'm calling the station."

"You going to wake up a judge?"

"For what, a search warrant? Come on, Fenway, a kidnapping means exigent circumstances. You know that."

"I just thought we should cross all the T's and dot all the I's."

"Not on this. I gotta go."

Fenway hit *End* on the phone. She felt amped up, and wanted nothing more than to be at the warehouse when they found Olivia, even though she knew it wasn't a good idea. She texted the address to Dez.

She tried to think of how she could justify her presence there, and realized the first step was going to get her car.

"Well," Fenway said to herself, "speaking of bad ideas..."

She called McVie's number.

It rang three times before he picked up. "Hello?" He sounded groggy.

"Hey, Craig."

"Fenway? What time is it?"

"It's about eleven," she said. "I know where Olivia Jenkins is being held."

"What?" Just like Dez, all traces of sleepiness left his voice. "Where are you?"

"I'm downtown at a dance club. I ran into a dealer who had come into the office a couple days ago to talk about the, uh, economic climate for the burgeoning pill trade in Estancia."

"What did he say?"

"That the guy who he gets his Red Skies from took him to his warehouse and he heard a little kid crying in there."

"Did you get an address?"

"Eleven fifty-seven 28th Street, right near La Crescenta. It's supposedly behind a bunch of other buildings; I guess the building numbering is all messed up there."

"The heart of the warehouse district," McVie mused. "I know it. Anything else?"

"Isn't that enough?" Fenway said defensively. "No way is a screaming little girl in that part of town after dark of her own free will."

"There are a *million* explanations," McVie said. "Any employee who works there could have had to bring their kid. Their babysitter could have fallen through, or they just came in to drop off a check or something. Did your guy actually *see* the little girl?"

Fenway narrowed her eyes. "Not really."

"Is that a 'no'?"

"But I know for sure there's a ton of pills there," Fenway said. "That's enough for probable cause, right?"

McVie paused. "Yeah, I think that would pass muster with a judge," he said.

"Dez is getting everything together," Fenway said. "I think she's going to take some officers over there and raid the place."

"It's not like a SWAT team, Fenway."

"Whatever. Do you want to go watch?"

He sounded exasperated. "Fenway, I'm still on administrative leave, and even if I wasn't, your presence there would endanger Olivia more than it would help her."

"Me? What about you?"

"One of us is a pretty good shot. And the other one has rescheduled firearms training three times."

Fenway was silent.

"You still there?"

"Yeah," she said. "And I still need a ride home."

"From the club? You too drunk to drive?"

She scoffed. "I wish. I took an Uber down here." She almost told him about Zach, but then stopped herself. "After I ran into that guy with the pills and he told me about the warehouse, I thought I needed to get out of there and call Dez. I didn't even get my second whiskey sour."

"Oh, that's right, your car is still up at Sea-Tac."

She laughed. "It's actually not. My father flew someone in his private jet up there to get it."

"But you took an Uber there?"

"I was kind of *planning* to drink. I just never got around to it."

McVie laughed lightly. "You asking me to come get you?"

Fenway hesitated and drew a figure eight on the sidewalk with her heel. "Not really. I mean, I know it's past eleven. I probably woke up Amy with my call. You can stay home."

McVie didn't say anything.

"Craig? What is it?"

"No, you didn't wake Amy up." He paused. "I'm—uh—not at home. She and I thought it would be best if I stayed in a hotel for a couple days."

"Oh." Fenway's heel paused in mid-swoop. "Oh, Craig, I'm sorry."

"Don't worry about it. We tried. Maybe we're still trying, I don't know. This stuff doesn't happen overnight."

"Is she—" Fenway started, and then bit her tongue. It was really none of her business if Amy had cheated on McVie again.

"I don't know *what* she is," McVie said, with a touch of anger in his voice. "I'm not sure what's going on, to be frank. I'm working fewer hours, we went on a bunch of dates, I even did that whole concert thing with her when I probably should have been figuring out why your dad's private investigator didn't show up."

Fenway waited a beat. "Well, then, if I'm not bothering anybody, would you mind coming to get me?"

There was silence on the other end of the line for a moment.

"No, forget I asked," Fenway said quickly. "You're already in bed, it's late. I can take an Uber home."

"It's not that," McVie said. "It's that, uh, we've been working well together lately."

"Yeah," Fenway said, "we have."

"And the last time Amy and I were on the outs, you and I did something we probably shouldn't have." He cleared his throat.

Fenway waited for McVie to continue.

"I mean, if you remember, you and I fought the next morning. We jeopardized our working relationship before it had even started."

"And I like working with you," Fenway said.

"Right, me too," McVie said. "And I don't want to mess that up."

"It's just a ride home, McVie," Fenway said, consciously using his last name. "It's not like I find you so *irresistible* that I have to tear your clothes off whenever I think you might be available."

Now it was McVie's turn to be quiet again. Fenway pictured herself tearing his clothes off.

"I didn't mean that the way it sounded," Fenway said. "I just meant that, you know, I have at least a *little* self-control." She tried to laugh, but it came out weakly. "I mean, I'm not going to pretend I'm not attracted to you. I just, you know, I know it's not a good thing for our working relationship, and I value that more."

"Sure," he said. "Right. I mean, I'm not going to pretend that I'm not attracted to you either, but I've got enough smarts that I'm not going to do anything about it."

"Right. It's just a ride home."

"Okay," he said. "You're at that dance club on Seventh Street?"

"I just left," Fenway said. "I'm in front of Mustang Sally's Barbecue, kind of around the corner."

"I know it," McVie said. "Ten minutes."

He hung up and Fenway stood staring at her phone as the restaurant turned off a few of its interior lights. A woman in a white apron and white chef's hat, both with noticeable flecks and smears of barbecue sauce and a scorch mark or two, walked to the front door and turned the lock on the double doors at the front.

Fenway took a deep breath, now that her adrenaline pumped slower in her veins, and she started to think.

Just what was she doing with McVie, anyway?

Three days ago, she had desperately tried to get McVie out of her head. She thought he would reconcile with Amy for good. She had been with Akeel, ready to have a one-night (okay, maybe a weeklong) fling with him and his great abs. And a phone call from Dez changed all of that in an instant.

She knew she had already backslid into getting hung up on McVie, but she couldn't do anything about it.

And she probably should have been depressed to realize that, but she felt excited that McVie had left to come to pick her up.

The headlights of a beige Highlander swept around the corner. She recognized McVie behind the wheel. He saw her too, and she saw his eyes widen. He hadn't seen her in the black dress with the slink and slither before.

He slowed to a stop in front of her. He wore a polo shirt, tight around his biceps and chest. Fenway blinked a couple of times, telling herself it was from the brightness of the headlamps and not from steeling herself.

He rolled down the passenger window. "Hey, Fenway," he said.

"Hey, Craig."

"Didn't expect you to be so dressed up." He cleared his throat. "You look beautiful."

For a black girl, Zach's voice echoed in her head. Fenway had to fight back the voice. "What did you think, that I'd go dancing in jeans and sneakers?"

McVie shrugged.

Fenway opened the door. McVie couldn't take his eyes off her.

She slid into the seat, putting her purse at her feet, and looked at him expectantly.

"Thanks for the ride," she said. "I know you were in bed."

"Not a problem," McVie said.

He didn't move the car forward, resting his hand on the automatic gearshift.

"Oh, seatbelt." She reached back and put the seatbelt on.

"No, it's not that. I'm deciding something."

Are you debating whether or not you want to make a bad decision with me? Fenway thought. She leaned slightly toward McVie and lifted her hand to place over his on the gearshift—then she chickened out and put her hand on the center console.

"Screw it," he said. "You only live once."

And he put the car into *Drive* and turned down Eighth.

"My apartment is the other way," Fenway said, after a couple of blocks.

"I know," he said. "But I had a summer job when I was in high school in the warehouses around there." McVie looked over his shoulder and changed to the left lane to turn onto Burbank Road.

Fenway cocked her head to the side.

"That sounds like we're going to the warehouse."

"I will completely deny everything we're doing tonight, Fenway. So we're never going to talk about this again."

"Some Boy Scout you are, Sheriff."

The streets started to increase, one at a time: Tenth, Eleventh, Twelfth. They crossed the tracks and the street signs changed from being spelled out to being numerical. Soon they were past 23rd. McVie made a right on 27th, and they passed Los Feliz and La Crescenta.

"That was La Crescenta," Fenway said.

"We're not pulling up in front, Fenway. That would be asking for trouble."

"Okay."

He slowed and turned in between two scraggly Catalina ironwood trees.

Fenway jumped a little in her seat. "Is there even a road here?"

McVie nodded, slowed to a crawl, and killed the headlights. "A gravel road that leads to an alleyway. Me and my friends used to, uh, skateboard through this area all the time."

"Oh, for real? You were a skater boy?"

"I don't like to talk about it."

"You still have a *Skateboarding Is Not a Crime* bumper sticker? I could get you one and you could put it on your cruiser."

McVie looked at her out of the corner of his eye. "You're not old enough to know about that, Fenway."

Fenway scoffed. "Oh, please. I worked in an ER for a couple of years. You think I never saw a skateboarding accident? Or a parent who wanted to reminisce about their glory days while I checked for a broken clavicle?"

McVie smirked. "Spoken like someone who's never done a Madonna while bombing a hill."

Fenway shook her head. "I've seen too many swellbows and hippers to do any of that myself. But if you want to keep trying to impress me with your skateboarding vernacular, good luck."

McVie came to a stop at the edge of a vacant lot and killed the engine, right behind a low, wide electrical box that they could see over. The box hid the body of the car from the other side, and a few more Catalina ironwoods cast disruptive, fingerlike shadows all around them.

"Where are we?"

McVie pointed over the electrical box. "Across that lot on the other side of that fence. That's the warehouse you were talking about."

"Police aren't here yet," Fenway observed.

"It should take them another ten or twenty minutes, at least," McVie said. "Tuesday night shift is a little light, but they'll get the manpower."

"Looks dark."

"If anyone is home, they'll probably minimize the lights. They wouldn't want to draw attention to themselves."

Fenway nodded. "I don't see any cars parked in front."

McVie had a grim look on his face. "I don't see any either."

"What do you think? Think they'll find anything here?"

McVie shook his head. "If we have a mole in the department, they might have already warned the people in the warehouse."

Fenway sat silently.

They waited for ten minutes. The windshield started to steam up from their breath. Fenway wanted to make a flirtatious joke about something getting steamy, but she couldn't think of a good punch line. McVie turned the car on just long enough to roll the windows down.

Ten minutes turned into twenty, then thirty. Fenway unbuckled her seat belt and stretched in the seat. The dress was meant for dancing, not for sitting in.

"Are they coming?" Fenway said.

"I know Dez," McVie said. "She'll be here."

They continued to watch the warehouse, but everything was quiet and still. Then, they heard a low sound of engines in the distance, quiet and far away at first, then getting closer and louder. They saw the red and blue lights from the cars shining into the dark summer sky, then darkness again as the police vehicles got closer.

"Do you think they'll see us?" Fenway asked.

"I really doubt it," said McVie. "Between these trees and the electrical box, it's really tough to see over here. They'd have to shine a light right on us." He paused. "And, of course, we shouldn't do anything stupid like open a door."

"Look!" Fenway hissed, pointing. A door at the back of the warehouse slid open and two figures slipped out and crouched in the shadows, scurrying quickly into the trees.

"Did you get a good look at them?"

"It's too dark," McVie said. "I couldn't make anything out."

"They carried themselves like men, not women," Fenway said, "but that was about all I could tell."

"How tall?"

Fenway shook her head. "I don't know." She thought she saw motion in the trees but couldn't see anything in the darkness.

"We're staying put," McVie said. "We're too far away to pursue them ourselves, and even if we could, we'd put ourselves in danger of being shot by the good guys." He sucked in a breath through his teeth. "Plus, it didn't look like they had Olivia."

In front of the warehouse, Dez was the first one out of the cruiser. She had on a Kevlar vest. She walked around to the back of the car, opened the trunk, and lifted a battering ram out. Mark opened the passenger door and got out. Like Dez, he wore a Kevlar vest, and joined four other officers, also in vests, fanning out in a semi-circle behind Dez. Two officers sneaked around the side of the building to the back door, not realizing two people in the warehouse had already left that way.

"She going to use that herself?" Fenway asked.

"Dez is the best door key we've got."

"Not you? You with the muscles?"

McVie shook his head. "Dez has perfect technique."

Dez walked up to the metal door, turned slightly to the side, lifted the two handles up, swung it back just in front of her hips, and drove the ram next to the lock with a loud clang, metal on metal, then the sound of the back of the door hitting the wall.

"POLICE!" Mark shouted as he ran through the door. The other four followed close on his heels as Dez dropped the battering ram to the ground and drew her gun to guard the door.

Very faintly, a child's cry.

"Holy shit," said Fenway, grabbing McVie's hand. "I think they found Olivia."

McVie squeezed back.

Dez started to bark orders into the warehouse, but neither McVie nor Fenway could make it out. They heard a shout from inside that sounded like "Clear!"

Dez ducked inside.

"Please be safe," Fenway whispered, her eyes riveted to the front door, her hand still squeezing McVie's.

There were muffled voices inside.

Dez appeared at the door with a crying little girl with large dark eyes, light brown skin, and a mop of tangled black hair. The girl wore a white shirt, filthy with brown stains, rust or dirt or excrement. Dez pulled the shirt off in a fluid motion and handed it to an officer who put it in an evidence bag, then pulled a small blue blanket out of the trunk and wrapped the little girl in it.

Just like Isla, Olivia looked like she could have been Fenway's daughter.

"She's okay," Fenway choked out, a tear running down her cheek, still holding onto McVie's hand.

McVie nodded, blinking hard.

Fenway turned her head to look at him.

She had felt triumphs in her previous career: the woman who had been thrown twenty feet by a drunk driver, who Fenway managed to stabilize in the ER while waiting for the doctor to show up; the little boy in anaphylactic shock that Fenway saved with the epinephrine IV (getting the vein on the first try, by the way); the woman who Fenway saved after a myocardial infarction on the Amtrak up to Bellingham when she was still a nursing student.

But this felt different—somehow, better.

Fenway pulled herself on top of McVie, straddling him, her dress hiking up her thighs, her high heels threatening to catch on the gearshift or the steering wheel, but missing them both. She took it as a good sign.

She leaned down and kissed McVie with an open mouth, searching for the same thing she had been looking for with Zach.

McVie started to say something.

"Shh," Fenway whispered into his ear, putting a finger over his lips. "The cops will hear us. Stay quiet." She tossed her hair to the right-hand side, spilling over her right ear, almost to her shoulder, and leaned down and kissed him again. This time, McVie kissed her back.

McVie was a much better kisser than Zach was.

CHAPTER TWENTY-THREE

AFTER A FEW MINUTES, THEY HEARD A LOT OF COMMOTION IN front of the warehouse, and Fenway and McVie stopped kissing each other so they could see what was going on. An ambulance had arrived, and Dez stepped into the back of it, presumably to ride with Olivia to the hospital. Olivia's nightmare wasn't over just yet—Fenway knew she still faced a couple of hours of poking and prodding—but it had to be better than the warehouse.

She pulled herself off McVie's lap and half-landed back in the passenger seat. Her dress had ridden all the way up her hips, but she pulled it down and McVie didn't say anything. They both watched the scene unfold in front of them.

After the ambulance left, a CSI truck came in a few minutes later. Kav and Melissa got out with their kits, already gloved up.

"We're going to be here for hours," Fenway whispered.

Mark got in the driver's side of the cruiser Dez had pulled up in.

"O ye of little faith," McVie said.

Mark started the cruiser up with a roar. McVie turned the ignition as soon as he heard the engine start.

Fenway held her breath.

McVie left the lights off and backed slowly down the alleyway.

"They'll see the reflection of the brake lights," Fenway said.

"I don't think so. They're paying attention to a million other things."

It seemed to take forever to back out from between the two ironwoods, off onto 27th Street. They finally made it, and McVie turned the Highlander and drove away.

Fenway finally exhaled. "That was kind of a rush," she said.

"It's even more of a rush when you're the first guy running into the warehouse."

"Or the one swinging that battering ram." Fenway flashed a smile at McVie.

"Yeah."

Fenway wanted to invite McVie over to her place, but she wasn't sure how he'd react. The long kissing session was as passionate as anything she'd ever had with Akeel. And McVie was more of a grownup.

Fenway groaned inwardly. Of course McVie was more of a grownup. He was literally fifteen years older than Akeel, with a gorgeous blonde wife and a sixteen-year-old daughter.

She remembered how Dez had reacted when she had found out that Fenway and McVie had spent the night together a couple of months before. Dez hadn't gone easy on Fenway.

Fenway had justified it to herself back then because turnabout was fair play—Amy slept with someone else, so Craig could, too. But she hadn't felt good about her decision afterward. And they had just built their working relationship back up to where it wasn't awkward.

Well—sometimes Fenway still felt awkward. She hated the fact that she still carried a torch for McVie. And maybe he felt the same way.

So making out like a couple of teenagers in the front seat of the Highlander wasn't a good idea. At least she hadn't slept with him. Although there was a voice in the back of her head telling her that if she played her cards right, she might have a chance with him once he and Amy called it quits. And from his sleeping on the sofa a couple of nights ago to his sleeping in a motel tonight, Fenway wondered if that wouldn't be sooner rather than later.

And at least she hadn't had that second whiskey sour with whatever Zach may or may not have put in her drink.

She actually wished she had just gone dancing—not clubbing, not trying to get with a guy, but just dancing. Maybe with Rachel, although they had gone dancing before, and Rachel had been an even worse dancer than Zach.

Zach. Fenway shuddered.

When they had gone out before, Fenway had seen Rachel's eyes look up and down at her dancing, almost the way that the boys in the club had looked at her, but with envy, not lust. Fenway had moved effortlessly, really feeling the rhythm, feeling all the men's eyes on her, even though Fenway thought Rachel was the prettier of the two. But there wasn't any hate in Rachel's eyes—jealousy, perhaps, but more because she wanted to be part of what Fenway was doing, not because she wanted the boys' eyes on her.

Fenway sighed and her breath caught. She was glad Olivia was found and was somewhere safe. But Fenway missed Rachel. She tried not to think of what might have happened to her. What she might be doing, whether or not she was in danger.

Fenway stopped and thought. Rachel had disappeared without a trace, and that in itself was strange. Buprenodone overdoses affected many different parts of the body—but Fenway knew from dealing with a couple of buprenodone overdoses in the Seattle clinic, that the patients needed rest and time, not fancy medication. It was suddenly clear to Fenway that Rachel wasn't on her own; without money, she wouldn't have been able to go anywhere, and since she needed days of sleep and fluids to recover, she needed somewhere to stay put. The police had already searched her sister's apartment and Rachel's house. Where else could she be hiding out?

Rachel didn't trust a lot of people, especially after what happened with her father two months before. Her friends still avoided her; Jordan, her friend since fifth grade, had stopped returning her calls. Same thing with a lot of her old friends. Her former mother-in-law? Fenway supposed that was possible, but she didn't think they were particularly close.

Fenway was pretty sure Rachel trusted her, certainly enough to hide her if she needed it. But Rachel hadn't contacted her. Fenway was also positive that Dez was a good candidate for Rachel turning to in a bind; Dez was almost like a mother to Rachel, especially after her father went to jail. But Fenway had been over to Dez's apartment after Rachel's disappearance. There wasn't any sign of anyone there besides Dez—although she hadn't really looked. And Fenway was certain that Dez could keep a secret—from McVie, from Fenway, from everyone else at the sheriff's office.

Dez might be hiding Rachel somewhere. Fenway wouldn't put it past her.

Of all the people Rachel trusted, most of them were the friends she went through hard times with in the last couple of months.

Did that include Natalie Andrada—or Captain Elena Valenzuela, or whoever she was?

She kept coming back to Natalie through process of elimination. Rachel wasn't staying with her sister, or with Fenway, or with Dez—and she didn't have the financial footprint to be staying anywhere on her own.

Fenway snapped back to reality as bright oncoming headlights shined in her face. A loud growl in her stomach told her she needed to eat before she could think this through any more.

"I'm all keyed up," Fenway said. "You want to get something to eat?"

McVie shrugged. "Sure." He looked at the clock on his dashboard. "It's almost one. What's open?"

"Jack and Jill's."

"Do you actually eat anywhere else?"

"Dos Milagros."

McVie rolled his eyes.

"And my father takes me to all the pretentious restaurants in the county. But Dos Milagros closed at ten, and the pretentious restaurants are all closed on Tuesdays because that's when the wizards gather the unicorn tears to prepare the truffle foam."

McVie chuckled. "You sure you want to go to a sit-down place?"

Fenway imagined grabbing something quick from the all-night market and going back to her apartment with Craig. But she nodded.

"There's a whole bunch of information you haven't been read in on yet," she said. "It'll be good to have a place to talk it over."

"You sure you want to read me in? I'm still on leave."

"I'm sure," Fenway said.

"Anything you want to tell me now?"

"Well..." Fenway paused, gathering her thoughts. "Piper found out that Natalie isn't really Natalie."

"Natalie?"

"Rachel's admin. The one who let us into the office the day she disappeared."

"Hold on, Natalie isn't really Natalie?"

"This is kind of a long story." She paused. "Perfect for a late-night greasy spoon discussion."

"Good," he said. "I'm a little keyed up too."

They pulled up to Jack and Jill's at five minutes to one. There were a couple of big rigs parked in the back of the lot, perhaps on their way to or from Santa Barbara or Ventura. Late on a Tuesday night—or early on a Wednesday morning—there weren't any other customers in the restaurant except for the two truck drivers, both at the counter, staring bleary-eyed at their cups of coffee and half-finished burgers.

"Good evening," the hostess said, recognizing McVie. "You're in late." She looked at Fenway, still in her short black clubbing dress and the strappy high heels, and a look of disapproval crossed her face. Fenway did her best to ignore it.

"Big night," Craig said. "Knocking down doors, saving lives."

The hostess smiled and took them to a table on the side, a little away from the truck drivers.

"Coffee?" the hostess said, as she handed both of them a menu.

"Absolutely," McVie said.

The hostess turned away, and Fenway looked at the late-night menu, knowing she would just order eggs and sourdough toast.

The server bought coffee and cream. Fenway poured the half-and-half into her coffee from the small silver pitcher.

Fenway nodded. "So, I didn't ask you, Craig, when do you hear about going back?"

"Oh," McVie said, "that's not—"

McVie stopped talking and a shadow fell over his face.

"Going back *to work*," Fenway said, trying to keep the color from rising to her cheeks. He had thought she meant going back to Amy.

He cleared his throat. "That's not for another couple of days. Red tape and all."

The server came and took their order. Fenway waited until she went back into the kitchen before she spoke again.

"So," Fenway said. "About Natalie."

Fenway explained everything Piper had told her—how Captain Elena Valenzuela had just dropped off the map, how she had appeared in the back of a photograph of white-collar drug dealers, how she possibly spearheaded a new black-market prescription drug ring, how Nozithrapham could be the next Oxycontin, but even more dangerous because of its classification as a non-opiate.

"Nozithrapham? Is that what Red Skies are?"

Fenway nodded.

She also told him about the strange conversation she had with Natalie, and their plans to meet at Rachel's office later that morning.

"And I think Rachel is hiding out at her place," Fenway finished, just as the server came with their plates: eggs and toast for Fenway, a BLT and fries for McVie.

McVie salted his fries, then set the salt down thoughtfully. "Why would you think that Rachel is with Natalie?"

"Because Rachel only trusts a handful of people." She held up a forkful of egg but didn't put it in her mouth. "But she's not with me, she's not with Dez, and she's not with her sister, and there's been no movement on any of her bank accounts or credit cards. She's got to be hiding out, and it's got to be close, and I can't think of anyone other than Natalie." She finally ate the egg off her fork.

"There's no way you could get a warrant."

"Of course not." Fenway shook her head. "But you could park in front of her house. Take a look and see if there's any indication that Rachel is there."

McVie paused as he ate a bite of hash browns. "Fenway, remember that I'm still officially off the job. I don't have my badge or gun. I don't have backup."

"Maybe I could do it."

"No—my official status isn't the issue. Check that—it *is* an issue. But I meant my lack of a firearm."

"You're telling me you don't have a personal firearm?"

McVie sighed. "Yes, I do, but it's at the house in my gun safe."

"I'm not asking you to go there straight from here. You can go home first."

McVie paused. "You know I can't just waltz in there, not with the way Amy and I are right now."

Fenway cringed. She hadn't intended for this to come up.

"My point is," he continued, ignoring Fenway's discomfort, "if Natalie really is the one behind this, she's very dangerous. She might have murdered two people, kidnapped a child, and hired a hit man to kill Rachel. And if Rachel *does* trust Natalie and Natalie's the bad guy, can you think of a scenario where Rachel isn't dead by now?"

The sentence hit Fenway like a slap in the face. McVie was right; even if Fenway's theory about Rachel going to Natalie held water, Rachel probably wouldn't have survived an hour, let alone the three days it had been. She set her fork down.

"What are we going to do, then?" she said softly, trying to keep the hysteria out of her voice. "I can't think of any other explanation."

"You've had other leads," he said more like a question than a statement.

"Yes," Fenway admitted, "but everything about Natalie being behind it all fits."

"But we didn't see her leaving the warehouse last night," McVie pointed out. "We couldn't tell who those two people were, but neither of them had a wheelchair."

"You know as well as I do that whoever's trying to get control of the Nozithrapham market here doesn't do all their own dirty work." She shook her head. "No, I felt the same way about Stotsky—once I found out that he was Rachel's dad, everything just slid into place like the last piece of a jigsaw puzzle in my head."

Fenway could see McVie mulling over the options before he spoke. "I don't think I can convince anyone in the sheriff's office to simply go over to her place and take a look around," he finally said. "Especially not after what happened last night. We'll have to go through proper channels from now on. And it's too dangerous for either one of us to do it ourselves."

"We could go over to Rachel's and get her .22. And she might still have Dylan's Glock."

"Do you hear yourself talking?"

"Do you have a better idea?"

"We don't have any proof that Natalie has Rachel, Fenway. This is a stretch. I *do* have a better idea—it's to work the case until you have something that points to Natalie, or Elena, or whoever she is, actually being guilty of something."

Fenway thought for a minute. "Isn't there some sort of misrepresentation of, I don't know, military personnel or county employees that we could charge her with, so we can at least question her and see inside her place?"

"I'm not going to purposely skirt around the fourth amendment just because you—"

Fenway waited for a few seconds. McVie had a faraway look in his eyes.

"Because I what?" she asked tentatively.

"Hang on," McVie said thoughtfully. "Of course. A 470b."

Fenway looked plaintively at McVie and waited for him to explain.

"Sorry," he said, catching the awkward silence. "Fake ID."

"Same thing you catch the college kids with trying to buy beer?"

"Yes, but definitely a different application. If she didn't change her name legally, she might be in possession of a fake ID that allowed her to work for the county fraudulently."

"Ah," Fenway said.

"That would at least allow us to question her, and it might be enough to search her property."

"You did say proper channels," Fenway said. "What do you need me to do?"

"You said you were going to meet Natalie this morning at Rachel's office, right?"

"Right."

"So go there. When does she get in?"

"She said she'd be there at 7:30."

"Okay. While you're doing that, I'll call HR and see if I can get any information about her job application. You know, when she first applied for the position. If she didn't disclose that she's known by another name, it could be fraud."

"And talk to Piper," Fenway interrupted. "She's got a lot of info on Elena Valenzuela."

"Will do."

They ate in silence for a minute or two.

McVie took the last bite of his BLT, pushed his plate away, wiped his mouth, and sat back. "Did I hear you say you got your Accord?"

"I don't want to talk about it." She sopped up the remaining yolk on her plate with her last bite of toast.

McVie looked at her.

"My father," she said. "Sticking his nose in. Didn't even get my mother's painting, which is why I went up there in the first place."

McVie nodded.

The server came over to refill their coffee and Fenway asked for the check.

She felt like the moment when she could ask him to spend the night would slip from her grasp if she didn't do it soon. She could read his face and saw him planning his next steps for trying to get Rachel back. At least he was on her side.

"How long do you need with HR?" she asked.

"They get in at eight. I should have everything I need by half-past. Maybe a little later."

"So I've got to keep Natalie busy for an hour?"

"It's not like she's going to rush over to HR. Probably not, any-way. I just want you to be there to make sure she doesn't. I'm on leave, I shouldn't be there anyway."

Fenway looked at Craig across the table.

"How are you doing, Craig? On leave, I mean. You okay?"

McVie chuckled. "I'm keeping busy. I've had to deal with a corpse in a trunk in front of my house. It's been a crazy—" And suddenly, a painful look came over his face. He looked away.

Fenway wanted to comfort him, to leave her side of the table and slide into the booth next to him. She wanted to take him in her arms. Like she wanted him to comfort her after Stotsky attacked her in her apartment two months before.

For a fleeting moment, Fenway pictured herself doing that, wrapping her arms around Craig, feeling him sigh, exhaling the pain and breathing in her scent, her perfume, her comfort. She pictured herself taking his hand in hers and letting him lean against her. Leading him out of the restaurant, going back to his motel room, turning off her phone, turning off his phone, getting into the queen bed with him, hooking her leg over his under the covers and pulling herself on top like she did in his car, feeling his lips on her collarbone and her neck, feeling his fingers and hands run over her body, letting his worry and pain run off him and onto her.

She shuddered.

"Listen," he said, snapping Fenway back to the present, "I've gotta go back to the motel and get a few hours of sleep. I've gotta be on my game if I'm going to go through Natalie's files in a few hours."

She hoped the disappointment didn't register too much in her face. "No," she said, "I suppose you do need to be fresh. I guess I can get a few hours of sleep too."

McVie caught the server's eye, and she brought the check.

"I'll get it," Fenway said. "You're on leave."

"*Paid* leave," McVie said. "It's not a problem."

Fenway wanted to keep arguing about his expenses going up because of the motel, but then thought better of it.

She felt tension in the car as McVie drove Fenway to her apartment. She wanted to ask him to come upstairs with her, thinking hard about how to make it sound casual, but couldn't come up with anything. It seemed to take no time at all until they were turning into her apartment complex's driveway.

"Okay," McVie said, putting his hand on the gearshift as he stopped in front of her building. "I'll text you as soon as I'm done with Natalie's file."

"Okay," Fenway said, looking McVie in the eyes, trying to gauge whether to lean forward or play it coy. Finally she put her hand on top of his, on the gearshift. "I'm really glad you took me to the warehouse tonight. I really needed to see Olivia safe. It meant a lot to me."

"I'm glad I did too," McVie said. "Let's kick some ass tomorrow, Fenway."

She smiled, picked up her purse, and then opened the door and got out of the car.

She walked up the stairs to her apartment and wrapped her arms around herself.

PART VI

WEDNESDAY

CHAPTER TWENTY-FOUR

HER HEAD HIT THE PILLOW AT TWO-FIFTEEN IN THE MORNING, but she woke at five, an hour and a half before her alarm, wide awake. She could feel the nervous energy coursing through her. She lay in bed for ten minutes, trying to get back to sleep, but it didn't happen; her brain wouldn't shut up. She reluctantly pulled herself out of bed and put on some running shorts and a tank top.

She went for a run out through the butterfly waystation just as the first fingers of light were snaking over the mountains, and stood for a few minutes, watching the morning light play on the water. She wished again that her father had brought back the painting she had gone to Seattle to get.

When she returned, she took a long shower, making the time to put the shea butter and avocado oil treatment on her hair. She put her makeup on carefully and deliberately. She looked in the mirror and thought she had done a good job.

Fenway transferred everything back to her larger purse from her clutch, and saw Rachel's apartment key still in her purse. She reminded herself yet again to give the key back to Dez.

As Fenway drove to the parking garage at City Hall, she had a hard time figuring out what she would tell Natalie. She didn't want Natalie to think Fenway suspected her of anything, so she'd have to dust much of Rachel's office for fingerprints.

She got out of her car; she still had the thoughts of Craig and the motel room in her head. She closed the door and walked halfway down the ramp of the parking garage before she snapped her fingers and ran back to the car, getting the fingerprint kit from the floor of the passenger side.

She walked quickly, looking at her phone—it was 7:35. She was already five minutes late to meet Natalie—and she didn't think Natalie would look kindly on tardiness. Probably a great fit as Rachel's assistant, Fenway thought, if it weren't for the whole drug kingpin thing.

She went into City Hall and took the stairs two at a time to the second floor, catching her breath when she reached the landing at the top. She smoothed her blouse down and shook her hair out, then cleared her throat and entered Rachel's office.

Natalie looked up from behind her desk. "Good morning, Fenway," she said. She pulled a key out of her drawer. "Okay, you still need to get in there?"

"Sure," Fenway said, nodding her head, perhaps a little too enthusiastically, and pulling out her fingerprint kit.

Natalie wheeled over to Rachel's office door and unlocked it, swinging it open.

The scent of pine and rubbing alcohol tickled Fenway's nose. She looked at the desk, a single neat stack of papers in the corner. The post-it notes had been taken off the monitor, which looked polished and new.

"What happened in here?" Fenway said, dazed.

"Oh, no," Natalie said, putting her hand to her mouth. "The cleaning crew must have been in last night. Usually they just empty the wastebasket, but once a week they give the office a thorough cleaning. That must have been last night."

Fenway closed her eyes and shook her head, and had to suppress a laugh. She had thought she had been telling a lie about the cleaners coming last night when she persuaded Huke to get her the fingerprint kit. Not only had she been unwittingly telling the truth, but now there were no fingerprints to recover.

"I am so sorry, Fenway," Natalie said. "I didn't realize they'd be in here last night."

"It's totally my fault," Fenway said, trying not to break into sardonic laughter. "I knew yesterday that the cleaning crew would be in last night; that's why I came over here in such a rush. And then I just forgot about it when we got to talking."

"Do you think you can get anything useful?" Natalie said.

Fenway shook her head. "I specifically wanted to get prints from the monitor, where all those post-it notes were." She looked around. "I suppose I should dust for prints anyway. Just in case the cleaners missed something."

Natalie nodded as Fenway snapped on her blue gloves.

Fenway didn't really want to fingerprint everything; the dust got everywhere, and she had dressed more nicely than usual—certainly nicer than she would ordinarily be dressed to fingerprint an office. But in her experience, cleaners wouldn't get all the fingerprints wiped off; they were looking to make the room clean, not to eliminate all traces of fingerprint evidence. Her original plan had been to limit the dust to the desk and the monitor. But now, she'd be dusting some of the bookshelves, the light switches, and the metal arms of the guest chairs, even though they were curved surfaces. She sighed, resigned to the fact that this would take a messy hour or two. She couldn't see a way around it, however; Natalie—or Elena—likely would see through her ruse if she just gave up. She thanked Natalie and shut the door.

Fenway started with the desk, now cleaned off completely. She expected just a few fingerprints, probably of the cleaners themselves. She thought she would quickly find a corner that hadn't been wiped clean. She dipped the brush in the carbon and tapped off some of the excess. She held the brush just on the surface of the desk and spun the handle of it between her thumb and her first two fingers to spread the carbon powder on the desk's surface. The large desk made for tedious work, but Fenway exercised as much patience as she could muster.

But she found nothing. No traces of fingerprints at all. She even did the edges of the desktop, and not a single particle of carbon stuck to anything.

"Damn," she said to herself, "I wonder if these cleaning people are available for my apartment."

She did the light switch next. But again, the same thing—no traces of any fingerprints at all. And then the bookcase. Even the bottom shelf. Then the edges of the monitor. Then the back of the monitor. Then the squishy armrests and metal arms of the guest chairs.

Not a single fingerprint. Not a partial. Nothing at all.

Fenway sat in Rachel's chair and thought. This wasn't the work of a thorough cleaning service. The office had been cleaned by someone specifically trying to eliminate all traces of fingerprints. Someone who knew what they were doing. It took a level of patience, determination, and discipline almost *military* in precision.

She should have known as soon as the scent of pine hit her nostrils: she had underestimated Natalie. Natalie had convinced her to return the next morning, but had obviously come back and cleaned everything. She should have listened to Piper—Fenway wouldn't be able to rattle Natalie or talk her into a corner. Fenway was angry with herself; she should have seen this coming.

She wiped down all the surfaces and packed up her kit. It was past nine when she finally removed her gloves. The fingerprint kit had taken much longer than she had expected—but McVie should have called at least a half hour ago. As if reading her mind, her phone rang, McVie's name popping up onscreen.

"Hey, Craig," she said.

"I'm done with HR," he said quietly. "Sorry, it took me a lot longer than I thought."

"What did you find?"

"Nothing," he said.

"Nothing?"

"Well, that's not exactly true," he said. "I found a big red stamp marked 'Classified.' And a big brick wall where the information should be."

"All right," Fenway said. "I'm still in Rachel's office. I just finished up. Why don't you meet me in the plaza?"

"How about the coffee cart downstairs?"

"Okay. Give me five minutes."

She hung up the phone and got up from Rachel's chair, trying to see if she could work up the resolve to talk to Natalie, to try to catch her between a rock and a hard place. She took a deep breath. Maybe Fenway would ask Natalie about the Marines. Maybe some talk of rank, or how Fenway had toyed with the idea of the G.I. bill before she chose the route of massive college loan debt.

She picked up the fingerprint kit and walked to the outer office.

"Did you find anything?" Natalie asked, looking up from the computer, but still typing.

"I'm afraid not," Fenway replied. "Those cleaners did a pretty good job in there."

Natalie nodded sympathetically.

Fenway opened her mouth to talk—to try to get Natalie talking—and then shut it again.

"Did you need anything else?" Natalie's fingers finally paused on her keyboard.

Fenway shook her head. "Nope. I guess I keep hoping Rachel will just magically show up."

Natalie averted her eyes and nodded. "I know what you mean."

Fenway hated herself for being so indecisive, but finally said goodbye and went out into the hallway.

She trudged down the stairs. McVie, waiting at the coffee cart, watched her come down. She got to the landing and walked up to him.

"Hey," she said.

"Got you a large latte," he said.

She brightened. "Thank you, sir."

"Don't mention it."

"So," Fenway said, lowering her voice, "you didn't find anything at all?"

"I got Natalie's address from payroll. That's it."

"What did HR say?"

"They told me that they couldn't give me any more information unless I had the proper authorization."

"But you're the sheriff. You're leading this case."

"Not right now. And even when I'm reinstated, I don't get first dibs above the Feds."

"The Feds? They're the ones who locked Natalie's files?"

"I think so," McVie said. "I said I'd speak to the state attorney and they said she didn't have the proper authorization either."

"The Feds locked Natalie's HR files just because Piper nosed around a little?"

McVie shook his head. "No, apparently the files were locked down as soon as Natalie arrived. Whatever's happening has been going on for weeks, if not months."

"So—who do you think locked the files? You think the FBI is involved in catching Natalie?"

"If I had to guess, I'd say the ATF."

The barista handed both their coffees to them and they walked outside. The day hadn't heated up just yet.

Fenway took a sip of her coffee. "This isn't good, Craig. If Natalie killed Mayor Jenkins and if the Feds have a claim to her, we're not going to be able to give the city any closure."

"I know," McVie said, gloomily. "We'll have to think of something else. I kind of hoped you would've had better luck in Rachel's office."

"I didn't find anything either," Fenway said. "Not a single fingerprint."

"What do you mean, not a single print?"

"I mean someone went in there and wiped every single surface clean of prints. They did a very thorough job. Much more thorough than a normal cleaning staff would do. I'm positive Natalie cleaned that office last night."

McVie paused. "I think we're dealing with someone very good at this." He rubbed his forehead with the tips of his fingers. "I don't know who we can trust and what we can't."

Fenway shook her head. "It's pretty obvious to me that we can't trust Natalie. We know for a fact that she isn't who she says she is."

McVie nodded.

"I say we go over to her place now," Fenway continued. "Before she has an opportunity to get back there. Before she suspects that I know anything."

"It might be too late for that," McVie said. "If she's the one who cleaned the office last night, you're probably already on her radar."

"She might still be holding Rachel there," Fenway insisted.

McVie shook his head. "I don't think so. I think that would be too close to home. She'd be keeping her somewhere. She'd have people working for her guarding Rachel."

"You're probably right," Fenway said, "but I'm at least going to go look."

"That's dangerous. Didn't I just say there might be a guard there? Or the person who killed the private investigator might be there."

Fenway shrugged. "I can talk my way out of it."

McVie pressed his lips together. "Look, Fenway, I appreciate that you feel like you need to do something about Rachel, but that's just—" he sighed. "That's just *not* a smart thing to do. There's such a high chance of something going wrong."

Fenway tapped her foot. "Listen, Craig, if I *am* on Natalie's radar, that gives us until about five o'clock tonight to get whatever is at Natalie's house. If that's evidence, if that's Nozithrapham—or if that's Rachel. Once she leaves the office, the first thing she's going to do is move everything from her house. I need to go there. Have the police come with me if you want."

"No, Fenway," he said firmly. "It's too dangerous." He exhaled loudly, clearly irritated.

"Of course it's dangerous," Fenway snapped. "But I'm afraid the next place Rachel goes will be in a shallow grave. I don't think it's the safe move either, but I don't think we'll have another chance to get Rachel. Period." She crossed her arms. "I'm sorry, Craig, but our master plan didn't work. We didn't find anything to question Natalie about. No fingerprints. No nothing. And I think we're running out of time."

"Don't forget, no warrant," McVie said. "If we move now and we're wrong, or we're caught, we can kiss any chance of finding Rachel—and, by the way, solving Mayor Jenkins' murder—goodbye."

Fenway put her hands on her hips, ready to counter the argument, and then sighed and put her arms at her sides. "You're right," she said. "I want to find her, I want to pull her out of danger, but you're right. It's stupid."

"I said dangerous, not stupid."

"You said it wasn't smart."

McVie rolled his eyes. "Yeah, okay." He glanced at his watch. "I'm heading over to the prosecutor's office," he said. "I'm going to see if anyone knows when I can come back. Maybe they've scheduled a hearing."

"You're expecting them to do a hearing?"

"No," he said. "But I want to be prepared for the worst. I thought I took care of all the reports and paperwork at the scene, but I haven't heard anything."

"Okay," Fenway said. Then, trying to sound as nonchalant as she could: "You want to grab some lunch later?"

Craig looked into Fenway's eyes, paused for a moment, and smiled. "Yeah," he said. "Yeah, I'd like that." Then he turned and walked down the sidewalk toward the district attorney's offices.

Fenway watched him walk away, admiring his body in spite of herself, and went across the street to her building. She turned the information over in her mind. Rachel's office had just been cleaned. Natalie was probably still attempting to conceal her true identity—which meant that Natalie didn't know Fenway had seen the report from Piper.

Fenway set her jaw; she knew McVie warned her of the danger of going to Natalie's place, but she knew in her gut she'd find Rachel there, and she saw the window of opportunity closing quickly.

She walked in. Migs, Mark, and Dez were all behind their desks.

"Good morning, everyone. I hear congratulations are in order."

"They sure are," Mark said, beaming. "We rescued Olivia Jenkins from the warehouse district last night."

"How's she doing?"

"Physically, she's okay," Dez said. "Mentally, I don't know. But some kids are really resilient. I couldn't tell if she really understood what had happened to her."

"Everything okay with the warrant, Migs?"

Migs nodded. "Yeah, the anonymous tip looks to me like it'll stand up in court, and the judge agreed."

"So I know why Mark and I didn't get here till nine," Dez said. "But you're not usually late, Fenway."

Fenway shot a look at Migs, wondering if Migs had said anything about the screaming match she had gotten in with her father, but Migs' lips were pressed tightly together and he avoided eye contact.

"I dusted for fingerprints in Rachel's office this morning. Natalie and I met at seven-thirty."

"I thought we got everything we needed from the guest book."

Fenway shook her head. "I thought there might be something on her monitor. There were a bunch of post-it notes on there."

"You heard the news?" Dez said.

Fenway paused. "You mean there's more than Olivia's rescue?"

"Yep, good old Mr. Smellsgood," Dez cackled. "He sent out a press release this morning announcing his candidacy for coroner. Apparently he had the press conference at Carpetti in their boardroom."

"Now that Dr. Klein is running for mayor," Migs piped up, "Everett Michaels is going to need a challenger to keep him honest."

"That's not me," Fenway said defensively. "No way. He's handsome, he's charismatic, he's rich, and he's—"

"He's an entitled sonofabitch, is what he is," said Dez.

"Sure," Fenway said, "but he's also my father's preferred candidate. Talk about swimming upstream. And besides, I've got my state nursing boards next month. I need to start studying."

"Your dad isn't the superhero he thinks he is." Dez tapped her foot. "He endorsed Michaels this morning, and I've gotta say that the audience reacted, uh, *tepidly*. The public might not trust Ferris anymore after his right-hand man turned out to be a murderer."

"*Alleged* murderer," said Migs. "Trial date hasn't even been set yet."

Dez gave Migs a nasty look and Fenway laughed. "Okay," she said. "Let me know if you need anything." She walked into her office, shutting the door behind her, and woke up her laptop. She typed in her password, then did a web search for *U.S. Marines Keepsake Clock*.

She found it on the third link—a clock with all the Marines paraphernalia that Natalie had on hers, and the exact same design. She clicked on the order form and scrolled down to the section for the soldier's information for the nameplate. Fenway entered some phony information—"Barry Klein," with a rank of "Major Pain in the Ass"—and clicked the button to continue.

A mocked-up graphic of the nameplate appeared—with no indication that it would be checked against a master database. Only a credit card information form stood between Fenway and a U.S. Marines keepsake clock with false identification data. She leaned back in her chair.

There was a knock at the door and Dez stuck her head in. "Fenway?"

"Come on in."

"This just came over." Dez walked in with a few sheets of paper and set them in front of Fenway. Fenway glanced at it; there were graphs and chemical names and phrases like "TLC densitometry" and "analysis of aqueous solutions of synthetic dyes."

"Forensics came back with the ink analysis?"

"Yes," Dez said. "Just the fake suicide note that they found at Rachel's, though. The credit card receipt from Maxime's was lower priority."

"They're analyzing that too?"

Dez held up her hand. "Hey, I know, it doesn't seem like it would tell us anything, but Kav was insistent. It's San Miguelito's budget, not ours. If they want to set fire to their money, so be it."

"So what does it say? Bic ballpoint, only a bazillion of those in the world?"

Dez looked at Fenway, a half-smile on her face. "No," she said. "It was Montblanc ink, the blue-black. Some sort of special blue dye in it that turns black after it oxidizes."

"Sounds fancy."

"It is."

"Sounds like the kind of ink you'd use in a keepsake pen set." She turned the monitor around to face Dez. "The kind of keepsake pen set that would come with a U.S. Marines keepsake clock."

Dez looked at the monitor and looked at Fenway. "That's the same kind of clock Natalie Andrada has on her desk."

"Yep," Fenway said.

Dez noticed the nameplate on the mock-up. "Nice that you can keep your sense of humor about Dr. Klein."

"It's not humor, it's misplaced rage," Fenway said, smiling sweetly.

"Do you think Natalie has something to do with all this?" Dez asked incredulously.

"I should have told you about this yesterday, Dez," Fenway said. "This is a long story. It might take a while."

"You know you're talking about an ex-Marine," Dez said, shaking her head. "She lost both her legs fighting for this country. You're saying she's behind everything? From the mayor's murder to the little girl's kidnapping to Rachel's disappearance?"

"Don't forget the murder victim in the trunk of the car at McVie's house."

"You think she's behind all of that?"

Fenway nodded. "And if you can believe it, that's just the tip of the iceberg."

A knock sounded at the door.

"Yes?"

Migs opened the door. "Everett Michaels is here to see you, Fenway."

Fenway rolled her eyes. "Did he say what he wanted?"

"He said it was important that he discuss an 'action plan.'"

"Whatever he means by that," Fenway muttered. "Okay, Migs, tell him I'll be right with him."

Migs nodded and shut the door behind him.

Fenway turned her attention back to Dez. "While I'm getting rid of Mr. Smellsgood, call the sheriff. Both of you should go see Piper—she's got all the intel on this. I couldn't believe it either, but she can show you all the evidence—fingerprints, photographs, false identities."

Dez cocked her head to the side skeptically. "You're sure about this? It's hard evidence, not just circumstantial?"

Fenway hesitated. "Most of it *is* circumstantial," Fenway admitted, "but there would have to be a lot of coincidences for Natalie to be innocent."

"I don't like coincidences," Dez said quietly.

"Not even when veterans are involved?"

Dez paused. "No. Not even then."

"Would you ask Mr. Smellsgood to come in?"

"Sure." Dez walked out of Fenway's office.

CHAPTER TWENTY-FIVE

EVERETT MICHAELS LOOKED READY FOR A MAGAZINE SHOOT IN A neatly pressed charcoal gray tailored suit, with a white dress shirt and a patterned tie in dark red and navy that somehow managed to look patriotic without trying too hard. Fenway marveled at his command of the room even though he obviously planned to ask for a favor.

"Mr. Michaels," Fenway said, rising from her chair.

"Please, call me Everett." He flashed a charming smile and Fenway felt her heart lurch. His charms were beating down her defenses, and she wondered just how many women had succumbed to his unique combination of sensory gifts.

Fenway nodded. "Okay, Everett. And you can call me Fenway." She saw Everett glance at the monitor, still swiveled around to the front of the desk. He smiled. "I see you're no fan of the new mayoral candidate."

Fenway quickly turned the monitor back around. "That's no secret," Fenway said. "And you know he doesn't much care for me either."

"To be honest, I'm really glad I don't have to run against him in November. He doesn't like your dad, he's a scrappy fighter, and I'm sure he'd do everything he could to win." Everett sat down in the guest chair in front of Fenway's desk.

"So what can I do for you?" Fenway asked, taking her seat as well.

"There are one or two things I'd like to discuss." He cleared his throat. "You see, I expected to go the full twelve rounds with Dr. Klein for the coroner election. I could have outspent him, of course, and I have the backing of your father. I have been quite direct in asking for your endorsement, but even without it, I remain confident that you wouldn't have endorsed Dr. Klein."

Fenway smiled. "True."

"But now," Everett continued, "I'm running unopposed."

Fenway nodded.

"What do you suppose my chances are for continuing to be unopposed?"

Fenway chuckled. "You mean, am I going to run?"

"Yes, and I must say, I'm wondering if the row you had with your father last night will affect your decision."

"Just to spite him and his handpicked candidate?" Fenway ran a hand through her curls and gently shook her hair out. "I think you overestimate my desire to spite my father, and you underestimate my need for self-preservation."

Everett smiled.

"Can I assume that's a no?"

"No current plans," Fenway said. "I have the nursing boards to study for, and the filing deadline is just three weeks away. So unless you really do something to piss me off, you won't have to worry about me opposing you."

"In that case, Miss Stevenson—I apologize, *Fenway*—maybe you and I can start some information sharing to make it a smooth transition in January."

Fenway narrowed her eyes at Everett. "Information sharing?"

"That's correct," he said. "If you could, say, introduce me to the staff, acquaint me with your open cases, and give me a bit of training on the procedures and expectations in the coroner's office, particularly the unwritten rules, as they say. I would hate to find myself knocked down by a cultural misstep that could have been avoided."

Fenway put her elbow on the desk and rested her chin in her palm.

"It makes quite a bit of logical sense, don't you think?" he continued. "You're quite well respected by your peers. You've been able to navigate the politics of this office, you've had some very public successes, and—well, you've been able to carve out an identity for yourself that's separate from your dad."

Fenway shook her head. "I'm not sure that's been successful. Everyone who loves my father now hates me, and everyone who hates my father *still* thinks I'm in his pocket."

Everett smiled. "So the real reason you're not running is because you think you'd lose?"

Fenway smiled back. "Of course I would lose, but I never intended to do anything but babysit this position anyway." And then she felt a pang of regret. Even though the deaths were hard to deal with, she enjoyed the puzzles of piecing together the information—time of death, drugs in the system, enlarged hearts, and so forth. And of course she'd miss the people she worked with. But she didn't care for the politics of the position, and could only imagine that running for office would be a nightmare. People would finally see how young, naïve, and underqualified she was, and the idea of a humiliating election defeat turned her stomach. But there were jobs in forensic nursing, surely; she had already toyed with the idea of staying in this field after she passed her state boards. Maybe as an assistant to Dr. Yasuda. And maybe she'd move to San Miguelito so she could get a little distance from her father's sphere of influence.

Everett nodded. "If you're up for it, and if you have time, I'd like to start getting up to date on your cases as soon as possible. Especially the Alice Jenkins murder. You've got her son in custody?"

Fenway shook her head. "No, Everett, I apologize, but I don't think that's appropriate right now." She paused. "In fact, I've been meaning to ask you a couple of things for a while."

"Ask me?" The confidence in his face drained. "Ask me what?"

Fenway cocked her head. "This Nozithrapham," she said. "For one thing, the man who shot up the hospital had his mother in the clinical trial."

Everett sat up straight. "You think it's connected?"

Fenway shrugged. "I don't know what to think."

He smiled radiantly. "I can give you assurances that it's not. Those clinical trials are double-blind. Neither the doctors nor the patients know if they're taking the drug or the placebo."

"But Carpetti has access to all that information, don't they?"

He paused, looked up at the ceiling, and considered for a moment. "I suppose our clinical trial manager does," he conceded. "But the woman's son—the one who shot up the hospital, you say?—would have no way of knowing."

Fenway narrowed her eyes at Everett. "Okay," she said. "I'd like to see the information you have on that, anyway."

Everett shook his head. "No, no," he said. "That would be a health information privacy violation. We'd get fined. Give me a court order, sure, I'll be happy to comply. But Carpetti can't share that information with anyone outside the patients themselves."

Fenway sighed and remembered all the health privacy forms she'd handed out over her career. "Of course," she said. "I guess I assumed clinical trials were different, but obviously they're not."

Everett had a sympathetic smile on his face. "You're welcome to speak to the clinical trial manager."

"Right," Fenway said. "You mentioned him at breakfast. A German name, right? Gottfried something."

"Austrian, actually. Gottfried Ebner."

Fenway tapped her fingers on the desk. Maybe this Ebner character was Natalie's inside man for Blue Skies. It made sense: Ebner might have skimmed the Nozithrapham from the clinical trials, or ordered more than they needed. With the double-blind test, the doctors and patients would be none the wiser. Then Ebner would pass the drug to Natalie, who would take care over the black market in Dominguez County, and maybe all of California.

Fenway debated bringing up the dinner at Maxime's, but knew she had to. "Just one other thing."

"You found out I had dinner with the mayor," Everett Michaels said, nodding.

"Yes. When you came with my father and me to breakfast, you didn't mention you went to Maxime's with her the night she died."

Everett nodded. "Of course."

"Why didn't you tell us about it?"

"I wasn't obligated to; surely you know that."

"Of course," Fenway said. "But it's odd. It's odd that you didn't say, 'Mayor Jenkins, I can't believe she's gone, and she and I had just had a wonderful dinner Friday night.'"

Everett paused and ran a hand over his face. "Surely you've done things you're not proud of, Fenway."

Fenway thought back to the night before with Zach. Thought back to sleeping with McVie two months before. She nodded. "What aren't you proud of, Everett?"

"I took her to dinner to tell her that Carpetti decided to sunset a scholarship program that she'd championed. Scholarships for twenty Estancia High students who can't afford college."

Fenway briefly thought of her own crippling student loan debt.

"She, shall we say, expressed her displeasure with me. She had sob stories from students who counted on that money. I believe she told me I had to make it right."

Fenway breathed out. "Yes, I'd heard that exact phrase from one of our witnesses."

"Witnesses?" Everett chuckled, slight crinkles appearing around his eyes. "Surely you don't consider me a suspect? Not with someone already in custody who has confessed to the crime?"

"We're leaving no stone unturned," Fenway said. "I expect you to do the same when you're coroner. Otherwise, I won't vote for you. Even if you *do* run unopposed."

Everett smiled, a smile that made Fenway melt a little bit, and leaned forward. "It's obvious that I'll have some pretty big shoes to fill, Fenway," he said, a little bit softly, so Fenway had to lean slightly forward to hear him better. She breathed in. He smelled wonderful, a hint of cardamom in his cologne. "Listen, after you've finished doing your due diligence on me, I hope you reconsider sharing what you've learned on this case. Just an outline of what evidence you've found. Surely with a suspect in custody, you don't need to tell me a whole lot more than the news has already reported."

Fenway cleared her throat.

"Listen, we don't even need to make this official," Everett said, turning slightly to the side, leaning his forearm on the desk, and moving closer to Fenway. She caught his enchanting scent again; bergamot layered underneath the cardamom. "We could just have dinner together. People talk about work when they have dinner, don't they?"

"They do," Fenway admitted.

"Maybe we can head to a nice dinner tonight," Everett said. "Perhaps Origato?"

Fenway breathed in his scent again, but thought about due diligence, and gently leaned back, away from Everett.

"I love sushi," Fenway said, making her voice buttery. "And you're an incredibly—uh, your offer is incredibly generous." She forced herself to put a wistful smile on her face. "But people talk in this town. The two of us together having an intimate dinner wouldn't be politically good for either of us, as much as I might love to, uh, break bread with you."

Everett leaned away a bit also. "I can't say I'm not disappointed."

"I'll take a rain check in three weeks," Fenway offered.

Everett nodded, but Fenway could tell he had already moved on, the gears in his head turning. That broke the spell. She stood up.

"If that's everything, Everett, you'll need to excuse me. I still have a few open cases I need to be working on."

"Of course," Everett said, and turning the charm back on, stood, leaned forward slightly and looked deep into Fenway's eyes, and shook her hand, holding it a few seconds longer than necessary.

"Three weeks," Fenway said.

"I'll be back," Everett promised.

He left the office, leaving the door open. She could see Migs at his desk, looking at her with a question on his face. She shrugged and put her palms up. Migs nodded.

Fenway turned to her computer and logged into the system. She went into the county address database and found Natalie Andrada's house, on Mountain Lion Road in a town called Tukem. She knew neither the street nor the town, although Fenway didn't know much local geography beyond a few neighborhoods.

She pulled up Natalie's address on a web map and paused. Tukem wasn't much more than a crossroads in the foothills, off a side road from the road up to Cactus Lake. A winery stood about a mile before the turnoff, but she saw no gas stations or stores for a few miles in any direction.

It looked like Natalie lived on ten or twelve acres, almost forty-five minutes away from the office. She noticed the house had some back roads that could provide quick—and relatively private—access to the Cactus Lake Motel.

Perfect for getting away after she stabs the mayor to death, Fenway thought.

She looked at the satellite image. It didn't look any different than the neighboring houses. There were no signs of cement walls or gun turrets or anything else that Fenway associated with a compound. She didn't see anything that looked suspicious in the brush behind Natalie's house, either. There was a smattering of outbuildings: two large structures that could have been garages or barns—or storage units to hide drugs, Fenway supposed—and then a couple of smaller units that looked like utility or feed sheds. The house itself looked fairly small, although Fenway couldn't tell if the house had one story or more. She assumed it was single-story given Natalie's situation, but she didn't want to jump to conclusions. *A little late for that,* said a voice in the back of her mind.

She closed her laptop and grabbed her purse, walking out to Migs' desk.

Migs hung up the phone.

"I'm going to the sheriff's office," she said to Migs. "Gotta get the fingerprint kit back to Officer Huke."

"I was just on the phone with the district attorney's office," Migs said. "The warrant finally came through on Carpetti's financials."

"Oh," Fenway said. She had been so focused on Natalie that she had almost forgotten about that line of inquiry. "Great. You have an investigator on it?"

"Yeah. A consultant. Someone from Aperture Consulting. The D.A. told me that this is the second time someone from the county has called to look at Carpetti's financials."

"Second time?"

"That's what the D.A. said."

"Who did it the first time?" Then she remembered; Fletcher Jenkins worked for Aperture. Did the mayor ask him to look into the financials, and did something happen to warn Natalie, leading to the mayor's murder and Olivia's kidnapping?

Migs noticed Fenway's faraway gaze. "You know who the first auditor was, don't you?"

"Fletch."

"Yep," Migs said.

"We need to talk to that clinical trial manager," Fenway said. She pulled the fingerprint kit out of her purse. "Migs, I changed my mind. Would you go take this over to the sheriff's office, and then have Mark or Dez track down a man named Gottfried Ebner at Carpetti Pharmaceuticals? I have something I need to take care of."

"Sure," he said, taking the kit from her. "Need help with anything?"

"No, I got it."

Migs scrunched up his face a little. "You're not going to do anything that will make me wish I gave you a refresher course in legal search and seizure, are you?"

"No, of course not," Fenway lied.

"Good," Migs said. "I'm going to lock up."

"You'll only be gone for five minutes."

"Yep. So I'm going to lock up."

Fenway nodded and left the office.

She walked through the plaza toward the parking garage, thinking hard. She pulled her phone out and dialed her father.

"Nathaniel Ferris."

"Hi, Dad," she said. "I need a favor."

There was silence on the other end of the line.

Finally, Ferris spoke. "You've got a lot of nerve calling me for a favor after the way you treated me last night."

"Yes, I do," Fenway agreed. "Unfortunately, it's important. Can you spare one of your security guys to help me out?"

Ferris paused. "One of my security guys? What for?"

"I know where Rachel is. And I think I only have a little while before she gets moved."

"Shouldn't you be getting the sheriff's department to give you backup?"

"We don't have a warrant," she said.

"For the love of God, Fenway, you shouldn't go."

"I think I have to. I can convince Rachel to come with me. She might think she's safe, but she's with the main suspect."

"Main suspect for what?"

"For all of this. The mayor's murder, the hitman at the hospital, the murder of your P.I."

"You're not going, Fenway."

"Or what, you're going to ground me?"

Ferris scoffed. "Take this seriously, Fenway. If this guy did what you suspect, it's too dangerous."

"First of all, Dad, it's not a guy, and second of all, she's not home, and that's why I've got to do it now. I *am* taking this seriously. Time is running out."

Ferris was quiet.

"You think I *wanted* to call you up after our little talk yesterday?" Fenway walked up the stairs to the second floor of the parking garage. "Are you going to help me out or am I going up there alone?"

She heard her father take a deep breath and exhale, like he was deliberately trying to keep calm. "Okay," Ferris finally said, "I can send them up there right after work."

"Right after work?"

"They're all at a field training exercise in San Miguelito right now."

"Can you call them out of there?"

"I don't think they even have cell signal out there. And they're probably an hour away from their cars on foot. They're supposed to be done by three-thirty, though, and they can be back to Estancia by four-fifteen or so. Can you wait until then?"

She sighed. "No, Dad, that's too late." She saw her Accord and pulled out her keys. Fenway saw Rachel's apartment key at the bottom of her purse; Fenway had once again forgotten to give it back to Dez.

"Promise me you won't go by yourself."

"Don't be silly." Fenway unlocked her car. "Would I have called you for help if I were planning to go by myself?"

"Okay," Ferris said. "Look, I know we're fighting right now, but, uh, just take care of yourself, okay? I don't want anything to happen to you."

"All right." Fenway slid into the car and started the engine. "I'll take care of myself."

She ended the call and drove out of the garage. She thought for a moment; without McVie or her father's security detail, she knew she shouldn't go to Natalie's house—in the middle of nowhere, no less—without protection.

She knew she should do the safe thing. She should go home. She should figure out next steps later.

But she also strongly suspected the opportunity to save Rachel would be gone if she waited any longer. It wasn't the safe thing to do—but she knew it was the *right* thing to do.

She steeled herself and turned left, taking Estancia Canyon Boulevard across the freeway, and drove to Rachel's townhouse.

Fenway parked in a visitor's space and looked around the deserted lot. She got out of the Accord, walking quickly, and unlocked Rachel's front door with Dez's key.

She took the stairs two at a time and entered Rachel's bedroom. From the drawer of the nightstand, Fenway took out Rachel's Smith & Wesson Model 41. It had the five-and-a-half-inch barrel, not the longer seven-inch, which meant it could fit in Fenway's purse. She looked for the magazine release, and finally found the switch above the handle. The magazine came out faster than she thought it would and she caught it just before it fell.

There were eight bullets in the magazine. The other two bullets had been shot into Rachel's father's arm and shoulder two months before. Fenway hoped this gun might save her life again.

Fenway looked through the drawer for other bullets or maybe a full magazine, but she didn't find any more ammunition.

She pressed her lips together. Eight bullets would have to do.

She went downstairs and pulled back the front curtains to glance out of the front window. The parking lot was still empty. The clock on Rachel's wall read a quarter to eleven. Everyone was probably at work or school or running errands. Fenway slid the magazine into the gun and put the safety on before dropping it into her purse. It just barely fit, and the barrel didn't even stick out.

She opened the front door, then thought better of it, and started looking around the room. There was a desk and a chair in the alcove between the living room and the kitchen and Fenway made a beeline to it. She pulled open a couple of drawers and found an empty manila folder. She flipped through a stack of papers before she found several press release drafts. Putting them in the manila folder, supposedly for Natalie's review, she hoped it would be a good enough ruse if she needed to explain her presence at Natalie's house.

Fenway stepped out of the townhouse, locking the door behind her and walking quickly to her car. She started the Accord, typed Natalie's address into her car's navigation system, and drove out of the driveway, turning toward 326 and the road up to Cactus Lake.

Her heart pounded. Despite suggestions by Mark, Dez, and McVie, she had kept postponing her firearms training, thinking that she wouldn't need it in the few short months she'd be on the county payroll before she went back to nursing. But now she wished she had taken a few days out of her schedule to do it.

She turned on the radio to a pop song she didn't recognize. She turned it to the jazz station, and the opening notes of *A Love Supreme* greeted her. She laughed—her father's favorite song *would* come on at a time like this when she had pretty much lied to him about going up to Natalie's house herself. But she figured she had at least three or four hours before Natalie would return.

She turned off the radio and tried taking some deep breaths to calm down. "You know what you're doing is stupid and dangerous," she told herself. But as much as she tried, she couldn't shake the feeling that she was in the crucial window, the only chance she—no, that *anyone*—would get to save Rachel. Natalie would likely put additional safeguards in place as soon as she got home, the opportunity would close, and Rachel would be lost.

Her instincts were loudly telling her that she'd find Rachel there, either in the house itself or in one of the outbuildings. But if Rachel were there, that might also mean guards. And most certainly more firepower than Rachel's .22 had to offer. She promised herself if she saw any signs of guards, or of Natalie, she'd turn around and hightail it out of there.

She passed the winery on her right and kept watch for Mountain Lion Road. She saw the sign and turned; the road hairpinned almost immediately and went uphill at a steep angle. The Accord's engine began to complain.

She looked at the navigation system, which showed another three miles to Natalie's house, and she had to slow to twenty miles per hour. Fenway could hardly believe Natalie would choose to live out in the sticks like this when she was missing both her legs. But then, Fenway reasoned, the ex-Marine had fifteen-inch biceps. Fenway had preconceived notions of activities that would be difficult for a wheelchair-bound person, when in reality she supposed Natalie could do them better than most people *with* legs.

The road narrowed to a single lane, and Fenway slowed to about ten miles an hour. Some of the curves were blind, so Fenway turned her lights on and prayed no one was driving down the hill the other direction.

With about three-quarters of a mile to go, the asphalt ended and she heard gravel crunching under her tires. She came upon a three-slat split fence, painted white, and going over the next ridge—the beginning of Natalie's property, she thought. As she crested the ridge, she saw a small house, several outbuildings, and a concrete driveway. Her navigation system dinged, announcing her arrival.

She knew she couldn't sneak up on the house, and she hoped she'd find no one but Rachel there. She saw no cars in the driveway, but one of the outbuildings was a three-car garage. All the doors were closed.

No sign of guards. No sign of Natalie.

She took a deep breath.

She drove up the large concrete driveway and turned around so the nose of her car faced out. She thought of the Buick Verano in the hospital parking lot.

Fenway turned the car off. She picked up her purse. She put it over her left shoulder and arranged the gun handle up, so she could take it out quickly. She tried it; it slipped easily out of her purse and didn't catch on anything. But Fenway noticed her hands were shaking as she put the gun back in place.

She closed her eyes and took a deep breath.

It's good that you're scared, she told herself. *It means you realize that this is a dangerous situation.*

Keenly aware that she didn't know what she was getting into, she knew Dez and Craig and her father would all be very angry with her for putting herself in harm's way. She just hoped that she wouldn't be another victim needing to be rescued. Or another body on Dr. Yasuda's table.

She got out of the car and walked halfway up the driveway before she realized that she had left the press release folder—her ruse for being here—in the front seat. She went back and got the folder, walked up to the large maple front door with two rectangular smoked-glass windows in the top half. She reached for the doorbell, hesitated, and pushed it. Electronic chimes sounded, two of them in a lazy interval, high then low.

She waited, her heart pounding in her ears.

A shadow behind the glass.

The door opened.

CHAPTER TWENTY-SIX

A YOUNG BLACK WOMAN WITH SHORT TIGHTLY-CURLED HAIR stared back at Fenway. Fenway had seen her before—both in Natalie's office and at Dr. Barry Klein's press conference.

"Sascha?"

She nodded. "Come on in," she said.

Fenway hesitated. She hadn't expected to see the reporter from the *Estancia Courier*.

"This is what you came for, right?" Sascha asked. "So come on in. I'm kind of surprised someone put it together."

Fenway followed Sascha into the living room.

There, on the sofa, with two bowls of soup in front of her on the coffee table, was Rachel.

"Hi, Fenway," Rachel said quietly.

"Are you okay?"

"For now." Rachel nodded. "I'm safe here, for the time being."

"What are you talking about?" Fenway said, exasperated. "This is one of the least safe places you can be."

"I guess you haven't figured *everything* out," Sascha said. She pulled a badge out of her purse. Gold with dark blue lettering, with an eagle, wings spread, the badge had a small seal in the middle, a large U on the left and large S on the right, and just below the eagle, the letters ATF.

"Craig was right," Fenway muttered. "The ATF."

"Special Agent Robin Orlando," she said. "You probably also know me as James Monroe."

Fenway blinked.

"We're working on taking down a new opioid network before it gets up and running."

"Red Skies."

"Right. The sheriff's department made a grab of part of the last shipment last night when they rescued Olivia Jenkins."

Fenway nodded. "I heard."

"And you might have heard of one of the shell companies associated with it."

"SRB."

"Right."

"But what is Rachel doing here?" Fenway asked. "Shouldn't you get her to safety?"

Special Agent Robin Orlando squinted at Fenway. "This *is* safety," she said. "This *is* well-protected. Rachel's going to stay here until we catch the man trying to kill her."

"The man?" Fenway was incredulous. "Isn't the head of the network Elena Valenzuela?"

Agent Orlando cocked her head to the side. "What do you know about Elena Valenzuela?"

"I know that it's Natalie's real name," Fenway said. "I know that somebody classified her personnel file. And I know she's been missing ever since her discharge from the Marine Corps. And I'm pretty sure she took over El Magnate's network after he went to jail."

Agent Orlando shook her head. "No, Fenway. Elena Valenzuela has been working for the ATF since she got out of the military. She's the one who took down *El Magnate*."

Fenway's eyes widened.

"She's been undercover for over a decade."

Fenway looked at Rachel. She nodded.

Agent Orlando folded her arms. "We recruited Elena into the ATF. She's helped infiltrate several opioid distribution networks. We got word of a new, hot opioid coming out on the market—especially dangerous because it wasn't *classified* as an opioid."

"Nozithrapham," Fenway said, automatically.

Agent Orlando nodded. "And they worked really hard to keep it off the ATF's radar. Falsified clinical trial data, for example."

"Like the mother of Alan Patrick Scorrelli," Fenway said. "Gottfried Ebner falsifying all kinds of data, right?"

"For coming to the wrong conclusion, you sure figured out a hell of a lot," Agent Orlando said.

"But who's *they*?" Fenway asked. "If not Natalie, then who's trying to become *El Magnate Nuevo*?" As soon as the words left her lips, she knew. "Oh," she said. "He just announced his candidacy for coroner this morning."

Fenway's phone dinged. She pushed the Model 41 aside in her purse and pulled the phone out. It was a text from Kav.

Ink from Rachel's suicide note matches credit card receipt from Maxime's – same ink batch

Then about ten seconds later:

APB on Everett Michaels – we want him for questioning

Then one more:

I know he's friends with your dad – call and warn him

"Everett Michaels is behind everything?" Fenway asked.

"That's right," said Rachel.

Fenway turned to Agent Orlando. "Why haven't you moved on him yet?" she demanded. "You've let him kill our mayor and a P.I.—and kidnap a little girl?"

Agent Orlando shook her head. "We can't just scoop him up off the street," she said. "For the last few weeks, we were trying to get him through Carpetti's financial records. He's overseen literally thousands of hidden payments."

"And Fletcher Jenkins brought you the information."

Agent Orlando nodded. "And his mother."

"So how did she end up dead at Cactus Lake Motel?"

Rachel sighed. "I don't know," she said sadly. "I assume Everett Michaels found out some way to get her there."

"We have a theory," Agent Orlando said. "And we've found a couple of the pieces that fit. There were two calls from a throwaway cell phone to the mayor on Friday evening. I believe someone pretended to be a friend of Fletcher's concerned about him backsliding. Preyed on one of the mayor's worst fears."

"And who killed her?"

"Michaels had brought some people with him the last few days," Agent Orlando said. "You met one of them—well, after the sheriff shot him dead."

"Alan Patrick Scorrelli."

"Right."

"And the guy in the track suit."

"We've identified him as Wilson Bai."

"Did he have a relative in the clinical trials for Nozithrapham too?"

"His mother."

"But he seemed to be more dangerous."

"He's wanted in connection with several stabbings in Los Angeles, yes. The short dagger, the kind that killed both the mayor and your private investigator—that's his weapon of choice."

Fenway turned to Rachel. "And you knew about this all along?"

Rachel hesitated. "I knew that *someone* high up at Carpetti Pharmaceuticals laundered money and bribed senators so that he'd be able to control the pill market."

"Estancia was basically his test market," Agent Orlando said. "If he could do well here, and squeeze out Norco and Oxy, we think he planned to expand to Los Angeles, and maybe the whole West Coast."

"So why kill the mayor? And why try to kill you, Rachel?"

"About two months ago, Fletcher Jenkins found thousands, and I mean *thousands*, of financial anomalies in the Carpetti records," said Agent Orlando. "It had been hidden very well, but Fletch did a bunch of digging on his own, and found all the holding companies and tracked all the payments to the senators and to many of the dealers. He went to his supervisor, and she told him to bury it."

"Bury it?"

"We think she's on the take too. She just paid off a bunch of credit cards. So he went to his mother, and she went to the state attorney, and the state attorney went to the ATF."

"Right about the time that I got offered the PR job at Ferris Energy," Rachel said, "and then right after that, this job. That didn't seem right, so I talked to Mayor Jenkins about it. And she had a plan."

"We had to keep the Carpetti Pharma stuff out of the press or risk Michaels getting away," said Agent Orlando.

"And voilà," Fenway said, "Rachel accepts the public information officer job, you go undercover as a reporter, and another of your agents goes undercover as a veteran who needs the pills for PTSD."

"Right," said Rachel.

"And of course," said Fenway, "you, Agent Orlando, are the owner of the 'classified' fingerprints in Rachel's office."

"If you found classified fingerprints in Rachel's office, yeah, they were probably mine." She winked. "Or James Monroe's, if you prefer."

"You're so undercover even your fake identity has a fake identity," Fenway said.

Agent Orlando's face turned serious. "We were really close to solving it," she said. "But we didn't think they would see Fletcher as a threat." She pressed her lips together. "Obviously, we were wrong."

"But why not just retire from big pharma to become a drug kingpin?" Fenway asked. "Why did Everett Michaels make a play for the coroner job?"

"Because," Rachel said, "of the side effects of Nozithrapham in those clinical studies."

"Like Scorrelli's mom," Fenway said. "She had an episode of violent rage."

"And then died," Rachel said.

"But if you're the one in charge of figuring out what caused all the suspicious deaths in the county—" Agent Orlando began.

"Then you can throw all the investigations of those drug-related deaths off the trail of Red Skies," Fenway finished. "But why the hell did Michaels kidnap Olivia?"

"Leverage for Fletch's guilty plea," Agent Orlando said. "If Fletch had gone to jail, Michaels would have been untouchable on that murder."

"And," Rachel interjected, "we think that Michaels figured all the financial anomalies that Fletch caught would have been swept away, especially since they bribed his supervisor."

"Of course, Everett Michaels didn't know the feds were on to him," Agent Orlando said. "But I suspect that was his motive."

"Didn't you have eyes on him?" Fenway asked. "How could he kill so many people if you were following him?"

"He doesn't do the dirty work himself, Fenway," said Agent Orlando. "Scorrelli and Bai both owe him big. They've been promised distribution. But Michaels keeps his hands clean. We can't touch him."

"Well, now you can," Fenway said. "The ink from the fake suicide note and the ink from a credit card receipt are matches from the same ink batch from Montblanc."

"It's great that it's a match," Agent Orlando mused, "but that doesn't necessarily prove anything. There are lots of rich people with Montblancs in the area."

"Not with that specific batch, I bet," Fenway said. "And it's enough to bring him in for questioning. We've got an APB out on him."

The window behind Rachel exploded.

Fenway felt a searing pain in her left forearm.

"DOWN!" Agent Orlando yelled, jumping into a low crouch. She pulled out her gun. "GET DOWN!"

Fenway and Rachel both dove to the floor.

"Who else knew you were coming here?" Agent Orlando demanded.

"No one," Fenway yelled. "I didn't tell anyone." She felt wetness and pain from the top of her arm. The bullet had hit her.

"What about your dad?"

"My father didn't know where I was going." She rolled onto her back and grabbed a dishtowel from the top of the coffee table.

"Did anyone follow you?"

"I don't know." But Fenway's heart sank—she hadn't been paying attention. She knew Michaels could have followed her without her registering it. She pushed the dishtowel down on top of her wound and held her arm up, above the level of her heart. It bled steadily but didn't gush. She hoped she could get it to stop.

"You two, stay down," Agent Orlando said. She pulled out her radio and pushed the button. "Monroe on fire, Monroe on fire. Request immediate backup."

"They're half an hour away," Rachel said quietly to Fenway.

Fenway hooked the handle of her purse with her foot and pulled it up. She took her right hand off the dishtowel just long enough to take the Model 41 out and slide it over to Rachel on the floor.

"Fenway, is this my gun? What the hell?"

"Sorry," Fenway said. "I thought I'd need it."

"Do you even know how to use it?"

"I know *you* know how to use it," Fenway said. "I'm trying not to lose blood here. Think maybe you can defend us?" She felt around the wound, a through-and-through in the muscle and tissue about two inches away from her elbow. Fortunately, it hadn't struck bone, but she thought the bullet hit her radial artery.

"We know you did it, Everett," Agent Orlando shouted. "The sheriff's office just pieced it all together."

Another shot. This one buried itself in the wall on the other side of the room.

"How do you think you're going to get away?" the agent called out. "Do you really think you're going to murder three people in this house and then drive five miles back to the freeway like nothing ever happened?"

Agent Orlando paused, listening carefully.

"Do you think you're going to be able to win the election with all this blood on your hands?" she yelled. "Do you think you're going to be able to go back to your two-thousand-dollar suits and your Montblanc pens?"

Another shot came from the other side of the house. A second window broke.

Agent Orlando called out again. "How do you think this is going down, Everett? What's your escape plan now that everyone knows you had the mayor killed?"

"What is she doing?" Fenway whispered to Rachel. "Doesn't she know there are two of them?"

"I think she's trying to get him out of here. Take his private plane to Central America, maybe, without killing us first."

"Well, tell her to stop. He knows he won't be able to escape anywhere if he leaves us alive with cell phones and radios." Fenway started to feel the blood seep onto her fingers. She grabbed another part of the towel and folded it on top of the wound.

"There's two of them and three of us," Rachel whispered. "And two of us have guns. Maybe we can take them." She looked across the room. "Shit."

"What's wrong?"

"I don't know where Robin went."

Fenway turned her head. Agent Orlando wasn't there.

Fenway heard another car pulling up to the house.

"Is that another car?"

"I think so," Rachel whispered. "I don't know if that's us or them. But we're too exposed here. The kitchen is better. We can get in the corner behind the breakfast table and see what's in front of us. I'll have something to shoot. Now I'm trying to cover the window and the door and two other entrances."

"And I'll have more dishtowels," Fenway said under her breath.

"Okay, start moving," Rachel whispered. "And keep quiet."

Fenway moved backward toward the kitchen, trying to keep her arm up, and didn't get very far. The pain in her arm intensified, and she grimaced. After about ten seconds, she turned over to her hands and knees, taking the towel off her arm, and crawling as quickly and quietly as she could into the kitchen. She left a smeary trail of blood everywhere her hands touched the floor.

She saw the kitchen table and the corner she thought Rachel would want to use. Fenway scooted around to the left side of the table, next to a set of drawers. She opened the bottom drawer and found several cloth napkins. They looked expensive. Fenway promised herself she'd replace them as she pulled out the folded napkins and put two of them together, eight layers of fabric over the wound, again elevating her arm.

Three gunshots—*pop, pop, pop*—came from the front of the house.

"Was that Agent Orlando?" Fenway whispered.

Rachel shrugged her shoulders.

I'm not doing much good here, Fenway thought miserably. Not only had she gotten Natalie's role in the whole thing completely wrong, but she had led the actual bad guy right to Rachel. She pursed her lips and tried to concentrate on stanching the bleeding in her arm. She started to get a little lightheaded and fought the feeling. She tried to slow her breathing so her heart rate would lessen, so she'd stop pumping the precious blood out of her body, but she couldn't calm down.

"I'm sorry, Rachel," she said. "I led him right to you."

"You were trying to save me," Rachel whispered. "Now quiet."

There was another sound of breaking glass.

Fenway looked at Rachel.

Rachel held the gun out in front of her, calm and relaxed—just as steadily as she had held it on her father two months before. Fenway marveled at how Rachel's hands could be so steady under pressure.

"The Marines are here to back us up, Everett," Agent Orlando shouted. "Your buddy in the track suit is down. This won't end well for you unless you give up."

Natalie—Elena—had arrived, Fenway thought. And she shot Everett's henchman.

Fenway and Rachel stared at the doorway to the living room, not moving, not daring to breathe.

Fenway started to drift.

The blood flow slowed but didn't stop. It hadn't soaked through the eight layers, though how much longer she could do this, she didn't know.

"Is he gone?" she whispered.

Then she caught the scent of cardamom and bergamot.

She went on high alert.

And then Everett Michaels appeared in the doorway, gun out.

His head turned the wrong direction.

Rachel pulled the trigger on her .22.

A click. Then nothing.

Everett Michaels spun toward Rachel, seeing her sitting on the floor, and lowered his pistol to aim it right at her.

Fenway screamed, a guttural snarl, as she jumped to her feet, hands holding the two bloody cloth napkins taut in front of her, and launched herself at Everett Michaels.

He jerked when he heard the scream.

The cloth napkins caught him right over the eyes and he pulled his hands up and dropped the gun.

Fenway kept driving with her legs.

He clawed at her hands, trying to get the napkins and the blood away from his eyes.

He took two steps back and then fell backward.

Fenway had her whole weight behind herself as they fell together. He whipped his head from side to side, trying to free his eyes from the bloody napkins. Fenway tightened her grip and pushed harder.

Crack.

His temple crushed against the corner of the coffee table. Fenway smashed her left hand against the edge of the table as she went down.

He landed on the floor in an awkward position.

Fenway landed on top of him. She put an elbow into his neck and the blood-soaked napkins fell off his face.

His eyes were open but unseeing.

A trickle of blood ran onto the floor from the side of his head.

Fenway pushed herself off him. She saw Rachel, Natalie, and Agent Orlando appear above her.

"That psychotic motherfucker still smells fantastic," she said.

Then she passed out.

PART VII

THURSDAY

CHAPTER TWENTY-SEVEN

A SOFT BEEPING PULLED FENWAY INTO CONSCIOUSNESS. SHE gradually became aware of other sounds: faraway voices, echoes of footfalls, wheels from carts scooting across tile floors.

She opened her eyes. A beige room greeted her.

She looked to her right. An IV went into her arm, an oxygen monitor on her finger. A few machines quietly whirred; one beeped with every heartbeat.

She looked to the side. Her left arm, heavily bandaged over the bullet wound, ended in a boxer splint over her left hand. Dez sat in a straight-backed chair next to the bed, a book of crossword puzzles on her lap, eyes closed and head back.

"Hi, Dez," Fenway said. Her voice came out as a croak.

Dez's eyes popped open. "Oh, you're awake," she said. "Thank God. Took you long enough."

"Nice to see you too."

"The nurse is going to want to see you," Dez said, pushing the call button.

"How long was I out?"

"About fifteen hours," Dez said. "It's half-past six."

"In the morning?

"Yes."

"What did I miss?"

Dez nodded. "Well," she said, "Olivia is getting out of the hospital tonight, going back with her mom. She's having nightmares, scared out of her mind, but Tracey's taking her home."

"Good."

"And just a few hours after y'all took down Everett Michaels, with Rachel showing us the evidence that the mayor and Fletch had, we finally found the other accounts that SRB—and Mr. Michaels—had been hiding on the whole Red Skies distribution network."

"Did Natalie kill that other guy at the house?"

"No, she shot his leg pretty good, though. He's talking, too. His mom came here from Seoul just to get into the Nozithrapham clinical study, just like Scorrelli's mom, but *she* recovered. Michaels seemed to have a bunch of henchmen he paid off with free pharmaceuticals for their parents."

"Is Nozithrapham coming off the market?"

"I don't know what the FDA is going to do. That'll take months." Dez crossed her arms. "Anyway, we've got names of a lot of the people paid off through SRB. The two senators who took the bribes deny everything, of course, but everyone is calling for their resignations. The ATF has taken over, though. I expect a hard slog."

"Has Fletch been released?"

"His paperwork is in process—he should be released later today. He's none too happy about how this all went down. He's talking about suing the sheriff's department."

Fenway nodded. "At least he's going to be with his daughter again."

When the nurse came in, she asked Fenway a barrage of questions. An internist came in as well, and tapped her on her knees and wrists and feet then asked more questions. They nodded grimly but seemed satisfied by her answers as they left.

"So what else happened in the last fifteen hours?" Fenway asked.

"Funny you should ask," said Dez. She pulled a folder out of her case, took out a paper, and handed it to Fenway.

Fenway looked at the sheet for a moment. "Dez, this is a candidate filing form."

"Yep," Dez agreed. "Deadline is in two weeks."

"And it's all been filled out for me."

"It certainly has," Dez said. "All you've got to do is sign at the bottom and hand it into the county clerk."

"But I'm not running," Fenway protested. "I've got the nursing boards to study for. I've got other jobs I need to start applying for."

"Well, that's all well and good, Fenway, but the people need you here. We need you here. Rachel, Mark, Migs, Piper, me—and especially McVie. We need you here."

"You might need me here," Fenway said, shaking her head, "but there's no way I'll win this election. Too many people against the idea. Believe me, I can think of a lot better ways to spend this three hundred dollar filing fee."

"Oh, it won't be three hundred dollars."

"Sure it is. That's the filing fee, isn't it?"

"You'll want to look at this other paper," Dez said, pulling a second sheet out of the folder. "See, the filing fee gets waived if you get three percent of the voting population of the county to sign for your candidate nomination."

Fenway looked skeptical. "There are half a million people in this county. That's fifteen thousand signatures."

"Four hundred and twenty-two thousand people in Dominguez County, if you want to get technical," Dez responded, "but only fifty-two percent of them are registered voters. And three percent of that is—" Dez looked at the sheet, "six thousand, five hundred and eighty-four."

"There's no way you got sixty-five hundred signatures in two days," Fenway said.

Dez handed her the paper, a printout from the county registrar.

Number of signatures required   6,584
Number of signatures submitted 17,708

Fenway's mouth dropped open.

"And it wasn't two days," Dez said. "We've been gathering signatures for weeks."

Fenway pressed her lips together and averted her eyes.

"What is it, Fenway?"

"Dez, you might want me to run for coroner, but I really screwed up on this," she said. "I went to Natalie's place by myself. I thought Natalie was the bad guy, when instead she was the best of the good guys. I didn't realize Michaels followed me there. I almost got Rachel killed. I almost got us *all* killed."

Dez sat back in her chair. "You ever heard of something called *impostor syndrome?*"

"I'm serious, Dez. I was a liability."

"No," Dez said. "You forced his hand. He would have kept under the radar, moving the chess pieces around, and we'd never take anything but pawns. You disrupted everything he tried in the last week."

"But—"

"But nothing," Dez said. "If it weren't for you, Fletch would be locked up for a crime he didn't commit. Olivia might be dead—we might not even have known she'd been kidnapped. Rachel might be dead. The feds might have egg on their face. And we might have gotten a drug kingpin as coroner, in a position to cover up drug overdoses, murders, you name it. You seriously think you were a *liability?*"

"I almost got them killed," Fenway repeated, softer this time.

"And then you *saved* their lives and made sure Everett Michaels will never hurt anyone again."

"Natalie took the other one down. Don't forget about her." Fenway paused. "Will she forgive me for thinking she was the kingpin?"

Dez laughed. "Natalie thought it was *hilarious*. She couldn't stop laughing. I think everything is okay with her."

"Do you think I could see her and apologize?"

Dez shrugged. "She's already gone. Moved on to her next assignment. Probably has a whole new identity being set up as we speak. Oh—she told me she'd see you in Valhalla. Whatever that means."

Fenway smiled wistfully.

"So," Dez continued, "are you going to take that down to the county clerk and get it signed?"

Fenway looked at Dez, then nodded.

<hr/>

The hospital discharged Fenway that afternoon, and McVie picked her up to drive her home. Fenway's hand was starting to throb as she got in the car, but the doctor had said the fracture to the fourth metacarpal was lined up well. If she was lucky, she wouldn't even need a cast. He offered her a few Oxycontin for the pain. She refused.

"You know," McVie said as he drove, "you were a no-show for our lunch date yesterday. I don't usually take getting stood up very well."

"Yeah, sorry," Fenway said. "I was unconscious from a loss of blood, and I totally lost track of time. Plus someone tried to kill me."

"If you're going to lie, Fenway, at least make your story realistic."

Fenway laughed. "So, are you back?"

McVie looked sideways at Fenway. "You mean..."

"Are you sheriff again?"

"Oh," McVie said. "Yes. They reinstated me this morning."

"Good," Fenway said. "What did you think I meant?"

"Uh, I thought you might have been asking if I'm back with Amy."

Fenway nodded. "Well, I guess that's something I'd like to know if you're going to call it a lunch date."

"She served me with separation papers as soon as I got reinstated," McVie said.

"Oh," Fenway said. "I'm sorry. That must be rough."

McVie shrugged. "At least I know it's over. The last couple of years have been such a roller coaster."

"What's going to happen to Megan?"

"She'll get to choose who she wants to live with. I hope it's me, because Amy doesn't really set boundaries with Megan. But it probably won't be."

Fenway was quiet.

"So, I mean," McVie continued, trying to sound casual, "I was sort of half-joking when I said we had a lunch date, but, uh, if you wouldn't mind it being a real date, then I'd like that, too."

"You have literally been legally separated for six hours," Fenway said. "Isn't there a rule about that?"

"I don't think so," Craig said. "It's probably not a rule that Amy's following, anyway."

Fenway smiled. "Well, part of me thinks it's a bad idea, just because you're the closest thing to a boss that I have."

"Not really," Craig said. "You report to the people of Dominguez County, not to me. Just because I appointed you doesn't mean I'm your boss." He cleared his throat. "And besides," he continued, "I'm going for another position."

Fenway looked at Craig. "You're not going for re-election?"

Craig shook his head. "I'm submitted my paperwork this morning. I'm going to run for mayor."

"Against Barry Klein."

"Yep," he smiled. "Your dad has already told me he'll endorse me. That's gotta get under Barry's skin."

They arrived at Fenway's complex and they walked up the flight of stairs to Fenway's apartment. A large, flat box leaned up against the wall in front of 214.

"What's that?" Fenway said. "Did you send that?"

"Nope," Craig said.

She looked at the box; the return address was Seattle. "It's from Akeel," she said.

"Akeel?"

"One of my old friends from Seattle," she said, opening the door.

McVie took the box inside, and Fenway opened up one end. She saw a picture frame.

"Oh, this can't be what I think it is," Fenway mused. She grabbed ahold of the frame with her right hand. "Help me take this off, Craig." He took ahold of the box from the other end and pulled; the box slid off easily.

It was the painting of the shore on the other side of the butterfly waystation.

"This is the painting I drove up to Seattle to get," Fenway said, "and Dez called me home about the mayor before I could get it. I didn't think I'd be able to go back for a few months."

She picked up the box to move it and an envelope fell out with her name on it in Akeel's handwriting. She picked up the envelope and opened it; her key to the storage unit fell out, along with a handwritten note.

And you thought we were just about mindblowing sex, didn't you? You don't think I'm paying attention, but I do. You told me how important this painting of your mom's was to you. When I realized you left the key to the storage locker here, I thought I'd do something nice. I hope the painting makes it to you in one

piece, but I insured it with the shipping company for a ridicu-
lous amount of money, so I bet it got to you fine.
Next time you come up here, you can plan to stay for more than
one night. I'd like that, as a matter of fact.
—Akeel

McVie looked at Fenway expectantly.

She cleared her throat. "Akeel obviously got the painting and spent an obscene amount of money shipping it to me."

McVie paused. "Is there something I should know about?"

"No," Fenway said. "Well, the guy is an ex-boyfriend."

"And he's doing above-and-beyond things for you?"

Fenway shrugged. "We're a thousand miles from each other, and we broke up two years ago. It's ancient history."

"Okay," he said.

"Come on, Craig," Fenway said, "don't start getting all jealous on me when we haven't even been on a real date. As if you've forgotten that you were officially married yesterday."

McVie smiled. "You're absolutely right," he said. "Okay, real date? Tomorrow night, dinner."

Fenway considered for a moment and then shook her head. "Not tomorrow," she said. "Give me a few days to recover. I've lost a lot of blood and my hand is broken. And I have to figure out how to get dressed with only one hand. And—I'm exhausted. I don't want to fall asleep on you."

"Oh, sure. I understand." She could hear the disappointment in his voice.

"But soon," Fenway said, taking hold of McVie's hand. "Before my hand is fixed, but after I figure out how to manage."

"Sure," Craig said. "I'd like that."

They stood there for a minute.

"Anything else you need before I go? You want me to hang the painting for you?"

"I think I can do that," Fenway said.

"I've got two good hands."

Fenway remembered back to the night they'd spent together two months before, and the kiss they shared in the front seat of his Highlander. Yes, yes, he did have two good hands.

"Jars I can open, anything like that?"

"I think I'm good," Fenway said. "You're still at the motel?"

He nodded. "I'm apartment hunting tomorrow," he said. "Forty-three years old and I feel like I just got out of college. I haven't shared a common wall with anyone in years."

"You know, there might be an open unit around here. We could, you know, be neighbors." Fenway gave him a coquettish smile.

"Yeah, just what I need, your dad as my landlord," McVie said.

She walked him to the door, and they smiled at each other. They shared an awkward hug, not quite sure what to do, before McVie turned, smiled, and walked out.

She made some coffee, struggling to pour and grind the beans with just one good hand. It took a few extra minutes, but she finally got it brewing. She went to her computer, thinking she'd try to find what she needed to know about running for coroner. But she thought about the folder Dr. Klein had put on the counter in her office a few days before. She thought of the pain and regret and anger she felt.

She typed *Professor Solomon Delacroix* into the search box.

She didn't know what she expected to find, but after learning about the video stills, she was absolutely positive that her Russian Lit professor had other victims.

The first hit, though, linked to a news story from the *Seattle Times* from the day before.

He was dead.

Professor Solomon Delacroix's body had been found by a boater in the Squalicum waterway, just a couple of nautical miles from the Bellingham marina. Professor Delacroix, an avid swimmer, hadn't returned from his usual early-morning swim at the university pool on Wednesday morning.

Police speculated that the cause of death was accidental.

Fenway, stunned, looked for additional stories, but could find nothing else online, except that Delacroix had been teaching a summer session class on *The Brothers Karamazov*.

The coffeemaker beeped, and Fenway stood at the kitchen counter, drinking her coffee, piecing together the timeline. The accident had occurred only about thirty-six hours after she had told her father about being raped. She found herself wondering if he had a reason besides retrieving her car to send his private plane to the Seattle area.

She sat down on the floor, heavily, being careful of her broken hand, and put her good hand over her face. She felt like she should have been grateful that the man who did that to her couldn't hurt her—or anyone else—ever again.

But she didn't feel grateful.

The tears started, and she didn't know where they came from. Anger, relief, resentment, anxiety for the future—she couldn't untangle the emotions to pinpoint the cause. But she couldn't stop. And for the first time in a long time, she allowed herself to be overwhelmed. Tomorrow she would regain control. Tomorrow, she would file her paperwork with the county clerk and officially begin her campaign for coroner. Tomorrow, she would revel in the fact that McVie was suddenly, wondrously, available and interested. Tomorrow, she would allow herself to wonder if her father had entangled himself in her professor's death.

Not tonight, though. Not tonight.

UPCOMING RELEASES

I'd love to hear what you thought of *The Incumbent Coroner*. Please leave reviews on Goodreads, BookBub, and your favorite online bookstore site.

Want more Fenway Stevenson?

Buy Book One, *The Reluctant Coroner*, available in paperback or e-book, on your favorite online bookstore, and available for special order from your neighborhood bookstore!

I'm hard at work on books three and four! Join my mailing list and be the first one to know about the new releases: title and cover reveals, previews of the first chapters, and more! Visit www.paulaustinardoin.com.

Want more Sergeant Dez Roubideaux?

Twenty-five years before she met Fenway Stevenson, Dez was finishing her criminal justice degree. *Bad Weather* is a novella chronicling Dez's experience with a mysterious writer who isn't what she seems, to be released in late 2018. Join my mailing list and get the cover reveal, launch date details, and more! Visit www.paulaustinardoin.com.

ACKNOWLEDGMENTS

I'd like to thank my editor, Max Christian Hansen, and the early readers and proofreaders who made a huge difference: Siobhan Ordorica, Blair Semple, Timarie Shelton, Debbie Degutis, Devin McCrate, Monique Koll, Charlie Lemoine, Tom Sykes, Alexis Marcom, Christina Bellinger, Michelle Damiani, Erica Root, Emily Fluckiger, Carolyn Ardoin, Beverly Ange, and the members of Wordforge Novelists. The feedback, input, criticism, and corrections you gave me made this a much better book, and I sincerely appreciate it.

A thousand thanks to the tireless efforts of Cheryl Shoults, my marketing manager, who gets the word out about Fenway Stevenson.

And I very much appreciate the support of my wife and kids, who put up with my excited ramblings about my mailing list and my book reviews, as well as the hours I've put in.

BY PAUL AUSTIN ARDOIN

FENWAY STEVENSON MYSTERIES

•

The Reluctant Coroner
The Incumbent Coroner
The Candidate Coroner (coming soon)

Bad Weather (coming soon)

22039458R00239

Made in the USA
San Bernardino, CA
08 January 2019